ON THE JAVA RIDGE

Jock Serong is the author of *Quota*, winner of the 2015 Ned Kelly Award for Best First Fiction, and *The Rules of Backyard Cricket*, shortlisted for the Victorian Premier's Literary Awards 2017.

@JockSerong

JOCK SERONG

ON THE JAVA RIDGE

TEXT PUBLISHING MELBOURNE AUSTRALIA

textpublishing.com.au

The Text Publishing Company
Swann House
22 William Street
Melbourne Victoria 3000
Australia

First published in 2017 by The Text Publishing Company

Cover design by W.H. Chong
Cover photos by iStock
Page design by Jessica Horrocks
Map by Simon Barnard
Typeset in Minister Light 10/16.5 by J&M Typesetting

Printed in Australia by Griffin Press, an Accredited ISO AS/NZS 14001:2004 Environmental Management System printer.

National Library of Australia Cataloguing-in-Publication entry:
Creator: Serong, Jock, author.
Title: On the java ridge / by Jock Serong.
Subjects: Australia, fiction. Australia, politics.
ISBN: 9781925498394 (paperback)
ISBN: 9781925410662 (ebook)

On the Java Ridge

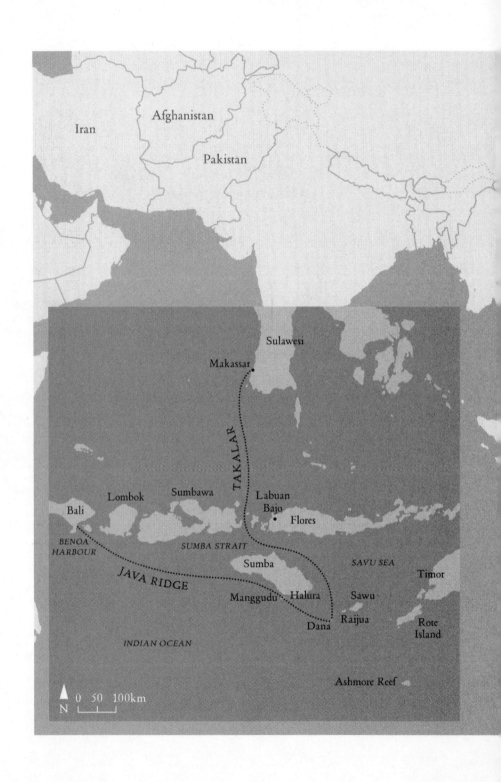

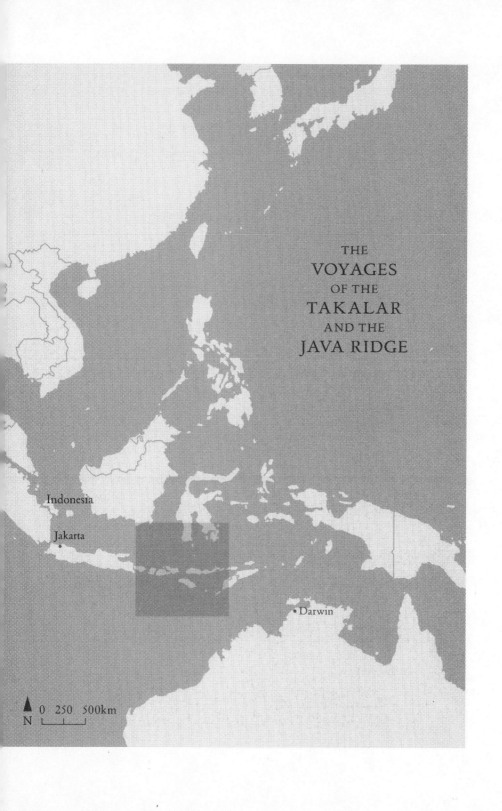

THE
VOYAGES
OF THE
TAKALAR
AND THE
JAVA RIDGE

Indonesia

Jakarta

Darwin

0 250 500km

N

PROLOGUE

Six Australian flags hang rich and solemn, three each side of the doorway. The doors stand open. Beyond them is a corridor in gloom; before them, an empty lectern. The light of Canberra winter throws cold geometries on the high walls: triangular shadows, blades of light.

Closer, an overcoated herd circles on the damp flagstones. Breath suspended over busy phones, footfalls making darker patches on the frosted lawn as the dew works its way into open footwear. Cables snake forward between the huddles to microphones laid gently, like floral tributes. The walls spear high above the cluster. The crowd on the lawn, seen from a currawong's eye, make dark specks on a green square. The day slowly dawning over the mountains sweeps sunlight, warm and generous, over the city; but it will reach this little enclave last of all.

Three figures stride through the doorway, arranged in formation with the tallest in the centre. As they emerge the light strikes them. Two flanking acolytes a step behind the man at the apex: a tall man, lean and angular in a pale grey suit. The triangle of white between his lapels so bright that the shirt has surely never been worn before. Hair slightly receding but still a youthful brown, the bones of his face making a robust frame for his easy smile. An open face, for a politician.

One of the two advisors is a woman in her twenties. She leans in towards the lectern, leaving her shoes securely planted to its left: she is not the focus here.

'Morning ladies and gentlemen, thank you for coming out. The minister is ready. Thanks for your patience.'

He squints once at the light from above and begins.

'Unauthorised boat arrivals have been a scourge on our society for many years, and for many years we have fought them vigorously with a range of policies: mandatory detention, excision of territorial islands and tow-backs to name a few. The Bali Process has been in place for twenty years now.

'The countermeasures adopted by people smugglers have been brazen and ruthless. The destruction of personal documents, assaults upon the hardworking men and women of our Border Integrity Unit; even setting fire to their own vessels. January's incident, in which a young Border Integrity officer was tragically killed while lawfully boarding such a vessel, is only the latest in the long series of outrages perpetrated by these people.

'Plainly, a new way forward is required. Which is why, at the recent Jakarta Summit, I signed the diplomatic communiqué between Indonesia and Australia that transfers to our Indonesian friends the responsibility for all maritime departures from their territorial waters into Australian waters. All of them. All checking of registrations, of passengers and of cargo, and the communication of that information to us, will be the responsibility of the Indonesian navy. In return, Australian government vessels have undertaken not to cross into Indonesian waters at any time.'

He pauses, looks up from his notes, chin high with defiance. The cameras start crunching, as he knew they would.

'It follows that any vessel entering our territorial waters from the north, which has not been specifically cleared by the Indonesian navy, has breached our borders illegally. This much you already know.'

He stops again, scans the press pack, knowing his eyes are filling screens across the nation. Behind him the staffers are nodding furiously.

'I want to make this very clear: I will not have our personnel endangered by the reckless conduct of criminal people smugglers. So today I am proud to announce a significant new border security measure ahead of next week's federal election.'

He waits just long enough, settles the cold breath in his lungs.

'From this point forward, no unidentified vessels in Australian territorial waters will be offered any form of maritime assistance. None. No contact will be made with these vessels on the open sea, either by the Border Integrity Unit or, indeed, the navy. Any future incursions into territorial waters will be met with remote measures by our private sector partners, Core Resolve.

'I want to repeat that for absolute clarity: there will be no further boarding parties, no rescues. Advertisements will be placed on Indonesian television, in print media and online. It will be made absolutely clear that unauthorised boat journeys into Australian waters are the sole responsibility of those who organise them.'

He pauses weightily once more. The experienced correspondents brace themselves for a new campaign talking point.

'No Australian will be placed in danger.'

The brief silence that meets these last words is suddenly strafed by a volley of shouted questions.

'Yes—Daniel.'

'What if the people on board are seeking asylum and mean us no harm?'

'Recent experience has shown we can never make that assumption. But in any case, the question doesn't arise. Indonesian personnel will already have prevented their entry.'

'Well, what if they're fishermen?'

The minister's face reveals the faintest trace of impatience. 'Indonesian personnel will have prevented their entry.' His eyes shift right: the ABC. 'Yes?'

'What exactly are "remote measures"?'

'Obviously I'm not at liberty to discuss the on-water methodologies that Core Resolve may choose to employ. That is a matter for them. Suffice to say, there will be no Australians placed in danger.'

A rush of questions begins and he raises his hand to silence them.

'Make no mistake: you are either on the side of these criminal gangs, cynical traffickers in human misery, or you are on our side. Some in the media already have hundreds—*hundreds* of deaths at sea on their consciences. I won't allow them to add Australian citizens to that number.'

The shouted demands resume. One question cuts through the noise and heads turn. The questioner is a respected press gallery veteran.

'What about the caretaker conventions?' she asks. 'It's highly unusual to announce a measure like this so close to an election.'

'The caretaker conventions are exactly that: conventions, born of easier times. Let me say again, I will take robust action to protect our borders *whenever* the need arises—during parliamentary sittings or otherwise—and to ensure that no Australians are placed in danger. That's what I was appointed to do.' A purposeful nod. 'Now if you'll excuse me...'

A shadow crosses the minister's face—he touches his temple gently. The young advisor appears again, a deferential hand not quite touching the flank of his suit jacket. The minister taps his notes into a neat pile and turns from the lectern.

Parliament House, Canberra

The Honourable Cassius Calvert MP, federal Minister for Border Integrity, swept past his executive assistant's desk. He was already through the door into his own office as he called to her.

'Hey Stell, did you watch?'

Of course she'd watched. Stella never missed anything. Until he met her, Cassius had assumed that people who make a lot of noise are incapable of observing the world, but somehow she did both.

Big and loud, maybe twenty-five, Stella Mullins was the one condition Cassius had set for taking the job. She'd known nothing about how to be the executive assistant to a federal minister and not much about his political portfolio but she was a ferocious learner. Anyway, he had a departmental head and a chief of staff for that: the twin ogres of policy and politics. What he needed was a buffer between them—a fighter in his corner—and he knew Stella had the mongrel for it. He'd known that since they met, him on a post-retirement contract with the Olympic chef de mission, Stella an economics student and cornerstone of the rugby sevens squad.

'What's this shit about "remote measures"?' she yelled back.

A man on a stepladder in the far corner of Cassius's room jerked his cordless drill out of the plasterboard and recoiled. Stella's voice could do that.

On a table inside his door a bottle of Grange lay like the infant Jesus in a straw-filled presentation box. Cassius picked up the card.

Cass—Congratulations on a groundbreaking policy. We look forward to many years of service to you and the Australian people— With kind regards, the Board and Staff of Core Resolve.

Bloody Grange—how imaginative. Stella was standing at the door now, crisp in executive-tier tailoring but still wearing the sneakers in which she'd walked to work.

'You seen the Core Resolve share price? Just gone up nearly two bucks. That's...' she looked at the ceiling while she did the numbers, 'about four million their CEO just made.'

Cassius nodded. 'Put that wine in the register of interests, will you Stell?' he said. 'Then go drink it with a friend.'

He reached the desk and unlocked his screen to reveal a column of unanswered emails. 'Have you been filtering these? Holy shit, there's...' he scrolled down. 'Nearly four hundred! I cleared this last night.'

Stella folded her arms. 'I got rid of another three-fifty. Hey, you want to ask me why there's a guy on a ladder in your room?' The tradesman stopped the drill again; looked around uncertainly.

Cassius sighed and started tapping the down arrow. 'Stella, why is there a man on a ladder in my room?'

'He's putting in the video-conferencing. Two cameras up there, microphones on the table, secure links within Cabinet. I can control it all from my desk for you.'

'Wonderful.'

The ladder guy finished what he was doing to the ceiling and took himself off with a nod to Stella.

'Hey seriously,' she said, 'what's all this remote measures crap?'

'We...ah...' He didn't look up. 'We needed something vague so the company's got room to run their own show. And no, it wasn't in the draft you typed last night. Came from the PM's office this morning. Needed plausible deniability.'

'Hah! Deniability…get that from those crooks I s'pose. Anyway, I better give the FOI desk a heads-up.'

'They'll be using the exemptions pro forma, referencing the new commercial-in-confidence provisions. Ron Smedley's all over it.'

'Okay. You want coffee?' She clumped out of the room, humming loudly. He took the briefing notes that had arrived on the desk and sorted them on the side table—department, electorate, miscellaneous—with the ones marked *urgent* at the top of each pile. His eyes roved over the shelves behind the desk. The flag, the trophies and plaques. The Olympic gold in its heavy glass case. Framed pictures: him with Kofi Annan, him with Schwarzenegger, the Dalai Lama, Blair, Susan Kiefel.

He spoke loudly again in the direction of Stella's doorway. 'Can you get the electorate office to run the numbers on that announcement? I want to know how it played.'

'Already on it,' Stella called from her desk. 'The guy from Pollwise said he's tracking it live.' Then, moments later, 'You'll be fine, I'm sure. The nine per cent haven't gone anywhere.'

'I want you…' He was sick of yelling. He got up and marched to her cubicle outside the door. 'I want you to put together some follow-up quotes for online.' His eyes roved over her workspace; the functional stuff, the personal shrines to family, team-mates, assorted dogs and cats. He plucked a large sticky note off the wall: *Mikey and Mel Make My Morning.*

'Who are Mikey and Mel?'

'You don't listen to breakfast radio, do you? They're giving away five thousand bucks. Gonna call someone Saturday morning, and if you answer and you say that, you win the five grand. So it's just a, y'know, a reminder. In case I'm in here.'

She set up a blank page on her screen and her fingers hovered over the keys, waiting for him to start. He spoke slowly, staring into the middle distance.

'I am aware that today's policy announcement will have created disquiet in some quarters. I do not pretend that this is a kind policy. It is a firm and necessary one, and it will help to bring an end at last to this pernicious trade. I expect to hear commentary from the usual quarters about our human rights obligations. To them I say—Australia does not have an obligation to assist criminals in profiting from human misery. Quite the opposite.'

She nodded. 'That all?'

'Can you boil that down to a tweet as well?'

'Yep.'

'Get it around to the PMO to top and tail it with some approving stuff from the PM, then through to media for a final once-over. Thanks Stell.'

He checked the time on her screen. If he was quick he could change and get through a gym session before the party-room meeting. It took work to be in such great shape for a man of his age.

Makassar City, Sulawesi

Roya knew when her mother had had enough. The tilt of her head, her tendency to look away. The past few months had been enough to teach her the limits. Before, she had thought her mother inexhaustible, as nine-year-olds do. She'd thought her impervious to pain, even to mere irritation. But that was before.

When her *madar* was herself, lit up with joy and tenderness, she would look deep into Roya's eyes. But it had been cities and nights and long empty roads since she'd done that, and the baby's time was drawing nearer. And now they'd been sitting in the main room of this hotel for hours and hours. Tiled walls, an uneven cement floor. Rugs and a whimpering dog.

The man had told them to wait here after the car trip. Someone would be along to collect them, he said. They were not to leave, nor talk to anybody, not even to answer the door. He'd left abruptly and she watched the lock turn over with a small click. Went back to studying the streaky walls.

An old Pashtun man was reading the Qur'an, cross-legged with his back straight against a doorway. His face was creased like the flesh of a walnut; his eyes dark slits in the wrinkled skin, neither lashes nor even eyelids to be seen. His nose seemed to be growing towards the Qur'an, and his hennaed beard quivered above his throat, moving slightly as he murmured the words. Two younger Pashtun men sat beside him. She guessed they were his sons. Their dress traditional like his, their eyes a bright, vigilant green. She looked away quickly before either pair of eyes could find her.

There was a fat man dressed in a Shinwari *kurta shalwar*, with a delicate pair of silver-framed glasses perched on his nose. She thought he would have been a trader. All these people were something else at home. Pious or clever or strong; fathers, aunts, students. Here they were just people in a room.

Nobody looked like they would want to talk to her, though she would have liked to know how they felt. Excited to be going on the boat? Scared, maybe? Some of them would have probably seen the ocean before, some might even be able to swim. The mother in the big green shawl, holding the fat baby: had she seen the sea? The baby nuzzled discreetly in the folds of her clothing. She had turned her shoulder away from the men, but the impertinence quivered in the air.

It was now deep in the night. Roya had thought they'd arrived— this was Indonesia, the word they'd been hearing and repeating for weeks. But people were now talking about Australia. She'd tried asking other children what they knew about Australia—she didn't dare ask the adults—but it was clear they had no answers for her and would only make up silly stories. She would save the questions she had for all these interesting people. She was sure there would be time later on.

• • •

She dreamed of home.

She was no longer in the tiled room. The smells were no longer those of close bodies, but of familiar foods and the adult fragrances reserved for particular times. Thursday nights, eating and listening to the women's stories, her inclusion part of the gradual process of ushering her into their world. Treats like this were the incentives to put an end to childish ways.

Women on cushions around the walls of a pocked and chipped room, the heavy floor mat on the floor between them. Cups and saucers tilting on someone's laughing belly, spilt tea, the crockery riding a storm. And when they could collect themselves, the racket would subside and they'd go back to their murmured gossip.

As the remembered world turned to sorrow, Roya unsettled herself into waking. Footsteps now, and low voices. In the dim light she looked at her mother, whose head was nodding on drifts of wretched half-sleep.

'Wake up, *Madar*. Someone coming.'

Her mother clutched at Roya instinctively and struggled to consciousness, reflexively checking her head-covering.

The lock tumbled and two men entered: Indonesians, but younger and wearing surf shorts and rubber sandals, T-shirts. Peering through various windows over the long hours, Roya had come to realise that much of the world dressed this way.

Their faces reminded her of her brother Anwar, though they weren't smiling like he did. Friend or enemy, she and her mother had no control over who came through the door or what they did. Their best hope lay in remaining quiet and small, a way of being that came hard to her. Among her friends she was strong and confident.

The men gestured. The people in the room rose wearily to their feet and began to shuffle out.

Outside the streets were quiet, unhurried in the darkness. The smell of baked concrete and dirty water was still there, but the cooking smells of the previous night were gone. A white van waited by the door, unmarked aside from some torn surfing stickers, the windows blacked out. The driver wore sunglasses, the lights of the city swirling over their big lenses. They were hurried into the back of the van, and found it already contained two other women and a boy who looked slightly older than Roya. By the time all of them had climbed in, there were no seats left and she had to curl onto her mother's lap, squirming to tuck herself beside the dome of her belly.

The door slid shut with a bang and the van moved off. New smells: the chemical tang of a car deodoriser. One of the men leaned over the front seat and looked over the group. He spoke to Roya's mother, repeating a single word as his head jerked about with the gear changes and the bumps. She knew the word from her book.

'Documents, *Madar*. He is saying "documents".'

Her mother dug in her bag and produced their two identity cards with the grainy photographs. Taken by the police chief the first time they'd been arrested. They'd had to hand over their *taskera* to get them, along with cash. She remembered the Taliban fighter behind the desk, his stained teeth and his pale eyes. His pale, pitiless eyes.

The man in the front looked at her and grinned, comparing the identity card. 'Roy...ya Say...ghan.' He paused, thinking. 'You,' he pointed. 'Nine!' He counted out nine fingers.

She nodded and formed a tiny smile to be polite. He studied the card again.

'Herat?'

She nodded again.

'You Hazara?'

Another nod. He looked at her mother. 'Shafiqa. *Shah-fee-kah*. Okay. *Madar*?'

'Yes.'

'Where you *bobo*?'

She shrugged. She could say *Hezbe-wahdat*, but he would not understand. She wasn't sure she did, really: the Wahdat were her father's friends, but then some of them weren't. He'd long since left the Wahdat behind: he worked as an interpreter for the aid people. But she knew something profound had shifted the day she mentioned the Wahdat friends to her father and he scolded her with unusual ferocity, jabbing a finger in her face. They were never to be spoken of again, he warned her. So nobody ever did.

She could say he was taken in the night, along with Anwar. But she didn't know if she had the English for it and she was unsure whether she could bring herself to explain anyway. Discussing it was painful, and best avoided.

That unbearably hot summer night: Roya and her brother shifting on their mats, whispering fragments of conversation into the restless dark. The hammering on the door, her father's sleepy movements then his polite *salaam alaikum* in the doorway. The sudden urgency of his voice as he tried to reason with the three men there, awake and fierce. Them coming in despite him, bandits in the robes of authority. Picking up objects and weighing them in their big hands, their greed and disdain. A moment later they were officials, too, reading something formal from a piece of paper while her father protested how ridiculous it was.

Then time bucked like a horse they'd kicked. Angry words, the crash of a rifle butt. Her father dropped near her feet, bright blood from his nose separating like rivers over his cheek. His cheek, how dare they? She knew it to rub her nose over it.

They cursed and hauled him out like a sack of meat. Her baba and all his love and stories, his jokes and his calm authority.

They were shouting at her mother, and she was screaming back at them, unafraid. One of them slapped her. *Bas*, they roared at her. *Bas!* The screaming didn't worry the Talibs: none of the neighbours would be coming to their aid. But Anwar, propped on his elbows on the *toshak* beside her: he needed to move. He needed to go but he was lying there silently, too afraid to do anything. One of them saw him and leapt onto him: she could hear Anwar whimpering as the man tore down the front of his *perahan tunban*. He examined Anwar's chest, found the strands of dark hair that had appeared the previous summer. The Talib roared with delight, slapped him hard across the face.

'No more basket for you, little dog!'

And so he was marched out, a muzzle pointed into his ribs. Roya's mother wailed at the closed door and it was over. A burst of violence in the fractured light from the windows and their family had been halved.

The man in the front seat turned back to face the windscreen. He rummaged on the seat beside him and shoved a cassette into the stereo. Pakistani pop music. Roya thought the man had probably chosen it to put them at ease. She wondered if they would get their identity cards back. The night went past outside: an occasional motorcycle, a dog, a yellow streetlight.

Then the van was moving out through scatters of older housing. People moving about on their motorcycles, on foot under the bright moon. Roya had a sense, stronger than the day before, of how foreign they were. Or no...the people in this van—Roya, her mother and the rest of them—they were the foreigners. Hazaras might be different among Afghans, but all of them were different here.

• • •

They stopped among containers and nets and crates on a wide concrete apron. *Last stop! Last stop!* the man in the front was saying. She'd dozed a little and couldn't tell how long they'd been driving. The man reached in among the bumping hips and lifted her down, then took her mother's hand as she stepped out. He crouched to bring his eyes level with Roya's and smiled.

'Be good for you *madar*.' His gappy teeth shone under his dark hair. Then he was in the van and gone and Roya realised there were crowds of people hidden by the darkness: women with their children, old people; but mostly men. Men laughing and placing their hands on one another; men standing forlorn and broken by themselves; men in secretive huddles.

She could pick the Afghans by their clothes and beards; sometimes the drift of a word or two in Dari. She could pick the Hazaras from the Pashtuns and the Tajiks, of course; and, she found, the Pakistanis from the Iraqis. She knew that other people had fled from Herat: from the bombed and charred countryside around it. She hadn't known that people in other countries were doing likewise, even drifting in the same direction.

A smell closed in around her, unlike anything she had ever smelled before. Both dirty and clean; something like a food smell but also like the desert sand. She concentrated. The smell was the sea.

And now she made out the ripple and gleam of the water in the middle distance. It shone where the lights caught it, as it would at home. A puddle under a streetlight or a washing dish in a gloomy courtyard, reflecting the stars. The map in her mind told her they would be companions from now on.

• • •

Afghans were good at waiting, Roya's father sometimes said. They could queue for a ride on a truck, for a loaf of bread, for some sort of official questioning. They could outlast the sky's pale stare for a few drops of rain. They'd waited out the Soviets, he'd said, then the mujahideen, then the Talibs and the Americans. Afghans were a patient people, he told her, and they would wait out the Talibs again. But it was the Talibs who lost their patience with him.

There were police standing around in their grand uniforms, Roya saw. Casually, not because anyone was in trouble, and they were smiling and shaking hands with other men. The police in Herat wore robes, and they certainly didn't smile. These police had gold stars and badges and all sorts of decorations on their tight shirts. They looked like American police. *Cowboy*, she mouthed silently. *Sheriff.*

She watched them smoking, turning their backs discreetly to shuffle wads of money. One of the men was older than the others, dressed like a businessman. He laughed like he'd heard a rude joke. Something sparkled among his teeth. He clapped his hands sharply now and everyone turned to face him. He barked some orders and the crowd began to drift towards the edge where the concrete ended abruptly over the water.

A crush developed near the edge. Roya and Shafiqa found themselves in the centre of it, careless elbows knocking sharply into Roya's head. Her mother kept her close, arms linked protectively against the shouting and pushing. This only irritated Roya; it should be her protecting her mother, not the other way around. A boy fell and someone stepped on him so that he squealed in pain before his father hauled him up again.

She'd seen pictures of boats in books, but this—it was so tall! The bow, a dirty timber wall sweeping upwards in a great curve from her right to her left. The cabins were stacked on top of each other like cigar boxes, and atop the front deck a small red and white flag hung motionless in the lazy night air. The Indonesian flag, Roya knew: her English book had a page devoted to the flags of the world—*Union Jack, Hammer and Sickle, Maltese Cross*—and the one that filled her with such mixed feelings: the mosque, the golden leaves and sacred words. *Afghanistan.*

The boat was a thing of wonder: its dark bulk, its subtle movement against the wharf, bumping lightly on the slimy tyres that were slung as fenders. She could feel its enormous weight suspended by the water, an immensely powerful animal testing its leash. Greeny-blue paint, flaking now; dark spills of rust weeping under the metal fittings. A little tired; but perhaps this was the way of all boats. It had been important to people, she thought, but was forgotten now. Forgotten people on a forgotten boat.

Shafiqa gripped her hand tightly as they approached the edge. One of the men had moved closer, pushing people onto the gangway plank. Roya placed her feet carefully on each of the small steps that had been nailed across for traction, the heads of the nails pressing through the thin soles of her sandals. Cigarette smoke made clouds overhead; voices hurried them.

Her mother guided her to a space behind the high sides of the boat. Roya sat cross-legged on the deck, feeling the alien swaying for the first time: they were no longer of the land, but now of the sea. A man came past, handing out bright orange jackets with reflectors on them, clips and buckles. Roya sniffed the clumsy object, as she often did with things that aroused her curiosity: plastics and mould, and old diesel like the generator at the library.

She checked her treasures, the things from which she would never be parted: her father's ring, heavy and scrolled, tumbling like a snail in the pocket her mother had sewn into her dress; and her English book—a worn copy of the *Pocket Oxford Dictionary,* between the pages of which she kept the photograph she loved.

Her mother. The ring. The book and the photograph. Between them she strung the globes of her hope.

She checked over her mother once more and received a smile in return. Satisfied, she curled up and turned her face back to the orange jacket. A single word had been written across it in heavy black capitals. She rolled the new word around in her mouth several times:

TAKALAR.

Indian Ocean, south of Lombok

The sun splayed through the rum bottle, casting a bar of golden light on Isi's feet. The stern deck had a tendency to draw in diesel fumes when they were under way, but tonight there was a faint breeze to carry the exhaust away from them, and the only smell in the air was the releasing warmth from the timbers.

They were heading east, away from the sunset. The guests had crowded up onto the deck above the stern and were cutting limes for their duty-free spirits, talking over each other as they sluiced through the iceboxes for beer. Hands on the stereo, hands gripping the overhead metal frame of the sun canopy, hands in motion telling stories.

They were hyperactive; first-nighters always were. Clean and pale and brand new, but experience told her they weren't a tight group. Some groups were bound by lifelong friendships. Some, like the company-sponsored team trips, had a kind of corporate familiarity about them. But this lot were ones and twos, loose acquaintances: a polite distance in their words and movements around each other.

She leaned against the bulkhead, looking back at the spreading wake. She was the smallest person here, thanks to what her father called the *paesano* gene: her skin dark by birth and by constant exposure to the tropical sun. Her feet were splayed flat and even darker than her legs, with white margins between her toes. Joel had laughed when he first saw them. Island feet, he'd said.

Isi waited until the group had settled, drinks in hand. Sanusi had the helm, and would sit there watchfully until she took over at midnight.

'Hi everyone,' she began. 'I'm Isi Natoli—I think I've met you all now. Joel wishes he could be here but as you've heard he's busy sweating out a dose of malaria. So seeing as I'm Joel's partner in the business and in, um, life...You've got me.' She flashed a modest smile.

'So, introductory stuff. We're steaming east from Benoa Harbour and we've got a fair voyage ahead, so get yourselves comfortable.' A wave at the colourful bottles; a couple of the guests waved their drinks back.

'Okay. Welcome aboard the legendary *Java Ridge*. As you might know, she was built for us by the Bugis people up in Sulawesi, who are boat-builders and sailors from way, way back. They got as far south as the Australian coast on trading runs. The Bugis were also fearsome pirates who liked slashing up the Dutch in the old spice-trading days, which is thought to be where the idea of the Bogeyman came from... Bugis Man, Bogeyman, yeah?' No response. 'Anyway, we had her built along traditional lines, so the idea was from the outside she'd look exactly like a traditional fishing vessel, but on the inside—luxury!'

A little cheer went up. Raised Bintangs again.

'So this type of vessel is called a *phinisi*, and they go back, as I say, about five hundred years. All timber, very long, stretched bow... the whole boat's made without computers, without even power tools. It's a piece of living history.' And they'd managed to duck a welter of engineering regs by building it up north. Joel and his instinct for the path of least resistance.

'Okay, so we're travelling east towards Sumba, then Rote and Timor, generally in the direction of PNG, if you know your geography. Now there's plenty of people who've surfed Rote, and there's plenty who've surfed Sumba—that's where Occy's Left is, if you've ever seen *Green Iguana...*' Appreciative hoots and chuckles. They always loved it when Joel dropped the *Green Iguana* reference. 'But we're not taking you there.' Mock booing. 'We're going somewhere a little bit wilder and you'll be able to tell anyone you've surfed a place they haven't. It's an island called Raijua, between Sumba and Rote, and believe me, there's something there for everyone.'

She knew how the chorus would go and it went exactly that way. *Yew! Sick! Yeaah!* Sometimes, but not very often, the sameness of this culture wearied her.

'It's about four hundred nautical miles out of Bali, so it's going to take us forty hours or more, depending on conditions.' They groaned collectively, as anticipated. 'Now there's a few rules to observe while we're motoring across. Have a few beers by all means, but be conscious that you're on a fast-moving boat on the open sea. Be careful around the ladders and if you take a piss over the side'—she felt their eyes on her when she said *piss*. A tiny encroachment—'be very careful to hang on. Remember, one hand for you, one for the boat. If we don't know you've gone over we might never find you out there. Okay, what else? Beers in the iceboxes—we'll keep topping them up as fast as you can drink them, but please write down what you take on the clipboard. You're going to eat really well, but if you want to troll a lure and catch us a fish, the boys'll love you for it.'

She nodded towards the two Indonesians lounging behind her against the cabin wall. Grins and finger-waves. Sanusi had politely turned up for the briefing, leaving the *Java Ridge* on autopilot. Isi's confidence rested heavily on Radja and Sanusi. They knew the cycles of a surf trip: the build-up of first-night anticipation, the routines of the days to come, periodic elation and the gradual onset of exhaustion and injuries. Their mood, as steady as the diesels below, would never waver.

'They're Batak people, from northern Sumatra—a long way from home just like you guys, so be nice to them. Radja will be looking after the Zodiac—it's on the crane up the back there. When he's taking you out to the lineup, please don't jump out until he gives you the nod. You can wave to him from the water and he'll bring you sunscreen or wax or whatever. Beer, if you can signal that.' More cheers. 'So Radja's your chef, and he's a good guy to know. He'll even whip you up something in the middle of the night if you're on a session.'

'Bagus,' offered Radja with an easy smile.

'Sanusi there is our engineer. He can operate anything on this entire vessel and he can fix your boards better than they do back home. Don't, whatever you do, mix these two up and ask Sanusi to cook you something. He's fucking terrible.' Again the minor ripples through the group, a smirk here and there. The spiel played differently for her than it did for Joel.

'There's snorkelling stuff, so go for a swim if you're bored with barrels. These reefs are live coral, so they're worth a look. Stand-up paddleboard...' It was hung neatly under the awning where they were gathered. She knocked on its deck. 'Help yourself to that. It's aircon-ditioned down below, and if you notice the aircon's on during the day, please close the hatch behind you. There's gases and other flammables on board, so—have we got any smokers?' The heavy, red-haired one who'd introduced himself as Fraggle raised his hand and realised he was the only one. He'd turned up with Pelican cases, said he was a photographer. He also looked the most easygoing of them.

'Not a crime, Fraggle, but please make sure you only smoke where the boys do, down the back. Yeah?'

She pointed to the young guy with his shirt off, sunnies pushed up into his hair. He'd introduced himself at the airport...Carl. He had his hand raised.

'You got wi-fi?'

'No.'

'Are you gonna sink shots like Joel does?'

She knew it was a bait. 'No, Carl, I'm not. That all right with you?'

A faint *ooh* passed through the group and Carl revelled in his direct hit.

•••

After the talk the surfers stayed on the high deck over the stern, slouched on cushions and laughing loudly. Radja worked his way to and from the galley with trays of fish in lime juice. For their families, Radja's and Sanusi's employment with a surf charter company was a cause for unconcealed pride in their home villages. Their children would boast about it at school: their wives would thread it into conversation in the street.

Fraggle had found the box of Beng Beng bars in the fridge and was somehow alternating the chocolate with mouthfuls of beer. He waved the box at the person next to him. It was the tall girl, Leah. She peered into the box, drew a long strand of brown hair behind her ear and smiled at him. 'No thanks.'

Isi retreated to the wheelhouse and leaned both elbows on the instrument display. She spooned out the rest of the avocado she'd started earlier, flicked the husk out the window into the sea. Congratulated herself on the malaria line, a momentary inspiration. She'd been worrying how she would explain Joel's absence. He was legendary to them, a word-of-mouth phenomenon whose reputation grew over coffees among the marooned city surfers back home. *How long you got for lunch? You wanna try that joint in Little Bourke Street? Hey, did you email the Indo guy?*

The fact that it was him, not her, that they spoke of in hushed tones was of no concern to Isi. They'd talked once or twice about marketing her directly to women looking for an all-female charter, and she liked the idea. But with the steady demand for Joel, who required no marketing, the idea never became a reality. The obvious risk, of course, was that when Joel wasn't available the clients felt they'd been had. They needed a cover story, and malaria was a pretty good one: it conjured the great surf explorers like Troy and Cooney. A bag of rice and a motorcycle; a fateful mozzie one jungle night.

Whereas in fact Joel was talking to bankers, because the business was bleeding money. Credit cards, fuel bills, people with their hands out for cash all over the place. The old Javanese man who'd sleep on the boat at the wharf in Benoa to ensure it wasn't pilfered, even though it was his own cronies doing the pilfering. The capital partners required by Indonesian law—businessmen from Jakarta who appeared only on holidays, wearing the wrong batik and as foreign to the locals as Isi and Joel were. The 'taxes' paid in cash to a revolving cast of local officials; the casual handouts to make business happen quicker; the kid on the motorbike...the workshop...the food wholesaler.

Indonesian banks were liberal with their credit, but the Australian end had had enough. Every extension or limit increase meant a trip to Perth and another twelve hundred dollars in flights.

Isi went sometimes. She could dress the part and spout the commercial buzzwords. But when Joel did the trips he came back hungover and irritable, and sometimes empty-handed. She could trace his exhaustion through the online banking: casino, nightclubs, favourite pubs with his old schoolmates. Shouting the bar and making a big fella of himself. *Yep, I run a charter business in Indo. It's epic. You should come over.*

She glanced over the pictures of Joel on the cabin wall.

Joel surfing, Joel drinking. Joel always, always grinning. There was the one someone took of them the night they got together—the night he pulled off his best feat of salesmanship. She was first year out with an engineering degree, determined to break into the boys club, and the resources boom was pulling all the available talent into its orbit: even a few women like her. She'd flown to Jakarta for an interview with an oil and gas joint venture, gone out drinking with the recruitment people and stumbled into this bullshit artist along the way. A week's growth, red eyes and a crinkled smile, buying her drinks and asking why she wanted to analyse load tolerances in a dirty city. She'd looked at the ends of his brown collarbones, visible in the frayed neck of his T-shirt, and realised he probably spent almost as much time under the open sun as he claimed.

Within four days she'd moved into his crappy apartment, armed only with a bag and a credit card. She didn't go home for another year.

'Imagine it,' he'd said that night, his hand on her forearm, selling her the dream. 'All the waves you could ever want. Money, freedom…I'll be your backup guy. Just run the boat while you look after the clients.'

She burst into laughter at that. The audacity of him.

'Look around you.' He swept his arm around the room full of bellowing expats. 'Worker ants. They're nothings. You could have the ocean for the rest of your days.'

Don't look away, said the eyes, green and pale and burning with something. *Don't laugh and brush me off. This is the truth.*

And he was right of course, in a way. Life on the water—the image they fed to the wailing baby of social media—was magnificent.

But the life they really led was one of photogenic poverty. Rented lodgings in Kuta, a mattress on the floor and the same blackouts and internet failures as everyone else who lived back-of-house to the tourism. The traffic, the litter and snarling mopeds, the smell of broken sewers.

So, the begging trips.

But this time, as Joel walked away from the van at Denpasar airport, Isi saw him in sharp focus. He was a drifter. He could live on nothing much, burn the lot and start again. His instinctive response to any kind of hardship was to move on—she'd seen him do it already. That easy version of friendship he practised...all his clients were 'brother' until the financial hooks were set, then they were 'mate'. Shortly afterwards they were forgotten entirely, and none of it was worth a pinch of shit in the hard times.

His vast knowledge of the islands, his mind-map of the reefs— they were real. They would always be in demand. He didn't need to grind out the sheer hard work it took to build a business. Someone would pick him up to skipper their boat and he'd do it until he'd stashed enough money to start again. Open another business, screw another partner. There was enough ocean out there that he could indefinitely avoid the people he burned. Her included.

• • •

In a drawer to the left of the navigational instruments she'd stored the clients' passports, as she was required to do until she'd entered them in the government register. This was a good time to start on them, before the demands of the surfing took over.

Neil and Luke Finley.

The surgeon and his son. The resemblance in their photographs, as in life, was remarkable. Joel had warned her about the father, who'd travelled with him before. The Vaucluse vowels, the aloofness. Polite, but only as an expression of his superiority. He drank very little, listened more than he talked. *Snob*, said Joel, but there was something to be said for having a doctor along. Injuries happened. Usually minor, but not always.

She looked down from the wheelhouse windows at them, side by side in the hammocks on the foredeck. They'd both shaved their heads down to a number-one. Both wore the same brand of boardies, coathanger-new with the stitching still sharply white. And they were fit. Stringy, mung-bean fit. The lamps lit their ribs. Like brothers separated by a generation, the young bloke's body was an exact replica of the old man's, right down to the bony knobs over his shoulder joints. Neil had a light silver fuzz over his flat pectorals: the youngster was hairless. Six weeks out from his seventeenth birthday.

She carefully entered their details in the ledger and took up another passport.

Timothy Wills.

A trip to India at eighteen and a border crossing into Nepal. A couple of Indo entries. Twenty-six now. In his emails booking the group, he'd been eager to establish their environmental cred—*I hope you don't mind me asking: do you use sustainable anchoring practices?* The whole group were copied into the queries, though the tone of their replies suggested only Tim was concerned. He'd been on the boat before. *Harmless*, was Joel's assessment. *And you won't see him on the big days.* She took another passport from the pile.

Carl Simic.

She leafed through the pages. Nothing. His first overseas trip.

Right now he was stretched out on a yoga mat, sipping at the rum he'd been poured. Short but strong, tanned on his forearms and neck. As he reached for his ankles she could see a Southern Cross tattooed on his shoulderblade. But she'd also seen the brands of his board and his gear, bought online from overseas. Not so patriotic with his con-sumer dollar, then.

Joel had said Tim and Carl were cousins. In the exchange of emails about ethical anchoring, Carl had responded—probably for-getting the whole thread was going to Isi's email—*Right behind your environmental push cuz—will make sure I only shit in your board bag.*

They were bickering down there: Carl wanted a rum and Coke, Tim was starting in on a lecture about sugar. *Coke's just toxic sludge*, Tim said. *Cleaner than the water here*, Carl shot back. Over ten days at sea the heat and fatigue and close-quarters living normally brought out the worst in people who couldn't reflect on their own behaviour. One or two mishaps—an infected cut or a broken board—and these two would be at each other's throats.

She hurried through the passports for Fraggle (*Alan James Veal*— no wonder he'd cooked up an alias) and Tim's girlfriend Leah Hogan. Fraggle had been everywhere: Morocco, Spain, Hawaii, Mexico, Chile. The perpetual wandering of a journeyman photographer. As for Leah, she'd had a gap year in the UK at eighteen and passed through Denpasar on the way back. It didn't tell Isi much.

Below her, Radja was talking to Carl. Trying to joke around, the body language said, while the Australian eyed him suspiciously. She wondered if Radja was incapable of reading the hostility. Or maybe he saw it clearly and was setting out to dismantle it.

Sumba Strait, north of Sumba

There was a feeling of anticipation on the *Takalar* as they passed through a sea gap between mountainous islands. The lights of a distant city warmed the night sky. *Labuan Bajo*, the captain said to someone. A rumour swept the boat: the crowds of small islands were behind them: ahead was the great open expanse of the Indian Ocean and beyond that, Australia.

But as the long night hours passed and they chugged eastwards into the Savu Sea, the festive mood subsided and something more irritable took its place. Roya withdrew from the sound of the fractious passengers, curled herself instead into the familiar folds of her mother's *chador*. She rested her fingers over her mother's forearm and allowed sleep to take her.

• • •

She and Anwar had hidden themselves in the storage space by the well, looking out over the courtyard. Her father had shooed them away when the butcher arrived, herded them out with the other animals, while ensuring one sheep remained. It was this, the act of selecting, that spelled the animal's doom. The *dhabihah* must not take place in front of the other sheep, any more than in front of the children. They were dumb beasts and nothing more, but she knew them. It felt like a betrayal to be watching this happen, yet it was too terrible and forbidden to pass up.

The butcher sharpened his knife, talking calmly to her father while he did so. He had his back to the sheep, which was now tethered to a peg, and the animal seemed unaware of the sliding blade, even though the sound, the steel on steel, carried to where Roya and her brother were hidden, breathing softly. At a word from the butcher, her father took the sheep in his arms, kneeled beside it and ran his fingers gently, gently over its neck. Roya had done this many times but not this way: not looking for the courses of its blood under that warm fur.

He took a tin cup and placed it under the animal's snout, keeping two fingers on its neck as it drank, marking a place. He lowered the cup and withdrew; the butcher moved in deftly, and pushed the knife into the spot that the fingers had indicated. When it had gone in all the way, he drew it around the sheep's throat as it kicked and thrashed, holding it firmly by one of the soft ears.

Roya tightened her grip on her brother and held her breath.

The butcher's words drifted towards them, *Bismillah Allahu Akbar*, as he completed the circling of the knife. He lifted the animal's head back and the blood came gushing forth onto the sand. A final kick raised dust that settled on the blood's bright pool, then it shuddered and its legs collapsed. Her father had his arms around the animal now and he caught its fall and eased it onto its side, taking the utmost care of it—as the laws required him to do.

• • •

She shuddered as she woke. Dawn, and the sky was choked with a high gloom. Smoke from forest fires, the captain said. It made a halo around the rising sun, mixed with the diesel fumes that wafted over the deck and made people cough. The gas stove burned noisily in the kitchen doorway: some of the women were preparing tea. It had been Roya's routine, every dawn. Collect the pile of sticks at the door, left by her brother the previous night. Light the stoves in the kitchen and the bathroom, blow on the struggling flame until it took. Set the water to boil, fill the washbasins, cook the bread. Chase the endless grit that settled over every surface of the house. It had felt unremarkable, faintly tedious until the Taliban took it all away. Now it felt like lost comfort.

As the sky began to glow in front of them, Roya found her mother awake, standing heavily on the boards of the deck to stretch herself. High above Roya, her mother's reaching hands wavered slightly with the movements of the boat. The light was weak over the quiet sea. They were out of sight of the other passengers, many of whom were still below decks. There was a timber floor down there for people who wanted to escape the weather, covered with old carpet and cushions. Roya had been in there but she didn't like it: the lighting was dim and the older people jealously guarded their share of the floor space, snarling at any child who came near. The tiny kitchen area was even less welcoming: a chaotic huddle of women heaving sacks and crashing into each other as the unseen movements of the ocean confounded them.

Roya had discovered a gap where a trickle of seawater ran onto the deck from each passing wave. She took her plastic sandals off and examined her feet, letting the water run over them. There were stripes of dirt where the sandal straps had been, and she carefully rubbed her wet hands over them until the marks were gone. Then she wet the sandals and rubbed at them until they were clean again, revealing the tiny sparkles in the plastic. She left the sandals to dry and watched Shafiqa unfurl herself in the gathering sunlight.

'Mama, can you tell me the little verse about the egg?'

Her mother looked down at her thoughtfully. 'The egg? Hmm. Was it Rumi?'

'I think so.'

Shafiqa sat down and drew Roya into the folds of her *chador*. 'See if I can remember,' she muttered. Roya thrilled to the tracing of her mother's fingertips across her forehead and into her hair—

Like the ground turning green in a spring wind
Like birdsong beginning inside the egg
Like this universe coming into existence,
the lover wakes and whirls in a dancing joy,
then kneels down in praise.

'What do you think it's about?' asked Shafiqa when she'd finished. Roya was reluctant to answer in case her mother stopped stroking her hair. But she said, 'It feels like he's talking about the morning.'

'Yes, that's what I think,' said Shafiqa. 'Or maybe it's about starting again.'

'I spoke to a boy and he said we have to go in camps when we arrive.'

'Camps?'

'He said they're like jails, and no one knows when they will be let out.'

Shafiqa's fingers ceased their linear strokes and began to trace circles. 'I don't think so. But even if there is something like that, we will be together. It can't be worse than what happened at home.'

'I want to see the beach,' said Roya.

'The beach?' Shafiqa's tone was gently scornful. 'We'll see.'

• • •

As the passengers awoke they each took a bowl of rice and passed a cup of water between them. There were awkward attempts to defecate over the side, out of view. During the night Roya had heard some of the adults getting up and moving about for this purpose so they wouldn't be seen. It made her worry that they would topple over and never be seen again. There was a lookout posted overnight, a short, silent Iraqi man. But he was only looking forward, not behind.

The sea was getting up now as the expanse around them grew larger, the land more distant. People sitting together were knocking against each other and the tiny, constant adjustments needed for balance made them tired. Many of them weren't sleeping at night either—the heat, their private torments. They would move about the deck, settle and writhe and grumble and re-settle.

The old Pashtun man with his hennaed beard was seated against the stern of the boat, his sons immovably flanking him. Like watchful dogs, Roya thought. From eavesdropping, she had learnt that the old man was called Irfan Shah and that the family came from Khost. She wondered how they had wound up on this boat: surely Sunnis should have enjoyed the favour of the Taliban? Something must have gone wrong for them.

There were boys climbing on the roof. The captain was telling them off. *The navy will see you, you idiots.*

The man to Irfan Shah's left was trying to eat rice and he had no hands. Roya couldn't tell his ethnicity because his face was so shattered, scars expanding like a sunburst away from where his nose used to be. The little dark tunnels and pocks in his skin, Roya knew, were the paths of shrapnel. He scooped at the bowl with his two stumps, pushing his face into it and groaning in despair as the bowl flipped over and landed in his lap. He tried now to push the sticky grains with the shorter stump onto the side of the longer stump—his left—to lift a few morsels to his torn mouth. Roya wondered how he had fed himself until now.

Irfan Shah stared openly at the spectacle. 'What happened to your hands, brother?' The man looked up at him, didn't answer. Whatever his background, he clearly didn't feel the older man's authority.

'You have no hands. Have you maybe lost your ears as well?' Again the man ignored him and continued to fumble the rice around. Roya felt a helpless anger stirring inside her. This was an exchange between adults—none of her concern. And it was not as if it was new to her, seeing someone missing a hand, an eye, a foot. A person could be damaged, just as a building might be: ruptured by an explosion and left with a stairwell that went nowhere, or a balcony that hung by twisted rods of steel. But the problem here, the man trying to eat, could be fixed so easily.

A bigger feeling had been working away at her for some days now—a feeling of boldness, the loosening of old rules with so much adrift. Without even glancing at her mother for permission, she scuttled across to where the man sat and pressed the spilt rice into a clump on the palm of her hand. Then she placed the clump delicately on his forearm. It felt daring. He barked at her and she withdrew, but then he lifted the arm to his mouth and got the rice in.

'Be gone, little girl! Have you lost your manners?' Irfan Shah was outraged. One of the sons muttered something that Roya missed. The old man stared at the amputee and asked again. 'So what happened?'

Again there was no answer. Mucus trickled from a dark hole, the ghost of a nostril. 'Were you making a bomb? Looks like it blew up in your face.' He shook his head in mock pity. 'Hazaras. Dumb as donkeys, the lot of you.'

The man's tongue appeared, cat-like, and slowly licked the remaining rice grains off his forearm before he spoke.

'Shut up, you old fool.'

Roya was knocked down as the two younger men rushed forward, piled onto the man and tumbled him backwards. Other men threw themselves into the fight and women screeched at them: in seconds a crowd had formed around them on the deck, voices shouting in Arabic, Urdu, Pashto and Dari, drowning each other out. The amputee couldn't grapple with the young men, and they quickly overpowered him, pummelling his face with their clenched fists. The back of his head resounded against the boards of the deck as they hit him.

'*Wadrega!*' The single word from the old man Irfan Shah brought the brawl to a halt. 'Aluddin! Mahmud—*bas!* Remember your place.'

Calm was restored but nobody moved off. Roya saw a wisp of hair on the captain's head lifting in the breeze made by the boat's progress. He was watchful, that captain, secretive. Moments like the fight—and there had been a few along the way—were nobody's fault. Yes, Irfan Shah had taunted the no-hands man. But he had done that because he was bored and worried and tired. He'd probably never had to speak to Hazaras in anything but the most passing manner. Now he was stuck among them.

Within minutes, a mother was anxiously brushing her children's hair 'so they look nice for the officials'. A man commented to Roya's mother that it was bad to travel without a husband.

The whole boat was on edge.

• • •

Roya liked to go to the front of the boat, to the point where the curve of all the timbers led, and one great heavy timber joined them together and pushed vertically through the sea. If she lay at the very point of the boat and looked down she could see the whitewater curling either side of that timber, the swoop of an old man's whiskers. From here, the sea stretched out in every direction like a wide plain of moving grass—and they were passing through it in a great caravan that trailed streamers and glittered in the sun and rang with the sounds of *tambor* and cymbals.

There was a boy lying there this morning. He wore shorts, like she thought an American boy would. And he had glasses, with thick lenses. She had never met a child with glasses before; she'd only seen them on television. He shuffled across without comment, offering her space. He had his chin on his knuckles as he peered over. His assumption of ownership irritated her.

'You are from Afghanistan?' he asked.

'You're sitting in my place.'

He rolled from one side to the other, checking the timbers. 'There's no sign here.'

'I've been in this spot for days,' Roya insisted. 'It's mine.'

'What's so good about it?' the boy asked, calm as a glass of water. 'It's no good without a friend.'

Roya sighed and rolled her eyes. 'You're very annoying.'

'No, I'm Hazara. Same as you, I think.'

He was smiling at her. She concluded that he could be both annoying *and* Hazara.

'Are you travelling with your parents?' she asked him eventually.

'Don't have any. My uncle is that man over there.' He pointed down the line of the starboard side, where a man with a dark moustache sat cross-legged and silent, lost in his own thoughts. 'That was funny, wasn't it—the fight?'

'No it wasn't, it was awful. That poor man...'

'I know, but at least something interesting finally happened. This is very boring.'

She looked at him sceptically. 'What happened to your parents?'

'My father had a helicopter,' he said gravely, 'and a tank, a massive one with rockets and guns. My uncle sold them so we could go on the boat.'

'He did not,' laughed Roya, though anything was possible, she supposed.

'It's true. He was the commander of all of Kandahar.'

'The whole city? *Pffft.* So where is he then?'

'They killed him. Hung him at the football stadium.'

Roya caught her breath. Would anyone make such a thing up? Maybe there really was a helicopter and a tank.

They watched a distant landmass slowly growing on the horizon, listened to the wheezing and banging of the engine below them. The boy spoke again without prompting.

'I'm going to be a chef in Australia.'

'Really?' She was beginning to like his grand statements, true or not.

'Yes, and I'm going to learn to swim.'

Roya considered this. 'But we will be in camps, won't we? I don't think you can learn to swim there.'

He shrugged. 'That's okay. Just play computer games all day long.'

'Will you really be a chef?'

'Why not? Their food is simple, and you can cook it on television and become famous. That's what I'm going to do. You will hear them say "Hamid" on the television and you will look up and it will be me. I'm going to own two restaurants, or three or four, and everyone will know me.'

'Can you actually cook?'

He shrugged again. 'Not yet. But I'm only eleven. It can't be too hard.'

'Well I hope you are successful.' She got up to leave. She needed to check on her mother.

He rolled over to look up at her. 'I will see you again, Roya,' he smiled.

'Um, yes,' she responded, stifling a laugh. 'We're on a boat.'

...

She found her mother where she had left her, sitting alone against the cabin wall on the shaded side of the boat. Shafiqa smiled as she saw her daughter approaching, and took her hand lightly. 'I saw you talking to that boy.'

Roya blushed. 'Hamid? Hmph. He is ridiculous.'

'Do you like him?'

'Mother! Stop it. No I do not. He tells tall stories and he has funny glasses.'

'Yes, just as I thought. You do like him. Very well, the two of you have my blessing.' She laughed a little, then mocked a frown as she saw that Roya was cross with her. 'Oh honey, I'm just...'

'I'm not talking to you anymore!' Roya put her hands on her hips and stormed away. She knew that when she was angry her bottom lip would stick out, and that would make her mother laugh and there was a risk that her mother laughing would make her laugh, so she put her head down and didn't look back.

She would hate it if she really didn't talk to her mother anymore.

She walked uphill, straight to the bow. Hamid was still there, looking out to sea through a pair of toy binoculars blobbed with army camouflage colours. For a fleeting second she considered that he must have brought these with him all the way from home. That he might have a bag of treasures, as she did. He lowered the binoculars when he heard her approaching.

'Ah, you are back! Come and join me!'

Roya stood there, hands on hips again. Her irritation and worry boiled over: she aimed a swift kick at the binoculars in his hand and watched them spin from his grip and over the edge of the boat. She erased the image of his shocked face by flicking her hair and turning her back on him, but she saw enough of that look to know how cruel she'd been.

Indian Ocean, south of Sumba

Isi wasn't particularly prone to superstition but time on boats gave you a feeling for trips that worked and trips that didn't, and an eye for which kind you were on. She was steering the *Java Ridge* between the two small islands off the southern tip of Sumba when she first felt a shiver of misfortune hovering. She shrugged it off. She had a group that would have preferred Joel, that was all.

The passage between the two islands—Halura to the north and Manggudu to the south—was less than two miles wide but the water was deep off the edges of the atolls, and it would give her a chance to show her guests some scenery after the monotony of the overnight crossing from Bali.

She slowed the *Java Ridge* as the colours of the reef on Halura's southern side rose from the blue. The powerful diesels burbled at low revs and the bow-wave became sluggish and loud. The boat pitched and rolled with the swells passing under it. In the distance they could see the thatched roofs of the village on Halura's western tip. On the steep hills behind the houses, the jungle was so thick that nothing—not a fence, an aerial or a roof—disturbed it.

Sanusi appeared with a heavy tuna rod, slightly taller than he was, and offered it to the surfers as they lounged on the shaded front deck.

'Good here.' Sanusi pointed along the edge of the reef.

Leah folded her paperback face down on her towel and dropped a water bottle next to it. She stood to take the rod. Isi, watching the exchange from the wheelhouse, had decided she liked Leah—her physicality and her lack of airs.

'You want big lure,' said Sanusi. A statement, not a question. He disappeared below decks and returned with a colourful plastic squid that trailed streamers and two large treble hooks. He looped the line over his cracked index finger and tied the lure on, then handed the rod back to Leah. She sat herself on the bow, directly in Isi's line of sight, and flicked the lure out towards the reef until the line extended well wide of the boat, then snapped the reel into gear. Sanusi took himself halfway down the same side and sat in the shadow of the cabin with a handline and a cigarette both sprouting from the same fist. Between them was an open stretch of deck, the wide timber boards slick with seawater.

Isi could see them both without leaving the captain's chair. If she looked out wide she could even see the surface disturbance made by the lure. Nothing much happened for a while. But then as the *Java Ridge* mounted a swell, the rod whipped down and Leah strained her arms to keep it under control. The reel fizzed with each bounce of the rod tip and she stood, thighs braced against the rail so that it left white marks in her flesh, winding the reel and working the fish towards the boat as Isi backed off the throttles.

Isi could see the silver flank of the fish making urgent circles down deep in the clear water. Ordinarily Sanusi would be up and waiting with the gaff hook to haul it in, but she could see that he hadn't moved. Maybe he'd fallen asleep in the sun. She considered calling out to him but thought better of it. Fishing was Sanusi's department, and he wouldn't welcome the intervention.

Leah had wrestled the powerful fish to the bow of the boat, and now she was trying to winch it vertically through two metres of air to get it to deck level. It was a Spanish mack, long and slender. The graceful tail sliced at the air as Leah wound the reel and walked back, shrieking with excitement. Isi could see the eye of the fish screaming panic behind the wolfish rows of its teeth.

With a final heave, Leah lifted the fish over the rail. It thunked down hard on the timbers and began to thrash wildly. In an instant the lure had been tossed free and the mad convulsions of the fish had pointed its head down the deck. Leah dropped the rod and groped at it, trying to keep her fingers clear of the ferocious mouth. Then the *Java Ridge* mounted a new swell and the bow lifted so high that the bowsprit pointed at the sky, and the mackerel began to slide.

Isi could see what was unfolding but was powerless to intervene. She flew to the window and yelled Sanusi's name as loudly as she could. He woke, looked around and immediately took in the heavy fish sliding towards him. Rising to a crouch, he began to leap away but the last part of him to move was his left hand. The gaping head of the mackerel slammed into it and he cried out in pain. The impact deflected the fish, speared it through one of the deck scuppers and it was gone.

Isi ran down the gangway to find Sanusi's hand was sliced through the large muscle at the base of his thumb, as cleanly as if someone had slashed it with a scalpel. It was bleeding freely. He held the arm over the rail to allow the blood to run off, talking to himself fast and low in Bahasa: Isi followed enough to know he was cursing his own carelessness. A circle gathered around him—Neil Finley's long fingers appeared over the hand and the others withdrew. Isi went and found the two plastic tubs Joel kept in the main cabin: the one marked *Medical* that she'd used only on coral cuts, sunburn and ailments of overindulgence; and the one marked *Surgical*, which she had never opened and never wanted to open.

She set them up on the table in the lounge and Finley brought Sanusi in. Within minutes, and with barely a word to anyone, he'd washed the wound out, jabbed it with lidocaine and stitched it up. Half an hour later, Sanusi was seated in exactly the same position, smoking away sedately with his left hand wrapped in bandages. Finley brushed off his thanks: such tasks were often the lot of a doctor on a surf trip. Even Leah's apologies eventually abated—Sanusi was clearly self-conscious about the whole thing. But Carl must have assumed he had some licence in respect of his cousin's girlfriend.

'What were you fucking...what were you *doing*?' he sneered.

Leah looked back at him, her mouth open in surprise. Then, just as a retort might have formed, she changed her mind, smiled and turned her back.

But the incident stayed with Isi for hours: the tiny misjudgment and its consequences. Would it have happened on one of Joel's trips? Maybe, she decided eventually. But he wouldn't have told her about it.

Canberra

Cassius pushed hard to catch the bunch as it sped northeast on the Federal Highway. The last of the houses at Watson fell away behind as he reached the other riders. He took the stragglers first: the unfit ones, the ones on cheap bikes. The firm silence of carbon fibre and the wind under his helmet whispered predation: the feeling of taking down the weak, a finger raised on the bars in greeting as he passed. He stood on his pedals, pumping harder as the road steepened ahead of him. He could work past anyone on this ride: he knew them all. He could run cadences that would ruin them utterly, could push until he threw up if he had to. But the reality was he never had to.

The incline was slowing him now. He returned to the saddle, thumbing through the rear cassette until he had his revs right. More of them falling behind him, and the bunch up ahead on the crest. He directed his thoughts through his thighs, disengaged his mind from his arms.

And there at the rear of the bunch he could see his quarry, bony arse high over the saddle, chewing extravagantly as his stringy legs pumped. Ron Smedley: his departmental secretary. A nothing in a suit, and a sub-nothing in lycra. Cassius powered up to him and hung quietly in his slipstream, banking energy. A quick glance over Smedley's gear confirmed so much about the man that was irritating.

He was rolling twelve grand's worth of space-age touring machine, emblazoned in green with the manufacturer's logo. Nice bike, but perched on it in an Italian racing jersey he looked like a poser. He was still using Look cleats after all these years—*rocking them*, Cassius smirked to himself—despite how they made him walk. Skittering through cafes like a yearling on a frozen pond. And none of the head-gear—the rainbow-tinted plastic shades that wrapped gigantically around his cheeks, the aero helmet—could conceal it: Smedley had a weak chin. Cassius slipped round from behind him and pulled alongside.

'Ron.'

'Cass.'

'Pulling hard mate. You're a little out of breath.'

'No I'm not.'

'Mm. Hey, did you see my announcement the other day?'

'Yes of course.'

'What'd you think?'

They'd crested the hill near the New South Wales border now, and Smedley shifted through the gears to set himself for the downhill. He gave it a dozen firm cranks—Cassius matched them easily—then held the pedals parallel to the road.

'Not up to me to think, is it? Just there to carry out your commands.'

'Must have an opinion.'

'Look, Cass, if they drag me in front of Senate Estimates, I'll defend it to the hilt. But privately...' He looked down at the asphalt blurring past under his pedals, then jabbed at his Cateye with a gloved finger. 'Privately, I think you're courting disaster.'

'Why?'

The Minister for Environment and Conventional Energy drew level with them and began to pull ahead.

'Boys.'

'Bob.'

'Bob.'

They waited until he was clear.

'Because I have a kind of old-fashioned insistence on the government doing its own dirty work.'

'Oh come on mate, this is a much cheaper option. The BIU and the navy are out of harm's way. And we don't have to front the media and explain what they're doing.'

'Yeah. But has it occurred to you that…' he sucked in a breath, '…being in harm's way is what our armed forces actually do? It's like, their job. The SOLAS rules? Safety of Life at Sea, Cass. Look it up.' He drew a series of short breaths. 'And, um…you're s'posed to front the media and explain things. That's *your* job.'

'Taxpayers want us to be frugal, Ron. That's what we're doing.'

Smedley snorted. It cost him a breath. 'Let's be honest, hey? You're motivated by nothing but popularity, Core Resolve's motivated by nothing but profit—and when Mr Popularity hands over the controls to Mr Profit, you've got chaos.'

Cassius was pumping harder, but disguising it. He could feel Smedley straining to stay level and he loved the secret animal politics of it: Smedley didn't want to talk to him, but was compelled by deference. And now he was having to work harder to stay in the unwanted conversation. He pushed the pace again, walking Smedley around an invisible room from which he couldn't escape. He liked to make people talk when they were trying to control their breathing.

'So here's what I want from you, Ron. I want a chain of communication, but with deniability. You understand?'

'Well…as far as that's…understandable.' He was puffing now. Cassius was breaking the fucker down. 'You want to be told what's going on and you want to say you had no idea.'

'Yes, exactly. You can manage that?'

'Don't compromise me, Cass. It'll come back to bite you.'

Cassius couldn't help but laugh at the gasping skinny-arsed bureaucrat. This was what settled the long debates about his future: this right here—a contest of wills. And if they kept feeding him contests of wills he'd win every one of them and he'd die happy.

'You're right Ron, you are old fashioned. How long till the retirement?'

'Long enough…to give you the shits…till the electorate's sick of you.'

Which was not a bad rejoinder for an old bloke, thought Cassius, as he cranked down the gears and left Smedley behind.

West of Pulau Dana

The going was smooth once they cleared the inshore chop near Sumba. Isi separated herself from the surfers and did the rounds of her plants.

She'd seen them glancing at the greenery. It didn't fit with their preconceptions, the rows of planter boxes, foliage spilling down the outside walls of the cabin. It was perfectly normal to Isi, of course. Life in the Kuta apartment with Joel was incomplete without her plants. In Perth, even in Jakarta, she'd managed to find enough space and sunlight to surround herself with pots and buckets and troughs—anything that would hold soil. Mostly she liked to grow edible greens, though sometimes she'd follow a whim that made her happy: jonquils, frangipani, orchids.

Joel, to his credit, had understood her need and even encouraged it. They were both aware of the abundant herbs and spices at the local markets in Denpasar: fresh, dried, packaged or handed over in clumps, trailing wet roots and tied with string. But buying them wasn't the point of it. It was the nurturing and gathering, the tactile business of handling living things—her living things. The pungent smells, the watering, feeding, pruning and re-potting. She picked seeds out of salads when they ate in restaurants, hunting with thumb and forefinger for chillies, capsicum, tomatoes. She could propagate a mint bush from a sprig in a drink, grow lemongrass from the slivered stalk on a curry. Adrift from her upbringing, often adrift at sea, the delicate mooring of a seedling to its soil made her feel centred somehow.

But in Kuta all they had was an upstairs flat: dark, trapped between concrete walls. The shopkeepers had offered to keep her plants on the small allotments behind their stores, but everything she planted there disappeared.

The idea had come to her one day as she sat on the wharf, chatting to Joel while they scrubbed grime off the deck with wire brushes. The sun was ferocious: clumps of fat cloud wandered across the sky but never managed to shade it. Isi was sweating freely. Every ten minutes or so she'd stop her work and run the outdoor shower that sprayed cool rainwater from the *Java Ridge*'s tanks. Under the stream, her clothes soaked and everything glittering in the reborn rain, she knew what to do.

First she tried a small experiment with basil. Delicate and temperamental, if it could survive on board she felt that more ambitious planting might be possible. She went to the truck depot and bought hose clamps from a man in an Iron Maiden T-shirt. She screwed these into the wall of the *Java Ridge*'s cabin, high up, away from the salt spray. Then she dropped a plastic pot into each and stood back to admire the crayon-green of the basil leaves against the timber of the *phinisi*. Next she took a cordless drill and made a fine hole in the sill of the cabin roof above each of the pots. The shavings smelled mysterious and beautiful. She glued short lengths of hose onto the holes so a little rainwater would trickle down and into the pots without disrupting the collection of water for the clients at sea.

Clean air, sunshine, rainwater. The seedlings would need nothing else, provided she could keep them up out of the hull's spray.

For two weeks she fretted over them while Joel took a group of South Africans out to sea. He radioed in frequently—sometimes for business and sometimes for company—and each time she resisted asking him about the progress of her plants.

When he returned she sped down to the wharf on the scooter, to where the *Java Ridge* knocked patiently against the bollards while fishermen yelled over the slicking water. And there, lit by the sun's energy, were her seedlings: a foot taller and vividly green. The only flaw in the operation was the abundance of sun: they'd bolted to seed.

She harvested a few shoots and immediately set to work: fifteen pots, arrayed along both sides of the cabin this time, and planted with an assortment of coriander, chillies, a peanut creeper, lemon balm, stevia and even a knuckle of ginger under its own veil of shadecloth. She added aloe vera for sunburn and garlic for everything. On the window ledge in the galley, where the filtered light would reach them, she lined up jars of alfalfa and mung beans. She armed Radja with secateurs so he could snip shoots for his cooking, and taught him how and when to prune. And this time she added slow-release fertiliser. It took her three hours in the cool of early morning to get all the pots arranged, Joel watching from the wheelhouse, amused but indifferent. He'd been reading the permaculture book she'd left on board. He told her she was a heliotrope—a flower that followed the sun. She'd giggled like an idiot—only Joel Hughes could find a pick-up line in a book about worms.

• • •

Now she swept the fronds aside to make her way into the wheelhouse. In the haze of early afternoon, she could see land on the horizon, a low dark line between blue and blue.

As it neared across the shining surface of the ocean, Luke Finley stood alone, staring at the beach that had materialised, the thin white lines of breaking waves. Spray haze low in the sky, birds wheeling. The island was tiny, maybe only a mile long, rising to a peak of bare boulders at one end. It grew larger but in detail it only looked wilder.

Just the fringing reef, the beach and the trees. So unlikely, so far from anything, that this shocking explosion of life and colour should rise from the abyssal plains of the ocean floor.

The engines grew quieter and Luke skipped up the gangway to the bridge. Isi was standing at the controls, gazing at the approaching island. She wanted to take them close enough to have a look, without tangling with some random pinnacle of reef. She looked at him briefly and caught him regarding his reflection in the glass of the wheelhouse windows. She nodded towards the atoll.

'Dana Island.'

'We going in?'

'We can cruise past it. I want to get a sense of what the swell's doing. It hardly ever breaks here.'

They watched Dana growing before them. Past the small Indonesian flag fluttering on the canopy over the bow, the coral made a graceful arc around the northern side of the island. Each incoming swell found the edge of the reef and followed it.

'Anyone live there?'

'No. The Savunese have beliefs about the place. It's an island of the dead, you know, lost souls and all that. I think you can get a permit to stop there, but no one ever does. They mostly steam through to Raijua.'

There was a loud clattering sound as heavy feet ascended the steps outside. Carl appeared in the doorway, shirtless and smearing sunscreen over his face like a squirrel grooming.

'Oh my God! That thing is *sick*! We stopping?'

Isi sighed. 'I'm just getting a look at the swell. You'll do better at Raijua.'

'What? You're kidding me...' He watched through the front windows of the wheelhouse as a set formed on the encircling reef. She silently cursed its timing.

'Look at that one! Oh *faark*!'

The first wave of the set had lifted majestically, before peeling down the edge of the reef, hollow and perfect. They were close enough now to see the path of whitewater it left in its trail, to draw the imagined lines of their own surfing over its contours. It expelled a cloud of spray, like the exhalation of a living thing, as it collapsed in deep water further on.

Carl's tone darkened. 'Seriously, we have *got* to get on that.'

Isi was about to answer him when Neil Finley arrived, stern and watchful behind Carl. He spoke quietly; a man accustomed to being heard. 'I think the consensus is we're surfing this.'

Carl ducked under the arm that Finley had propped against the doorway and disappeared.

'Raijua's going to be every bit as good and there's a mooring there. If I anchor here I'm going to damage the reef. And the locals don't like people visiting.'

Finley assessed the island over his shoulder. They were close enough now to hear individual waves among the distant roar. 'Locals?'

Isi stood firm, hands on hips. She knew she was being tested.

'I don't see anyone around. Is there a pass in the reef? Let's put it in the lagoon.'

She knew there was a pass. She hesitated, long enough for Finley to press his momentum. 'Good girl. So take us into the lagoon and anchor there. I'm sure there'll be sand.'

If he wins now, the entire trip's going to be a nightmare. 'No. I'm sorry, but I'm the skipper and I'm not go—'

'I'm the client. I don't need to remind you how much money we've paid.' His voice was flat and even, reflecting the glacial certainty of those pale blue eyes. Absurdly, she imagined them over a surgical mask, no other point of reference on his face. No wonder he thought he was infallible.

'No.' Her voice rose slightly. 'We're twenty nautical miles from Raijua. You'll be there in two hours.'

As she spoke there was a splash. She looked out the port window and saw a shake of brown hair in the water and a floating board. Carl. He slung a few strokes of freestyle to retrieve the board, laughing, then saluted the boat and started paddling towards the island, the rest of them cheering and whistling from the bow, scrambling for fins and wax. She knew she'd lost them.

'Get out,' she said to Finley. To her surprise, he obliged. Out in the sun, she whistled to Sanusi and pointed to the Zodiac. He tilted his chin slightly in acknowledgment, and began craning the rubber boat into the water. In a few moments he'd circled the *Java Ridge* to collect the surfers. Isi stood at the rail as the two-stroke exhaust drifted over her, and called down to him in Bahasa. She would take the boat inside the reef and look for an anchorage. He was to come around and join her when he'd dropped them all off.

The last to leave the boat was Fraggle, smeared in zinc and carrying a heavy water housing for his camera. So ill-adapted to the tropical sun, so freckled and pale. He smiled awkwardly at her, his teeth showing yellow against the chemical white of the zinc.

'Not your fault, eh. You're not Joel...' He shrugged and tried the smile again. When she didn't respond, he took a pair of swim fins in his other hand and jumped overboard.

Bringing the *Java Ridge* through the pass in the reef was easy enough. Joel had marked their charts: coordinates that involved lining up a tall dead tree with the odd-shaped pinnacle of red rock at the far end of the island. No trig markers out here, no beacons. Nothing but the accidental symmetry of nature.

The stern swung around to bring the two features into alignment, the deep passage appearing as an inky stripe through the stained glass of the fringing reef. Beyond lay an emerald pool of calm water, then the white beach and the jungle. As the boat rounded the tip of the reef she could see the six of them in the water, clustered close together waiting for a set. The Finleys, shoulder to shoulder and shirtless. Tim and Leah, also side by side, the female form distinctive among the square male bodies. Fraggle kicking his fins over the coral mosaic of the shallows, pushing the bulky camera housing ahead of himself. And Carl, who'd paddled all the way up the line to sit furthest out. Waiting, staring at the horizon and ignoring the conversation around him. *First surf of the trip and he's already a ball of tension.*

Radja silently moved around the boat to stay in the shade as its angle to the sun changed. The bigger swells breathed as they passed underneath, setting the hanging towels fluttering in the heavy air. Isi had been presented with a choice between Joel's way—his easygoing accommodation of people—and hers. Her way would be to fight for authority, to lay it down. But what would it gain her to crack the shits so early in the trip? They were expecting her to do it, goading her to. There was no prospect of fellowship from Leah, welded as she was to her boyfriend.

The *Java Ridge* slipped into the sheltered lagoon inside the reef. Deep below her, the drone of the diesels reduced to a purr and the bow settled in the water. A lumbering turtle hurried out of the way.

For now, at least, she had to defy expectation and surprise them.

• • •

Once she and Sanusi had carefully anchored in the sandy bowl of the lagoon, she went aft to the high deck over the stern where the stereo was. One of Joel's indulgences: huge Japanese lounge speakers bolted to the bulkhead. She lined up a playlist—heavy on bass because it carried further. Then she cranked the dials to send the music over the water to the surfers. Below her, Radja grimaced at the volume.

Sanusi's favourite downtime was crosswords—his way of working on his English. The deafening music would probably irritate him too, but they'd both just have to cope.

Next, she piled the gear she wanted into the Zodiac and drove it ashore. Her feet sank into the heavy coral sand as she hauled the load up the beach and between the palm trees. Behind the palms she knew there was a clearing, an open flat area with a natural grass cover where she and Joel had camped in the past.

She went back to the *Java Ridge* three, four, five times until she had everything piled up in the clearing and sweat was trickling down the small of her back. A high-pitched whistling sound rose from the jungle around the clearing, unwavering like a jet turbine. Sometimes as she worked she would cease to hear it, then a momentary distraction would cause her to focus on it again. Insects, she figured. The spirits of the dead.

The sweat was stinging her eyes. She could smell her own body now, mingling with the scent of sunscreen. In a little over an hour she'd put up four tents: one for her, one for the couple and two to be shared among the remaining four. The Indo boys would sleep on the boat. She walked the beach looking for stones to make a fireplace. The surfers were visible in the distance, and she let the ripples wash over the tops of her feet as she watched the unwrapping swells on the reef. It was still hypnotic, no matter the hours and the miles; the very idea of this reef, stretched around the point of the atoll. Innumerable tiny lives clinging to a foothold in the empty sea.

The margin between the deep-water channel and the dry reef platform was narrow, meaning the rideable part of the wave was no more than a couple of metres wide. It was a pocket of physical possibility that was itself travelling at high speed down the side of the reef and the threading surfer had to hold it somehow. Too far forward and momentum would be lost as the wave shouldered over deeper water.

Too far back, and the cyclonic whirl of the barrelling wave would deposit the rider in the razorblade gardens of coral.

A white blemish appeared in the distant line of blue as someone paddled. She stopped and watched, the music floating past her. The surgeon's son, behind in the race as the wave gathered power and hollowed out, rushing forward onto the shallowest part of the reef. She knew instinctively he'd passed the point where he should have let go, but the kid was still pushing for it. The wave wasn't offering an entry anymore but he was still paddling as the guitar line curled into a death spiral. In an instant the sparkling lip picked him up and slammed him down, hard. He went over head first, the board following soon after. Jesus. Going down that way could drive him into the reef, with the heavy back of the wave behind him and shallow water in front. She lost sight of him for a moment, imagined him somersaulting down the line, his body spinning in a cloud of aerated seawater.

Then he reappeared in the shallows; he'd snapped his legrope and the board had continued on without him. He was swimming—swimming the wrong way because at water level he couldn't see which way the board had gone.

Now he was standing and hopping between coral heads, arms outstretched for balance. She could see Sanusi at the stern of the *Java Ridge*, watching. Sanusi cared a great deal about his work. He unloaded a paddleboard from the deck and made his way over to the surfboard, which had come to rest deep inside the lagoon. He tied it to the paddleboard and set off after Luke, who by now was treading water in the lagoon and catching his breath.

When Sanusi reached him, Luke rolled onto the board and paddled it towards the *Java Ridge*. Sanusi dipped slow paddlestrokes beside him, chatting and smiling, untroubled by his injured hand. Isi watched them for a moment then turned back towards the camp with an armful of stones.

With the tents arrayed around the clearing and the fireplace made, she sat with a towel over her head, watching the others surf. Luke was visible as a lump in one of the hammocks suspended under the awning on the *Java Ridge*'s main deck. She'd left her sunnies on the boat and now the glare was screwing her face into a squint. Thunderheads were building to the north—the radar had indicated bad weather up there. The system was pushing new swell ahead of itself, each new sequence of waves standing taller than the last: the addictive suspense of the ocean before a front. The waiting.

Well, if she was going to roll over, she might as well do it properly. She looked at her watch: 3 p.m. She had time. A few minutes later she stood on the gunwale of the *Java Ridge* in a bikini with a five-ten van Straalen under her arm. This wasn't an indulgence she allowed herself very often. She threw the board onto the dazzling surface of the sea and jumped after it into the body-temperature water; paddled the distance to the reef, swells rising and falling more sharply under her. Sea lice prickled now and then around her ankles. Her whole body was talking back to her, as every practical demand fell silent.

As she reached the takeoff she found only Leah and Tim waiting at the top of the line, the rest of them in various stages of paddling back from rides. The heat of the day had reduced the surface of the ocean to an oily mirror scattered with strange flotsam: a slick of tiny dead fish, leaves, a half coconut. These little ghosts floated past her in streaks between wide stretches of flat water.

And then the sea rose. The first wave of the set was small, forming wide of the reef, but it was only there to announce the larger swells behind. She started moving quickly out to sea, before Tim and Leah knew to react. As she rose over the first wave she could see the second, already darkening much further out. It was big enough and moving fast enough that she struggled to reach it and yet she had time to appreciate the exquisite curvature of the sloped ocean coming forward. The flat water in front of the wave tilted slightly down and into it as it drew the sea towards itself. It moved without violence, its tremendous weight and energy made sinuous by deep physics; a glass escarpment that was concave in two dimensions, trough to peak and end to end, a bowl reflecting the wide convex of the sea floor.

Now it was lifting and the lip of the wave began to fizz. When it reached her, the pitch of the steepening wall would be perfect. She locked her eyes on the exact space she wanted to occupy, then turned and stroked into it. Tim and Leah were wide of her and still sprinting to avoid being run down. She'd be able to weave around them once she was up. It lifted her, tilted her downwards as she paddled, and she swept to her feet.

Rushing under her, the water surface became a transparent lens, the coral heads clearly visible and rising as if to break the surface. She knew they were deeper than they looked: if she held her nerve she'd pass safely over them. Coloured stripes between the corals resolved themselves into reef fish, pulled helplessly around by the powerful suction of the wave. The board accelerated silently as she angled downwards into the bottom turn. She banked onto the inside rail and felt the fins grip tight into the foot of the wave. From here she could see only the great blue wall before her and the wide expanse of the sunlit ocean everywhere else, dotted with the upturned heads of the other surfers.

She swung off the rail and speared the board up the face, unaware of herself and conscious only of the wave's propulsive will. At the peak of her speed, as the board crested the lip, she stood hard on the tail and flicked it back down again, fanning the air with spray. The board slowed momentarily then began to accelerate again and she wove it gracefully down the line, looping the others as they lingered to watch her pass.

The wave rocked and spilled several more times in front of her, curves upon curves. Movements in her hips and calves and feet, tiny contractions her conscious mind had abdicated to experience, took her through the end sections of the wave, faster and faster over coral that rose ever nearer to the surface. Until she kicked over the wave's dying edge and let herself fall face first into the deeper water, where a circle of golden fish were delicately inspecting a coral head.

• • •

Later in the afternoon they all slumped themselves over the front decks in hammocks, on yoga mats and towels, enjoying the faint breeze that picked up over the water. The boards had been returned to their racks by the crew, each with its legrope wound around its tail and buffered against the other boards by an interleaved board bag. Only her van Straalen wasn't there—it lived under Joel's side of the bed in the private cabin.

Fraggle had clipped a camera to the drone and filmed the last of the surfing. Now he was using it to cut high circuits above the boat, filming the reclined bodies on the deck. 'Lifestyle,' he told Isi. 'I'll shoot you a copy of this stuff.'

She was grateful that at least the gadget was being put to a practical use. Joel had outlaid fifteen hundred US on the damn thing, and so far had only perfected the art of taking a cold beer can from the *Java Ridge* out to a surfer in the lineup. It was a popular trick, but no more or less effective than the old way—putting Radja in the Zodiac and running the beer out by surface mail. Somehow the beer-delivery drone typified Joel's approach: do it the flashy way rather than keep it simple and hang onto the money.

The surfers had found the rhythm that settled over every trip: they'd helped themselves to beer from the fridges and were laughing and heckling, reliving the afternoon. Isi was listening to Carl and Tim, sparring like they were at one of their deckchaired family Christmases. What caught her attention, as she pretended to fiddle with a hand-held radio, was their pushing towards an unspoken line.

Carl didn't mind, he was busy telling Tim. He didn't mind. What he minded was Tim bringing *her*. Isi figured this could only be a reference to Leah. She was just about out of earshot, though the boat wasn't a big place. Tim had sold the trip to Carl as a boys' trip, his birthday present to himself. 'You're my one cousin,' Carl was arguing. 'I don't have a brother. Couldn't you have left her at home for ten fucking days?'

'She's not causing you any trouble.'

'She's so bloody picky. Have you watched her eat? Won't eat the chocolate. Won't eat Indo food. Swear I haven't seen a drink in her hand once this trip. I mean, she lives on salads! A bird like that...salad chicks do not deliver.'

Isi marvelled at Tim's self-control. He was screwing his face up but his voice remained calm. 'You don't know what you're talking about, my friend.'

'You're right. I don't. She's probably into like, activated charcoal enemas or something.'

'Freak.' Tim was trying to suppress a smile.

'Me? Mate, it's you I'm worried about. Friends like that, who needs enemas?'

Tim lost the battle and started snorting with laughter. But Carl wasn't done. 'Seriously, how's she gonna have an authentic Indo experience if she won't eat the food?'

'Well how are *you* gonna do it if you won't engage with the Indonesians?' Tim stopped and thought for a moment. 'Things change, Carl. You've got your footy and your work, and I've gone off into—' He made a vague detouring motion with his hand.

'Into what? Chasing causes? What you do, right, it's like the latest fad you've found at uni turns into something that everyone around you has to take up.'

Jumped from the girlfriend to the big issues pretty quick, thought Isi.

'And that's fine,' Carl was saying, 'but I'm not gonna go fucken weeping for people I'm never going to meet. Bad shit happens everywhere. Nothing I can do in my lifetime is going to change that. I'm not going round thinking I'm such a big deal I can change the world.'

Isi could imagine the two of them retreating year by year into their own versions of conscience: Carl and his family (which by extension included Tim); Tim and the world.

Carl had his index finger extended off the beer can now, pointed at Tim for emphasis. A good-looking prick, she thought. Still a prick. 'What about you emailing all your fucking admirers with your—your press photos from getting arrested in the city at your rallies and shit. I delete 'em, you know. I don't even wait for the fucking things to finish loading.' Tim laughed again, despite himself.

'Remember your crush on the Dalai Lama? Then what you called land rights, so we'd go "land rights" and then you'd correct us and go "nah, it's called native title."'

'I get it, Carl.'

'Nah, mate, you know there's more. Bloody boat people...gay marriage, sweatshops and Nike and battery chickens, and what the fuck have chickens got to do with Nike, Tim? Coal seam gas...what else is there? Naomi Klein: what is she, like Calvin's missus? Assange and Snowden...oh, and that poor bloody tranny Manning. It's fucking exhausting mate.'

'Assange is alt-right these days. And yeah, they all matter, even if you deliberately mix them up.'

'They matter to *you*, Timmy.' He took a big slurp from his beer. 'You make the mistake of thinking they matter to everyone, like it's compulsory.'

'Hey, at least I never fell for that Kony 2012 shit.' They both fell silent, then Tim chuckled. 'Fuck, your memory is prodigious. I can't believe you can list all that. You wasted your brain being a landscaper.'

Carl didn't answer him, chose to look out over the sea. *He's hit a nerve*, thought Isi. But there was an underlying affection between these two: maybe Carl loved the way Tim had no idea how he came across. Maybe he loved the fact that he was passionate. The night before the *Java Ridge* had sailed, when they were all laid out in the dormitory at Legian, he'd been talking shit right up to the point that a honking great snore cut off his sentence and he was out like a light. Carl had worn him out with his obstinacy.

The clouds she'd seen earlier were now stacked up on the horizon, an ominous gloom forming under them. Sanusi was watching them too, cross-legged in singlet and boardshorts, absorbed in thought.

'Weather coming in?' she asked him in Bahasa.

'Yeah,' he said, waving his bandaged paw at the clouds. 'Nasty up north, huh?' Then he smiled. 'We get swell though.'

Neil Finley had seen them talking, seen them both watching the dark horizon. 'Is that trouble?' he asked quietly.

'Not for us in the lagoon. You wouldn't want to be out in it though.'

He reached behind him into the icebox and produced two Bintangs, handed her one and prised open the other.

'I've set up a camp on the island,' she said. 'You think everyone will be okay sleeping on land if it gets ugly?'

'Yes, I'm sure they'll be right.'

'Sometimes, when it gets gusty, the boat swings a bit on the anchor chain. It's probably a better night's sleep on land.'

He nodded, took a swig. 'You can surf.'

His tone was so perfectly neutral that she had no idea how to take it. If he meant to be condescending she didn't care anyway.

'Yes. I can.'

...

Once night fell, they sat around the long table in the main cabin, eating big white chunks of reef fish in a salad that Radja had made from Isi's greens. The crew reclined in the shadows away from the clients, eating with their hands, chatting softly in Bahasa.

Isi watched Neil Finley's precise use of his cutlery. 'What kind of surgery do you do?'

He stopped chewing and touched his lips neatly with the knuckle that held his fork. 'Plastics.'

'Must be very interesting work.'

His smile was thin and dismissive. She looked at his son beside him. The boy's face bore the remains of the day's zinc—applied in exactly the same pattern as his father.

'And you, Luke? What do you do?'

Again, that look with its trace of superiority. 'I'm doing year twelve at Scots.'

'You going to be a surgeon too?' she asked, unsure if this was awkward territory.

'Yes.' A tiny smirk. 'That's the plan.'

They were both drinking water, ploughing through the salad. Father and son. *Whose plan, little man?*

Leah sat between Carl and Tim, who were arguing about climate change. Smiling painfully as she attempted to steer the topic away from their differences. She was eating fish without the marinade. The photographer, Fraggle, sat alone at the far end of the table, unnoticed by the others. Isi wondered about him. He'd paid full fare for the trip, but his gear looked professional. Joel reckoned the guy was trying to build up a folio to get magazine work. He was scrolling and tapping at a computer, turning the screen around now and then to show the others his shots from the afternoon. Each was greeted with a chorus of hooting, then conversation would re-form around Fraggle as though he wasn't there, and he would return to his work.

When they'd finished, Isi ferried the guests two by two over to the beach in the Zodiac. When she climbed in she found Sanusi's smokes and lighter resting on top of the plastic fuel tank. She'd told him before that this wasn't a good look, but Joel would've laughed it off enough times that Sanusi was now habituated to ignore her warnings. Someone else waiting for her to finish her shift so life could go back to normal.

•••

These were urban surfers, and this beach was a puzzle. Nothing demarcated it from the jungle behind. Not an erosion barrier, not a fence or a warning sign. There was water, then there was sand, then the jungle crept forward as far as it dared. Nobody would ever build a walkway here. The foliage obeyed no one.

So they wandered across the sand, away from the spill of the shoreward ripples into the heavy grasses and back to the sand again, unsure of where to put their belongings. It was like watching a dog make circles in its bed.

By now, everyone had noticed the towers of cloud soaking up the night's first stars. Lit occasionally by spears of lightning, they'd grown much taller and more menacing, occupying at least a third of the northern sky. The air hadn't changed: it was still and heavy, as it had been all day. Isi was unconcerned. The storm would probably miss them, but even if it scored a direct hit, the boat was safe in the lagoon and they were safe on the island. Carl's selfish dash for the water that afternoon had ended up being the best move for all of them. As she landed the last boatload, a distant rumble echoed over the ocean. The reef had been roaring under the impact of ever-larger swells, but this was different: a vast, alien booming.

This was thunder, and it was coming their way.

North of Pulau Dana

The ocean was no less gigantic by moonlight, a great expanse of restless land. Hills and gullies and cliffs and dunes, cut from some gleaming substance that shifted and fought itself.

Roya watched it with her chin resting on the smooth wooden rail, trying to understand what she was seeing. This changing mood: she had nothing to compare it to. She wondered if the sea had its own mind and had become angry over something.

She was hungry now—they'd started the voyage with bananas, canned fish, rice and bread and water. But the bananas and the fish were eaten rapidly and the bread went mouldy. People were becoming sick.

Her mother had slumped under the rail with an arm extended so that it wrapped around Roya's waist, leaving her enough room to twist her body and watch the sea, the growing chaos that was making the men nervous too. There were so many of them, men of unfamiliar kinds laughing and playing *fis kut* during the afternoon when the ocean was flat.

Their faces tensed when the engine trouble started around sunset. They'd crammed themselves into a hatchway that led into the dark belly of the boat. Those who could argue in a common language were doing it now. Others looked sullen; they spat and glowered.

However it was that the sea was supposed to behave, none of them had expected this.

She listened for familiar words. Some of them were Urdu but still made no sense, because they were the words of men; words about the engine, curse words. It was possible to know a language and still get lost in its corridors.

This much she understood: the bolts that held the engine in place had broken, and the beating heart of the boat had gradually worked its way off its mounts, shifting its great weight into the well of the hull, still connected to the shaft that drove the propeller. The men disagreed about exactly what this meant, but it seemed the engine could no longer drive the boat without everything overheating and jamming up. Some of them were furious, bent on violence. Some were panic-stricken, some beyond caring. She thought about which to avoid and which to trust, how best to protect her mother and the sister she hadn't met.

Her mother still slept. This was good, Roya decided. She didn't want her to worry. She studied the timber under the rail, the little corner formed where the upright held the timber of the rail in place. A collection of old fishing muck had formed there; scales and snipped pieces of fishing line, a mealy-looking pile of something rotted. The timber there had fresh marks in it. It had been gnawed. Roya knew what did that.

The men down below made metal sounds with their tools, yelling curses at the men above. A mother held a small boy over the side, her arms locked through his armpits, while he emptied his bowels into the ocean. In Herat, catching a boy in this position would have been excruciating, both for the boy and for the observer. Now it was beyond embarrassment: it was something to pity. The boy's face, looking back towards Roya, was racked with shame then caught by spasms as his body ejected the filth. A man sat slumped on the opposite side of the deck, vomiting helplessly between his feet, thin and watery; pale solids stopping on the timber boards as the fluid streamed away.

The deck was heaving now, not only rising and falling over the oncoming waves, but twisting from side to side so that the timbers groaned. Meagre belongings slid away from people and they crawled to retrieve them. Hours earlier, an orange had rolled from one woman to another and an argument broke out when the second woman claimed it as her own. Others handed back the wandering items in good humour; even with a smile.

Two teenage boys were hunched over the big plastic tub scooping water into their mouths with a cup. The water had started running low because everyone used it to wash when they prayed, in addition to the quantities they were drinking. The boys scooped greedily, spilling the water on their feet in their rush and scrapping to take turns with the cup. Neither of them noticed the figure approaching them from behind, but Roya did.

Ali Hassan, the man who called himself the captain, was one of the three Iraqis on the boat, but he was fearsome to her in a way the other two weren't. His eyes were barely visible under his angry brow. He never smiled, never stopped moving—checking, issuing instructions, tugging at a rope, pushing a crate, smoking, smoking, smoking. She wondered if perhaps he wasn't a bad man, but that something was burning inside him, causing him pain he couldn't hide.

His pace quickened as he approached behind the two boys, then he was on them, barking rapidly. He grabbed one by the back of the basketball singlet he wore, and cuffed the other one hard across the face. They were too shocked to react, open-mouthed and still dripping. She could feel it in her own mouth, the need for that water, and she watched one of the boys, even as he was being shamed, stuffing the hem of his singlet into his mouth to wring the last of it from the fabric.

Roya moved down the gunwale to where the edge was closer

to the surface of the ocean. With her knees on the slimy deck and her elbows on the wooden rail, she reached down into the blackness because she wanted to know about the water. She tasted some from a cupped hand and spat it in alarm—she hadn't expected that. She peered down again. How deep was it, she wondered. What was on the bottom? Were there lost cities down there? Places like home that had been swept over by the mighty sea? And if that had happened, what had happened to the people?

She'd thought about this as they'd travelled. So many people out there, out the windows of buses and on the streets. So many different people, fighting with each other over the complex disagreements they had. Maybe the only way it could all be sorted out was by the rise and fall of terrible things. The war was a terrible thing, so probably there were other terrible things, like maybe a great upwelling of the ocean that smothered a whole country. It would be sad for all the children, because they weren't involved in the war. And it would be sad for their parents, because they would miss their children. It made her feel confused, paralysed, to think of all this: such thinking surely wasn't the way of the Prophet.

The sea slid past the slimy timbers of the hull, slower now but still moving away behind them. Roya wanted something else to think about, and nuzzled closer to her mother. She held her hand to the great belly and her mother pressed it there. 'This little person in here is for you. Your sister, I think.' She smiled. 'And wherever you go from now on, you will never be alone. There will be me, but I will become old and tired and slow. But here inside me is someone who will always be with you, as long as you both live.' The murmured words floated over her, soothed her. 'You will know each other's ways as closely as anybody can ever know another. Do you feel her? Move your hand a little, up, up. There. Your sister.'

She fixed her eyes urgently on Roya. 'You must look after her, though. An older sister is always responsible. She watches out, sees danger. It will be a burden sometimes.' She stroked Roya's hair slowly, stopping at the foot of each stroke to run the strands of hair between her thumb and fingers. 'But you are my wise little one, hmm? My special one…and this will be how everything starts again. A whole new family of you and me, and this little girl in here.'

Roya understood. She knew what it all meant and why her mother was saying it. Her hand still rested on the warm, hard dome of her mother's belly, feeling the tiny insistent thubbing, the bumps and kicks that could be the pulses of a heartbeat itself.

I am here for you, she whispered inside.

• • •

She must have slept; her mother too, because when she woke the day was under way. She was aware of a new sound but not its origin.

The world had changed: the sky was glowing a sickly green like there was something poisonous under the clouds. The boat was rolling high and low, the tops of the waves slapping hard into the hull. People were skidding and falling as they tried to keep their balance. Roya had become accustomed to the way the swells rolled across the sea towards them, coming from ahead and to their right. But their silent rhythm was gone, replaced by a mass of angry chop: chaotic triangles peaking and disappearing. Her eyes tried to predict their passage but they lurched and hid in all directions. Sometimes the nose of the boat would spear high over a hollow so the belly came down flat from a height, causing everyone on board to jolt and groan.

The man in charge, Ali Hassan, was moving around the deck. He had a small wooden box under one arm, steadying with his free hand as the boat tried to upend him. 'You have lifejackets?' he said in Arabic to the cluster of bearded men nearest to Roya. They nodded, held them up. He jabbed an impatient finger at them. 'Put them on!'

One of the men was yelling at him again in Arabic, pointing and waving his arms. She couldn't catch it all, but it was something about the broken engine, the storm, the money he'd paid. His voice rose higher as the captain argued back, trying to reason with someone who had long since passed that point.

'I can't swim!' the man insisted. His friends joined in—they couldn't either. Nor could Roya, but surely it wasn't going to come to that. The captain turned his back on them and looked down into the box as Roya watched. There was a delicate instrument of some kind in the box and he was trying to keep it level as he studied it.

'Where are we?' the men demanded. 'Where is Australia, you thief?'

He snapped the lid shut over the box and fixed them with a glare. 'We passed Sumba hours ago. We go southeast, so two days' sailing to Pulau Pasir...what the Australians call Ashmore Reef. It is their territory. So Australia, see? I have stolen nothing!'

His voice had failed to convince even him. There was a burst of sarcastic laughter from the group at the captain's feet. 'This piece of shit won't make it that far!'

'There are supposed to be islands out here. If I can find one that has a lagoon, I can steer us in and get out of the weather, make repairs. If you want to be useful, look out for land.'

He staggered his way back to the wheelhouse. As he did so, the boat dropped into a trough and Roya's empty stomach lurched. She clutched at her mother without thinking, and stirred her awake. A wave topped the gunwales and came spilling over the deck, washing over their feet and sweeping away the congealed remains of the old man's vomit. The wave was met by screams from the women and children. All sorts of loose objects came sliding down the deck from the bow towards the stern, bouncing when the hull slammed on the water, rolling when the deck pitched. The plastic water bottles that everyone carried, random tools and fittings, even a large steel bolt that tumbled painfully into a woman's knee before dropping through a hole in the deck.

Roya willed herself away to her home, mapped her way around it. Sunshine, warmth, ground that didn't shift under her. The high stone wall that surrounded the block, keeping out the windblown sand and the rubbish that scattered in the wind. The kitchen with its kiln, and the water fountain under the almond tree. She tried to picture them eating together again, the four of them, on the rug her mother kept specially for dining. Some *kabouli*, beef and rice or maybe a little bread. She and her brother would drink water from plastic cups, while her parents sipped tea and spoke about complicated things, things she tried to follow but couldn't. The smell of the bread was still with her. The dry grit of flour under her fingers.

And then the damp reality of the present.

Quietly at first, one of the men was saying something specific. He had wide Hazara cheekbones like Roya and her mother, and he was speaking Dari. He was looking out to sea: others began to look at him and to follow his gaze out from Roya's side of the boat.

'An island! I see an island!'

Roya turned over again and looked: there in the gloom between sea and sky lay a thick black line on the horizon, humped at one end into a little peak. In front of the black shape she could make out a zone of white and she understood enough now to know it was breaking water.

And beyond the whitewater, something else. She thought it was a building at first, a hut maybe. But as she stared and let her eyes work on it she recognised the lines, familiar to her now. It was a timber boat.

A boat just like theirs.

Canberra

Cassius sometimes thought of Kevin Waldron as his punishment for being insufficiently mediocre. Mediocrity, he'd realised quite early, being generally rewarded by things like, to take a random example, getting to choose your own damn chief of staff. Not having a duplicitous turd like Waldron foisted on you by the PM's office.

In a world where ages were not discussed, Cassius placed Waldron somewhere north of fifty, but there was little damage to indicate he'd seen much of the sun. His skin was soft-looking, barely lined, and his frameless lenses glinted on the soft pillows of his cheeks. He was neat and contained, a veteran of the role and a still point in the chaos. Maybe he liked to watch birds. Or club fur seals. Where his true allegiances lay, Cassius had no idea.

Now, on one of those crisp, clear Canberra Sundays when normal people were stripping the shelves at Bunnings, Waldron was leading someone into Cassius's office. The rooms were all empty but for the three of them: the press people, the staff room, reception, all of it deserted.

'Ron's sent Nigel up to have a word,' Waldron said. 'Can't wait, apparently.' His expression betrayed no opinion about Smedley's known tendency to brief compulsively on sub-crucial developments.

Nigel had turned up before. One of Ron Smedley's new graduates, media studies major with a tech game; a few tiers down but rising. Neat beard, lacquered hair—Smedley's crew were made in his image, well-presented even on the dog shifts. It depressed Cassius to think that Smedley had an army of these pop-outs coming after him.

This one's job was to liaise with Australian Signals Directorate over specks and dots in the sky. Right now he looked edged with grime, like he'd been working in the same dull suit through the dark hours of Saturday night.

'Coastwatch have picked something up sir. The assessment is that you need to be informed.' He placed a briefing folder on Cassius's desk. Stepped back from it. Cassius made no attempt to pick it up. He was tired of being made to read what the person in front of him knew in detail.

'What does it say?'

'Indonesian boat approaching our waters. It's probably a *phinisi*, big timber fishing boat. They come from up round Sulawesi mostly. We can have the Core Resolve people fly over it to get a better look, but at this stage we'd be saying it shouldn't be where it is. In those latitudes, sir, if it isn't people smuggling, it'll be trochus poaching.'

'Do you know how many on board?'

'No. And that'll be the difference between fishing and illegals.'

'All right. Is that all I need to hear?'

'It is, sir.'

'Hm. Keep it classified for now. Don't write it up. I'll talk to the PM.'

Waldron had watched their exchange in silence, but his face betrayed mounting unease. The man turned to leave, then reconsidered. 'There's one other matter sir...'

'Yes?'

'It's, it's not making much headway. Not quite dead in the water, but...the weather's nasty out there at present.'

Cassius paused, chewing his lip. 'Do we need to be concerned?'

'Well, at a technical level, no. Under the new protocols, their welfare is Indonesia's problem right now.'

'Do we know what they're doing about it?'

'No. We're chasing that up.'

The man left the folder and Waldron walked him out. Cassius closed the door behind him. Ringing the PM was an ordeal at the best of times. On the weekend before an election it was going to be all but impossible. He started the process, calling one number to be diverted to another to be told to call back another. Like Maxwell Smart passing through endless slamming doors. Cassius's star was still bright enough, his portfolio high-profile enough, that he stood some chance of getting through on a Sunday. Others, he knew, weren't so fortunate.

He was told to wait for a call back. He checked his emails: polling numbers, talking points for Monday, social media petitions from lefties...messages from the electorate office. A sticky note from Stella on his monitor: *Pollwise want you to use the word 'strikeforce'.* Papers on the side table, waiting for him as always. One item caught his eye—a heavy bundle of documents emblazoned with the British royal coat of arms. Above the lion and the unicorn, a with-comps slip was stapled to the front sheet:

Warren Carmichael, Policy Director, Institute of Social Justice Advocacy.

A hard-left think tank created to feed ideologues into the Senate: the IPA with better haircuts. The crossbenchers—bumblers and eccentrics though they might be—were for Cassius less of a danger to democracy than these institute-raised faith healers. And they were not much different on either side, he was fairly sure.

On the with-comps slip, Carmichael had scrawled in fountain pen: *Do your people send you this stuff?*

The bundle of papers was headed *Report of the Whittaker Inquiry into Core Resolve UK PLC*—and no, Cassius hadn't been sent a copy. The document would have meandered through the departmental system and eventually got diverted into one of Smedley's information billabongs: *not something the minister needs to see.*

He'd known of the inquiry's existence for over a year but it was news that the report had come down. The institution formerly known as the national press, now the national clickbait, was so demoralised by sackings and funding cuts that it didn't follow overseas inquiries anymore. Not unless they related to gruesome acts of terrorism. No one had asked him a single question about the British inquiry. No one had thought to inquire about the fact that a company now responsible for critical Australian government functions was under investigation overseas, and might be the subject of prosecutions. It made some aspects of his job easier than they should have been.

He studied the index, unsure what he was looking for.

Cartel Conduct

Deaths in Transport Van

Employee Safety Breaches

Failures of Reporting

Human Rights Violations

Of course, these were the acts and omissions of a different entity: a separate subsidiary of a global parent company. Even if the rump of local journalism looked into it, they lacked the ticker to put him under any real pressure. It was ordinary human curiosity that prompted him to open the bundle at 'Deaths in Transport Van'.

The deaths of fourteen asylum seekers on the Albania/Macedonia border were deliberately concealed from investigators until their occurrence could no longer be denied. This Inquiry notes that the concealment first took the form of active hindrance of local police, and then moved to a bureaucratic setting, whereby officers and agents of Core Resolve sought to invoke commercial privilege to resist disclosure of documents relating to the fatalities. Coupled with that resistance, there were proven instances of the seeding of misinformation in both traditional and social media.

Such was the effectiveness of this strategy that it is no longer apparent to this Inquiry whether the deaths were the result of deliberate acts or mismanagement or a combination of the two.

The misdeeds of a faraway body. Executives he would never have to deal with. Distasteful, nonetheless.

He checked his emails on the phone: it was loading faster than he was deleting. Something from Monica. His finger hovered over the delete button. Subject line: *Rory.*

Cassius: as we discussed you will need to take Rory this week as I'm enrolled in a professional development course in the city. I am booking him on the 5pm flight tomorrow—you can see flight details in the account here. Please avoid a repeat of last time—be there punctually to meet him and do not use babysitters/nannies etc. You remain his father and he is your responsibility when he is with you.

The phone lit up and the PM was talking before Cassius had the handpiece to his ear. He was still thinking about Monica's email manners, still wondering what the hell he was going to do with a nine-year-old during the worst week of the entire three-year electoral cycle.

'Where is it?'

Cassius scrambled up to pace. 'Coastwatch can give you the lat and long, but it's basically southeast of Sumba and about a quarter of the way between there and Ashm...'

'Anywhere they can land?'

'No. Well...there's a couple of little islands, just reefs basically. Even smaller than Ashmore.'

'How far are they from the line?'

'Territorial? Don't know exactly but they've got a fair way to go yet.'

'Well, what's "a fair way" mean? Overnight? A week? We're six days out from a federal election, Cassius. I don't need a bunch of illegals crashing the party.'

'I know, I know.'

There was a long sigh on the other end of the line. 'Is Core Resolve onto it?'

'I believe they are.' Cassius knew this would end the conversation.

'Look, this is why we wrote the fucking protocol. So the Indonesians can sweat on it for a while. And if they can't deal with it, then Core Resolve will. With the greatest respect, I don't know why we're even discussing it.'

The line went dead. Sometimes the job left him precious little room to move between Smedley's mealy-mouthed worrying and the PM's bullishness, but this was the first time Cassius had ever been on the receiving end of the PM's famous brand of displeasure.

Had he done something wrong? No, he hadn't.

The PM was standing on the brink of electoral reckoning, with a plummeting personal approval rating and a photo finish on the two-party preferred. Cassius was right to tell him: he needed to know there was a potential problem floating around out there, just as he'd need to know if there was a sex scandal or some shitty little expenses problem. They were all of a species: distractions that made the job of selling the government to the punters that little bit harder.

His head was starting up again. He slid open the desk drawer, grabbed the pills and swallowed them dry.

If he was jammed between a pessimist and a blind optimist, then he was probably about right. If they were going to be re-elected on Saturday then the odds were he'd have harsh words with the PM again in the future. And he knew from Pollwise that his own position was secure—he was seen as firm and decisive; the No Duty to Rescue policy already an electoral winner, aided by the online advertising with a boat full of actors playing brown people looking dirty, poor and sinister.

Even if the Opposition tipped them out they'd have to adopt the policy—any change of government represented an escalation where boats were concerned.

He scrabbled around in the kitchenette and found coffee capsules, shoved one in the machine, stood there contemplating his knuckles on the sink. He reminded himself this election held no fears for him personally. His seat was safe. A win paved the way for steady advancement through Cabinet; a loss just changed the scene to the shadow ministry. Which might make for better timing where his personal goals were concerned.

The coffee trickled dismally.

It had almost surprised him, to be honest: a cleanskin like him having a knack for politics. But elite sports could burnish a career in a way that hacking your way through law firms and unions never could. All those years in the boats, stroke of this crew, bow of that one. Hard fucking work. Done for the love and the companionship. Dodging the boozers and the journeymen, pulling ergoes till you collapsed. Such a long road, so much of it torture, all of it done in obscurity—King's Cup, even the World Champs and still it was for the love.

The crema was forming—it looked fake.

Standing on the Olympic podium, though, head and shoulders over the British and the Americans. That's when the offers started to come, seemingly from everywhere: consultancies with finance houses, TV slots, motivational speaking (the hypocrisy of that—actually, you *can't* have a life like mine, no matter how hard you believe in yourself). Sports media, which seemed kind of cheap; charities, a book offer...

Then the discreet approaches at social events. *Cass, you need to meet this guy*...Both major parties and a couple of moist-handed operatives suggesting something independent. At first he baulked at politics. Just a crude popularity contest—sycophancy and begging. But the party assured him they could engineer a by-election to drop him into a safe seat, and he could see how that would look more dignified. Statesmanlike. Or at least not desperate.

What they wanted, of course, was a celebrity face: a nodder for other people's press conferences. A long career in backbench glad-handing, yelling *Hear, hear!* and collecting the super at the end. But he'd learnt fast that there wasn't such a gulf in talent between him and the men—they were mostly men—in Cabinet.

And one day he thought, why not? Why not me? The competitive drive in him waking, stirring.

Shit. The coffee was too full.

He held it level as he returned to the desk, like a child carrying a Mother's Day breakfast, and landed it safely. Only a couple of drops on the carpet: the infamous wattle carpet that had done for his predecessor. A great idea that might have played well to the rural-sector whingers, until it was pointed out that the wool came from New Zealand and the weaving was done in China. One of many stumbles for poor Victor. They brought him into the party room's embrace and sank the blade between his shoulders. And once they'd mopped the tiles they welcomed Cass in, a result that suited his opponents and supporters alike.

Border Integrity. Even back in the days when it was called Immigration, it was a political graveyard, a place to bury rivals in a septic pit of controversy and complication. Like no other portfolio, this one was a lightning rod for hatred.

But for Cassius Calvert, the cascading name changes that had preceded his tenure—*Immigration* to *Immigration and Border Control* to *Border Control* to *Border Integrity*—spoke of an evolution that led inexorably to *him*: a man of integrity with no interest whatsoever in immigration. This ministry was no burial but a rare political opportunity to remake the portfolio in his own image: rigorous, disciplined, deliberate.

He asked himself the foundational questions for a few days and then he saw it clearly. You have a border. Desperate people on one side of it who do not consider themselves amenable to the rule of law. On the other side, the rule of law.

So enforce the law. And if the law is inadequate to cope with the situation? Change it.

How this portfolio had brought about political ruin for so many of his forebears was beyond him.

• • •

By late afternoon he'd covered everything with the electorate office in a teleconference. They wouldn't need him until election day, when they would want him to come over and meet the film crews at one of the booths. Casting his vote, smiling for the cameras—his borrowed son would have been an asset there; shame he was going home on Friday—while the onions sizzled and he stuffed the paper in the slot. The local volunteers would get the job done under their own momentum. Passionate people, happy to serve someone they believed in.

He'd pick up the boy tomorrow, do the father thing somehow, despite the demands of the week. Fatherhood was about setting an example, really. Being a template. He hadn't seen Rory since June but he imagined the kid got a lot out of it. Christ, his father was a federal minister and an Olympian. How many kids got to say that in the schoolyard?

He checked in with Media to ensure they'd covered the morning cycle: unauthorised arrivals numbers well down compared to the same period under the previous government. Follow-ups from the policy announcement; the photo from yesterday of him on the bridge of the naval destroyer. And his time for the Lake Run, leaked to the fitness mags. Their deadlines would be after Saturday, of course; that one was pure vanity.

Offshore, Pulau Dana

The *Takalar* had circled the island all day. Now night had come again.

Roya could hear the disputes between the captain and the other men, sometimes in words she understood, and sometimes exchanges she had to figure out from gestures and reactions. He had been search- ing for a way into the lagoon, limping along on the disabled engine and trying to stay clear of the breaking waves that she felt were deliberately keeping them out. They'd see a break in the relentless white lines and think they'd found deep water, edge in a little closer to the spot and then turn tail when it exploded into spray the same as everywhere else. The frustration was tearing at all of them.

It was a very small island. Their full journey around it each time took only a couple of hours, even at the poor speed they were making. But the air had become impossibly heavy, so thick that the *Takalar* seemed to be pushing through the atmosphere as much as the sea. There was no way of distinguishing the edge of the sea from the beginning of the sky: they had merged in the darkness. The damp was settling over everything: the timbers of the boat, people's clothes, their itching skin.

Halfway around their second lap, the rain started falling, gently at first but enough to obscure the details of the landmass.

Eventually, a hubbub of voices indicated the men had found the opening in the reef that they were searching for, a place where patient inspection had revealed no breaking waves but a darker spill of deep water. When they stopped the boat directly off the opening, Roya could see straight in. There was the boat inside the lagoon. She could see a tiny light burning on board, could make out the gleaming wet links of the anchor chain.

Hamid lay in his usual spot on the tip of the bow, looking out into the darkness towards the other boat. She had apologised to him for kicking the binoculars away and he had accepted it, but he seemed wary of her now. She'd sat down with him, his hair wet from the rain: he pretended to flinch and she laughed at that, but he had no more tall stories to share.

Others had seen the boat and were now calling to it, waving their arms over their heads. But if there was anyone on board they didn't stir, and soon the captain ordered them to be silent until they were safely inside the lagoon, in case the boat belonged to officials who might prevent them entering. He wanted to wait until well after dark before making a run through the reef pass. Roya could tell that the dark was a cover for sneaking around, and she didn't understand that. They weren't doing anything wrong. She sat on the deck beside her mother, unconcerned about the rain but increasingly worried about the ocean.

Near the mouth of the narrow channel she had a clear view to each side. The waves curling along the sides of the reef were frightening, much taller than the boat and gouging hungrily at the sea before them, like they wanted to tear the reef off the end of the island. She could see them churning great boulders of foam in their bellies, reaching out towards the boat, trying to grab hold of it. The sea was alive; pocked with heavy raindrops, angry and cunning—it wanted to dash their hopes.

A boy of about her age was watching the same waves, held tightly by his father. They were Hazaras too: he was the kind of boy she might have seen in the street. He looked briefly back at Roya, his big green eyes pleading. Amid the clamour of voices, shouting, arguing and crying, he suddenly wailed in fear.

Even where they were, in deep water, the boat rode clumsily over the swells, wallowing like a sick animal. Roya stood up and steadied herself against the wall of the cabin. Her mother watched her with concern.

'Darling, be careful. The waves are coming over now.'

They were. The waves were coming over, and the voices were growing louder and more panicked. The rain was drumming harder on the roof of the boat and trickles of water were running off its edges onto the people standing below. They had nowhere to move to: they looked up in frustration at the water coming down on them but could do nothing.

Someone in the engine bay demanded a lighter. Someone else roared back *You'll blow us up you fool*. A young man produced a glowing mobile phone and passed it through the hatch.

'The engine mounts!' came the dismayed cry from below. 'They've been filed off!'

Roya turned the words over in her mind. She wasn't sure what engine mounts were, but she knew about metalwork from her father, knew what filing entailed. So this was why the engine had worked its way loose, but she didn't understand the logic of it. *Filed off*. Deliberately? Why would anyone do that to these engine mounts if they had to go to sea?

An angry knot of men confronted the captain at the wheelhouse door. Roya could see that he had drawn his knife and was holding it low at his hip. The group were shouting at him, threats and curses over the noise of the rain. They were approaching the point she had seen before, when a mob can no longer help the headlong rush into violence.

'Why would I harm the boat?' he yelled back. 'I'm depending on it, same as you are!'

Blub. Blub. Blub. The engine's heartbeat was feeble and irregular. Her mother pulled her closer against her hip, either to shelter her from the rain or to protect her from the angry men. The captain pushed the nearest man hard in the chest and he staggered against the others. 'This is not the time. Why don't you concentrate on fixing it, and let me work out how to get in here.'

He pointed over his shoulder. The island was getting closer, and so were the breaking waves. Everything was racing towards something, but Roya didn't know what. The captain fought the wheel again. His movements were forceful but the boat responded only to the sea: its high, sweeping nose was rising and falling, but it was pointed towards the reef. The deafening clatter of rain on the roof of the boat made conversation impossible.

And then, at the worst possible moment, the engine stopped. There was a grinding sound then a muffled bang, followed by a cloud of bitter black smoke escaping through the hatch.

Sudden silence. The darkness closed in.

Then another chorus of shouting, another stampede up the deck as a wedge of men rushed forward to renew their grievances with the captain, and others began clambering into the hatchway that led to the engine, coughing, their shirts around their mouths as they went. Enough of them had moved that the boat began to ride alarmingly down at the front, and the captain again emerged from the wheel-house to yell at them, *get back*. He scared Roya with his furious voice, his hard face, but she had a feeling the failure of the engine had surprised him as much as the others.

She understood, though she had never been through this before, that the boat was paralysed now. It could only await the will of the sea. There were people praying, loudly beseeching Allah to deliver them.

The white foam of the biggest waves was only a few boat-lengths from
them. It made devouring sounds: this giant faceless malice was something new to her.

The men had resorted to tearing timbers from the decking and
using them as paddles. But their thrashing at the sea was futile—it
had them in its grip. Roya bent to her mother and reached around her
back. Her hair was wet through. The straps of the lifejacket hung limp
because tying them had been too uncomfortable for her. Roya made
the knots fast and her mother hugged her. The lurches of the boat
pressed her into her mother's chest and then pulled her away. She held
onto the straps a moment longer so they wouldn't separate.

Then, simultaneously, a loud noise and a violent shudder.

The sound and the feeling were both unfamiliar and unmistakable to Roya—the front of the boat had slammed into something hard.
People who were standing fell over. People sitting slewed across the
slippery deck and tumbled onto their backs. Immediately the boat
swung around the axis of its bow. Timbers cracked and popped as the
weight of the hull in the current twisted them free.

Roya's eyes, straining in the dark, could make out the line of the
next wave coming towards them. The wall of whiteness was a horizon-
tal avalanche, growing larger as it approached.

She grabbed for a hold. So did her mother, but their hands were
weightless, like the futile screams of a nightmare.

The nose of the boat, almost perpendicular to the swell, sliced
deeply through the whitewater and the wave was unable to force its
will upon the sides of the hull. The boat rose up and floated free again,
but now it was caught in the spill of water returning to sea off the
back of the reef. Without power, and because the torrent of water was
pushing them from behind, the boat fishtailed from side to side and
raced helplessly out to sea.

Roya imagined that the island might be home to some rescuer, waiting out there in the darkness for them. But this far from Herat, she felt sure they wouldn't understand Dari. She knew the English word from her book, and she hurled it into the night with all the force in her slight body.

Help.

Her mother clutched her harder in response. She had held Roya through bombardments and house searches, through the screams from unknown horrors in other homes. The strength of her embrace was the core of Roya's world.

The next line of foam was rushing forward, bigger than the last. Roya could see it because she was standing, though her mother could not have known it was coming. She could feel the tight grip of her mother's fingers on her thigh, hear her chanting something quietly under her breath. She nuzzled into her warm belly once more, searching for her sister.

Some of the passengers had gone below, though it felt like the wrong instinct to Roya. Amid the furious ocean there was no human sound on deck: some people standing, watching the wave, but no one capable of words. The boat swung faintly left then straightened as the distance closed. For a second Roya felt relief, thinking the nose would again spear through most of the impact. But something took hold of the dying boat and this time threw it to its right, so that the whole starboard side of the vessel faced the impending blow.

Roya could feel it, that this was the worst possible way for the wave to meet the boat. She counted down the final breaths before the impact, looked at her mother and dropped to the deck. The last move she made was to wrap her arms around her mother's ankles.

They were up high for an instant, the rain in the air around them. Then the furious water descended and the night disappeared.

The force of it was the combined anger of the whole sea and sky. The great roaring of the fist coming down, the timbers in agony, shrieking and splintering. Crashes, voices calling, rushing water and the ringing of struck metal and the deck was tilting up and up and up and people were sliding past them, some falling weightless through the air, and Roya and her mother were wedged against the small timber support that had been their resting place. The boy, the little one who'd been so sick, came racing past with his limbs flailing, his mother still reaching for him. He tumbled and slid across the deck until his head met one of the heavy timber buttresses with a dreadful thud. He remained there limp beside the fatal timber, palms upward beside his small hips.

As she slipped and grabbed, Roya looked down at the water surging beneath her, people already clambering to regain a hold on the boat while the sea pulled them away. There was another massive impact as the next wave hit the underside of the boat. Again it rode high and vertical for an instant, a ladder to the dark sky. Roya and her mother clung on, as others fell and cursed. The air filled with the smell of diesel, and the people in the water coughed and retched as it filled their lungs.

She saw the captain hit the water on his back.

A baby floating face down.

Empty lifejackets swirling.

She turned her face into the dark wooden corner they were hiding in, but fear drew her to look down again, to see the rushes of white from the exploded wave. Silent fingers curling up towards them, reaching for them.

In that moment, the boat stood tall on its end. Then it shifted straight down onto its stern, crunching hard onto the reef. *Now the land is attacking us as well*, she thought. There were bombing sounds again; crumpled air, giant forces. The stern had broken off and the boat was teetering over. The sea rushed forward to take them, and Roya felt only sadness. Her sister, the one she had never met but felt that she knew. Her mother, herself.

Their resistance had ended.

Onshore, Pulau Dana

Isi had passed in and out of a restless sleep for a few hours. Her day would often end this way when she was working on the boat: thinking about forecasts and navigation and supplies and personalities. Joel managed to make these routines invisible, as though everyone simply woke up and fell into perfect conditions by accident. That smiling insouciance of his.

It was him she was thinking about, once she'd run the various checklists in her head. His absence. The opportunity to let go of him, to take a realistic view and call it a day. She'd thought that maybe she loved him, briefly one late afternoon when the sun was casting shadows from the waves back out to sea towards them, and with each passing line of swell they would disappear together into a half-lit world before the tired sun found them again. She'd let him float away that time, absorbed in his thoughts as her mind sifted the evidence: the long shadows, the drift and disappearance of each new line that approached; the way she felt about him and, in short bursts of a harder realism, the contradictions. He'd rescued an entire village after a typhoon. He'd burned down his first flat in Kuta after nodding off on a straw mattress with a lit joint. He'd stared down an American frigate after he was ordered to leave a 'secure exclusion zone', making headlines in Australia. He'd walked out on her and drunk himself insensible for three days when she told him she wanted to go off the pill. The answer had eluded her that day in the water, just as it eluded her now.

She'd veer close to bringing all these strands together, and then the sleep would take her again, robbing her of a conclusion. She'd wake again, add a layer. The rain started, drawing her attention with its small sounds against the tent. Then it intensified, and the steady drumming worked her into drowsiness.

Finally, she slept.

• • •

The first sounds to reach her were the voices.

For a time—Isi couldn't tell how long—the voices were merged in her dreams, irrational and ghostly. But now they were becoming real, taking form.

Cries.

They were cries. Male and female, deeper and higher in pitch, but frightened. Pleading. That was what woke her, dragged her mind from the fog. The rain was much heavier now, and the cries wove in and out of its roar.

She struggled to understand—were they pleading for her personally, or were they just crying out? At first her voice cried back to them, but her dreaming mind couldn't give form to her replies. She rose from sleep into a restive semi-consciousness, and there were words. Words of supplication, none of them familiar. It was a foreign language, she realised, maybe more than one.

Now she could hear the surf over the rain, and the voices persisted.

Now she was emerging from her confused state: now she was conscious.

She opened her eyes in the darkness and listened. Drops ran

down the sides of the tent above her, dimly visible. The voices were rising and falling with the wind that moved the trees overhead and smacked the dried palm fronds of the shelter she'd made between the tents. And now she could hear more than the voices—she could hear a heavy thudding, like a construction noise, heavy banging against something immovable.

She was tired still, shoulders aching from the work of the previous day. The small coral cuts on her feet stung faintly. It was well before dawn and part of her wanted the sounds to cease, for deep and restorative sleep to return. The trees were slapping and tilting this way and that as the turbulent air rushed over the island.

She reached out and found the zipper that opened the tent. A feeling of unease was building in her. The voices were real. The dream was now behind her. With her head out, the rain stung her eyes. There were already puddles outside. And then, with perfect clarity, her ambivalence was swept away by a single word.

Help.

She threw back the net and found herself running, barefoot and still in the previous day's boardshorts and singlet. Her thoughts lagged some distance behind her, and she hadn't yet formed an idea of what she was doing. Out through the scrub around the camp and onto the beach, in the direction she guessed the sound was coming from. She slid sideways in the wet leaves as she broke free of the scrub. Standing on the narrow beach, she tried to hear over the stippling of the downpour on the surface of the lagoon. She'd lost the sounds.

Then they reappeared, coming from her right, from the point where she knew the reef was. She ran again, landing painfully now and then on half-exposed rocks in the cool white sand. The moon slipped free of the thunderhead and the sea was a great pool of silver. Anything that didn't reflect the light—the inshore rocks and the nearside of passing swells—appeared to her as black silhouettes. And now she could see there were shapes out at the point, shapes that were starting to define themselves as she neared. She already wanted her suspicions to be wrong.

The slope of the land towards the point. The clattering palm trees. A single, square rock sitting high on the platform of the intertidal reef and the sea beyond. The night-time shallows pale and phosphorescent like a swimming pool illuminated underwater. A large dark object, out on the reef among the waves, clearly visible through the curtain of the rain. Every line of swell that swept in, reaching shallow water and unfurling from right to left, each of these was a streaking black line that grew thicker as the wave peaked and hollowed. Each would grow, lay claim to the reef and die, but the large object remained in place, an unmoving reference point in the shifting shadows out there. It stayed in position for long enough that she could recognise its outline.

It was a boat.

Visible by its profile only, but distinctively a boat of Indonesian manufacture. As it reared up over a foamline, she could recognise the high bow, the low-swept sides and the squared-off timber cabin. It was a big vessel as Indonesian boats go, wallowing squat and cumbersome in the very place the surfers had sat yesterday, a place where a large boat had no business to be. As she watched it she saw that it had begun to move. It was being drawn into the teeth of the breaking waves. The stern was swinging from side to side, a motion that told her the boat was adrift.

New swells gathered in front of it: first a small wave that spanned the full width of the reef—the one that indicated larger waves would follow—raising enough energy to lift the boat slightly. Its bow lifted again as the wave worked its way under, tipped level then plunged with its stern high in the air. It slumped back down onto the trough as a bigger wave gathered behind.

Isi was a hundred metres from the end of the beach, where the sand met the low-tide reef. And from there, the boat was another hundred out to sea.

The voices were louder now, high and low, young and old, and it filled her with horror to hear so many of them. Laid over each other in differing pitches and volumes, marked by their unmistakable distress. Of all the foreign words and phrases being called into the night by all the humans she couldn't see, she was fixed upon the lone voice that rang clear between and among them: a girl, a small girl surely, crying in perfect English the same word she'd recognised from her bed:

Help.

The reef pointed out into the lagoon, narrowing as it extended into the deeper water of the pass. On the open side, the rushing lines of whitewater rolled through a field of white, the chaos of previous waves, and over the shallow coral. On the lee side, in the sandy bowl of the lagoon, the water was calm and darkening again as the moon disappeared.

The boat was slumped at the stern, the bow pointing skyward. As Isi watched it, the bow climbed towards vertical and she could see people, people falling *Christ they're falling* from the cabin roof and the decks. Dark figures against a dark background, but taking form in the helpless splay of their limbs.

Running now, she squinted harder and her horror mounted.

There were heads in the water. Dozens of them.

The splashing of those people was not the ordinary motion of swimming. They were thrashing, all the ones she could see. Thrashing and going nowhere. She stopped, breathing hard. She had to think. She could get in the water but the moment she did she was going to be overwhelmed.

The rain was licking down her spine. She started turning back towards the camp but took one last look at the boat before she ran.

It was hanging high and vertical with a huge wall of foam bearing down on it. As the foam struck its exposed belly the boat shuddered and came down hard on its stern. Then its downward motion stopped abruptly and the grinding sound reached her soon afterwards—it had struck the reef end-on, and now the shape looked wrong. The stern had broken off completely.

The boat settled briefly on its starboard side, shook a little under the impact of a smaller wave, then capsized.

The last glimpse Isi saw before she started running was the upturned timber belly, the wet timbers gleaming with the first light of dawn.

• • •

She ran through the camp, yelling at the tents.

'Get up! Get up!'

Carl appeared first, followed by Tim and Leah, the Finleys; lastly Fraggle, emerging like a sea monster with his red-brown dreadlocks tumbling over his face and a wrap tied hastily around his waist. Confusion appeared to be his natural state at this hour, but the rest of them looked just as shocked.

'There's a boat on the reef. People in the water. Heaps of 'em,' she rushed between breaths. 'I need...I need five of you to run up to the point and start getting them onto the beach. Someone come with me and we'll get boards and things from the boat.'

It took a static moment for this to sink in. Then each of them fished around for clothes and footwear and began to move off, sluggish, whether because of the hour or their disbelief at what they were hearing. Tim appeared at her side and they ran for the Zodiac. The voices were audible again on a swirl of the breeze, and as she ran she heard Tim mutter *shit*.

As she raced the inflatable across the lagoon she was tempted to turn directly towards the heads in the water, but she knew it was the less effective option. From the *Java Ridge* they piled surfboards into the Zodiac. The crew were already moving, either roused by the cries, as Isi had been, or alerted by the noise of the outboard. She grabbed the two medical tubs that Neil Finley had replaced neatly under the bench after his work on Sanusi's hand.

Back in the Zodiac she saw that Tim had gathered a pile of towels and a torch. They raced across the lagoon, and again Isi was forced to ignore the pleas for help coming from further out. She ran the Zodiac up onto the beach and threw out everything except the boards. There were people wandering in the half-light now, she could see, some of them the *Java Ridge*'s guests, and some of them from the stricken boat. Those people were silent: they were wraiths, huddled, or stumbling nowhere in particular on the beach. They didn't react at all to the rain. The sounds were still behind her, out in the lagoon and on the reef. Voices, growing feeble as the light grew stronger.

The Finleys appeared on the beach and took the tubs and the towels. As Isi wrenched the throttle to leave the beach behind, she could see Carl and Leah swimming towards a group of exhausted men. She threw the boards over the side near them and sped away.

On the far side of the lagoon they found an old man, coughing and retching, and hauled him aboard. Because he was light, they kept looking while he lay slumped in the floor of the Zodiac. The dawn was spreading fast now in the east, making a burnished lens of the inshore water. The storm was letting go of the island, moving off to somewhere else over the troubled sea.

Splashing nearby, hoarse shouts: two teenage boys, unharmed but exhausted. She steered them over the fizzing shallows of the reef. The air moving over her wet clothes chilled her, the first time she remembered feeling cold in weeks. They wove out of the path of an incoming wave, slowed now by the weight of their passengers.

Isi was gripped by confusion. The voices had stopped. She looped this way and that, searching the surface. Where had all the people gone? They had three. Carl and Leah might have found more than that first group, but there were dozens out there—what had happened? She knew if she and Tim remained near the surf, they could be caught by a wave themselves, so she drove back into the lagoon and ran up onto the beach in the same spot she'd left the gear.

The rain was finally backing off. By now, the Finleys were working together, bodies laid out before them on beach towels. She could see that Neil had the two tubs open and was sorting through them.

'How many?' he called to her without looking up. He was counting plastic packets of something. His voice had no more urgency to it than it had in conversation the previous afternoon. *This is how he lives*, she thought to herself.

'I don't know,' she stammered. 'There were a lot of dead out there.'

'How many *living*, you idiot?'

She would've flared at him if that wasn't such a fucking indulgence in the circumstances. 'Not many.'

He returned to counting and laying out supplies on another towel. She looked back to the Zodiac on the beach. Tim had heaved the old man out and sat him on the sand.

'Neil,' she said, hating herself for sounding tentative. 'I don't know where they all went.'

He looked up impatiently. 'Who?'

'Well there were…heads in the water. Heaps of them. Now I can't find them.'

Finley sighed, screwed up his face before he replied. 'You've got three. Carl and Leah got six. There'd be, what, fifteen on the beach. The rest have drowned. They'll be on the bottom. Forget them—twenty-four hours they'll re-float. You can collect them then.'

He turned back to what he was doing without another word.

Isi took Tim again and sped back out to the surf zone, spurred by disbelief. She found a few of the dead, swaying among the coral heads where they'd been entangled by their clothes in the spikes and horns of the reef. Others were wound around pieces of wreckage, or knotted up in each other, like the father she found who'd tied his tiny daughter to himself by his clothing. Gone together. The love in that desperate knot—maybe he'd spared her some terror.

But for Isi the numbers still didn't add up. Finley had to be right: they would all be bumping along the floor of the lagoon. In the time she'd been doing this job she'd never had to deal with a drowning, let alone dozens. But it had to be about the living right now.

She was about to head back when another silhouette broke the surface. A boy, maybe twelve, pushed out wide from the end of the reef.

Isi saw him from a distance, washing in towards the lagoon with each swell, sucked back out again as the water withdrew. His head was bobbing over and under the surface with the ripples of spent waves, his body floating face-up. His mouth was clear of the surface, still gasping at life. She turned towards him and moments later Tim was pulling him up into the bow of the Zodiac. He was shirtless, his wet hair hanging down over his face, jaw clenched shut and moaning quietly. At first it appeared there was nothing wrong with him, but as Tim lifted him clear of the water and he fell into the boat, he suddenly became quiet and limp.

'Christ!' blurted Tim. 'What the fuck just happened?'

'Tim!' yelled Isi. '*Tim!* Lie him on the edge where it's soft—gently in case it's his neck. And hold him steady.'

For an instant he was frozen in shock and the boy remained awkwardly slumped in the well of the boat.

'*Now*, Tim.'

He finally hauled the boy into position and wrapped an arm over him, holding one of the knots on the rope that encircled the boat. Isi throttled again for the beach.

The Zodiac bounced faintly on the choppy water in the channel, stirring the boy into consciousness once or twice, but it settled again on the sheet glass of the water nearer shore. She had time to look at the boy, his ribs in stark relief as they rose and fell with his shallow breaths. He was wearing boardshorts, a market stall rip-off of the designs the guests were wearing. On his dark skin she saw the scars of childhood cuts that hadn't healed well. He'd lived a hard life already.

The light was stronger now and Isi could see Carl and Leah on the sand. They ran into the shallows and carefully lifted the boy out of the boat and onto a vacant towel amidst a line of them higher on the beach. *Finley's set up a triage,* she realised.

As the boy was lifted past her she saw that he was conscious again. There was a lump over his temple, striped with a dirty-looking abrasion. She heard him say *thank you* in English, though it wasn't clear who he was saying it to.

'What's his name?' Isi called to Tim. She wasn't sure why it mattered.

Tim looked down at the clenched face. 'Your name?'

'Hamid.'

'You're doing well, Hamid.' He placed a hand on Hamid's shoulder, smiling false cheer. Isi saw through it, to the trauma that was churning in him. He looked nauseous with shock.

Back out again. Back across the lagoon, which was filling gradually with wreckage. Isi poked her foot into the middle well of the Zodiac and hooked a mask and snorkel that were lying there.

'Tim, you know how to drive these?' she yelled over the motor. He nodded. 'I'm going to jump off at the boat. I want you to get clear of the surf, then come back in if I find anyone. Okay?'

She angled in from the deep, choppy water of the channel towards the upturned belly of the wreck. The keel profile was instantly familiar to her—it was a *phinisi*, much like the *Java Ridge*. The fluted timbers and the curvature, the rolling from side to side; it was more dying whale than boat now.

The water was shallower in here, moving fast over the coral. With a last look for bodies in the water, she swung a turn next to the hull and jumped off as Tim scrambled down the boat to take the tiller.

The relative silence underwater suspended the chaos. Rushing bubbles, muffled thumps. Her hair drifted in front of the mask. It took a moment for her eyes to adjust to the early-morning gloom beneath the surface, the cloudy fizz of the passing waves. The reef was a gorgeous field of plate corals and digitates, parallel crevasses pointing in the direction of the prevailing swell. But the plates were obscured by the turmoil of the breaking waves now.

So much death. She needed to breathe.

On the surface, the energy of the surf had concentrated a great raft of floating refuse: the aggregated muck that would ordinarily float by when the ocean was at rest. Branches, coconuts, litter, froth and leaves, broken-off weed and soft coral fragments. Drinking straws, chocolate wrappers and twigs; all held in mucosal suspension. A frond caught on the upper edge of the mask, draping itself over her forehead.

She bumped her knee on a coral head, felt the sting.

For the first time since she'd woken, Isi was afraid as she approached the upturned boat. It was every bit as big as the *Java Ridge*, swinging erratically from side to side as the swells battered it. She ducked under and could see where the cabin was wedged into a shallow canyon in the reef, leaving enough space for the hull to wallow on the surface. On one side, the reef was high, almost breaking the surface, but on the other it fell away to deeper water. A strong enough impact could shake it free and send the boat tumbling into the deep. She didn't want to be anywhere near it if that happened.

She surfaced again. Tried to steady herself with one flat hand against the slimy curve of the timbers while she banged on the hull with a closed fist, wondered how she would possibly hear a reply as the world roared around her, the howling of the ocean pitched to obliterate any specific sound.

And she didn't hear it. She felt it.

Directly under the hand she'd laid palm-down against the hull, a rapid, fluttering knock: the heartbeat of a bird. For a second she remained there, waiting to feel it again, wondering if she'd imagined it. Then it came again, more insistent, and she knew she had to go under.

Tim stood at the stern of the Zodiac on the edge of the deeper water, cutting impatient loops. She caught his attention and made a signal that she was going under the boat. She took a breath and dived.

The access wasn't difficult. Swimming just above the coral, there was room for her to get under the gunwales, low to the reef with the deck of the boat above her. In the shadow of the boat the light was dim, but she made for the point where the *Java Ridge* had its hatches, a couple of metres aft of the cabin, and there she found a dark opening above her.

Inside, her head banged hard against something before she burst loudly into an air pocket. In the darkness she slowed her breathing to regain equilibrium. She could see nothing, but the smell of diesel oil was almost overwhelming. She swept a hand around and felt timber on two sides, then touched a curved metal surface. Greasy. She was in the engine bay.

She spoke into the darkness. There was no answer but the loud sloshing of water in the confined space.

She thought about the position of the engine as her hands continued to creep about. It didn't make sense: the motor was hard up against what would have been the ceiling of the engine space—it had fallen with gravity towards the sea floor. That could only mean it wasn't moored to its mounts. If it had somehow come adrift and malfunctioned, that might explain why none of her party had been woken in the night by the sound of an approaching vessel—it had been dead in the water.

Her hands continued on, found something soft. Fabric, flesh beneath.

She grasped at it. An arm.

Her fingers darted onwards, found the neck and head. A shroud of billowing shirt. The body drifted limply away from her touch. Reaching out again she felt a bearded jaw, found his eyes and pressed one of them. The feeling of it made her want to retch, but she needed to make sure. No reaction.

The space was barely wider than her arm span and she knew that his body and hers, and the engine, had left no room for anyone else in there. She took a deep breath of the foul air and dived.

On the surface again, outside the confines of the boat, she wanted to stay among the sunlit world. But she knocked again, and the reply came once more from inside the hull. This time she thought about the position of the sound. It was much further forward than where she'd been.

She ducked a wave, measured the distance to the next one. On a heave of new air she went under again, and this time forward, past the dark engine-bay hatch.

The cabin door. She'd seen *phinisis* made this way before. The short stairway into the main hold was accessed from inside the wheel-house. She swam into the tight square space of the wheelhouse and turned herself over so she was facing the stairs. The glass of the cabin windows had shattered, leaving vicious shards in the frames. Plastic bags and water bottles and loose articles of clothing swirled about her like ghosts. She caught a glimpse of the bare and broken console behind the helm, the cavities where navigation equipment had once been mounted. It was completely stripped—as though someone had dumped it in a park for children to play on. *What on earth were they thinking?*

She struck her shins once or twice coming up the stairway and saw the moving limbs underwater before she surfaced in the trapped air. Faces. A woman, heavily pregnant, and a small girl. Both in lifejackets.

She pushed the mask back on her forehead. It was dark, lit only by a vague glow from the stairway and the reef outside. The water sounds were loud in here, the air pocket expanding and contracting with the movements of the boat. Neither the woman nor the child expressed any alarm or relief at her presence. The mother—Isi concluded they were mother and daughter by the way they clung—eyed her with cold exhaustion. Her face, her lips, heavy with the late stages of pregnancy.

The girl's eyes were so dark they were visible only by the triangles of white either side of her pupils. Her hair was swept back, probably by the mother's caring hand, so that it was out of her eyes. She was clutching a plastic shopping bag with very little in it, a knot in the neck of the bag to keep the water out.

'Hello,' she said. In English, to Isi's great surprise.

'Hi there. I'm Isi. What's your name?'

The woman was watching the exchange in silence.

'Roya. This my mother.'

'What is her name?' Isi was exaggerating her pronunciation like the tourists in Kuta.

'Shafiqa,' said Roya. *Shah-fee-kah.*

Shafiqa darted a tiny smile in Isi's direction. '*Salaam alaikum.*'

'Okay Roya. How did you get in here?'

The boat jolted as a wave hit the hull. Roya looked around in fright, then concentrated.

'Wave come. Boat go over. We go inside here, water come up.'

They'd have to go out the way they came in. If there was another exit they'd have found it by now.

'Roya, I'm going to take you out of here first. Then I will come back and get your mother. Do you understand?

'Yes,' she replied carefully. 'Please wait.'

She translated for her mother. Isi didn't know the language. It wasn't Bahasa, or any of the island dialects. The woman suddenly grabbed her daughter and pressed her face into the girl's wet hair. She uttered one small word that sounded like consent.

'Yes,' said Roya again.

'I will go *one*, *two*, *three*, then under—' She counted off her fingers and mimed a deep breath.

Roya smiled. 'Yes.'

Isi pulled the mask down again but didn't use the snorkel for fear it would confuse the girl. She was about to go when she realised Roya was still wearing her lifejacket: she carefully untied the straps and lifted it over her head. No light, no whistle.

Then she counted down, took a breath and grabbed her by the waist, pulling her under. The stairway was directly under their feet, and by inverting her small body Isi was able to point Roya through the opening and out to the open space roofed over by the deck. She followed behind her, again banging her knees and shins on the edges.

The light was better underneath the deck, and she could see the girl floating against the timbers above her head. She took her hand this time and watched a tiny stream of bubbles escape her mouth. Her eyes were wide with fear but something about her movements suggested to Isi that the girl was able to control it. She pulled her wide of the gunwale and out over the reef, the sunlight now streaming down on them from the open sky.

Isi held Roya down a moment longer as she watched a shadow

gather above them: a pulsing grey cloud of foam raced overhead, leaving its lacework on the clear surface. Tiny yellow fish around them swirled in response to the pressure change. As soon as it had passed she kicked for the top, pulling Roya with her.

On the surface, Roya dragged in a hungry breath and was composed again, her huge dark eyes watchful as Tim raced towards them in the Zodiac. She must have seen a great deal, thought Isi, if the night she'd endured hadn't completely unravelled her. But there was something more than that about her. Something in the child's eyes; a stillness.

Isi let the thought go as Tim grabbed the girl's arms and swept her into the Zodiac.

Back in the darkness of the hold she surfaced next to Shafiqa and listened to the urgent pace of her breathing, held both of her hands and breathed with her until the tempo slowed. Then she started by undoing the lifejacket: moving closer to work on the straps, she placed one hand on her belly, the other around her shoulder blades. They were hard and bony despite the swell of her pregnancy.

'Baby?' she smiled.

Shafiqa nodded, tried to return the smile.

'Soon?'

A look of faint puzzlement, apology.

Isi was nervous this time: Shafiqa was a much bigger object to shift than Roya had been, and they had no language to use. But she had come in this way, and somehow she would have to get back out. Isi mimed the counting and the breath again, and the woman clearly understood.

She took the mask off her head and ripped off the snorkel, then fitted the mask onto Shafiqa.

'Look,' she said, and gently tipped her head towards the water. Shafiqa looked from side to side with the lens of the mask in the water,

her mouth still clear, like a child inspecting a rock pool. Isi waited for
her to look up again.

'Okay?'

She nodded.

Isi counted. They breathed. They both slipped under.

She peered into the blur and knew immediately that they had a
problem. Shafiqa had seen the light coming from the stairwell and was
trying to turn herself head-first, as Roya had done, to climb through
it. But her buoyancy was centred over her hips, and no matter how
she tried she couldn't invert herself, and she wound up curled into an
awkward ball. Isi slipped a hand under her and pulled her back into
the air space.

Shafiqa slapped her hands at the surface in frustration as another
wave struck the outside of the hull with a *crump* sound. The water
level rose around them and they pressed their heads up towards the
hull timbers to stay with the changing space. Isi saw the light from
the stairwell change: the wave had shifted the hull. Now she feared
their exit could be blocked if the boat slid itself onto some anvil in
the reef.

Her feet kicked into something that felt like cobwebs. She
scooped it from her ankle: a nest of tangled fishing line. It could have
killed either of them a moment ago.

She started again with the charades, this time trying to demonstrate that she needed Shafiqa to go feet first. Unbidden thoughts: Joel
at a bank somewhere in Perth.

The counting. The breath.

Shafiqa plunged straight down, her feet leading vertically into
the opening of the stairwell. Working by feel and by a vague sense of
where the light was, Isi found the woman's shoulders and pushed down
on them until she was sure her whole body had passed through into
the light. She followed, and found her too deep, low against the surface

of the reef where the coral was likely to tear into her flesh. Isi gripped her arm and pulled her upwards, but exactly as she did so, a billow of Shafiqa's robe caught itself on the reef.

She tried to kick herself free but it made the entanglement worse. Isi knew Shafiqa wouldn't have much breath, that her terror would be stripping it away even faster. She took the robe in both hands and tore at it, thrashing and kicking and flailing until she felt it come free. Shafiqa's thigh appeared, a pale flash against the dark canyons of the reef. Forward, forward she hurried her on, as behind them a crowd of fish came in to sift through the grit they'd stirred up in the struggle.

Isi took hold of the woman's hips and pushed her towards the sky. Raised around water and intimately adapted to its physics, she couldn't understand how anyone could be unable to seek the surface. She bashed her knee, yet again, on the coral heads. She couldn't see the damage without the mask.

Shafiqa was rising now, clawing at the bonds that held her. Isi wanted to stop and watch the surface, time their run so that they wouldn't be hit by a wave when they came up, but she couldn't see enough without the mask, and the urgency of Shafiqa's thrashing had increased.

Something was moving across the surface above them. Rhythmic splashes, the stabbing of limbs. Someone was swimming. The current pulled them into the deeper water of the lagoon and the swimmer was gone.

There was no time for fine judgments. They both broke the surface simultaneously.

Isi ripped the mask off Shafiqa's head and secured it around her own neck. Swung round behind Shafiqa and took hold of her, across her chest and under her arms. She floated well, despite her weight, but she was instinctively fighting off Isi's firm grip. Isi was close to going under. Shafiqa was elbowing her in the head, even landing one stinging blow in her eye. She slapped her once and wondered what the hell they were both doing.

Where's the fucking Zodiac?

She spun around and realised the swimmer on the surface was Tim. He'd anchored the Zodiac in the lagoon behind them, leaving Roya in it. She could see him still stroking hard towards the wreck. He hadn't seen them.

She yelled at him but he kept going. The wash off the reef was taking them further into the lagoon, towards the anchored Zodiac and away from the wreck. Tim was going in the opposite direction, slower now as he reached the reef. She yelled again, and again he didn't hear. As she grappled with the struggling woman in her arms, she watched him step up onto the coral on the inshore side of the hull. It was only knee deep where he stood, and he was bending over, trying to find an opening under the hull.

Oh God, she thought, *he thinks we're still under there.*

She yelled again, and this time he looked around. As he did so, a heavy avalanche of foam crossed the reef towards the wreck: behind the hull, obscured from his view and rolling fast.

Panic rose in her throat. He couldn't see them—why couldn't he see them? Jesus, their heads were on the surface in the blinding reflection of the sun...The wave was about to hit the hull when he spotted her and raised an arm; shuffled his feet around to dive off the coral head as the wave struck. The wrecked boat shifted forward, chaotic foam washing around it, and Tim disappeared. As the water receded, the hull now lay over the place where he had been. For a long moment he was nowhere to be seen.

Then he reappeared, screaming. Isi struggled to unscramble her racing thoughts.

They were drifting steadily nearer to the Zodiac. She couldn't swim forward to help Tim because she was supporting Shafiqa. She couldn't swim at all without letting her go. She was going under, sipping at half-breaths as Shafiqa's panic sapped the strength from her limbs. She lay back and tried to let Shafiqa's weight rest above her on the surface, kicking her legs to inch them towards the Zodiac.

By the time they reached it, Isi had caught sight of Tim several times, his head submerging and reappearing as the waves washed through. He hadn't moved—he *should* have moved in that current—and his cries were wild and uncontained. She led Shafiqa's hands to the guide ropes slung around the Zodiac. Satisfied that she had a good grip, Isi climbed aboard and hauled her over the hull and in. Roya watched this process in silence, but immediately cradled her mother's head once she was safely aboard.

'Are you all right Roya?' Isi asked as she pulled the anchor.

The little girl nodded silently.

'Okay, hold on.'

She drove the boat over to the lagoon side of the wreck, killing the motor to let the boat drift near to Tim. He was shrieking in agony.

'Get it off me!'

She could see through the shallow water that his right leg was pinned between the gunwale of the boat and the reef. The boat was shifting slightly up and down, but not enough to release the leg, and each downward shift in the hull sent spasms of pain through him.

'Okay,' she said. 'Roya, stay here with your mum. Tim, I'm gonna drop this next to your foot, all right?'

With great care she dropped the anchor into the reef beside the trapped leg. Then she let out enough of the anchor rope to ensure the Zodiac would float inside the lagoon and not stray into the surf.

Pulling the mask onto her face again, she rolled over the warm rubber of the inflatable hull and back into the sea. Her hands reached down the rope until her fingers found the chain, then the anchor, lying beside the big plate coral that Tim had been standing on when he was hit. The curved timber of the gunwale lay across it, and she could see his ankle disappearing under it.

She pulled the anchor free, reached under the plate and rammed it as hard as she could into the neck that supported the big coral. The first couple of times she succeeded only in raising a cloud of debris, the reef fish again swarming in to inspect her work.

She surfaced and took a couple of deep breaths. Her next blow cracked the pillar of coral and the fourth broke it. The plate collapsed and the leg tumbled free, Tim's arms windmilling on the surface to regain his balance. The foot drifted at a sickening angle to the damaged leg. Swirls of blood in the cloudy water drew a mob of the boldest fish to pick at the wounds. She tried not to look: grabbed him at the surface and repeated the sequence she'd used to get Shafiqa aboard.

When he lay with his body in the well of the boat and his leg up on the red rubber side, she could see the foot was crushed, an ugly scarlet colour between the gouges that the coral had torn through his flesh. Bright blood mingled with the trickling seawater and ran in every direction. And above the foot, near the wide point of his ankle, a blunt stub of bone had broken through, skewing the foot to one side like the end of a broken branch, festooned with little blossoms of coral. Tim was hissing through his teeth, wide-eyed with fear when he raised his head to look at the injury.

There was nothing she could say. She hauled the pick and started the outboard again, racing the overloaded Zodiac for shore.

The sky was a furnace now, the sun high enough to hammer down mercilessly, to reach into every dark place and reveal it; to wilt the leaves and beat the birds into tired retreat. The creatures of the low tide reef had scurried for cover, closing over their shells and withdrawing their delicate filaments.

The tropical sun would not find its way into the hellish confines of that boat. No one would ever retrieve it. Nothing could intervene in the long saga of its punishment by the ocean. Until the waves beat it to pieces and its timbers split and opened new entrances to the cavity of the hull, until its fragments roamed the open seas and gathered barnacles, no light would find the dead man whose face was still there under her fingers. The invertebrates would find him first; take his eyes, his tongue and his genitals, and then start on deeper flesh. The fish and the eels would compete, would reduce him to bones. And all this before the outside world broke through.

The darkness rose from her heart, clotted her vision as she retched and vomited over the side. Looked up to see the small girl peering at her from her side of the Zodiac. As though it was her natural place to feel concern for the stranger who'd rescued her.

Canberra

He'd called out to Stella three times from his desk; no answer.

With a sigh, he stood and walked to the door. She had her headphones on again, blasting fruity pop into her skull. She'd been told off in her first week for playing the music out loud and gone straight out to buy the headphones. By Friday afternoon she'd be dancing out there, literally as though no one was watching. Compulsively outgoing, she'd condemned herself to a working life in an office full of quiet, industrious people. She was mouthing the lyrics now, bobbing her head as she typed.

Cassius smiled and turned away, then grunted as the pain shot back, tendrils that crept wide of his forehead like the grip of something clawed.

He tried to concentrate on scrolling through emails on his phone, then saw the time.

Shit. Rory.

He scooped up his suit jacket and a pile of briefing notes: was stuffing them in his briefcase when Stella stuck her head around the door. It was her way of prefacing an interruption: by not presenting her whole self around the doorjamb she was only half-interrupting.

'You've got the appointment at six,' she said.

'Which one?' His life was nothing but appointments.

'The one you put in the diary and you wouldn't tell me who it was with,' she said pointedly. 'That one.'

He thought for a moment. Clenched his teeth as the pain surged again. 'Ah yes, that one. Thank you.'

The appointment she knew nothing about was an appointment with a neurologist. He ran down the corridor, yelling a random scramble of instructions her way. He hadn't told her he was supposed to get Rory. If he had, she would have reminded him two or three times by now. The obligation infuriated him so much that he'd pushed it down, buried it beneath layers of other commitments and thoughts, and eventually it had disappeared altogether.

The court orders gave him one weekend a month, Friday afternoon until Sunday night, or otherwise by agreement. It was the *otherwise by agreement* that regularly undid him. In the four years they'd been apart—roughly corresponding to the four years he'd been in politics—Monica had worked assiduously to create a life without him. Her instructions about Rory were delivered by text message, always curt and polite. In flippant moments he had tried to break open her defences with a joke or an anecdote about something Rory had done. If she responded to these at all, it was with a polite deflection: the same tone, he realised one day, that he himself used when communicating with the lawyer at six hundred dollars an hour.

So now she needed him to take Rory for the week. Unscheduled, and impossibly placed in the last days before a goddamn federal election. Did she not have any sense of the pressure? He was a Cabinet minister, for fuck's sake. Did she not think at all?

On reflection he knew she had thought. She had devised this as the most exquisite torment she could deliver, one that didn't cost her a cent. If he refused, if he took *agreement* literally and said no, she'd get him back: refuse him next time he asked, or save it all up for her next affidavit or their next session with June the Mediator.

Running out through the House of Reps entrance, he waved a frantic arm at the nearest Comcar in the queue. The driver eyed him caustically, unimpressed at being hailed like a taxi, as Cassius threw himself in the back seat and thumbed the phone. The flight had landed eight minutes ago. But he'd have luggage checked. The poor kid was pretty good at airport logistics—better than he should have to be in grade four.

The headache was coming on again. Down Kings Avenue and over the bridge, his mind flickering irritably back. The affidavits she'd filed, one after the other, the wounded legalese reciting the rumours her friends had circulated. Drugs, sexual encounters with perilously young interns at previous jobs. Explosions of rage and self-aggrandisement. Utterly baseless references to his mental health.

In the narrowest, most literal sense of the word, she had told the truth: she had repeated faithfully the hearsay that was reported to her by others. The fact that those others were lying—extravagantly—was immaterial. She didn't allege anything that she herself would have to make up: no physical violence or belittlement of the boy. No personal accounts of sexual transgressions. She truthfully related the circumstances of her pregnancy: the conception they had decided, at the very least, to delay; his fury at the news, his tirades about how it could have happened. All of that was true.

And the most damaging bit, the bit they'd leant on in the mediation: him insisting she terminate the pregnancy. It creased his face, it sent the blood rushing to his head every time he recalled it. He had done that. He'd regretted the words the instant they escaped him, but they were his. *It's a pregnancy, not a person, Monica. For God's sake be rational.* Her face had fallen; of course it had. In retrospect, it was probably the moment he lost her for good, though the endgame took a few years.

He kept the affidavits in a folder, hung in a filing cabinet in his office. The legals were done now—there was no need for him to keep them, and his lawyers had copies anyway. But occasionally an odd mood settled over him—he re-read them with wounded bewilderment. *Why did they need to go after me like this?* The whole episode had been a cold, hard revelation. A window onto a new place where the willingness to lie was locked into escalation, like an arms race.

She had correctly surmised that he couldn't take it to court, couldn't put her and the people behind her in the witness box. Because of the need for him to be politically clean, he could not have this muck repeated on oath. So he'd gone to mediation, conceding everything, winding up with a weekend a month in which to be a father.

East along Morshead Drive, following the river. He looked out over the wetlands, the birds rising. Passing through shadows where the Monaro Highway speared overhead. The most sustained and vitriolic attack on his character he'd ever experienced. None of the warnings about the rigours of politics held any terrors for him after that.

The boy had grasped none of it. Which of course was the way the system was designed, and Cassius had no problem with that. But sometimes he wondered how much Rory grasped of anything. He breathed through his mouth and muttered to himself. The sole occupant of a world concealed behind cloud banks, Rory offered few glimpses of his true nature, at least to his father.

The Comcar swung into the waiting bay at arrivals, and he leapt out. Rory was there on the tiles in a Chicago Bulls singlet, his Quiksilver bag beside him. His shoulders pale, marbled by the cold. For a second Cassius wanted to wrap his jacket around the bony frame of his son. Was it the spikes of his chaotic hair that somehow made him look lonely? Airport terminals were like that, though; solitary. Rory's mouth tilted into a half-smile at the sight of his father. Cassius checked his phone.

When he'd cleared the screen, he bent down and offered Rory a handshake. The boy took the hand uncertainly, made a flummoxed imitation of a man-face. Cassius picked up his bag and slung it over his shoulder.

'How are you, mate?'

'Good, Dad.'

'Flight okay?'

'Yep. It's too short for a movie though.'

'Yeah. How's Mum?'

'Good.'

'School?'

'It's okay.'

Christ, this is going nowhere. He looked down from the great height he occupied, at the crown of his son's hair where the cocky's crest originated. Forced a smile.

'So where's Macca?'

'They sent her to oversize again.'

'You're kidding. I thought your mother spoke to the airline about that.'

'Yeah, I think she did.' Rory shrugged. 'Anyway...'

They walked together to the oversize baggage counter, waited for the stubbled clerk to look up from a clipboard.

'Scuse me,' said Cassius.

The attendant looked up. 'Yeah mate.'

'We're after a chicken.'

Eyes down to the clipboard again, the attendant looked dubious. 'Does it have a name?'

Cassius sighed. 'How many chickens have you got back there?'

'Security mate. Can't let you walk off with the wrong bird.'

'Macadamia,' said Rory gravely. 'But she likes it if you call her Macca.'

The attendant disappeared and returned with a pet carrier.

Inside, Cassius could see the white bulk of the hen, the rubbery head jerking at the grille. The chicken glared back at him. It was turning into a hell of a week.

· · ·

Rory sat in silence in the back seat next to Cassius with Macadamia perched regally on his lap. Now and then his slender hand would stroke the bird's back, eliciting a contented sound that Cassius heard as *brookle*.

He stopped first at the neurologist's, and installed Rory in the waiting room with his chook, under the receptionist's withering stare. They'd been willing to take him straight through: nobody wants to see a minister of the crown waiting on the couches of a brain specialist.

She had nothing to offer him in any event: the latest round of scans was inconclusive. Cassius had a hatred of uncertainty that was related to his hatred of mediocrity. A result that was a wavering guess between 'safe' and 'not safe' was unsatisfactory to him. The doctor watched him from behind thick glasses, heard him out as he demanded a plan and a conclusion. It didn't work like that, she told him. All we can do is keep eliminating things.

The medication would continue. The tests would continue. They needn't do anything further until the election was over, but they needed to ensure there was nothing sinister going on. *I'm a politician*, he thought as he rolled his eyes at the ceiling. *There's sinister shit going on everywhere.*

When he emerged, Rory was holding court in a large vinyl armchair, explaining the chicken's ovulation cycle to a grandmotherly type.

Cassius found them a pizza joint in Kingston and the chook waited in the car, voicing her displeasure at being stuffed back in the cage. Rory started pulling the congealed cheese off the crust of his margherita and eating each component separately. It infuriated Cassius.

'Mate, you've got tomato sauce on your cheek. Can you...' He offered the boy a paper napkin. 'No, the other cheek, mate.'

He sighed. The boy hadn't spoken since the car. He sucked at the straw perched in his Coke, hollowing his cheeks. 'You can have the rest, Dad.'

Cassius looked at the twin piles of cheese and dough. He'd planned to eat at home, later. After Rory was asleep. The boy was swinging his legs under the table, and every now and then the toe of one of his sneakers would kick Cassius in the shins.

Cassius checked his phone again. Rory watched him.

'Mum says you've got the election this weekend.'

'Yep.'

'Are you gonna win?'

Cassius lowered the phone, tried to conceal his reluctance with a hard smile. 'We should be okay.'

'I saw you on the telly yesterday.'

'Yeah? What was it about?' Cassius knew what it was about.

Rory looked puzzled. 'Well, you said that the boat people...that the boat people from Indonesia would be on their own from now on.' He screwed up his face. 'Is that right?'

'Sort of. I said that the government won't be getting involved anymore.'

'So what happens if one of the boats comes?' Rory was stretching apart a handful of cheese.

'There's a special company whose job it is to go and deal with it.'

'What do they do?'

Cassius imagined himself telling Rory what they do, the boy repeating it to Monica later on, and the conversation finding its way via a kid in the schoolyard into the fucking media.

'I don't know. They deal with it. They're kind of—experts—at doing stuff like that.' Cassius made the smile again: he remembered his own parents doing it when a topic was too complex for children and needed to be closed. But the kid wasn't letting go.

'So why is there a company that gets rid of the boat people? Are they bad for Australia?'

'No. Well, they can be in some situations. Mostly they're just desperate.' He immediately regretted that choice of word, knowing he'd opened up another avenue.

'If they're desperate why doesn't the government help them?'

Cassius caught the waitress on the way past. 'Can I have the bill please? Mate, it's complicated, okay? We can't let them reach Australia because there are bad people in Indonesia who'll send more boat people if the boat people are getting through, see?'

'Cos you're the person in the government who does that stuff, aren't you?'

Cassius studied Rory for a moment. He'd stopped eating now, pushed the plate aside. Cassius felt in some distant way that he was looking back at himself: the tangle of stubbornness and sensitivity he carried at the same age. But different, physically. So different.

'What's bothering you mate?'

Rory fidgeted with the tablecloth, rolled his eyes theatrically. 'Got a detention.'

'What for?'

'A kid called you a name after you were on TV last time, so I smashed him.'

Cassius contained his shock. 'What did he say about me?'

'He called you a Nasty, and he did a weird-as salute like this.'

'Mate, put your arm down. People are looking. *Nazi,* you mean Nazi.'

'What's that?'

'Oh, it's an insult. Kind of old fashioned. I reckon the kid's picked it up from his parents, hey. You mustn't hit people Rory. It doesn't solve anything.'

But the boy was reddening, looking down. Cassius began to panic as he realised tears were forming in his eyes.

'*I don't like it when they do that,*' Rory whispered ferociously. 'When they say mean things about you.' He hawked back a great childish glob of snot. Now his thin shoulders were rocking. Cassius took his hand across the table, awkwardly.

'Rory, it's my job to be unpopular. With some people, anyway. It doesn't hurt me, whatever they say, so you can't let it upset you.'

'But you said the company does the mean stuff to the boat people. So why does everyone pick on you?'

'Hey, I didn't say it was mean.' He peered down low, trying to lock eyes with his son. 'Who said it was mean, Rory?'

Rory was silent.

'Was it Mum?'

Rory looked at his lap.

'She did, didn't she. What else did she say?'

'She said I shouldn't repeat stuff or there'll be trouble.' His lower lip shuddered as he pulled in a breath. 'Can we go home?'

The Comcar waited under a streetlight outside, the driver reading the *Daily Tele*.

'Yeah mate, let's head off.' He took the bill up to the counter, where the waitress took his card. She was maybe forty, dye growing out of her part and a chain around her neck with *Alyssa* in cursive at its centre.

'Your boy?' she said as she waited for the terminal to approve the payment.

'Yes.' Cassius was looking at the business cards in the fishbowl.

'He looks so much like you,' she beamed.

No he doesn't, Cassius thought irritably. *He's got that ridiculous spiky hair and he's shorter than I was at that age, and I was never that pale, and...*

He looked around at Rory, waiting with his hands in his pockets by the door, now wearing the jacket his mother had sent with him. His reddened eyes clearing, looking straight back at Cassius with uncomplicated adoration.

'He looks up to you, doesn't he,' she was saying behind him. And an unfamiliar state swept over him, like a wave of nausea.

He was not a man who often felt self-loathing.

Pulau Dana

The morning sun stretched shadows from the jungle onto the water.

Isi waded into the shallows, holding her T-shirt up around her ribs and kicking little stubs of coral on the bottom as she went. Silver darts circled around her, interested but wary: they turned on their sides in the bubble trail made by her hips, visible then invisible like spinning coins. The sand was entirely made of coral grains: heavy and white, ringing with tiny metallic harmonies underfoot. On the beach it had preserved the overnight tracks of furtive creatures—the crabs and lizards, the drag marks of the Zodiac and all of yesterday's panicked footprints. She could feel, as she rarely did, the aching, heavy air.

A group of Muslims—they seemed to be in the majority—were praying in the clearing between the tents. Someone had managed to keep hold of a Qur'an. Isi had seen an old man carrying it to the clearing: weathered and gaunt, he stooped as he walked. He had wrapped the book in a tea towel that Radja had supplied from the galley, and he bore the small bundle before him in both hands like an offering. The children avoided him, as they avoided the prayer session.

Leah was singing something with a few of the girls in the shade. Their words were a linguistic muddle but the rhythms of clapping and slapping thighs were universal. Isi felt a warmth towards her: she'd folded herself up to reduce her intimidating height, her long legs crossed in front of her, and the traumatised children were responding to her smile. Two thin girls with hollowed eyes and sores on their arms. A toddler who giggled and cried alternately. Another girl with the scars of terrible burns over her face and neck. Leah's chanting game wasn't the most obvious thing to do in this situation, but it was a kindness nonetheless.

The Finleys had set up a makeshift field hospital in one of the tents, and the survivors were now huddled in the other tents for the shade. Tim was lying under the hunched form of the surgeon, his foot raised on a tub and draped with a T-shirt, a legrope wound tightly around his calf as a tourniquet. The small dark feet of the injured boy Hamid were visible next to him. He was conscious—his hands were moving about—but he was quiet. Finley must have found drugs to deal with their pain.

Two boys stood toe to toe nearby, fighting listlessly in the heat. Their ribs flared as they puffed and grunted, twisting arms, seeking advantage. The bigger one got a hand free and shot his fist into the other's mouth, rocking his head back. Blood appeared on his chin but he didn't cry, just kept twisting and writhing, more determined than ever. No one got up to intervene. No one appeared to know what they were fighting about. One of the men interrupted his praying to shout at them: the older boy kicked out once at his opponent and sent him tumbling backwards. They both sat themselves down in sullen silence.

And as these things went on around her, Isi was watching the lagoon. It had been thirty hours now since the boat foundered, and according to Finley the corpses would be on the move. It was serene just now. But one dark hump marred the tranquillity, halfway between her and the reef.

She took the Zodiac, alone this time, and made a direct line towards the shape. She backed the outboard off, and as the Zodiac settled next to the shape she realised it was a woman's shoulders. Isi leant over the side and took hold of her clumped garments, turned her over and pulled her onto the side of the boat. A gasp escaped her before she could contain it: the woman's face was pulped, smashed beyond recognition. The injuries were bloodless now, the torn muscle and skin softened into trailing skeins of white. The sea lice had taken her eyes overnight.

Isi had to think for a minute. She took the dive float that was always kicking around in the Zodiac and clipped it to the woman's clothing, then released her back into the water. She looped around to head towards the *Java Ridge*, but had to swerve to avoid ploughing straight over a pink tangle of limbs suspended under the surface, beyond her reach. Shreds of clothing, an eye turned wide to the heavens.

They were rising, as Finley had predicted.

Next was a naked boy of eight or nine. His neck was broken: as she lifted him from the water, his head lolled back. His mouth was open, the way children's mouths fall when they sleep, in other places, in safety. He had kept his eyes overnight but they were wide with terror, staring back at her, green as the lagoon under the sun. His body was so slight that she was able to lift him easily over the side of the Zodiac.

She ran the body in to shore. Fraggle waded out with a bedsheet and took the boy from her. She whispered when she spoke to him, like some instinct in her had been tricked into believing the boy was merely asleep.

At her next attempt she made it to the *Java Ridge* without encountering another body. On board, she collected all the plastic bottles she could find and tied a long rope to each. On the other end, a weight: a heavy pot, a spare anchor, a dive lead, whatever she could find. She loaded all of these into the Zodiac and located the mask and a new snorkel. Then she motored out into the centre of the lagoon, nearest to where she could remember seeing the tangled bodies under the surface.

She anchored the little red boat, flopped over the side and waited for the bubbles to clear.

And there they were, gathered in a crowd like a dozen strangers on a railway platform. The hours and the current had brought them together by gravity in the deepest part of the lagoon. Some resting on the sand, some tangled in the limestone that speared out from the bottom. Some were starting to lift away, levitating in mid-water with their clothing in swirls. The fish sparkled among them, making spirals around the foreign shapes. They pecked occasionally, flashing in the sunlight as they turned on their sides.

Isi waited on the surface, treading water slowly and looking down at them. They'd been crushed together on the boat, she imagined, then torn away from each other by the storm and the wreck. And now they were together again, randomly collated by misfortune. She dropped one of her floats to mark the position and returned to the Zodiac.

There were humps appearing everywhere now. She motored from one to the next, tying on the bottles, dropping the weights. When she had finished with those on the surface she swam a series of straight lines across the lagoon, checking for any more bodies that hadn't surfaced. She climbed on top of the cabin of the *Java Ridge* and scanned the water for any she'd missed.

Lastly she launched the drone and swept high over the lagoon, watching the bird's-eye perspective on her phone. It was so bloody beautiful it made her eyes hurt. But no more of the dead reappeared.

She recruited Sanusi and Radja to help her gather the bodies she'd found. The survivors on the island were assembling on the shore, looking out over the glimmering field, the bodies with their little floats attached. Some of the women were wailing, perhaps recognising a shape in the water. Isi felt the pressure now, to get the bodies to shore before grief turned to hysteria.

The three of them took turns driving the Zodiac and swimming, hauling the victims out and driving them inshore. Sanusi had tied a plastic bag over his hand and secured it with rubber bands. He never mentioned it, never even looked at it. Luke Finley and Fraggle took the bodies onto the beach on surfboards, working patiently through the crowd that would gather around each new arrival. For those people there could be no prospect of good news—either the body was their loved one, or their loved one remained missing.

• • •

Hours after she'd begun, Isi ran the Zodiac up onto the beach and collapsed in the shade. She could not erase the images she'd seen: what the violence of the wreck and ravenous nature had done to fingers and lips and eyes and scalps and viscera. But the lagoon was emptied of its ghosts and now the dead lay in a neat row on the beach. The sun had dried them, and already the insects were noisily investigating what the ocean had delivered.

An old man with a pointed white beard, eyes agape and chin jutting in some kind of defiance. Children, a baby, two toddlers. Young women who might be their mothers. Young men—by far the most numerous—those merely drowned, those subjected to various traumas by the boat and the reef: head wounds, mangled faces, broken limbs that poked up like the disorderly roots of mangroves. Crushed and cut and torn flesh of every imaginable kind.

Isi walked the length of the row in silence, her feet scrunching in the sand. The heads rested near the edge of the grasses beyond the high tide line, yet the beach was so narrow that the feet of some of the taller ones lay within inches of the lapping water. Towels and sheets had been laid over their bodies where the ocean had ripped away their modesty. She saw the boy with the green eyes and felt a sadness for him that she knew was disproportionate. The line of corpses was a bottomless well of such pity, but the boy was deep at its centre.

Twenty-three humans.

And standing, sitting, lying around the tents where the Finleys were now working, the survivors.

Isi hadn't counted them yet, but Roya had counted fifty-six on board the *Takalar*, she said, so these silent figures must number about thirty, along with the injured boy. A handful might still be missing, but the odds on their survival were so faint that Isi thought it reasonable to focus on those living and present.

Radja had been back to the *Java Ridge* and brought ashore food, water and towels. He was methodical, efficient: no sign of the disbelief and panic that wrenched at Isi. In the shade she found Fraggle, head in hands and dreads spilling over his bare knees.

She sat beside him. 'Was it you who laid out the bodies?

He was silent a long time. 'Yeah.'

She could see his hands shaking. He still hadn't looked up. 'We're going to have to bury them at some point. Or the birds'll…'

He finally met her eyes. His were red from crying, fingers fidgeting with the latches of the camera case on the ground beside him. 'We should, like, identify 'em first.'

He opened the case and lifted out a camera body, chose a lens and clicked it into place. She walked with him along the row as he carefully composed a shot of each corpse. Where they thought some distinctive mark might identify the person—a broken tooth, a scar—they photographed that as well. It took a long time, and the heat rammed down on them as they worked. The insects had been keeping up their piercing whistle throughout, but it was only when they'd finished that she noticed how loud the sound was.

Fraggle rolled the thumbwheel on the back of the camera body, checking through the images. Once he was satisfied, he looked around again. At the bodies. At the flat lagoon.

'I've gotta go back to the boat and radio this in,' said Isi.

'Yep,' muttered Fraggle distractedly. He was moving left and right in the short scrub behind the beach, leaning against the trunks of the palms. The dried undergrowth crackled under him as he trod heavily. 'I just wanna get a shot that...explains this, y'know.'

When he'd found the perspective he wanted he squatted down on his haunches, heavy sunburnt knees swelling from the legs of his boardshorts. He pressed the camera to his face and Isi crouched behind him, seeing what he was seeing.

The *Java Ridge* was far off to one side, out of shot; lying quiet at anchor.

What Fraggle had framed was the flat lagoon, turning glorious indigo against the hard light; the overhanging coconut palms, the reef in the distance with the upturned boat amid the settling blue surf. And in the foreground, the nightmarish line of the dead, mottled and broken, their eyes unblinkingly fixed on the sky.

The photographer's hands made a few tiny adjustments to the lens, then he pressed the shutter.

• • •

Isi and Luke were fitting a hand pump to the plastic tub of drinking water she'd brought over from the *Java Ridge*'s main tank.

'Much water left after this?' he asked her.

'Yeah, we'll be fine. Ten thousand litres or something. You need a shower?' She smiled at him.

'It's just, I'm not sure if we should use it all on...' He stopped himself. He looked tired and distressed. 'I'd never seen a dead person until yesterday.'

'Me neither. How's Leah dealing with Tim?'

'Coping. Probably one of those people who always copes. It's her job.'

'What's she do?'

'Cop, she said. Senior conny at Bankstown.'

Isi looked at her sorting through a heap of personal belongings that had washed up, making a list of identifying details in a notebook. Beyond her, Neil Finley was visible in the shade of the tent, examining the pregnant woman. Her daughter, the girl called Roya, sat next to her, gently stroking her mother's hair.

He called from the tent.

'Leah, can you…er, the lady wants a screen in here. She doesn't want a man to do it.'

Leah scooped a towel that was drying on a tree and took it into the tent. Her attention diverted, Isi hadn't noticed that Luke had slumped beside her with his hands on his knees, the irregular shade of the palms making jagged patterns on his back. His head was covered in sweat and his face was red. Isi put a hand on his shoulder.

'How you feeling about that medical career?'

He laughed drily.

'Hey, where's Carl?'

Luke stood straight and shook his head in disgust. 'That fucking idiot. Have a look.' He pointed at the reef.

There, incredibly—Isi had to peer harder to believe what she was seeing—sat a surfer, bobbing between the perfect blue walls that had arrived with the passing of the storm. 'What an arsehole,' she muttered.

'You wait,' said Luke, and his vehemence surprised Isi. 'He'll have some reason for it. He'll have it all mapped out, the fuckwit.'

• • •

Fraggle was sitting in the shade, hunched over his camera.

'Tryin' to get the colours right on that shot,' he said, though she hadn't asked.

'Which shot?' She sat down next to him.

'The one of the lagoon and the bodies.' He returned to fiddling with the controls. 'You can do a lot of the editing on the camera itself these days. Cool, huh?'

He proffered the camera. She looked at the display but could only see the awful reality of the dead.

'Did you raise anyone on the radio?' he asked.

'Nah. The VHF can do thirty-five or forty miles in a straight line, but the only thing within that range is Raijua. There's a couple of villages there that might've picked us up, but there's another storm between us and them. You can just see it—' She pointed northeast where a thick pile of cumulonimbus lumbered behind the haze. 'The HF goes longer—we reached Korea once—but it's a bastard to tune. I've done a basic message a few times over but no one came back.'

'So no one knows?'

'Nope. And there was no radio in the console of their boat, so they haven't told anyone where they are.'

'Shit.'

'But our government watches this area pretty closely. We're near the edge of Australian waters, so you never know. They might be onto us.'

They watched Carl in the distance, hurtling free with the spray from a wide glossy barrel. She hated him specifically for that pleasure.

'I was thinking maybe that rock in the middle of the island,' said Fraggle. 'I know it's a long shot, but we could take a phone up there. I mean, it's nice and high…'

Carl picked off another one. Even from this distance Isi could see that he surfed with the kind of aggression that revealed irritation, annoyance. His turns were flicked rather than drawn, like he was swiping at bugs. She'd seen enough surfers to know that, for better or worse, something flowed out of their souls and through their feet.

'Sure,' she said eventually, 'why not?' She stood up, brushing the leaves off her backside. She wanted to do something about the situation, however speculative it might be.

•••

They picked their way through the undergrowth, slapping at insects. Isi wished she'd brought the machete from the boat, as she tore at the great tangles of vines and dead foliage. There was no path, only a vague sense of where they needed to go. The leaves on the larger trees had looked brilliant and delicate from a distance, but were in fact quite massive, some of them sharply serrated. And between those trees was a morass of cane, strap and fibre; tangled and aimless, in varying states of growth and decay. Even where bare rock protruded through the greenery, the plants would take hold in any fracture, clawing at the hard surface as though to crack it open.

The sand underfoot turned to tough, matted soil, and the soil to rock as the ground began to rise. Thorns picked at their clothes; unseen irritants raised itchy welts on their flesh. Eventually the deep scrub and the heavy canopy of trees broke clear as the way became steeper and the view opened up around them. At the screaming peak of the sun's fury, the light had now turned the sea to silver. The birds hung in the air like wet laundry. She watched their lethargic forward motion as the sweat ran down her back, the resentment in their slow flapping. Only the intrusion of these rare humans had compelled them aloft at all.

The summit of the rocky hill was unmarked: a bare red boulder, small lizards scurrying away. They sat and drank tepid water and Fraggle produced his phone.

'Nothing,' he groaned.

'Well, that was a nice walk,' Isi said cheerfully.

Tiny electric-blue wrens darted about in the twigs at their feet. Isi adjusted her position as a column of ants advanced on her. Far below, they could see the tents, the fly-speck humans, even the lines of the dead. Out in the lagoon, banded in yellow to green to deep blue, the two boats were juxtaposed in savage irony.

The *Java Ridge*, sleek and proud at anchor, and the dead belly of the wreck on the reef. Wide of it, a tiny black blemish in the vast expanse of ocean. Carl Simic.

Fraggle held the phone up again, circled it at arm's length around his head. 'Thought I had something there for a sec.' He started fiddling with the camera again.

'What are you doing now?'

'I can Bluetooth the shots to the phone. That way if we get any signal I can fire them off. Or at least fire one off—they're bloody big files.'

'Why don't you just type out a message about what's happened?'

He shrugged. 'I'm a photographer. I work in images.'

They watched in silence for a moment as a sea eagle swept in from over the lagoon with a big lizard in its talons. It settled on the boulders below them and smashed the reptile against the rock with a few sharp blows of its beak.

'Well if you're going to send a shot, can I suggest you don't send the dead people? Maybe that one with the boat on the reef.'

'It's got bodies in it anyway,' he countered, thumb-typing into the phone. 'Okay, how's this: *We are on Dana island west of Raijua SE of Sumba. Boat, probly refugee, aground here. Many dead, 2 sersly injured. Pls send help URGENT.*'

'Good. Who you sending it to?'

'I've posted it to Vipe.'

'Holy shit Fraggle, is that going to find anyone? What about sending it to the authorities?'

'Well, *which* authorities? You know the number for the rescue guys?'

'Nope.'

'Yeah, well it's Vipe or I'm emailing it to my mum.'

They waited in silence for a while, Fraggle revolving with the phone like he was shooting a panoramic, squinting at the screen.

'So why didn't we get Joel?' he asked absently.

'You think he would've handled this better?'

'No,' he looked indignant. 'Shit, I was just asking.'

Isi saw that she'd overreacted. Fraggle's face was open and kind: there was nothing behind his question. 'I gather you've done a lot of surf trips,' she said.

'Mm. Last few years I've been away a lot.'

'Great seeing new places, hey.'

Fraggle didn't even glance at her. 'Travelling's a way of making sure you're not at home.'

He plainly didn't want to add to that. Isi drank some water and offered it to him but he declined. She felt the urge to push through his silence.

'Joel's in Perth. He's got problems. We've got problems. I wouldn't have said anything, but I guess it's pretty minor by comparison now, isn't it?'

Fraggle said nothing, and she found herself going on. 'It's just me and him, the business. And things have gone wrong, like the bombings and the political bullshit between our government and theirs. And there's big corporate players in the market now, and they can advertise and they can bung on all the luxuries. And when Joel spends money on the business he does dumb stuff, you know? Extravagant shit. The Indos rip him off pretty easy because he's generous.'

'So why are you in business with him? You could have a relationship with him without going into business together'—he laughed a little, then added—'in a place like Bali.'

'He's a bloody good surfer and people respect him. You know, people like the Finleys and Tim. That should be enough...'

'Yeah, but it isn't, eh.'

'I don't know what it is that Indo does to Australian blokes. Turn into bloody cavemen: aggressive, but faking all this matey bullshit. Burn themselves black in the sun. They're *physical* you know? Nothing on the inside.'

'Christ that's bleak.'

'You know it's true. You've seen them. It's what you get when you give blokes all the sun and waves they want, and cheap piss and good times and zero fucking accountability. That's what they'll ultimately turn into, into a—'

'I've got a signal.'

'Shit! Go go *go!*'

'Sending...' Fraggle watched the screen, shading it with his other hand. 'We're done.'

She whooped with delight and hugged him while he remained awkwardly rigid. Far below them, the reef was empty now and Carl was paddling back. The wrecked boat had slipped off the inside edge of the coral into deeper water and disappeared from view.

Canberra

Cassius stared at the first photograph until it blurred, but if it held any secrets it wasn't revealing them to him.

He pushed his papers away to both sides of the desk and laid the two images in front of him.

From high, high above the island, the surveillance image had been cropped down to show the lagoon, the reef and the hill behind the beach. The colours were beautiful, the leaching of one brilliant primary hue into another: deep water to shallow, coral to sand, beach to palms to rocks. In the middle of the bay a boat lay at anchor, the dark chain visible in the sunlight. Large tarpaulins extended over the decks, and the shadow of the boat made a triangle on the sea floor beneath it.

There were people on the beach.

Who are you? He thumbed through a phone list. Stella was yelling at him again from outside the room. Christ she was loud. He frowned at the phone list and sighed. But she wasn't going away.

'Hey! Rory goes for the Sea Eagles, yeah?'

'Aha,' he replied, absently. 'Like his ol' man.'

'You know they're playing here Friday night?'

'Oh shit! Of course.'

'You want me to get tickets?'

'Great, great. Yes, please.' Thank God for Stella.

'That's election eve of course. How bout I clear it with Media so we can call it a public appearance? Tip off the commercials—you and your boy, doing the family thing in your silly bloody scarf...'

He smiled to himself. 'I love you Stella.'

She appeared in the doorway with a sarcastic grin. 'I'm not your Moneypenny. Better talk to your ex—he's due home sooner isn't he?'

She was right again. Cassius typed an email while it was in the front of his mind:

Monica,

You might not be aware that on Friday night the Sea Eagles (Rory's team) are playing the Canberra Raiders here in Canberra. I would love to take him to the game. Seeing as he's already here, would it be all right if I kept him another 24 hours? C.

'Tell her I'll babysit the chicken,' Stella yelled from outside. He found the number he was looking for and dialled it, kicking the door shut while it rang.

'Sir?'

'Nigel. All right, I'm looking at the two images now. Do you have them in front of you?'

'Yes sir, I do.'

'Now, the first one. Where's that shot taken?'

'It's over a small island halfway between Roti and Sumba called Dana. Uninhabited. I mean, we're talking here, it's about a mile by a mile and a half.'

'How did we get the shot?'

'Core Resolve had an asset in the area. We put in a call to them after that Coastwatch report about a boat out there. So that's taken from high altitude, but obviously zoomed right in. We took a series of shots across that sector and this was the only feature of any interest that we could locate.'

'I can see a boat. Anchored?'

'Yes, we think so.'

'And people on a beach.'

'Yes.'

'Who are they?'

There was a long expulsion of air on the other end of the line. 'Well, we don't know. The boat's a traditional Indonesian design. It's timber, and you can tell the bow's very high by the shape of the shadow. We've had a few people looking at that aspect, and they think it's a *phinisi*, a fishing boat that comes from up in the north.'

'So why's it way down here in the south?'

'They use them everywhere. Could be fishermen, could be insurgents, could be illegals headed our way.'

'What's the…it looks green round the cabin. Is it painted green?'

'I thought that too. Not sure, sir.'

'All right. Is it the boat we'd tracked a few days ago?'

Again, hesitation, breathing. 'Well sir I don't…Mr Smedley prefers we don't speculate…'

'I'm not going to hold you to it. But I want to know what your gut instinct is.'

'Yeah, I appreciate that. Look, there's a lot of variables in this game…I, er…'

'But if you take the position where we located the boat on the… what's that?'

'The Savu Sea.'

'This is not far away, right? So it's the same one?'

'Maybe.'

Cassius resisted the exasperation that was creeping over him now. Everyone was ducking and weaving: they all knew it was his job to be in the firing line for this.

'What do you mean maybe? Forty-eight hours ago a boat

matching this description was wallowing around just north of here. There was a big storm and now a boat with an identical profile is lying at anchor in a sheltered lagoon. It's pretty compelling logic isn't it?'

'Yes. But that doesn't mean it's correct. Sir.'

Cassius began rubbing the surface of the desk with his open palms, willing himself to remain calm.

'We don't *get* boats anymore. We've sto—' Something he'd taken as a certainty for so long. 'Are we still getting boats and we're sending them back?'

'That's a separate line of inquiry, sir. I can find out but I'd need to go to Core Resolve. Do you require me to do that?'

'No, I just want to understand this. Why would anyone send a boat these days? It's obvious that it won't get through.'

'With respect sir, that confuses the people sending the boats with the people *on* the boats. If you're sending the boat and you're holding the money, you don't care much whether it gets through. And if you're on the boat and you've been lied to, then…'

'All right. Can I ask you a couple more questions? What are the squares on the ground, just behind the beach?'

'Four of them? We think they're tents, sir.'

'Tents? Why would asylum seekers have tents? Why aren't they sleeping on the boat, or on the ground? The boat's got tarps over it.'

'Well, some of these outfits are better equipped than others. They might've taken them with them, or the tents might already have been there on the island…could be lots of reasons. Also, there might've been a problem with the boat and they wanted to get off for a while. You know, something infectious, or a fuel leak, or a fight of some kind…it can get pretty tense on board these vessels.'

Cassius sighed and felt the claws tightening again. Twice in as many days. He waited a moment for the pain to ebb, picked up the other photograph with its beach and quiet lagoon and glorious tropical sky. And then—like biting into an exquisite fruit and finding half a grub—the overturned hull and the bodies. So beautiful, so macabre.

'All right, the other shot. Now what's this?'

'We're looking across a beach, sir, out to sea, and the question I guess is, is this the same location as the one that the overhead shot shows?'

'Where did it come from? Is there any explanation for it?'

'No. It's public domain, whereas the other one isn't. It was posted on an extreme sports social media service called Vipe.'

'Never heard of it.'

'The kids use it, sir. Skating, surfing, that sort of crowd. From there it was re-posted by the left-wing media, activist groups. We've looked at some of their communications and they...'

'What do you mean?'

'Well we've...we've gone through all their social media, done some work on their metadata, some emails...'

'Are we allowed to do that?'

'Yes, some of it comes within the user agreements these people sign when they join whatever the service is. And the rest comes under national security regs of one kind and another. There's a protocol we run to ensure all the checks are covered by something.'

He appeared to be waiting for a further reaction from Cassius, but as there was none, he pressed on. 'So we went through the followers on the account. You see, the company behind Vipe won't give us account-holder details, and the guy who posted it just describes himself as Fraggle. He's got a sizable following, but only under that alias: there's no indication of who the individual is. So we worked through the followers on the account to see what we could cross-reference. And there's a woman named...Veal. Joyce Veal in Rockingham. You want me to keep going?'

'Yes.'

'So Joyce Veal, it turns out, is the mother of a surf photographer called Alan Veal, and DFAT confirms he's currently in Indonesia. In other words, he could be Fraggle. We're trying to find a legislative basis to burrow into her comms and find the link.'

Cassius was struggling to keep up. The claws were digging in. 'So the activists, the—what are they called?'

'Open Borders.'

He squinted, then un-squinted. 'Open Borders...what do they say the photo represents?'

'They're claiming it shows an asylum-seeker boat that's wrecked on the reef. The caption with it doesn't prove or disprove what it shows.'

'Are those bodies?'

'Possibly. That's certainly what some of the commentators are saying. There must be a couple of dozen of them, which of course is too many for a fishing vessel. More consistent with illegals.'

'And the'—Cassius flipped between the two images—'the two shots. Do they show the same place? Because the calm water in the ground shot could be the lagoon in the shot from Core Resolve. I mean, it *could* be...' He tried rotating them. He tried squinting again.

'Yes, and the question then arises, is the upturned boat in the background the same boat that's at anchor in the Core Resolve shot? And if so, what happened to it?'

Cassius looked at the shape. It was, unmistakably, a capsized hull, slimed with marine growth like he imagined an Indonesian fishing boat might be.

'What do we know about the timing?'

'The aerial view was taken last Sunday. We know precisely that the ground shot was taken thirty-six hours later. We had our tech people burrow into the image file to work that out. And they found something else, sir.'

'Mm?'

'The image has been manipulated.'

'Manipulated?'

'It's no big deal. Just the colour saturation we think, but they're still working on it. I don't want to confuse matters with that, but you probably should know.'

Cassius thought fast, thought about the implications of the two shots, the clock running down to Saturday and everyone's political fate.

'All right. I want to go to the PM on this basis: the aerial view was provided via top-secret channels and shows an Indonesian fishing boat sheltering from a storm in a lagoon. The other shot is of unknown provenance and may show the same vessel overturned the next day. The incident is outside Australian waters and we have had no notification from the Indonesians that we have any cause for concern. Now is there anything about that that doesn't ring true to you?'

'Well, there's a lot left to explain. There's the bodies, the tents, and as you rightly point out there's the origin of the second shot. It may come to light over the coming days...'

'I can handle all that. So can the PM. But nothing contradicts me, right?'

'No sir.'

'Good. Thank you.' Cassius was already bracing himself for the call to the PM.

'Oh, sir?'

'Yes?'

'You said there were a couple of things you'd noticed about the overhead shot. The tents and...what was the other one?'

Cassius racked his brains. The headache was starting to subside but there was fuzz in its wake. 'I can't remember. I'm sure it wasn't important.'

He put down the phone, scrawled out some notes and rang the PM's office. He was assured a call would be returned to him within minutes. He spent those minutes comparing the two shots. What the hell had gone on here?

The PMO rang back: he was transferred from an assistant to the chief of staff and finally to the PM. Between the expected bluster and indignation, he made the points he wanted to make and they agreed that the PM would take care of the media briefing.

It should have brought him satisfaction. This slimy chain of inference clearly had its origins in some murky place. It was a grenade without a pin, and now someone else was holding it.

The PM wanted the win here. He needed to sweep aside the misty-eyed bed-wetters looking to generate a humanitarian crisis in the hours before polling day. And yet Cassius felt a residual sense of doubt. Something didn't add up.

Two hours later the PM faced the press, timed to cut live into the evening news. Cassius was still in his office, two of the neurologist's pills down his throat and the corridors blanketed in silence. He turned on the TV, found the ABC and watched as he fed his notes into a shredder.

The two photos, side by side.

The caption: *Is this a wrecked asylum seeker boat?*

Then the PM's head, framed in the same doorway where Cassius had made his policy announcement. He had thrust his chin forward as he liked to do when there was a stoush on.

'Some irresponsible members of the press have rushed to conclusions about these images that are frankly alarmist. I object—I mean, I really strongly object—to people trying to whip up hysteria when they are not in possession of the facts. So to lay this to rest once and for all: the aerial shot you see here'—he held up a laminated copy of the aerial image—'shows an Indonesian fishing vessel sheltering from a storm in a lagoon in Indonesian waters near the island of Sumba. Okay?' He looked pugnaciously out at his imagined enemies. 'We didn't have to release that image—it comes from classified sources—but we chose to in the interests of openness with the Australian public.

'And the second image, provided by certain groups with axes to grind, shows the same vessel, overturned, a day or so later. Case closed, ladies and gentlemen.'

A flurry of reporters' questions. The PM continued to speak.

'But let me tell you one other thing. One other thing. And this might be a lesson for some members of the media about judging a book by its cover. This image'—he shook the laminated copy of the ground shot—'has been electronically manipulated. We can't tell what was there, or what's been inserted, but it is not in its original form.'

Half a smile played on his thick lips as he stared into the camera.

'A drowning at sea—any loss of human life—is a tragedy, make no mistake. People may have died here. I don't know. I don't know if I can trust this image. I don't know where it was taken, or by whom, or for what reasons. People pick things up off social media and treat them like they're gospel. I don't know why someone chose to fiddle with this image, or what their motivations were. My job, and minister Calvert's job, is to protect our borders. And we do that based on evidence. Reliable evidence from the men and women of our Border Integrity Force, and our commercial partners at Core Resolve. Not this…this rubbish.

'The boats have stopped, ladies and gentlemen, and despite what some interest groups might wish, they ain't coming back.'

The questions came again, each one deflected with a combative monosyllable. Cassius tuned out and took himself home.

• • •

He'd hired a nanny for Rory but hadn't had a chance to check in with her.

'What a lovely boy,' she said now as he paid her and showed her out.

The kid was asleep on the couch with a tablet propped in the folds of a doona on his lap. The chicken was huddled in a box of torn newspaper at his feet. Cassius could smell its shit in the sterile air.

He lifted the device gently out of his son's fingers and studied the screen. Rory had been watching the PM's presser. *You're nine years old,* he wanted to tell him. *You won't find the truth watching this old crook spinning his lies.* He tapped back one screen, then another. Rory's original search was *Cassius Calvert.*

He transferred the boy carefully to his bed in the spare room, legs and doona trailing like a fire rescue, and shuffled into his own room, where neither tenderness nor deceit could find him.

• • •

It struck him deep in the night, as the claws woke him, tearing at the inside of his head.

The other thing.

His second query about the satellite photo. A red shape, vaguely triangular, on the beach directly opposite the boat at anchor. It had bothered him during the phone call, with its familiar but maddeningly elusive outline. He knew what it was now. It was an inflatable boat, a Zodiac.

And no asylum seeker boat he'd ever heard of carried a Zodiac.

Pulau Dana

There was a tacit acknowledgment that they were stuck for the time being.

The survivors sent an emissary to say they wanted to bury the bodies. *Custom*, said the man. He placed his hand on his heart and bowed slightly. Carl watched him from the shadows. The surfers looked to Isi to make a decision: she hesitated, thinking that anyone rescuing them might need to see the dead. The crabs and gulls were already growing bolder: they'd take care of them as surely above the sand as under it.

But on the first day at least, no one could summon the strength to dig such a hole; nor did anyone know what tools to dig it with. So the issue remained unresolved as night fell, and the two Indonesian crew brought food from the *Java Ridge* and prepared it on the beach.

When they'd all eaten, Isi called her group together. The clusters of people from the wreck sat away from them, around a fire that Sanusi had made them. Their voices were low and could easily be taken as secretive. But there was something else about them, something Isi had to turn over in her mind before she could make sense of it. There was a calm in their eyes, of resignation or weary scepticism. They'd seen suffering before: not a shipwreck, but certainly the violent sundering of lives. A rocket, perhaps, lobbed into a market out of a clear blue sky.

Not something you'd accept, but something you'd wrap your existence around and through. Life's grim forward motion.

For the Australians, every one of them, the last two days had been the most harrowing of their lives. Whatever resilience might be built by random tragedy, they had none of it.

Isi couldn't take her eyes off Roya. She'd watched her through the afternoon, bringing water to the adults, rubbing her mother's bare feet, shaking sand and grass out of the towel they'd been given to lie on. The presence of her, the quiet composure.

'All right,' she began. 'I want to work out what we do next. I think I'd said earlier, this island is called Dana. It belongs to Indonesia, it's uninhabited and the locals don't come here because there are, um, cultural beliefs about it. Now the people we've...these people. Does anyone know who they are?'

'They're asylum seekers,' Leah said. 'From what I can work out they left from Makassar—on Sulawesi—and they came south past Sumba heading for Ashmore Reef. All sorts of people—Iranians, Afghans, Iraqis and Pakistanis, but obviously some of them...' her voice trailed off as she inclined her head towards the bodies. 'Lots of them are deceased.'

Isi had done a head count and discovered that there were twenty-nine survivors, not the thirty-three she'd hoped for. Either Roya had counted wrong in the first place—which she doubted—or there were four still missing.

'So we're dealing with twenty-nine people,' said Isi. 'The *Java Ridge* will accommodate them no worries—we're carrying enough food and water. I've tried to radio for help but heard nothing back so far. We're in a bad spot for that. Fraggle and I went up to the top of the rock this afternoon and Fraggle got a little bit of signal on his phone, so we've posted a photo that shows the bodies and the wreck on the reef.'

'It's gone now,' said Carl from the back.

'I saw.' Isi knew her voice was terse and she didn't care to hide it. 'There's villagers on the island called Raijua to our east, only about two hours' sail away. At the moment we're Indonesia's problem, and Australia stays out of the way up here. But they'd be talking to each other, I guess. South of us is Ashmore Reef but it's more like thirteen hours at full speed. So we need to work out when to leave and where to go.'

Leah spoke up again. 'The when's up to the doc over here, isn't it?' She nodded towards Finley. 'But the where—I mean, wouldn't you go straight to the nearest point? Like, straight to Raijua?'

'It's not that simple,' Isi replied. 'We might go over there and find there's no facilities and everyone's scratching their heads. They might be able to call in a plane to do an evacuation, but they might not. And how much time do we lose getting in there through the reef and finding someone to talk to, compared to getting ourselves into Australian waters and linking up to an evacuation from Ashmore?'

'But if you take them to Ashmore,' Carl nodded towards the survivors, who were watching the discussion in silence, 'then they've got what they wanted, haven't they.'

Nobody responded. Isi pressed on.

'I think Tim's welfare is probably paramount here isn't it? Tim and the pregnant woman? Neil?'

He must be exhausted by now, she thought. But there was no outward sign of it. He sat tall on a deckchair someone had brought him, shoulders back and chin up. A faint silver stubble was appearing over his jaw.

'Well, Tim's got a compound fracture of his ankle and a crush injury to the foot from where the boat shifted onto it. Nasty injuries. In a proper clinical setting we'd open it all up and debride it, do some grafts, but we're limited here. I've stopped the blood loss by closing the main vessel that was affected, and I've tried to clean up the big fracture site. But there are lots of small fractures in his foot that I can't possibly fix here, and I can't set the big fracture without knocking him out. I'm reluctant to do that until there's a plan about where we're going. So at the moment I'm relying on sterile dressings from the medical tub. But those won't last indefinitely. Oh, and I've found a pulse in the foot which means we have circulation, so that's a positive.'

He took out a scrunched piece of paper where he'd been making notes.

'Who else have I got notes on...a nine-year-old girl and her mother. The girl's Raja...?'

'Roya,' Isi corrected.

'Roya. Speaks some English, which is a help. Her mother's pregnant, about thirty-two, thirty-three weeks as far as I can tell; it's not my area. I don't see any symptoms that she's about to go into labour anyway. Then there's an Iraqi male, about thirty, with minor lacerations that I've sutured. He might be your skipper, by the way. Won't give his name, bit aggressive. There's two older men: maybe forty, they don't know—both got dysentery. They're Iranians. They should both be all right if I can keep fluids up to them.

'The boy who came in on the Zodiac unconscious, er...Hamid. He's a bit of a worry. Probably twelve...he's had a big whack over the temple.' He pointed to his own head with a long bony finger. 'I can't get any English out of him, but I want to watch him closely in case his conscious state changes. So he's lying down, and if anybody wants to take a shift keeping an eye on him, that'd be great.'

Finley's voice remained as flat and calm as the lagoon. It could have been a ward round.

'If you find any injuries or illnesses among the others, please let me know. The upshot of it all is, Tim's the main concern and I'm not that confident about moving him yet. He's in a lot of pain, a lot. I've put him on codeine, and if that runs out there are other options. But I...'

He appeared to change his mind about saying something.

'Neil? What else?' Isi wanted it out, whatever it was.

Finley continued reluctantly. 'The limiting factor in all of this is drugs. We have a woman who could go into labour. We have a foot injury that might deteriorate because the thread I've used on that vessel is crappy silk stuff from the tub. And we have a head injury that may or may not be stable. It's a bit of a juggle, and I'm working with the codeine, but the only serious agent in that tub is one vial of ketamine.'

'What's that do?' asked Isi.

'It's good for a situation like this because it's a painkiller and an anaesthetic in one. Kind of an all-purpose third-world trauma drug. I think I can keep Tim stable like he is, but I'll review whether we can move him in the morning.'

'All right,' said Isi. 'Everyone comfortable with that?' No one responded. 'We'll bury the dead in the morning, and at this stage I'm saying we'll head for Ashmore. If you disagree you can come and see me.'

The listeners stood and moved away, including a handful of the rescued. As Isi watched them disperse into the night, she became aware of one man in particular: a man with a wide thin moustache and glossy black hair that sprung out slightly from his crown and behind his ears. He had medical dressings on his hands. *Finley's Iraqi*, she thought. *The skipper.*

The man was watching her, his mouth set in a firm line. The look suggested disapproval to her, but she couldn't read it clearly on a foreign face. He kept his eyes on her as he slowly turned his body away, then he was gone.

Sanusi was beside her. He'd seen.

'Not Indonesian?' she asked him in Bahasa.

'No, Iraqi. He looks angry.'

'Maybe you should have a talk to him. Ask Roya to translate. See what's going on.'

Sanusi lit a cigarette, held it in his wounded fist and squinted as he drew back the smoke. 'Okay boss.'

His was a smile that could mean anything from happy assent to deep gloom. Isi had a fair idea he was worried.

• • •

She found Carl sitting alone on the beach. He had his feet in the water, his knees drawn up to his chest and headphones on. Sitting down beside him would look empathetic, so she remained standing.

He either hadn't noticed her or had chosen to ignore her. She pulled the cup off one of his ears. 'What the fuck were you doing?'

'You sure you can talk to your clients that way?' he smirked.

'Don't fuck with me Carl. How the hell do you think it's appropriate to go surfing when this is going on?'

'What's going on?' She had his attention now. 'We got everybody out of the water. Doctor's fixing the sick people. What do you want me to do?'

'See that's the thing, isn't it—you didn't ask anyone what you could do. You just went.'

'Yeah, whatever.'

She found she'd put her hands on her hips. Her disbelief was showing. 'Seriously, how do you *do* that? Go surfing when there are dead and injured people everywhere? What kind of person does that?'

'You judging me? They probably put a hole in it deliberately. They do shit like that.'

'What do you mean *they*?'

Carl shrugged, momentarily off guard. 'I dunno. Muzzies. Foreigners.'

Isi couldn't believe what she was hearing. 'Foreigners? *We're* the fucking foreigners out here.'

'Whatever you reckon. Our boat still floats and theirs doesn't.'

'That's appalling. I swam under their fucking boat. There were no holes. The engine had come off its—' She felt her own doubt creeping in. How the hell had it done that? 'It'd broken loose. They didn't have a chance.'

'Bullshit. They're using us.' Carl was pointing his finger at her now. She could see the speech forming across his face. 'They're using us and making us feel guilty. Those people paid some guy to take 'em in a shitty boat. They made that choice, and you live with your choices.'

She was shaking her head in disbelief, but Carl was now venting something that had been welling up for a long time.

'For fuck's sake, Isi. We're this massive empty continent, all fucken sunny and bright, just sitting there. Hardly any of us and let's face it, we're half asleep. Time goes on, more and more of these cunts are gonna want to get in. They don't turn up in warships these days, they don't parachute out of the sky—but there's a shitload of brown people to the north of us, and they don't have enough food and they're ruled by arseholes and their drinking water's fucken filthy. There's disease and typhoons and beggars and three-legged dogs. You'd have to be a fucking idiot not to realise they're coming over the hill sooner or later. These people aren't refugees—they're migrants to a better place. And what about the others, huh? The poor silly fuckers waiting their turn in camps in Some-fuckistan. We help these people make it to the front of the queue, and what we're doing is encouraging the next lot to try it.'

He stood and turned to walk away, but changed his mind.

'You want to fucken—you want to be Mother Teresa and rescue the reffoes that's your business. Might be your politics or Tim's politics or whatsisname—Finley's job, but it's got nothin to do with me. I paid good money to be here. Good money. I dug fucken ditches for months thinking about this trip so I could give you my money and you'd get me barrelled. An' if you can't manage that yourself I'll be fucked if I'll sit by and cop it.'

'Charming.'

'Yeah, fuck you Isi. We were supposed to have Joel to start with. Just my fucking luck I get a woman in a man's job.'

He turned resolutely this time and marched off towards camp. She watched his retreating back, the muscles taut with anger. Surfing all the time created a certain shape in some people. She knew it well, the flared lats and sprung triceps. You could call it conditioning. You could even say it was evidence of physical discipline.

But she'd never met a bloke on whom it wasn't evidence of selfishness.

WEDNESDAY MORNING

Canberra

It was rare that Cassius slept badly. His self-assurance, his desire to squeeze the most out of life, meant that no matter how the day had gone he could expect a good night's sleep, untroubled by any needling from his subconscious.

Tonight was different. He woke from sleep agitated by a late vigil on the email and the phone, and interrupted by invasive questions. The photograph, the shot from ground level. It reappeared in cinematic detail, even as he padded into the kitchen and he realised what was bothering him. The image was composed, not snapped: as much the sum of shadows and light as it was of the elements. Someone had thought to offset the rows of wrapped bodies, to place the lagoon in the centre of the frame and the dappled foliage of a tropical beach in the foreground. Its brutal harmonies reminded him of a news photo from ages ago, one of the few times that journalism had ever moved him. A dead boy on a beach, the tragedy of the small sneakers a parent had laced carefully before hell opened.

Cassius didn't do doubt: accordingly, he wasn't practised at it. Someone *wanted* to affect him this way, him and everyone else who saw the image. It was persuasion, not mere reportage.

His head was starting up again. He flipped the kettle on, checked email on the phone with his free hand. Scrolled and scrolled and scrolled: the darting of his eyeballs adding to the pain. Nothing from Monica. She cleared emails obsessively; there was no way she hadn't seen his. What was she playing at?

He wandered into the bathroom to take a piss and nearly stepped on the chicken. Rory had filled the shower recess with more torn newspapers, and overnight a slow drip from the fitting had turned the papers into a sodden mess. The chicken looked as disgusted as he was: once it recovered from the fright of the descending foot it stared at him coldly.

'Fuck you,' he slurred. 'Take it up with Rory.' Then he saw it had left him an egg, so he scooped it carefully from the newspaper shreds and carried it into the kitchen. Rory wandered in, wearing the Green Edge road racing pyjamas that Cassius had bought him for his birthday. It didn't occur to him—although it would later—that Rory had packed them himself, for this visit.

'Rorkers.'

'Dad.'

'Macca left an egg. You want me to fry it?'

'Cool.'

'Sleep all right?'

'Hmm. Yep.' Rory yawned and then exploded into a wet sneeze that made Cassius cringe. He took a paper towel and wiped the bench where most of the fallout had landed, then cracked the egg into a pan. Rory was pawing through the food cupboard looking for cereal.

'Sea Eagles are playing Friday night mate, up here.'

The kid woke up, lit up, spontaneously. 'We should go!' Then his face fell. 'Ah but Mum...'

'Don't worry. I'm working on that. And I'm getting us some tickets.'

The boy clenched his whole body with unrestrained pleasure, fists squeezed into small blocks and elbows tucked into his sides. *'Yess!'*

'We'll get a pie, hot chips. You bring your scarf with you?'

Another wave of disappointment. 'No I...I didn't know we'd be going.'

'Fear not, my boy. I'll cover it. Go and get dressed.'

He dialled the Comcar.

• • •

They walked into the sports store at the Canberra Centre as it opened for the day: Cassius in his suit, black business shoes squeaking over the polished lino, the boy springing excitedly ahead in sneakers.

The phone kept ringing and Cassius kept dropping a few paces behind his son to answer. It was mostly Stella, mostly deflecting awkward press. One from Waldron, drier than a desert burial, telling him he needn't bother answering the emails from the ABC. Halfway through the last week of the campaign it had boiled down to a presidential contest between the two leaders. All that was expected of Cassius was that he stay out of the way and prevent anything going arse-up. That meant the bulk of the media knew to leave him alone now. A few of them had follow-up questions after the PM's performance about the photos, but he was able to dead-bat them. *The prime minister has explained all that. We won't be adding to the speculation.* And occasionally, for variety, *I'm not going to respond to hypotheticals.*

He lost the boy, felt a stab of wild panic and found him again at the colourful racks of NRL merch, darting round the aisles looking for a scarf. Cassius tried not to betray the fear that had shaken him.

'Hold on a minute matey. Don't you need a jersey?'

Rory's eyes widened. 'Well, yeah but...'

'Come on. Pick one out. What size are you, a ten?'

'Maybe an eight. Mum says I'm small for my age.'

'No you're not, fella. You're fine. Try the ten.'

Rory wrestled himself into it. It fell to his mid-thighs, cuffs flapping beyond his fingertips.

'Okay, maybe the eight.'

Rory stood mesmerised in the jersey. He plucked at the price tag. 'Dad, they're pretty expensive...'

'It's fine, Rorkers.'

'It's got the *badge* dad. It's like, official merchandise.'

'Yeah, that's the real thing—exactly what the players wear, just shrunk down a little. Now it's gonna be cold—what about one of those beanies?'

'Serious?'

He smiled indulgently. 'Go on. And you better get two scarves— one for you and one for me.'

A sales assistant wandered up and smiled as Rory studied himself in a mirror.

'You guys going to the game?' She was looking at Cassius like she knew his face but couldn't place him. Old enough to vote, he estimated, but the kids these days couldn't care less. She probably wasn't even enrolled.

'We sure are.'

She raised her voice a little so Rory would hear. 'Go Raiders!'

He booed back at her, a little self-consciously, then laughed. His teeth stuck out everywhere. Cassius felt the fierce jolt of his love for the boy, there under the shop lighting.

He checked his phone again. Nothing from Monica.

• • •

Stella had arranged a pile of papers on his desk, neatly stapled bundles of twenty-two pages. Each was headed *Border Integrity (Unauthorised Disclosures) Regulations: Ministerial Order.*

'Stella!' he yelled at the doorway. As usual, the mimicry started instantaneously, from several corners of the office. *Stella! STE-llaa!* He had no idea why it was funny.

'What?'

'What am I doing with these? There's...' he started counting. 'There's dozens of them.'

'They're the orders you make that stop people saying stuff in the media about boat people. You called 'em gag orders.'

'Who are these people?' He turned to the second pages of the first few documents, studying the unfamiliar names. 'So we're really doing this now. I thought it was a bluff.'

'They're mostly journos, some whistleblowers inside departments. There's one from Core Resolve, couple of random nuffies. They came from the department and they've been through the PMO. The department had the AGS check each one individually. So they're all advised and clear. They just need your signature. Follow the tags.'

She had indeed placed plastic tags next to each signature line. He followed them through and with a few swoops of his pen (*With Gratitude from the Australian Olympic Committee*) he had silenced the baying mob.

Pulau Dana

The voices woke Isi shortly before dawn. Foreign words, slow and quiet.

She'd slept in a board bag, the plastic lining sticky against her legs. The tents were taken up by Finley's makeshift hospital and the women and children among the survivors. The rest of them—mostly men—were still sleeping under a long blue tarpaulin, propped up in places by sticks speared into the sand. There were so many lengths of high-density foam on the *Java Ridge*, for lying on, for padding fragile gear, that it was easy enough to improvise some sort of bed for each person. Another tarp had been laid over the bodies further along the beach, pinned down with chunks of coral. The dead beneath it were reduced to formless mounds.

She turned over onto her belly and watched quietly for a moment. A tiny blue curl of smoke drifted from the campfire, and past it, through the trees, she could see the first glow of green in the eastern sky. When she'd woken during the night, she could see the reflected light of the storms wandering like malevolent drunks to the north. Another good reason, she thought, to run south.

The lagoon was still, the *Java Ridge* quiet at anchor.

She could hear the crunching of adult steps through the scrub, a pause, then the hiss and crackle of someone pissing. The steps returned, approaching from behind her, and Finley appeared in the gloom. He stepped past and went to the washing drum, splashing his face and making an elaborate effort at washing his hands. *He's probably been up all night*, she thought.

Shaking the water from his hands, he noticed she was awake and came to squat beside her.

'How was your night?' she whispered.

He sighed, ran a hand over his stubbled scalp, setting off a spray of fine droplets.

'I don't like where it's going,' he said. 'That ankle of Tim's is a mess. Circulation's going to be compromised if we don't get on top of it. So normally, as I said, you'd open it right up, get a good look at it, maybe fix the bones with pins and wires. Clean it up, staple it and plaster the limb. Injuries like that, they never quite come good but you can get a reasonable result.

'But *here*, see, things are different. Nothing's sterile. Your surgical tub isn't bad, but I don't have the gear I need. I don't even know what ketamine's like as an anaesthetic. Never used it that way. What if I'm in the middle of it and it starts to wear off? Do I have to ask Luke to hold the poor bastard down?'

It was all rhetorical, she realised. He was rehearsing his own capabilities out loud. He wasn't expecting her to respond.

'So the second line of defence is, I need to make sure it doesn't get gangrenous. And I'm watching the pulse in that foot last night, and at some stage it just bloody disappeared. Toes are white, dorsum's mottled...I really just...' He hesitated. 'I really don't know what to do.'

He looked at her with a stricken honesty she'd not yet seen in him.

'Can you imagine doing an amputation on a moving target with bush tools? I didn't sign up for this.'

She felt ridiculous engaging in this discussion while lying in a surfboard bag. His hand had returned to rubbing his head.

'To try to fix it, I'd have to knock him out, obviously. For that, I need a second person to do the airway while I work, and I guess that can be Luke, but I have to do the sums on the ketamine so I make him unconscious but not—well—dead.'

'Jesus.'

'And there's more to it than that. The boy with the head injury—I mean, no X-rays, right? He could have a skull fracture under there for all I know. Or a bleed. He vomited last night. He's lucid...slept okay without slipping right under, but shit, he gives me a bad...feeling.'

The blur in his speech made her look up at him. He was swaying, and his eyelids were coming down. The horizon was turning orange now.

'Neil?'

He awoke with a start. 'Mm.'

'What are you going to do?'

He turned his palms upwards in sorrow.

She thought hard. 'There must be a rule for situations like that.'

'Juss, jussa rule of logic: save the person most likely to survive.'

She didn't want to know the answer but she had to ask the question. 'And who's that?'

'Don't know. Either of 'em could live, either of 'em could die.' He absently brushed the large grains of sand from the top of a foot. 'Can you get me something?'

'Sure.'

'I need a green coconut. Not a ripe one.'

•••

Over the next few hours, as the sun appeared and the palms cast their long shadows over the camp, Isi returned as much of the gear as possible to the *Java Ridge* and started to prepare her for sea.

A group of the survivors had taken every implement Isi could muster—pots, pans, buckets, even ladles—and were digging a mass grave in the clearing where the camp had been. The going was difficult for them—there were tangled skeins of roots running in every direction through the sand—but they were gradually making a wide hollow in the ground. Isi had allowed them to take the rest of the drinking-water drum to perform *ghusl*. A separate group were now washing the bodies, the women braiding the dead women's hair.

Isi sat on the gunwale of the *Java Ridge*, transfixed. The tenderness of the washing. The attentive hands closing eyes and jaws, placing hands prayerfully across chests. She had given them every sheet she could find on board and they had taken these, along with the towels and tarpaulins, and were using them to wrap the bodies. Right side first, then left side. Lastly the oldest of the men walked along the row of wrapped bodies, binding the shrouds with short lengths of rope; once around the head, twice around the body, once over the feet. Ritual guided their every movement: it effected economy and grace. Their world had gone mad, but these people still had their pieties.

Once the bodies were all wrapped, the groups came together in a huddle to discuss something. Two of the men walked away to approach Luke, who was squashed into the hospital tent beside Tim. He climbed out of the tent and waded halfway out to the *Java Ridge*.

'Mecca?'

She darted into the wheelhouse and punched it into the GPS. Back on deck, she pointed in a line towards where the wreck had been, in the centre of the reef. The direction was acknowledged by a faint wave from the morticians, and they began lifting the shrouded bodies into the grave, placing them on their right sides. Sometimes the body would not yield to easy placement: they would consult and shuffle it as best they could, the hard light reflecting off their sweating foreheads. Each time they laid a body in position they would recite a phrase, somewhere between speech and song, which would drift over the water to Isi: *Bismillah wa 'ala millati rasulillah.*

When the bodies were all in the grave, they dispersed into the scrub and came back with palm fronds, which they laid carefully over the top until no trace of the towels and sheets could be seen. The old man who'd tied the shrouds walked around the perimeter of the grave, shifting a frond here and there until he was satisfied.

The women withdrew and sat in the shade with their backs to the grave. The men each took handfuls of sand and tossed them over the palm fronds, chanting once again. Then they began the long labour of filling it back in, scooping sand back from the piles they'd made with the pots and pans. The women rose from where they'd rested and began to wander the beach, dipping an arm into the shallows once in a while. At first Isi couldn't work out what they were doing, but soon she could see they were collecting rocks. They would confer in little clusters; reject one, keep another.

These people don't even know each other, she thought. *The living don't know the dead, the men don't know the women, the women don't know each other.*

Finley was whistling at her.

He'd emerged from the tent, waving her over. She stood and dived from the deck, and as her body cut clean through the water she wished she could remain below and never have to surface.

But the world returned as she stepped onto the beach and hurried to the tent. Under the survivors' tarpaulin she could see Shafiqa sleeping alongside some of the older women. Finley had gathered the others: his son, Fraggle, Carl and Leah. Isi could see the bitter resentment all over Carl's face: somehow, even in the face of this extremity, he was seething with wounded entitlement. Behind them, in the darker interior of the tent, she could hear Tim faintly groaning. There was no sound from Hamid.

Finley was about to speak when the Iraqi man appeared. He had Roya at his side, and he pushed her roughly forward, barking a command. Between her fingers she clutched a small, thick dictionary, its pages swollen and curled by having been wet then dried. She looked scared.

'This man name Ali Hassan. He is c-captain that boat.'

She pressed her little mouth into a formal smile and continued haltingly. 'Ali Hassan…is want to know what is this island please?'

Isi directed her reply to Ali Hassan, looked calmly into his glittering eyes. 'Dana.'

He leaned over Roya's shoulder and spoke to her rapidly again.

'He ask where we going.'

'Tell him we go to Ashmore Reef.' She hesitated. 'He would call it Pulau Pasir. Australia.' She was puzzled by her own words. There had been excisions: it was Australia for her and the other Australians on board, but not for the people they'd rescued. Would the nature of the coral atoll change depending on who stood on it?

Roya started to translate, but he had heard the word and was already shouting. Forgetting himself, he pointed at the northern horizon and jabbed his arms at the sky before he remembered language and shouted at Roya in Arabic. She cowered from him and took a moment to find something in her dictionary.

'He say Australia navy'—that was the word she'd been looking for—'say no. Push us back. He say go to Indonesia now.'

Isi was confused. 'But his boat was going to Australia, wasn't it?'

Roya did not translate this to Ali Hassan. She was thinking hard, her dark pupils unfocussed.

'Now can-not go to Australia. He in tr-trouble now.' Those dark eyes darted towards the gravesite. The message was clear.

Ali Hassan grabbed her roughly and shook her, talking fast. He knew she'd added something. His voice rose sharply and without warning he slapped her hard across the face. Someone yelled in shock. Carl jumped up. Tears came to Roya's eyes but she said nothing. Ali Hassan muttered a furious curse and stormed off. Leah began to shout something at his departing back but stopped herself. A stunned silence enveloped them: Ali Hassan's sudden aggression had shaken them in a way that the slow hours of suffering and death had not.

A calm voice placed itself deliberately in the silence.

'Can you all listen please.' It was Finley. Any hint of the doubt that Isi had heard from him before dawn was gone. 'I'm going to do a further procedure on Tim's foot. I believe there's some kind of vascular compromise in there and it'll get worse if I don't go in and try to fix it. I'm going to put him under this time. I've spoken to him about it and he consents. Tim, can you confirm that please?'

Tim's voice came from inside the tent, a hiss of agony. *'Yes.'*

'I'm not seeking your consent,' he said, addressing the rest of them. 'I'm telling you that that's what I'm doing. We're too far from medical help to leave it without surgical intervention.'

A small voice rose. 'Please. What happen to Hamid?'

They'd forgotten about Roya, who had sat down on the spot when Ali Hassan hit her.

'Hamid. Oh, the boy, the head injury. He's all right at present but I have to keep watching him.' It was clear from Finley's voice that he was unsure whether he was addressing Roya or the whole group. 'Anyway, Tim's foot, it's messy surgery and it requires more equipment than I have here. There's flies and bacteria and he stands the best chance if we get moving quickly after I've done it. Okay?'

Carl spoke first. 'What do you want us to say?'

'I don't want you to say anything. This is all pretty irregular, as you can imagine; I need to ensure it's witnessed.' He turned his back on them and returned to the tent.

...

Roya watched the tent from a distance, studied the shapes made by the sunlight passing through it, the shadows of the people moving around inside.

When the doctor came out to wash something, she stood and crept into the tent, picked her way past Tim and sat down next to Hamid. He was breathing fast, his glasses long gone and his eyes brightly attuned to some dreamscape she couldn't picture. She took his hand, laying her plump brown knuckles over his upturned fingers. He cried softly and she wanted to cry with him. She wanted to hear his tall stories again, to know that the spark in him wasn't extinguished. Seeing him there, it seemed more likely he was just some ordinary boy with a home and a family and a school, but that didn't help her. She couldn't bear the thought of them grieving for him, nor him grieving for them. No one had come to claim him when the people brought him in from the water. Maybe the 'uncle', whoever he was, had died in the storm.

There was a sickly sweet smell in the tent. She'd smelled death before, but death was outside, buried under the sand. This was something else, death that stalked the living.

She had to be strong like her mother would be. Did he watch football? All the boys she knew liked to watch football. They'd crowd the café windows to see the screen, scuttle away from the raised hands of the men as they tried to concentrate. Maybe he had a bike. He was old enough to have a bike.

She reached out her fingers towards the long angry bruise that had grown above his ear. She dared not touch it, but she wished she could erase it with her fingers, like it was drawn in pencil.

The doctor came back, bent low to enter and resumed his work. Either he hadn't seen her or her presence didn't register. She watched him making his preparations as she held onto Hamid's hand.

He'd put the other man's injured foot up on a plastic tub, flipped over to create a stable base. Above the Australian man's head he'd put a coconut in a string bag and hung it from the roof of the tent. Now he stuck a clear plastic tube into it, and the tube snaked its way down to a medical-looking plastic bag. From there, her eyes followed another tube that led down to a needle, which the doctor slid into the back of the Australian man's hand, fixing it there with some tape. He was talking low and steady, reassuring the man, calling him Tim.

She couldn't imagine what the coconut did. She'd thought Australian doctors might have better ways of doing things than getting coconuts involved. Her left foot was going to sleep under her bottom. She moved it carefully so as not to disturb Hamid.

The doctor took a roll of cling wrap and tore off five or six long sheets, laying them delicately on the floor of the tent bedside him, next to Tim's hip. He lined up all sorts of objects on the cling wrap: some of them, like scissors and scalpels, Roya recognised. Some of them were unfamiliar to her, and looked terrifying. A strange steel instrument like a pair of fine scissors, with the curved beak of a bird. Whatever the implement was, she knew it belonged to a secret world and that terrible pain was its companion.

The doctor had another man helping him: a younger man who came in after him, who Roya thought might be his son because he spoke to him with a tone that fathers use, telling him to hold this and pass him that. Then the doctor spoke to Tim, counted to three and rolled him onto his side. He took a pair of scissors and cut a line up the leg of Tim's shorts so that his bottom appeared. Quickly he produced a small syringe and stuck the needle into the big muscle. The man didn't flinch at all. *He must be in a lot of pain if that didn't hurt,* thought Roya.

'Tetanus booster,' said the doctor to Tim. 'We're nearly ready to go now.'

She found herself squeezing Hamid's hand as she worried for Tim.

'Did you get his weight?' he asked his son.

'Eighty,' he replied.

'Is that right Tim, eighty?'

'Yep,' came the answer, clipped. Roya could hear the pain in it.

The doctor had a pen and he jotted down some numbers on the back of his other hand. Next, he found a larger syringe in the big plastic tub, and a little glass jar. He was reading the label on the tiny jar when Isi came into the tent. Her eyes immediately darted to Roya.

'Neil, there's people outside who want to see you.'

'What do they want?' He was fighting to keep his concentration.

'They've got a boy who's been stung by something. Wasp, probably.'

'Look, tell them to fuck off, will you? For Christ's sake...'

'Just passing it on.'

He sighed, rubbed his eyes. 'Where on the boat did you keep the surgical box?' he asked her abruptly.

'In a cupboard in my cabin,' said Isi, puzzled.

'Locked?'

'Yeah.'

'Who has the key?'

'Just me and Joel. Why?'

'Because your ten mils of ketamine is down to six mils.' He held the little jar up to her eyes. 'Good times, huh?'

She sighed. 'Can I do anything?'

'Not unless you've got some more IV fluids hiding somewhere. I used your supply on the two old blokes with dysentery, and the coconut routine's not exactly gold standard.' He paused. 'Actually, you can do something. Find me some music. An MP3 player or whatever, and some headphones.'

While she was gone, Roya watched him unwrap the syringe and spike its needle into the top of the miniature jar. Clear fluid filled the syringe as he drew back the plunger. Twice he held it up and studied the fine black lines marked across it, until he was happy that he had the right amount. By then, the little jar was empty. He laid the syringe on the cling film and busied himself checking the coconut and its plastic tube.

'Is the water boiled?' he said to his son. The son peeled back a flap of the tent and looked out.

'I think so.'

'Don't think. Go and check. Bring it in here if it's boiled.'

He was moving faster now. He was talking faster. The minutes were rushing inwards. Roya squeezed Hamid's hand again. She knew it was good that they were helping the man with the terrible leg, but she wished they would help Hamid. He was not all right. The sweating had made his hair limp and heavy. It fell back from his forehead, framing his face. He lifted one hand to his head and ran the fingers lightly over the swelling, his eyes searching for hers, fixing, detaching.

Isi returned with the headphones. They were the ones she'd seen on Carl, before when he was angry. She also had a small shiny object that Roya guessed was the MP3 player. The doctor didn't look up.

'Why the music?' she asked.

'Ketamine causes nasty hallucinations. There's a theory that familiar music helps moderate the effect. Put the headphones on him and find him something he likes that's going to last about forty minutes.'

Isi darted around to Tim's head and carefully placed the cups over his ears. She scrolled through the player, reading names to him until he picked one he liked. Roya heard the music leaking faintly from the headphones. The doctor was rubbing his gloved hand over the surface of the shattered foot, frowning as he did so.

'Have a look at this,' the surgeon said quietly to Isi. She joined him, hovering over the foot. He ran his hand over the flesh again, and Roya could hear it was making a strange crackling sound, a sound she'd never heard human skin make.

'What's that?' asked Isi.

'Clostridium. Gas gangrene. You could go your whole life in city practice and not see it. Breakdown of tissues under the skin releases gases. Can you smell it?'

Roya could smell it. That was the sick-making smell.

'Why are you showing me this?' asked Isi.

'I want you to understand'—he shot a look at Tim, who had the headphones over his ears and was staring straight upwards—'how serious this is.' Finley was sweating. Roya watched him quietly and saw the fear in his eyes, the struggle to contain it.

Now the son came back with the pot of boiling water. Roya didn't dare move, sitting behind the doctor's back, unnoticed. She watched as he tore open some little paper squares and took out what looked to Roya like tiny tissues. He rubbed these all over the foot and up the leg. He pulled disposable gloves onto his hands. She knew these from the clinic at home. He pressed a button on his watch and it beeped. Then he took up the syringe and slid the needle into the crook of Tim's elbow, taped it in position and slowly pressed the plunger.

'Grab that tequila and pour it over my hands,' he said to his son. The golden fluid splashed from the gloves to the floor of the tent. Roya felt even sicker as the chemical smell wafted over her.

'Now go round to his head and hold his jaw forward. It'll go slack in a sec, and I want you to support it. Use a pistol grip and you'll find his pulse under your fingers. Tell me if the pulse changes. You understand?'

The son said something Roya didn't catch. The mingling smells of the alcohol and the sick leg were making her dizzy.

Hamid was still breathing softly beside them, his eyes fixed on the far wall of the tent. Roya was always in trouble for being unable to sit still. Now she would sit still. Now she would stay and wait for as long as it took.

Canberra

Cassius exploded like some sort of missile, out of his office and along a known trajectory towards his chief of staff's. People scuttled out of the way as he went.

'Kevin you fuc—'

He was most of the way into the office before he realised Kevin Waldron was on the phone. Waldron held up a hand, sober as a Methodist, to silence his boss while he finished the conversation: a succession of abrupt yes and no replies. In the handful of months they'd been paired to each other, this empty man had deployed an arsenal of physical gestures to keep Cassius at bay, and it infuriated him.

Unhurried, Waldron replaced the receiver when he was done. Touched a finger to the bridge of his glasses. 'Minister.'

'Kevin, who the hell runs this office? Me or you?'

Waldron looked momentarily nonplussed, then recovered. 'It's a technical distinction, but I do. You run the ministry and I run the office that runs the ministry.' He smiled faintly. 'Why?'

'Because someone's changed all the social media passwords.'

'Yes, that's right. I did.'

Cassius raised his hands impotently. 'Why?'

'We want everyone on message. I can have all the comms

co-ordinated for you so you don't need to worry about "is this today's talking points?" and so on.'

'Who's "we" Kevin?'

'The PMO, delegating to me. Relax, Cassius, it's only until Saturday, then the pressure's off.'

Cassius turned to leave, turned back and tried to stare through the light reflected on Waldron's glasses. 'I'm not going to have my independence compromised…'

'You're as independent as you've ever been.'

Cassius searched the face, its vestiges of an extinct smile. How the hell would he know if this man was mocking him? He pointed a finger between those steady eyes. 'Don't fuck with me Kevin. I'm not in the mood.'

There was no response. As if on cue, Waldron's phone rang again and he picked it up, still locked on Cassius's stare. Cassius had begun to wonder if he had a button under the desk that did that.

...

He reappeared an hour later, hovering spectrally in Cassius's doorway. Head down at his desk, Cassius didn't notice him at first, so Waldron cleared his throat.

And there he was, arms folded, the wings of his suit jacket flaring wide of his hips. 'The PM wants you to give me your mobile.'

'No.'

Waldron sighed. 'He's not picking on you exclusively, Minister. It's standard practice now across the Cabinet. We hold your phone for you, take your messages and filter your crap so you can concentrate on…governing.'

'Tell him I can multi-task.'

Another sigh, and Waldron gave up. Too easily: Cassius could tell he had a backup plan, and as he turned to leave Cassius called him into the room again.

'Hey, why can't we check with passports to work out what's happening with that boat?'

'Boat?' Waldron's face creased. 'Oh. Why passports? It's an Indonesian boat.'

'We're *assuming* it's an Indonesian boat, because it's in Indonesian waters. It could be anyone. Could be Australians.'

'It came from the north. It's an Indonesian design. It appears to have asylum seekers on it, or maybe fishermen. No one's coming to us to say their family members are missing. So on what basis would we be going through passports?'

'Kevin, do you spend much time around boats? That thing had a Zodiac on it. An expensive, motorised rubber boat. And it had tents. And we're expected to believe that it flipped over *inside* the lagoon, after it was anchored in there. How could that happen? It doesn't add up.'

Waldron took a chair at the desk, slumped into it and let his exasperation show. 'So, what, we just start looking for missing Australians in Indonesia? Do you have any idea how many of our kids are incarcerated, overstaying—Christ, hospitalised—in Indonesia at any given time? We're talking *thousands*. We can't even keep track of pissed teenagers in Kuta.'

'Yeah, but we're not doing anything. We're papering over it. It might save the election but if something comes out afterwards we're fucked.'

'You want to talk politically? Politically, we have to let it die off. Every single word you add to the pile—and it's a relatively small pile at this stage—every word gives life to the idea that there's something to worry about. The PM made the right move by slapping it down. You can't just stand up in the public square and start *wondering*.'

He was earnest now. Cassius felt satisfied that he'd finally found a way under his guard. Waldron hitched the chair forward and put both hands on the desk.

'This election is going to be fearfully close. You, the PM, all of us are within a bee's dick of losing our jobs. We need to keep it very tight: the economy, jobs, future tech. Hell, we can even talk climate if it keeps us away from anyone suggesting a boat got through. The one thing that is going to save us is discipline: staying on message with the electorate. Boring, Minister. But it works.'

• • •

After Waldron had drifted back to his office, Stella appeared in the doorway.

'What's the go with mobile phones?'

'Nothing, Stell. Kevin said the chiefs have to take the phones off all the ministers and I told him to fuck off.'

'Yeah, well he's just told me to divert yours to his number, so...'

Pulau Dana

Isi had been helping with the loading onto the *Java Ridge*. Sanusi and Radja were hauling crates of gear off the sand, Sanusi's bad hand wrapped in a new plastic bag, a ciggie hanging from one corner of his mouth. Whenever either of them finished one, the other would offer the deck, and they'd light a new one. *They'd smoke their way through the apocalypse*, Isi was thinking as Finley shouted her name from the medical tent.

The moment she swept the doorway open, she knew the situation had deteriorated. Finley had laid open the foot and it hung like a wilted flower, the vivid interior splayed and dripping.

He was stirring a scalpel through the pot of hot water, and he looked up as Isi entered. Luke Finley was at Tim's head, both his hands occupied under Tim's jaw.

'*Get that fucking kid out of here.*'

Isi hesitated; Roya clearly didn't want to leave her friend's side. She bent down and picked the girl up in her strong arms. As she did so, her face came near to Hamid's, and she saw he'd vomited. His pleading eyes roved over her face, searching for reassurance. She knew Finley had more pressing matters on his mind.

'Neil, Hamid's been sick.'

He shot her a look. 'Is he hot?'

She let go of Roya, laid a hand over Hamid's forehead. 'No.'

'Then just leave him, will you. Get rid of the kid.'

As she carried Roya backwards out of the tent, Isi saw Finley holding Tim's knee in one hand, drawing a dotted line around his calf with a pen held in the other.

'Come back when you're done,' Finley called to Isi. 'And you,' he was speaking to his son now, 'check that legrope and make sure it's tight.'

Luke tugged at the red plastic cord that was wrapped tightly around Tim's leg, below his knee.

Roya protested mildly as Isi carried her to her mother. She was worried for Hamid, and the atmosphere in the tent seemed to have unsettled her. Isi silently cursed herself for letting her remain in there as long as she had. But there was a secret kind of pleasure for both of them in carrying, and being carried. Isi's feet dug slightly deeper into the sand with the extra burden; she felt Roya tap her lightly on the shoulder, and she turned her head to find the girl pointing at the sky, where a single vapour trail sharpened into a moving point: a shining, faraway aircraft.

'Australians, coming home from Bali,' Isi said to her. Roya appeared not to understand, and merely nestled her head back into Isi's shoulder.

When they reached the shelter, Isi waited patiently while Roya arranged herself under the crook of her mother's arm, one of her hands placed delicately on the distended belly. It was hot but a breeze was moving under the tarp, affording a little respite. Isi watched the girl settle. Moments later, Roya had closed her eyes and was sleeping alongside her mother.

• • •

Isi did the rounds of all the communications again. It felt like the outside world had to intervene somehow, that all this was too much for them alone. She tried the HF, the VHF: blanketed in static. She tried as many different mobile phones as she could find, hoping for differences in signal strength. Fraggle had been back up the hill, trying to find the window of reception they'd used the previous day, but had come back disappointed. She resigned herself to the idea that until they physically moved they were alone.

She didn't know what she'd expected to find when she re-entered the tent. Exhaustion was starting to dull her wits. Her eyes took a second to adjust from the tropical light to the interior gloom.

Finley, crouched low over Tim's leg. A leg without a foot.

The exposed bone was pointed straight at her, yellowy-white.

Luke had pulled back, compressed against the side of the tent, a hand to his head, his teeth clenched. Finley was working fast with a needle and thread, somewhere in an indistinct territory between bone and skin.

Her panicked eyes roved over the scene. The foot lay separately on the cling wrap among a scatter of bloodied tools. She recognised a large serrated fish knife from the boat.

Tim was moving, twitching and uttering strange sounds.

'God, what's happening to him?'

'Dystonic muscle activity,' replied Finley without looking up. 'It's just the ketamine. He's not feeling it...'

The hands reached out at the air, pawing at nothing.

'The foot...'

'Had to go. Five or six minutes before he starts to come round. Make yourself useful. Check the boy.'

Isi knelt over Hamid. His chest rose and fell slightly, but otherwise he was completely still, eyes open, staring straight back at her. She jumped in fright. The grazed area over his temple had now swollen into a large dome that spread forward to his eye.

'He's breathing but he doesn't look right.'

Finley continued working. Isi watched him pulling a flap of skin over the end of the bone, racing the needle through the flesh in extravagant loops.

'Take a pen or something and press one of his fingernails. Hard.'

She did as he asked. The pressure of the pen raised a livid red spot in the white bed of Hamid's nail, but he didn't move. She stared at his knuckles for a moment.

'What happened?' Finley was working frantically on Tim but half-looking at her.

'Nothing. I think you need to look at him,' Isi said quietly.

'I need to do *this*,' Finley hissed. 'If I don't make a decent stump here, he'll never walk on a prosthesis. Think perhaps *you* could do it?' He returned to the thread work, his fingers darting about in search of information among the sinews. But his eyes kept wandering to Hamid, and presently his frustration overcame him.

'What did you mean, he doesn't look right?'

'I—I don't know,' Isi stammered, 'but he's making a groaning sound.'

Finley kept sewing, watching Tim's movements, studying the limb. 'Eyes open or closed?'

'Open.'

'Are his pupils the same size?' He flicked a small torch at her, and she shone it into each of Hamid's eyes.

'No. The one on the injury side is big, and the other one's small.'

Finley was applying pressure to something as she spoke, and without warning his hand slipped forward.

'Fuck!' He looked around in frustration, saw his son. 'Luke, take the f—*Luke!* What's wrong with you? Take the foot outside and bury it. I do *not* want him to see it when he comes round. You,' he gestured at Isi, 'get the tequila bottle and splash my hands again.'

She poured the spirit over his hands as he watched Luke's departing back. 'Fucking hopeless,' he muttered.

He looked at Hamid, holding his hands back, then took hold of the boy's head, peering intently into his unseeing eyes. 'Shit.'

His fingers searched through the wet hair, pressing occasionally. He looked back at Tim, at his unfinished work. Checked Hamid's pulse, his eyes again.

'*Shit*. Why did this have to happen right now?'

He exhaled loudly, pressed his hands to his temples. They left a slick of alcohol on his skin. 'Your Indo boys. Is one of them an engineer?'

'Yes,' said Isi. 'Sanusi.'

'He's got tools, right?'

'Yep.'

'Tell him I need a cordless drill and a hole thingy...um...' he searched for the word, his face racked by the effort to cut through the static. 'Spade bit. About twenty mil. And a water bottle, drink bottle. Quickly.'

'What's going on, Neil?' she pleaded.

'Intracranial bleeding, an extradural.'

Finley had already returned to Tim's leg before Isi left the tent, working feverishly and looking back at Hamid as he did so. She could hear him berating his son as she left, telling him to pull himself together.

Sanusi was on the beach. He understood the order for the drill, and if he was puzzled it didn't show. She came with him in the Zodiac out to the *Java Ridge* so she could search for a water bottle, wondering all the while how Joel would have responded in this situation. He was good in a crisis: a present-tense, resolvable crisis. It was the life issues he ran from. This fucking mess, she reflected, was a little of each.

She had the drill and the water bottle back to Finley before she had given any thought to what he was going to do with them. When she returned, Luke had the water boiling in the pot outside again, and on hearing her footfalls, Finley yelled out to her to put the drill bit in the pot. She watched it tumble in the bubbling water, still not understanding. When she entered the tent, she found to her relief that the severed foot was gone. But Finley looked ragged: bright red in the face and sweating freely. He'd closed the amputation wound and was dressing it.

'Well done,' she ventured.

He focussed on her as though he hadn't seen her come in. 'Well done, you reckon? Well *done*? You fucking idiot—I've got nerves and vessels and shit all over the place in there that I can't even find, and he's going to wake up this way, and you come up with *well done*?'

He snatched the drill from her and gave it a rev to ensure it worked. Hamid hadn't moved throughout, and he didn't move now as Finley took a disposable razor and shaved the side of his head. Despite his manic state, his strokes were sure-handed and efficient. Before long he had a clear patch shaved away without a nick. He worked over the bald area with the alcohol wipes and sat back for a moment.

Behind him, Tim continued to stir. The sound of his breathing was more pronounced now, and his movements looked more like the process of awakening than the involuntary spasms brought on by the drug.

'Roll him into a recovery position, facing me. You do know what that is, right?' She ignored the barb and rolled Tim over onto his side, bracing his back with a pile of rolled-up towels. The stump of his leg remained elevated on the plastic tub.

'And scoop some boiling water from the pot into the water bottle. Slosh it out thoroughly and then fill it again. Don't touch anything.'

She did as she was told. When she returned, Finley had laid out his tools on new sheets of cling wrap beside Hamid's head. He waited for her to put the water bottle down, then took up a scalpel and cut a half-moon into Hamid's scalp, right over the abrasion. The blood flowed fast over his hands and down the side of Hamid's head, into the corner of his jaw and around the back of his ear. It dripped on the mat under his head and grew into a pool. Finley took up a pair of silver forceps and pulled downwards on the flap of skin he'd created.

'Here,' he said. 'Put some gloves on and hold this.'

Once she had the forceps in her hand and the flap of skin was pulled clear, Finley squirted liberally from the water bottle, clearing the blood away for long enough for Isi to see the skull revealed beneath. Tim's movement behind her was urgent and frightening. She wondered how Finley could focus on what he was doing.

'Luke!' he yelled. His son reappeared from wherever he'd been. 'Get the spade bit out of the water and bring it to me. Don't touch it with your hands under any circumstances.'

Isi was starting to understand now.

But faster than she could process it all, Finley had fixed the bit into the drill, had gunned the trigger. He was up on his knees now, with one hand pressing down on the poor boy's head and the other holding the spinning drill.

Luke crawled back to his place against the wall of the tent, again sat with his head in his hands. Without warning—without energy—he vomited all over the front of himself. Tried to wipe the mess off his chest with disgusted fingers.

Neil Finley appeared not to notice him. He was thinking. He was thinking hard and sweating and muttering to himself. 'Fuck. *Fuck.* He's nearly gone.'

Why hasn't he drugged him? Isi wanted to ask. But she knew the answer. There was no ketamine left. Hamid had descended far from consciousness anyway.

The drill was screaming at full revs. Finley had the trigger clamped under the finger of his gloved and bloody fist.

And now Tim was bellowing behind them because he'd woken up and he was still off his face but he'd found the stump and Luke was weeping with his head in his hands and Finley wasn't even looking up as he pressed the spade bit into Hamid's skull and the blood sprayed around them in a perfect circular arc and Isi cursed Joel and all his profligacy and tried to summon the comfort of Roya's night-dark eyes, and wished to God she'd never left home.

Pulau Dana

When Roya woke up she found night was falling. The Indonesian men from the *Java Ridge* fed her some rice and fish they'd kept aside, along with greens from the pots on the boat. She ate hungrily with her hands, squeezing her eyes shut so she could think about the flavours. When she mixed the greens through the rice with her fingers it reminded her of the *sabzi challow* her mother made at home. It was the best thing she had eaten in a long time.

The survivors had placed themselves around a separate fire in murmuring huddles of three and four: men talking to men the same way they would sit outside their houses in Kabul, trading libels while the prayer beads slid between their fingers; women withdrawn among themselves too. The Afghans were with the Afghans, though the Hazaras stayed among their kind. The Tajiks sat together and, at a remove from them, the Iranians and Iraqis kept their counsel at opposite ends of the huddles.

Slowly they drifted off to sleep, but Roya found she wasn't tired: the long doze through the afternoon had left her restless and fully awake. She sat for a while with Hamid, who had now been moved out to the camp under the tarp, where the Afghan women had made him a bed of towels and clumped leaves. He was responsive, his head heavily bandaged, but confused and in pain. Soon enough he fell asleep, and

Roya found herself alone. She went back to her mother, but Shafiqa was also tired. When she'd been pregnant with Roya she would have been able to seek shade during the hottest part of the day. Here the luxury of shade was fiercely held territory, and the tepid seawater offered little refreshment.

Once her mother had fallen asleep, Roya wandered irritably down to the beach. She sat herself on the damp sand at the edge of the lagoon, thinking and watching the tiny bursts of activity in the water that had been invisible until the light was extinguished.

She had so rarely been alone: if her mother was working she would play with her brother. If he was in classes she would be working alongside her mother; washing clothes, preparing food, cleaning the house. At nights her father's presence had filled the place: stern, sometimes playful, but always dominant. Visitors came and went in a steady flow because of the high esteem in which her parents were held. Her parents referred to some of them as relatives, although Roya didn't think they really were—sometimes she quizzed their children and usually found there was no connection at all. It was about politics. The Taliban had picked up the scent: too many visits and the eye of that sleeping dog opened.

Once the Talibs took back Herat, they guarded it closely. They watched for movement, for the tiniest symptoms of insurrection, real or imagined. Her parents had made a poor secret of their politics, and weaker people needed something to trade: a name would do. So the darkness descended over their home. The neighbours ceased to deal with them, ceased even to greet them in the street. It was like they were marked in some way. Children were scolded by their parents for playing with Roya and her brother. The school asked their parents not to send them anymore. It all pointed with grim certainty towards the night they came.

A heavy scrunching tread approached across the sand behind her.

Roya didn't need to look up to know it was her mother.

'Are you all right, Roya *jan*?'

'I'm all right. Just sad.' Roya pushed her toes into the delicate edge of the water, watched them change shape with the ripples.

'What are you sad for?'

The moon had lit the edge of a heavy cloud in front of them. The surface of the lagoon was sleek and reflective, but here and there a coil of ripples rolled out from the rise of a fish, wobbling the moon's light as they went.

Roya was thinking, unsure how to respond. 'Everything went bad when the boat sank. I feel there's worse coming, Mother. I don't know how this will end.'

'These people are kind...'

'Yes,' Roya said without conviction. 'Some of them. Mother?'

'Yes?'

'Is it all right when I speak English? With you, I mean?'

'Of course it is. Why?'

'No reason.'

Shafiqa leaned down and placed one hand on the sand beside Roya so she could lower herself into a sitting position. The small noises that came from her in this slow process made Roya smile a little. Finally she was down, and she settled herself so that her crossed legs faced Roya's. She unfolded a closed hand to reveal a pale stone.

'I found some pumice,' she said. 'I think it washes up on the beach. Here, give me your feet: we can have a *hammam*.' She took one of Roya's feet and began to rub the sole with the pumice stone. Roya giggled a little and flinched. 'It tickles.'

'Yes, but nice?'

'Nice.'

Shafiqa continued her work, buffing the sides of Roya's heel as though she was polishing a shoe. Roya was crying a little. She tipped forward against her mother's breast, clutching at her forearm.

'So what do we have left, you and me?' Shafiqa stroked her daughter's hair as she spoke. Roya didn't respond, but began to draw swirls and dots in the sand between her mother's knees with the tip of a finger. One tear fell among the shapes she'd made.

'We have stories, you know. I'm carrying lots of them. Do you want a story?'

Roya nodded silently.

'Arabian Nights? I don't think I've told you about The Fisherman and the Demon.'

'Yes please,' said Roya. Laughing among the muffling of her mother's *chador* because Shafiqa had indeed told her this story, many times.

'All right then.' She paused, drawing the story together in her mind as her long fingers worked their way through the girl's hair. Roya was watching the sand, transfixed by the tiny sparks of light on the heavy grains.

'So. This is one of the stories that Scheherazade told the king in order to save her life.'

Roya's hands pushed the sand into hills and valleys. With each completed scoop, the grains fell away from her small fingers to leave them clean. The night was dense and still and heavy, the moon and the fish holding back the darkness.

'In former times, in the country of the Persians, there was a certain old fisherman,' Shafiqa began, as she always did.

Roya had taken up a shell fragment and was using it to draw on her mother's calf as Shafiqa continued with the tale. The poor man who couldn't feed his family and the net that came up every day with fewer fish; the strange object caught one day in the net; his excitement as he unwrapped it to find a beautiful brass jar capped with an ornate lead stopper.

Fish were gathering where they sat, where the sand dropped away to deeper water. Roya could faintly make out the shapes of their backs as they circled; as the poor fisherman prised open the jar with his bait knife.

'And what came from the jar,' breathed Shafiqa, 'was the strangest thing you could ever imagine: a wisp of smoke, which became a column, then a great cloud. The smoke kept coming until it towered over him like a thunderstorm. Finally it gathered and took shape and there in front of him was a demon: a terrible huge creature with a head like a tomb, fangs...'

'...like pincers.' Roya did a ferocious voice.

'A mouth...'

'...like a cave.'

'A throat like an alley and eyes...'

'Eyes like lanterns!'

'And the demon demanded of the fisherman: "You who have released me, tell me how you wish to die."'

Here, at the delicious climax of the story, Roya sometimes felt she could see the demon's point. Imprisoned by the prophet Solomon and stuffed into a jar for nearly two thousand years. Making all sorts of promises about what he would do for any man who eventually released him...

'He promised he'd make them rich. But nothing happened. He promised he would make them king...'

'...*but nothing happened*,' they chimed together. Shafiqa smiled down at her daughter.

'Hundreds of years went by. He grew angry, snorting and stomping and pounding the insides of his jar. He told himself that whoever released him, he would put them to death, giving them only the choice as to how they died. And so that person, of course, was the fisherman.'

Roya squinted at the mark she had made on her mother's leg:

a fine white vapour trail on the brown skin, like the one she'd seen across the sky yesterday.

'But the fisherman stayed calm, even as he realised he might die, and that he might not see his children again. He thought hard, and he remembered that even though the demon was terrifying, he had the advantage of human reason. So he tried applying reason.

'"Demon," he said, "If I ask you one question will you answer it truthfully?"

'The demon was in a hurry to get it over with, because he'd been in the jar a long, long time, so he replied: "Okay, okay, just make it snappy."

Roya giggled as she always did at her mother's bad American accent.

'"Here is my question then," said the fisherman. "Did you really come from inside that jar?"

'"Of course I did," said the demon.

'"It's just that I can't see how you could have," said the fisherman. "It's not even big enough for your hands and feet. I think you have been lying to me."

'The demon was furious! "Of course I was in the jar!" he fumed. "Look!" And he turned himself back into smoke and swirled around the fisherman and, little by little, poured himself into the jar.

'"See?" he demanded from within. "You fool! There is ample room in h—"

'And quick as a flash, the fisherman slammed the stopper back into the jar and rolled it into the sea. Then he carved a sign on a piece of driftwood with his knife, saying NO FISHING HERE. And he returned to his family, who greeted him with tears and hugs and kisses.'

'So the lesson is,' Roya intoned solemnly, 'that we can defeat the demon with reason.'

But her mother's voice dropped in a way it had never done when she'd told this story before.

'Maybe. Or maybe that the demon still waits in the jar.'

Pulau Dana

The fourth day on the island dawned bright and relentless. There was an unspoken consensus that it was time to go: Tim and Hamid were both stable, the bodies were buried and the dysentery cases were under control. Any longer and drinking water might become an issue.

Isi felt a glimmer of optimism at last, knowing that if conditions favoured them she could have the boat at Ashmore Reef shortly after sunset. It was reasonable to assume that the reef was closely watched by Australian authorities, given its reputation as a landing point for asylum seekers and border-hopping fishermen. Friendly or otherwise, there'd be someone there to meet them.

She plotted a course in the wheelhouse, ran the engines to get the pumps and the aircon going, soothed herself with the familiarity of routine. Outside, she could see Carl and Leah struggling to carry Tim across the beach and into the Zodiac. Leah, at the head end, had the bulk of the load and Carl had responsibility for the leg that ended nowhere. He cradled the thigh carefully, and in this, at least, he was useful: a practical task that didn't challenge any of his fixed positions. He was trying.

They were preparing the Zodiac. Leah sat on the beach, arranged herself under Tim so that his head was resting on one of her thighs. Even at this distance Isi could tell that Tim was in a stupor, the effects of the ketamine still wearing off. No matter how she tried, Isi couldn't grapple with the notion of going to sleep with an injury and waking up with an amputation. The overheard exchange between surgeon and patient had been brutal:

Your foot was ischaemic. The blood supply was stuffed because of the crush injury and the end of the limb was dying.

Tim's half-conscious mind, all snarled in shock and chemical residue, appeared to have no room for the logic.

You cut off my foot.

Your foot had lost its blood supply. It was gangrenous, and if I hadn't operated you'd have developed septicaemia. Blood poisoning. Which could have killed you.

But you cut off my fucking foot…

They lowered him into the Zodiac now, and Isi watched Sanusi ease the boat into the shallows then jump in and start the motor. Tim lay in the well, staring upwards as he had been in the tent, disbelief still etched on his features as they cut the short distance towards the *Java Ridge*.

If we'd left it, you probably would've died. Now that the foot's gone, you should be fine.

Hamid, by comparison, had never questioned why someone had taken a power drill and bored a hole in his head. It was even possible that he didn't understand what had been done to him—he didn't fully regain his senses until after Finley had packed the wound and stitched his scalp.

Fraggle and Carl had spent the morning ferrying small loads of people and gear from the beach to the *Java Ridge*, the blue smoke of the Zodiac's outboard settling as a haze on the lagoon. Sanusi and Radja were somewhere on board below Isi, assigning hammocks, bunks, yoga mats and piles of surfboard bags to sleep on. Parents and children were told to share. Storage wasn't an issue: none of them had any possessions beyond the odd plastic bag.

The crew had given handlines to some of the men and were teaching them how to pluck reef fish from beneath the boat: showing them which were good, which were poisonous. The results brought little bursts of laughter from among them, especially once the translation for something called 'poo fish' had been made. It was the first time Isi had heard laughter since the afternoon they saw Dana.

The women were gathered around Isi's herb gardens, picking at the leaves: biting, offering, laughing. They took particular delight in her upside–down tomatoes: buckets hanging under the eaves of the cabin with holes in the bottoms, out of which sprouted the tomato plants, their stems veering and twisting to find sunlight. A couple of the older men were studying the lines of the *Java Ridge*, running weathered hands over the planking and the seamless joinery. Isolated for months, maybe years, by language and geography, the timber spoke to them in some dialect that was secret and shared.

Leah had fired up the stereo, a thick tropical stew of Desmond Dekker's early reggae. The bass thudded into the slow air and the men with their hands on the timber glanced up in disapproval. Isi, too, baulked at the idea of music in the circumstances, but she let it go. It might lift the pall that hung over them.

But it wasn't the music that grated. Isi's eyes followed Leah as she walked back downstairs, tall and graceful in a cotton wrap and a bikini top. She passed a group of seated men, all of whom studied her closely. Unconsciously, she had made herself the centre of a moment. One of the watchers was Irfan Shah, the old Pashtun man. He stroked his beard behind his upraised knees and said something.

Leah stopped and spun, searching for the source of the comment. 'What did he say?' she demanded of the men.

None of them answered: none of them knew how. Irfan Shah and his motives were hidden behind the expanse of beard. He repeated whatever it was he had said, and Radja, listening from the rail above, called down to her.

'He say to cover yourself, miss.'

Irfan Shah stared at her, confident now that his rebuke had hit home.

Leah stood before him, his huddled shape barely reaching her knees, and stared back. Someone hissed. She had her hands on her hips. Isi was about to move forward to intervene when Leah appeared to reconsider: she lowered her hands and withdrew, her eyes never leaving Irfan Shah's. The demeanour of the men around him shifted: the old man's authority seemed immediately to have diminished, like static had dissolved its broadcast.

Isi waited until the Zodiac was craned up out of the water and tethered to its rack on the stern. As was his habit, Sanusi darted from the stern along the port side to the bow, where he waited for her to start up the windlass. She took a long, last look at the island, at the scuff marks across the sand where they'd made their exit, the disturbed ground where the burial site was; and at the otherwise serene image of the atoll.

It had taken so much from all of them in such a short time, absorbed their short and wretched piece of history as it had no doubt subsumed other mariners and their ordeals for centuries. The birds and the crabs and the insects would continue their cycles of fertility and predation. The sun would go round a thousand times more without human witness and the sea would continue to pound the reef. In time all trace of them would disappear.

She switched on the windlass when Sanusi raised his hand to indicate he was ready. The heavy steel links crawled up over the roller onto the winch and the anchor clunked into its cradle.

Never again, she promised herself. Time for an office job somewhere dull. Somewhere Joel would never reach her—if he even wanted to.

She eased the throttles forward and felt the *Java Ridge* beginning to cut the water. Leah appeared beside her in a shirt and smiled as though nothing had just occurred. 'Snake?' she smiled and offered Isi the brightly coloured packet of lollies. 'Don't tell the others.'

The shadows of coral heads, the rocks and shoals of fish began to slip past on both sides of the rising bow. With a roll of the wheel she pointed the nose at the reef pass and let the forward motion settle her mind.

• • •

Once she was clear of the atoll Isi set a course southeast for Ashmore.

Thirteen hours. Off the side of the giant undersea ridge that marks the southern edge of Indonesia, towards the slope of Australia's continental shelf. Into the maze of sandbanks and coral cays around Ashmore and finally to safe anchorage. Get these people off, unload the surfers with them, and she could sail home with Sanusi and Radja. Hand them their cash, tie off on the wharf and walk away. If Joel wanted to make an insurance claim he was more than welcome.

The sea was calm all around, as eager to forget as she was. The horizon mingled into the low-hanging clouds and the island receded to a tiny smudge behind them. When the music had been playing for an hour or so Isi decided to turn it off. She imagined it would be dis-concerting for the children especially—the random shuffle had cycled through some indelicate rap, and if they couldn't follow the English she felt fairly sure the aggression would be clear to them.

She skipped up the steps to the aft deck and rounded the corner to find Fraggle and Carl seated on the benches around the table. On the table's surface there was a scatter of empty beers and a bottle of whisky between them. Playing cards were strewn about, the remains of an abandoned game. Crown caps, chip packets and cigarette butts on Fraggle's side. She stabbed at the power button, killing the stereo.

'What the fuck?'

Fraggle put a finger to his lips and made a *shhh* sound. He tried and failed to suppress his laughter, and it burst out of him childishly. His dreadlocks swung as he laughed.

'Shuddup man,' said Carl. 'She's *meeean.*'

Isi realised she had her hands on her hips again. 'There's two dozen Muslims downstairs, you inconsiderate pricks. Do you really think this is a good time for a piss-up?'

'Why don't you have a beer?' Fraggle asked hopefully. He patted the cushion beside him on the bench. She ignored the gesture.

'Pull yourselves together,' she said, and hated the sound of it.

'Hey, what happened to all the "help yourselves to the beers" bullshit, Isi?' Carl was rolling a lighter over his knuckles and she wanted to snatch it off him and throw it at his head. 'We helped you out with your friends downstairs, and now we're back to normal. Still your paying customers, eh.'

'This charter was over the minute those people hit the reef, Carl. You'd know that if you had half an ounce of common…fuck, what? Decency? *Sense?*'

Fraggle raised a conciliatory hand. 'Isi, this whole thing's a big stress. We were just letting off steam. Okay? We'll clean up. All cool.'

'Cool,' she fumed. 'Cool. Try telling that to the old bloke downstairs who just had a go at Leah about getting around in bathers.'

She left them there, returned to the wheelhouse and tried to shake off her annoyance. The other boat's skipper, Ali Hassan, was pacing the front deck below her. He reappeared either side of the large tarp from time to time, smoking and flicking his butts into the sea. She didn't like people smoking on the front deck, but she felt wary of a confrontation with him. His whole body was springloaded with tension. He had the same small backpack slung over one shoulder that he'd had since he first appeared on the beach. He'd never put it down, never opened it as far as Isi was aware. She had a fair idea what was in the bag: passports, identity cards and cash, which led her to think that Ali Hassan must be weighing a dilemma. He could use the identity papers of one of the dead to claim asylum, then accept a paid flight home from the Australian government. The bureaucrats wouldn't look into it with any great vigour if the easier option was to deport him.

But he ran the risk that the other survivors would turn him in. Some of them must have relatives who'd drowned. Some of them must have grudges over the state of the boat, the whole fucking mess. He was risking jail time. But sailing the other way offered no greater solace. Who could tell what recriminations awaited him in Indonesia? The local political figures who must have been complicit. Gangsters, dealmakers, more grieving relatives.

Isi reached for the Sampoernas, lit one and wedged herself against the cabin wall, feet on the handrail. It was her roost. From here she could watch life on the front deck without being observed.

The bow rode high and effortless, and a cluster of small children had gathered at the rail, scanning the surface. Occasionally they'd squeal with delight and point at the air beside the fast-moving boat: flying fish were launching themselves alongside, whirring at cabin height then plunging back in again.

Leah sat on the bow with a group of the women and girls, exchanging fragments of language and what looked like scandalised giggling. She'd found a bottle of nail polish somewhere, and handed it over to the girls so they could do each other's toenails. Movement agreed with Leah: she'd come alive since they broke from the stasis of the island. She'd been darting to and from the galley making drinks, fixing medications, delicately applying sunscreen here and there. A rummage through the cupboards of the galley had unearthed a needle and thread and some scissors, and Leah had declared she'd make a 'stubby holder' out of one of Tim's old T-shirts, to house his stump. Tim lay in a hammock under the edge of the awning with the stump elevated and the headphones on. Isi could tell the headphones were not about music but about keeping the world at bay. The codeine had his pain just about covered but not his anguish. Eyes fixed on the underside of the awning, jaw muscles knotted in his cheek. Occasionally he looked down, straight at Leah. Isi wondered what passed between them.

Carl was on the bow with Sanusi, sorting through the pile of surfboards that had been used in the rescue and lining them up for repair. A puff of air carried the petro-fumes of the resin up to Isi. Board repairs came last on any rational list of priorities; maybe like the stump-cover, it was a gesture towards normality.

Her anger with Carl had subsided. In its place she felt something more like pity. The language he'd used when they clashed on the beach—it was calculated to inflame, the way a child would argue. *This will infuriate you. And this and this.* The drinking session would have been his idea. He was young, hadn't seen much of the world. If there'd been more left of this trip, she'd have worked away at him until she found his better nature. But as things stood, they'd be parting ways forever by sundown.

Fraggle had reverted to his resting state, compelled to record everything. He wandered around the deck, explaining the camera to the survivors and gently prompting them to smile; arranging their hands, his heavy auburn hair spilling over the task. He'd pull faces for the children, shrink into himself, passively, for the elderly. He had a skill for it, she could see. But even in conversation with them, he remained somehow alone.

Neil Finley had mostly slept since his marathon session in the medical tent. Isi tried to see the situation as he would: was he ashamed of his momentary loss of control? Was he even wired for shame? The taut lines of his body stretched out on a board bag in the sun, one graceful foot crossed neatly over the other. Such a strange kind of violence: Finley had maimed Tim in order to save his life. Isi had seen him once unwrapping the stump and checking it while Tim stared pointedly out the window—there was a kind of fog between them. Even if either of them had known how to penetrate it, they showed no inclination to do so. In a hospital, the awkward conversation would be skipped through: a suit talking to a bed, the horror dulled by medication. Here, they idled on the deck only metres from each other.

The men among the Iraqis and Afghans had taken themselves down to the bunks. They'd be deep in conversation again. What was there to discuss? Someone, probably Radja, had given them cigarettes. They were powering through the damn things down there, despite her rule, plumes of clove-tinted smoke billowing out the vents.

Hamid was lying on Isi's bunk, behind where she stood in the wheelhouse. He was conscious now, with his head heavily bandaged. It amazed her that he'd gone from death's edge to this calm state with the aid of nothing more than the codeine she and Joel had bought over the counter in Legian. They were optimistic then, stocking their boat for contingencies they'd considered laughably remote. Much like Tim would have been when he bought his travel insurance.

Luke Finley sat on the point of the bow, his legs either side of the anchor chain. Something had shifted in him since they picked up the survivors, something that Isi couldn't place at first. A movement away from his father. The striking physical proximity when they first boarded was gone now; the invisible tether of loyalty or adoration severed. Luke's shoulders had lost their square set. Before the island, his gaze had sought out reflective surfaces where he could admire himself. Now he stared at nothing.

So Isi had retreated into the wheelhouse and was standing at the helm, looking out at the sea and letting the panic go with each outward breath. They were all lost in their own worlds, dazed by a giant percussion. But she just had to get them to Ashmore. It wasn't her job to return them to their senses.

Then the handset crackled.

She looked at it in surprise. Radja and Sanusi both had handsets but they never used them. They preferred an intimate vocabulary of gestures from around the deck, looking up at her in the wheelhouse and waving. Tapping fingers, whistling. Rarely, Sanusi might put a call in from the engine room but she knew he wasn't down there.

Survivors and clients on deck. Men smoking in the bunkroom. Crew busy. So why was someone calling?

She picked it up and answered. It was Sanusi.

'Isi, can you come down?' he said, slowly and carefully.

She misread his formal English and laughed. 'Can't you bloody come up here?' But as she spoke, peering out the cabin windows towards the sunlit bow, Sanusi appeared from under the cover of the front awning. He had the handset in his extended hand and was edging away to his right, looking left. The others were alert now, looking also. After Sanusi, Ali Hassan appeared from under the cover.

He had Roya.

He had Roya in a headlock and he was holding a knife to her throat.

•••

It took him some time to get it done, to take control of the *Java Ridge* and its occupants.

He stood on the deck, the sunlight gleaming on the dome of his forehead in front of his thinning black hair, screaming and pointing the knife to the north, back the way they had come. His clothes hung limp on the angry points of his thin body. The tirade needed no translation:

he wanted them to turn around. With manic sweeps of the blade, he herded all the survivors off the front deck and inside, then down the steps into the bunkroom; the largest space on board. Isi could now see that he'd delayed doing this for long enough to figure out the internal dimensions of the vessel: where everything was kept, where the large and small spaces were.

The bunkroom was big enough to hold all of them, and Ali Hassan was sending them there because it had only one doorway. There was a hatch at the far end that opened onto the bow, but as she edged around the deck, following Ali Hassan and Roya, Isi could see that he'd thought of that: there was a weight belt looped through the handles of the hatch so it couldn't be opened from the inside.

His gaze was fixed, furious with intent as he walked the passengers through the lounge and down the steps. He held Roya in a grip that betrayed to Isi just a little of his concealed self: firm enough to terrify, with his arm around her neck and the blade of the knife glinting in the bright sun, but not aiming to bruise her, their progress marked by traces of unconscious care. He lifted her over obstacles as he careened around the deck. Hauled her around so he always faced the passengers, but swept the flies from her face as they tried to settle there. Always the knife, though: the one unalterable reality.

Finally they were all penned, unresisting, in the bunkroom. All but Roya and Isi.

Isi watched the girl eyeing her captor. Thinking hard, it seemed: engaged with a whirl of inner possibilities but never uttering a word. Her huge dark eyes swivelled to take it all in, lashes falling when she looked down, whites flaring when she studied her periphery. Isi thought about how painful his grip must be, how terrifying to sense the gleaming metal held inches from her ear. Isi had prepped meals with that knife, taken it clean through the carapace of a mud crab, so sharp it didn't crush the edges. How made of flesh the girl felt to her then; how made of vulnerable flesh.

From where Isi stood, shaded by the awning over the bow, she could only watch helplessly. The expensive boards no longer mattered. The new gear, the fittings, the paint...the equipment she and Joel had borrowed for and fitted to the decks in the smoky heat and clamour of the wharf. All of that effort she knew with cold certainty was now slipping away from her. Yet she was surprised how little it troubled her, compared to the fates of these strangers. Compared to what might befall Roya. Deep in her heart, for reasons she couldn't fathom, the child mattered more than anything.

The poor girl's mother, Shafiqa, had wailed and fought as the others lifted her down into the bunkroom when her turn came. She reached for Roya and slapped at Ali Hassan as she unleashed a stream of Persian invective on him. He tensed, wove back from her out-stretched hand but did not retaliate. For Carl and Luke, who kept a reluctant hold of her arms, she proved a difficult proposition—lumbering and awkward with her weight tipping forward, lashing out at all who approached and reaching simultaneously for Roya. The child seemed to understand better than her mother how all of this was going to unfold. She hid her distress, spoke quietly in response to Shafiqa's cries. Foreign words that needed no translation: words of reassurance and calm, a composure that only fuelled her mother's dismay.

Isi dodged and evaded and made excuses to ensure she was the last one locked up, an impulse he should understand, as a skipper himself. Where was he planning to go? How would he navigate? Language and his simmering fury prevented her asking. In the wheelhouse, he watched closely as she brought the *Java Ridge* around and re-set the auto-pilot on a course to the north which would take them between Raijua and Sumba and up to Flores, a long, long shoreline that stretched from east to west like a wall across the ocean.

Ali Hassan watched over her shoulder, apparently satisfied by the change of course. Then he hustled Isi downstairs and into the bunkroom, pressing her backwards against the mass of bodies already inside. His arm was wrapped tightly around Roya's shoulders, the knife never deviating from its line across her throat. Isi had only seconds to intervene.

'Roya, can you ask him what he plans to do?'

In the space between Ali Hassan and Isi, who dared not approach closer, Roya raised her eyes to find his, above and behind her; exposing the curve of her throat, pale and perfect. She translated for Ali Hassan, who responded with a guttural burst.

'He say it is not your problem.'

Isi persisted. She had to. 'Tell him we need to head for Australia. We can get help there.'

When the translation had passed to him, Ali Hassan laughed angrily.

'Now he say you do not watch TV,' Roya said. 'Australia not helping boats anymore.'

She spoke to him softly as he held her, a bird in a fist. The pressure of his grip had not lessened, but he now stopped moving and muttered more gently in response to her. Isi tried to read the cues in their movements. The wildness of his expression was subsiding a little. He nodded in the direction of the adults and spoke to her more loudly.

Roya's small voice took on a new kind of authority. 'He say we not go to Australia.'

'What?' spluttered Carl. 'Where the fuck does he think he's going then?'

Isi was ahead of him. 'He's got the IDs from all the others. He's probably carrying cash.' He still had the backpack over one shoulder. 'Guess he thinks he can disappear. Indo's a big place, and he hasn't committed a crime in this country.'

Another long exchange between Ali Hassan and Roya.

'He say seven Australian. He want seven...' she hesitated, searching for a word she'd rarely had to use, 'phone, *phones*, now. To throw out here.'

After some rummaging the phones thudded and bounced, one by one, into the stairwell. Ali Hassan gathered them and pointed at a small calico tote bag that lay at the foot of one of the bunks. Leah's bunk. He waved the knife. 'Give.'

Leah stood beside it. She looked confused, then alarmed. 'No. It's mine.'

Ali Hassan waved the knife more urgently. 'Give me bag! Now!' He pointed the blade at Roya's neck and his eyes widened.

'Leah! Give him the bag,' someone shouted. But Leah didn't move. Carl darted in from her left and threw the bag at Ali Hassan's feet. He scooped the phones into it and kicked the door shut. Isi rushed forward to watch through the small porthole in the door, felt him latch it shut. With Roya still trapped under his arm, he pulled a large fire extinguisher off the wall and wedged it between the last of the ascending steps and the door.

'Why the fuck did you let him have that?' screamed Leah.

It was the first time anyone had heard Leah raise her voice, and Carl was visibly rattled. 'It's a fucking *bag* princess. Settle down.'

The bunkroom was plunged into gloomy silence despite the crowd. They could hear Ali Hassan moving off through the interior of the cabin; the mismatched sounds of his frenetic movement. Carl was standing on a camera case at the skylight halfway down the room, inclining his head so he could peer through the narrow opening.

'What's he doing?'

'He's gone down the stern...he's...he's tossed the bag overboard.' The whole room was listening intently to him. 'So there go the phones.' Leah had her head resting on the frame of the bunk.

Isi turned to her. 'Why didn't you just give him the bag, Leah? He could've hurt Roya.'

She lifted her head. Her eyes were black with despair.

'Because my insulin pen's in it.'

• • •

Ali Hassan ran Roya up the external steps to the wheelhouse and pushed her into a chair. He pointed the knife at her as he backed away a couple of paces, his message clear. Roya didn't dare move.

There was another fire extinguisher up here, mounted behind the door. He took it and raised it over his head, one fist wrapped around its neck. He held it aloft a moment or two, selecting his target, then brought it crashing down on the console, fragments of glass and plastic flying in all directions. He swung at the panel again and again, not with rage but with apparent calculation. Chrome edgings twisted and speared upwards; the timber backing was revealed in bright splinters.

What's he doing now? Roya asked herself. He picked up the handset that was connected by a coiled cord to the console, clicked the button on it a couple of times, held it to his ear. Then he tore it from its mooring and threw it out the window. It landed with a faint splash on the sea. Roya understood now—he was getting rid of all the ways they could talk to the outside world.

There was a small screen mounted upright on the console, aligned so it would be visible directly above the helm. Ali Hassan considered this for a moment, reading the same strange word Roya was reading, embossed on the casing: RADAR. He hefted the fire extinguisher again, this time striking sideways. It broke off clean and tumbled from its perch to swing on the ends of its coloured leads.

He pointed the knife at her again—a reminder—then stepped out the door of the wheelhouse and locked it behind him. She watched him climb the steel frame of the doorway, gripping the heavy painted hinges with his toes. The soles of his feet had picked up a dusting of white deck paint. Roya sat perfectly still, listening to his footfalls on the roof above her.

•••

Isi had joined Carl at the skylight now, awkwardly cheek to cheek. They could see Ali Hassan on the cabin roof.

He stood upright for a moment, as if even he could appreciate the majesty of the view, high above a placid ocean in the sun.

'Fucking idiot's already looking for land,' muttered Carl.

'No he isn't,' Isi replied. Ali Hassan sat down, braced his feet against the tallest of the three radio aerials and began kicking out at it. The aerial refused to budge, so he stood again and bent it down with both hands, monkey-swinging until it broke, dropping him with a *clang* on the metal surface of the roof. He threw the broken piece overboard.

'He knows what he's doing,' said Isi. 'That was the HF. It's the one with the longest range.'

Next he moved to another, thicker aerial. This one he studied for a moment, then simply unscrewed the base and lifted it out of its mount. It went into the sea, trailing its umbilicus of electrical cable. A third, smaller aerial broke off in his hands with little pressure. Now he produced a spanner from the pocket of his shorts and began working on the one remaining fixture on the cabin roof: a small satellite dish. It took him some time to loosen the three bolts but eventually it too splashed into the water beside the *Java Ridge*.

Carl had reached an arm out through the slender opening in the skylight. His fingers found the assembly that held the cover in place. He was watching Ali Hassan carefully as he explored.

'What are you doing?' someone asked.

'We don't have to put up with this,' he muttered. He produced a multi-tool pocket knife, opened the pliers and passed it from the hand that was inside to the one that was feeling around on the deck. Isi watched him: she could see he wanted to be useful, but he couldn't understand the futility of what he was attempting. She knew every screw and bolt on the *Java Ridge*'s deck. She'd painted them. Not one of them was going to yield to a pocket knife.

But he twisted and squeezed, feeling his way, tongue compressed in the corner of his mouth. The bunkroom crowd were transfixed by his efforts. Isi watched through the gap without commenting; thinking how if it was Joel doing this she would've been into him. *Is that really achieving anything?*

She could see Ali Hassan climbing down from the cabin roof with his back to them. But the sea was so flat, so mirror perfect, that the small taps and bumps of the knife's contact on the steel fittings carried far enough to reach him. He stopped and turned around.

Ali Hassan could see clearly what Carl was trying to do. He leapt down the gangway and crossed the deck in an instant. In his hurry to get the pocket knife back through the opening, Carl bashed his knuckles on the lip of the cover and dropped the knife onto the timbers. By then, Ali Hassan had reached him and he plucked the knife with a look of vindication on his face and threw it overboard. He produced the wicked kitchen knife again, held it to his own throat and mimed a cutting motion. Then he pointed the blade at Carl, yelling words that were just shapes and sounds, undiluted fury.

Carl retreated and wound the skylight down a little. He peered out, summoning defiance. He looked ludicrous to Isi: the yapper behind the fence, cowed by a Rottweiler on the street. The hot, damp air from the crowded room rushed past their heads and out the opening. This bullshit was not going to be the answer. Carl slumped down on a pile of bags beneath the skylight. Leah regarded him sceptically.

'What?' he said, looking back at her. When she didn't answer he added 'And what the fuck was that with the insulin? Why didn't you tell anyone?'

'It's no one's business but mine,' she responded. 'Did you tell us all about your medical history when you stepped on board?'

He looked contrite, for just a second. 'I thought you were just...'

'Neurotic? Of course you did.'

'So what happens to you now?'

'Guess I'm in a fair bit of trouble. Ask the doc.' She tilted her head towards Finley. The surgeon had sat quietly next to Tim Wills' head since they'd been confined to the bunkroom, only leaving him occasionally to check someone who complained: eyes, infected cuts, nausea. He looked to Isi as though the ordeal in the tent had depleted him.

'It's not my area,' he said. 'But if she's type 1'—Leah nodded—'then she's going to go into DKA within about thirty-six hours. Depends when she had—'

Leah looked at her watch. 'Three hours ago.'

'Okay. So maybe a little longer then if there's still some insulin in your blood. I take it there are no other diabetics on board?' He looked around the room. No one responded. 'After that,' he sounded uncharacteristically apologetic, 'it's irreversible.'

Isi looked out the skylight again. Ali Hassan hadn't moved from where he stood. He appeared to Isi to be deep in thought, looking back at the stern and the Zodiac on its crane. Now he stepped that way, over the hatch, and sank the big knife into the inflatable hull, ripping it forward so that the whole air chamber was laid open. He moved around it, stabbing and slashing at each separate compartment in the red hull until the heavy rubber hung limp in the sun.

• • •

Ali Hassan returned to the wheelhouse, anger and adrenaline compressing his features.

Roya hadn't moved. She felt a responsibility she couldn't place. Even at knifepoint, she had a measure of freedom the others didn't have: a hostage rather than merely a prisoner. She watched him working on the electronics mounted under the roof: a series of grey steel boxes, held into mounting brackets by large wingnuts. With one eye on her and the knife jammed in the back of his trousers, Ali Hassan worked his way along the row of them and removed each one, heaving them over the side as he went.

She watched the knife as he moved. The grip was a kitchen grip, not something designed for fear like the Talibs would carry. She was meant to be scared of this knife, and she was. But for an instant it took her back to the kitchen at home with her mother, fingers slipping over washed vegetables, a pot boiling steam onto the window. Talking, asking questions as they came to her; her mother answering and inter-rupting herself. *Pass me the oil. Careful with your fingers.*

The things he'd thrown from the roof were aerials, she figured. So whatever these boxes were, they were connected to the aerials and weren't much use without them. But Ali Hassan clearly wasn't done. Slowly and methodically he made his way through all the cupboards and compartments of the bridge, turning things over in his hands and considering them. Occasionally he would toss them overboard—more often he left them where they fell. He held a cigarette lighter to Isi's carefully compiled logbook and watched it smoulder on the floor.

He found a bright orange plastic package that Roya recognised instantly from watching football on television. Flares. She didn't know why anyone would have them on a boat.

He locked Roya in again and disappeared briefly. She pressed her nose to the window of the wheelhouse and saw him standing at the rail below, using the knife to slice each of the flares lengthwise. He held them over the side and watched as they spilled iridescent orange powder onto the drowsy sea. The air was so heavy and limpid that the colourful mist hung there as the boat drew away from it. It drifted neither left nor right. It just descended like a swarm of something until it rested on the water's surface.

Canberra

Cassius was on the phone to Rory. He was avoiding the desk phone for the time being, and Waldron's diversion had rendered his mobile useless. So Stella had given him her SIM card with a handful of his most valuable numbers saved onto it. It felt treasonous at first, but he was grateful. Stella and her casual pragmatism—she'd borrowed another phone from her sister and said she'd get by.

Earlier in the morning he'd been making calls to Sydney: to the head of department, to Core Resolve, to Coastwatch. Each time he instructed Stella to find another number, she made tut-tutting noises down the phone. *They'll have your nuts for this.* The expression surprised him—*she mentioned my nuts*—and he wasn't sure if he should pull her up on it. But in the small guerrilla campaign he had begun she was as game as he was, and considerably more skilled. By eleven he had set in motion everything he wanted, which was when his thoughts turned to his son.

Today's nanny, a different one from yesterday, had taken Rory to Questacon in the morning and was aiming for the National Gallery in the afternoon. Questacon admitted the chook, in line with their enlightened views on animal rights, but the gallery refused and there was a stand-off with security at the front desk. Other than that, the kid had apparently enjoyed his day.

Rory wanted to know if Cassius was going to come home early (Cassius nearly laughed) and would he be on the TV for anything tonight? Cassius found himself spinning the wheels conversationally: it was his life's habit to wind up any phone call as fast as he could, but he felt a need to listen to the boy's voice. The curling inflection and odd little detours of his speech brought the image of his face.

He understood very little of Rory as a person—his hopes and pleasures and worries. He was merely *the boy*, an abstract idea he processed by reference to his own life: one of its many passages. *I am a father.* He had to actively consider the notion that Rory might have an independent existence of his own. Cassius was sure that he loved Rory because that was what fathers did: there was no occasion for deeper reflection on the matter. And yet something lingered, unexplained.

The boy's happy chatter washed over him until Stella darted in, making an urgent motion with a finger across her throat. The thumb of her other hand was pointing over her shoulder. Cassius apologised to Rory and cut the call; the desk phone immediately lit up. Waldron.

'Yes, Kevin.'

'PM's on his way. About the boat thing. Put away any sharp objects.'

Cassius hung up again as Stella fled and the PM absorbed the doorway. He took two giant steps into the room and slung a manila envelope on the desk.

'Open it.'

'Hi.'

'Open the envelope.' The PM was closing the room towards Cassius like a heavyweight looking to land a haymaker. 'Open the fucking thing.' He pointed.

Cassius did as he was told and tore the top off the envelope. A pile of large photographs spilled out. They were identical: pictures of what he now knew to be Dana Island. The only difference between the prints was the time stamp in the lower right corner. Calibrated to some standard that meant nothing to Cassius, he could tell nevertheless that they were taken two hours apart. There were—he counted them—twelve shots. He laid them in order across the desk and saw the light fading into pale blues and greens, then back to pinks and mauves as the sun died in the west. Darkness, and then the process repeating in reverse.

'That's yesterday, right? And that's your island, Cassius. No people. Huh? *No people.* No boats, no fucking tents, no bodies. Nothing, mate. You owe me an apology.'

Cassius suddenly felt more tired than he ever had. 'For what?'

The PM plunged forward, ramming a thick finger into the desktop. 'For fuckin…for sniffing around like a randy little bitch in heat.'

'*What?*' The PM's head loomed uncomfortably close across the desk. Cassius focussed on the black hairs that sprouted from the nearer nostril.

'I know you're asking questions, you cunt. You want a…a… fucking point here. Trying to be fucking cute. Well I've been playing these games a fuckload longer than you have, son.'

Cassius looked down at the photos again, to avoid the PM's belligerent stare. 'So the boat's underwater and the bodies are buried. What do these pictures prove?'

'What they *prove*, you turd, is that you're listening to the bleeding hearts, and you've forgotten about doing your fucking job.' He was leaning even further forward, his spittle landing on Cassius's arm where he'd laid it on the desk.

'Why do you say I'm in bed with these people? I'm just trying to adopt a healthy scepticism towards this…whatever it is.'

'No. *NO*. Scepticism is what I'm doing. Hosing down conspiracies. So there's a boat, going south, right? It shelters in a lagoon, in their waters not ours. It sinks in a storm. Fortunately the whole thing's captured by our private contractors on *un-manipulated* images, see? It walks like a duck, Cassius. Quacks like a duck. IT'S JUST A FUCKING DUCK, you moron.'

He turned sidelong, regarded Cassius with open contempt. The stabbing finger again.

'I don't like you. Fucking jacked-up Henry. Who the fuck rows boats? People with no ball skills, Cassius; that's why you ride bikes too. And you don't like me. We can both live with that. But I'm fucked if I'm going to let you derail this campaign because you want to float some self-indulgent, half-arsed thought bubble.'

It took him three deep inhales to settle. Cassius waited for them.

'There's something wrong about this. I don't think that boat is an asylum seeker boat. I don't acc—'

'THERE IS NO ONE OUT THERE, CASSIUS!'

The PM's volume was sufficient to silence all normal conversation in the hallway outside. It ripped the oxygen from the room like an incendiary device.

But Cassius had retreated somewhere too deep for these antics to scare him. 'I don't accept that those people just went to the bottom or got buried. Be reasonable—if someone buried them, then where are *those* people? And who took the other bloody photograph?' Cassius knew his voice was rising.

The PM watched him, his face scarlet and veined. 'If you wanna make moral judgments, put 'em on Twitter you credulous little fuckbag. Otherwise, stay out of my way.'

'I'm not going to get in your way but I am going to find out what happened. You can't afford to pick a fight with me in public—not now. You can't afford to dump me. Fact is, you can't move and we both know it. Now if you don't mind, I've got work to do.'

The PM scooped the photographs off the desk in a furious lunge, arched his back and threw them at the wall. They fluttered towards the floor, and by the time all of them had landed he was gone. Cassius regarded the random arrangement on the carpet: pieces of a puzzle.

And this, Rory, is what your father does for a living.

Savu Sea, West of Pulau Raijua

The air began to circulate in the bunkroom as the vessel gained speed, and the crushing humidity thinned. Separated from their supply of codeine, Tim and Hamid moaned and writhed until a search turned up a foil of painkillers in someone's bag.

The Australians had dragged clothes out of their bags so that the men could lie on the floor, though most preferred to stand. Groups of women and children sat on the bunks. Very soon the children were restless, scrapping and playing, hustling for space and complaining when they were outmanoeuvred. As there had been on the island, there remained a polite distance between the Australians and the survivors of the *Takalar*.

A boy watching the porthole said, *Man is coming*. The latch turned and Ali Hassan was there, standing well back with Roya again under his arm and the knife held close to her face. In front of them, arranged on the steps, were bottles of water and buckets of fruit. As the men moved them into the bunkroom, Isi called to Roya.

'Ask him how many revs he's doing.' Roya looked puzzled and Isi thought harder. 'Roya, I can hear the engine. Tell him he's going too fast.'

The girl reached for her dictionary, alarming Ali Hassan at first before he saw what she was doing. She worked her way through a number of pages, deliberately mouthing the words to herself before she felt ready to speak. When she'd done so, he fired back a short and irritable burst.

'He say it is not...job for you. He drive boat now.'

But Isi wanted to keep the pressure on him. Even cooped up in the bunkroom she was responsible for the boat—as surely as if she'd been in the wheelhouse.

'Roya, ask him if he's keeping a lookout.'

The girl translated again, and was answered with a sarcastic laugh and another spray of invective.

'He say he is drive boats longer than you.'

'I need water!' Leah yelled over the top of the crowd. Ali Hassan nodded disdainfully at the buckets that had held the fruit, and spoke again to Roya.

'He say keep buckets for toilet.'

• • •

Ali Hassan took Roya back to the wheelhouse and sat her again on the low bench behind the captain's chair while he studied the screen in front of him and scanned the horizon. The afternoon was getting old now, the light shattering into white glare in the west and fading to pastels in the east.

Roya could see land to their right. From the exchange between Isi and Ali Hassan she imagined this must be Raijua. But it was of no interest to Ali Hassan. He had pushed the big steel handles all the way forward, making the boat rise high above the water. The sound of the engines grew louder. His eyes were locked on the horizon.

After a long time had passed in silence, Roya began to ask him questions. Simple ones, conversational, like whether he had a wife and children. At first he didn't answer, just stared glumly ahead. But after several minutes, his demeanour changed and to her surprise he spoke softly.

'I am sorry I struck you.'

A slow conversation emerged across the awkward divide of their two languages. He did have a wife, he told her, and four children. All girls, her age and younger. He fell silent again for a while, lit a cigarette. Beautiful, he muttered as he flicked the lighter's wheel. He didn't want...what had happened, he said. But everyone needed to find money somehow. *You must understand, yes?*

She asked him what would happen to all the people on the boat. He frowned, pulled at the bridge of his nose with a thumb and forefinger. The ones from the shipwreck would have to find their own way once they reached land, he said. He would be going on. He would keep the westerners as hostages until he knew he was safe. Maybe ransom, he said. She said she thought he wasn't a bad man, and that he wouldn't hurt the Australians. She knew she shouldn't speak to an adult like that, but she wanted to hear his assurance. His eyes became hard and cold at that point. They meant nothing to him, he said.

'Where do you come from?' she asked him. Since she'd been travelling, she'd found that people liked to discuss their home. But Ali Hassan weighed the question, searched it for traps.

'Baghdad,' he said eventually. 'Shi'a like you, but my family were communists. Both my parents teachers...professors. At the university.' He took his eyes off the sea, looked directly at her. 'You understand that word, university?'

She nodded.

'I was going to go to the university too. But then Baathists, they come and take my parents from the house when I am sixteen.'

He was choosing his words carefully so she could keep up. They were more terrible for their simplicity.

'They torture them. Too much, they could not take it. Some

soldiers come to the house and tell me to come get the bodies or they throw them out.'

The afternoon cooled outside. The breeze slipped through the open cabin door.

'They arrest me three times, beat me up, make me sign papers because my neighbours are telling stories. See?' He lifted his lip and pulled it back to reveal the dark cavity beneath his pink gum. 'Hit me in mouth with a rifle, teeth gone.

'Then I escape in mountains. So cold for a long time, nothing to eat.' He patted his stomach to demonstrate, as though he was talking to someone much younger. 'Walking, trucks, more walking. Kurdistan, Turkey. Four years in Turkey, very bad.'

'You have travelled a long time,' she said.

'You are travel too,' he replied. 'Most people are travel.' He swept an arm at the smothering dusk outside. 'Most people want...going somewhere. Not many people already are home.'

He studied her face intently. 'These people,' he jerked a thumb at the bunkroom. 'You think they worry for you? You mistake. They worry for no one but themself. That is my warning.'

He didn't want to talk anymore, though she tried to encourage him. An hour passed that way; her trying to coax his attention again, him locked and bolted by the grim reality of the situation. She decided some time during that hour that he didn't want to be in charge of a boat full of hostages, that this was all a terrible accident. She decided Ali Hassan liked her and would do nothing to harm her. But she was convinced the Australians were in graver danger than they knew. She tried again.

'How do you come from Turkey to Indonesia?'

His face indicated surprise that she'd followed the geography. 'Plane to Malaysia, then boats, buses. Long way.'

'How do you know how to drive the boat?'

He stuck out his lower lip, like it was no big deal. 'I work on fishing boats. Learning, learning...'

'You learned Bahasa too,' Roya ventured. 'You live a long time now in Indonesia.'

His face said she'd overstepped. 'Long enough,' he muttered and would say no more.

When the sun went down, he picked up the knife and held it to her throat again as if their conversation had never happened.

He took her once more to the door of the bunkroom and again he removed the fire extinguisher that wedged it shut. He called out for Radja and took him to the galley, where he instructed him to cook rice. Radja took two huge stock pots and filled them from a water drum, then set them on the cooking range and lit the gas jets. He looked questioningly at Ali Hassan, who told him to stay put until the cooking was done.

•••

The *Java Ridge* cut lonely miles into the night, fast enough for those trapped in the bunkroom to know that it was labouring hard. The small quantities of water in various containers had been collected into one bottle which Leah gulped desperately. She had climbed into the bunk next to Tim and was holding his head in her arms, their expressions remote: somehow they had departed together, joined in circling mortality.

Isi had her face pressed to the skylight. She could see that Ali Hassan had not turned on any of the exterior lights; not even the port and starboard lanterns. The sky was rapidly darkening, the sea a pool of faintly reflected light. She strained her neck to find the first of the evening stars.

Yes, he was still bearing dead north. There was no land he could hit in that direction, not for many hours yet, but that gave her little comfort.

Finley had unwrapped Tim's leg, and now he tapped Isi on the shoulder. She could see by his torchlight that there was a problem. The stump, the shocking termination of an ordinary leg, was now shiny, the skin crimped and puffy like rotten fruit. A rope of pus had squeezed from the line of sutures, braided with slender streaks of blood. Tim's eyes were filled with fear. Unthinkingly, Isi laid a hand on the shin just above its sudden end. It was hot to her touch. She sniffed the air as discreetly as she could, but couldn't tell whether there was any addition to the general stench of their confinement.

'What do we do?' she asked Finley.

He looked back at her in sadness, looked at Tim and then at the floor.

'Nothing,' he whispered. 'We can't do anything now.'

* * *

Ali Hassan cursed loudly when the banging started on the bunkroom door. He looked over his shoulder towards the sound and then turned his back on it. The note of the engine rang higher and more urgent. Roya could smell the rice cooking now. Radja had been left by himself in the galley to cook it, after Ali Hassan made clear to him that if he tried to assist the others, the knife would be used on Roya.

It was dark outside now, nothing left of the sun's afterglow. Ali Hassan opened the small vent window in the wheelhouse door, and the warm air rushed in, displacing the cooking smells. Now Roya could smell only the sea.

The banging continued. Roya could see Ali Hassan's jaw churning. Finally he turned away from the controls, grabbed her sharply by the shoulder and rushed her through the lounge and down the steps to the bunkroom door. He stood at the top of the steps and waved the tip of the knife at her, indicating the door.

She pulled the fire extinguisher out of the way and unlatched the door. As she swung it back, the reek of confined people hit her like a headwind. She recoiled from the hot, wet air; the stink of shit and piss and vomit. But Ali Hassan stood firm at the stop of the steps, waving the knife.

'What is wrong please?' she asked into the darkness.

• • •

Isi came forward when she saw Roya's slight figure in the doorway. There were people pressing against the doorjambs, gulping fresh air, and she had to push them aside to reach the girl. Shafiqa was calling mournfully for her daughter, but Roya did not try to enter the room. Her face was graven with responsibility. Isi found her eyes: she pointed back at Tim, who lay on a bunk near the door.

'We need water very urgently. And Tim's leg is infected. We need to bring him upstairs.'

Roya struggled to translate, trying to pluck some Arabic or Bahasa word for 'infected' from the strands of vocabulary she'd acquired. But Ali Hassan had heard enough to understand. He looked past Roya and Isi to Tim on the bunk, racked by new agony. He answered Roya irritably, and made a dismissive wave in Tim's direction. He would not be moved.

Before Roya could translate, a voice came from the back of the bunkroom, an aggressive rejoinder that was coming closer. Sanusi had heard the exchange and was berating Ali Hassan, rushing forward up the passageway through the bunkroom, stepping over bags and small children. Isi smelled his breath, sour from the last smoke he'd blown through the skylight, as he went past.

Roya caught phrases and unscrambled them as the argument built between the two men. Isi's eyes shifted to her, and Roya repeated what little she understood.

'Sanusi say boat not for him,' Isi had caught that much in Bahasa. 'He say put knife down and do…do something help. Ali Hassan say no. He tell him stop or he kill. Oh no…'

Sanusi had stepped past Roya in the doorway. No negotiation, no strategy: he was mounting the steps, rushing up towards where Ali Hassan stood with the knife raised. From back in the bunkroom Irfan Shah roared at him to return at once, but he was gone. Ali Hassan was screaming at him, gesticulating wildly. Sanusi, coming from below, never had the advantage but he charged up two steps at a time and was upon him before anyone could react.

There were shouts and swift movements from several directions, too fast and chaotic for Isi to process. The knife came down and stuck high in Sanusi's upraised arm. It wedged there: Ali Hassan wrenched at it, pulled it free and swung again, this time punching the blade vertically into Sanusi's armpit. Ali Hassan was screaming as he did it, a high-pitched shriek of distress that issued from deep within him. For an instant he was other than a man who could do this, could open someone's artery—for a second he was a man who would shrink from such a thing. But it had happened.

Sanusi never said another word.

They appeared to wrestle briefly before he folded at the knees and fell down the steps, ending in a crumpled heap in the doorway. He knocked Roya over as he landed. She struggled to her feet, covered in his blood, and turned to face Ali Hassan, coming down the stairs with the knife raised again. But he ignored her completely and hauled Sanusi out of the doorway then kicked the door shut. The blood was everywhere now, all over the three of them and the doorway.

Sanusi's head hung limp on his neck. His eyes fell on Roya,

beseeching her, and she reached a hand out to touch his hair. Ali
Hassan spoke harshly: she withdrew the hand and he dragged Sanusi
away.

• • •

Isi rushed at the door and pressed her face to the small window as the
latch slotted home. She could see Roya cowering and the small man
struggling to drag the body up the steps by his blood-soaked clothes.
He'd tucked the knife into the waistband of his pants. Ali Hassan
looked up and met her gaze: he dropped the inert form of the engineer
and rushed at the door, slapping a bloodied palm on the window and
thrusting a finger at Isi.

'No more! No more! You next!' The hate on his face, the sobs
of fear and panic were like nothing Isi had ever seen. He returned to
Sanusi, manhandling him up and over the top of the steps. Isi could
tell from the turn of his hips that he was moving him towards the door,
towards the deck outside. The deck and the rail and the limitless ocean.

There was a loud bang which she recognised as the sound of the
galley door being slammed shut. If Sanusi had had any hope out there,
she realised, it was Radja. Now he was isolated. She ran back to the
skylight and pressed her face into the opening. Women were screaming now in the crowded space, toddlers crying; grief and mayhem that
would answer to no single voice and would have to run its course. She
stood again at the base of the bunks, beside where Leah lay gripped
by small spasms of pain and nausea.

Ali Hassan's legs appeared on deck, close to Isi's head. He was
working his way backwards, heels first as his hands appeared, clutched
around Sanusi's wrists. Dragging him. It was dark out there—Ali
Hassan had extinguished all the exterior lights—and she struggled
to make out the shapes of the two men. But she could see Sanusi's

outstretched arms, the spill of blood that had soaked through his shirt now, his mouth shaping a word she couldn't hear.

Ali Hassan's near foot—so near that Isi could almost reach out and grab it—came down beside Sanusi's neck. It slipped in the blood that still seeped from him, and Ali Hassan came down hard on one hip. He dropped the body, rolled over and cried in pain. The long smear from his slip reached almost to the lip of the skylight. Sanusi's head was turned away, though his face still moved.

The foot was right there, where Isi's fingers gripped the edge of the skylight. Within reach.

She didn't even try it. She knew he would only chop at the hand with the knife. And there was Roya, still out there.

Ali Hassan didn't get up from where he'd fallen. He sat on the deck with his back braced against the cabin wall and pushed with his bare feet, pushed Sanusi to the lowest wire beneath the rail. Pushed him under it. It took several determined efforts, the clumsiness of it only increasing the horror. The last Isi saw of Sanusi was the pale underside of his left foot as he lurched, finally, over the edge and was gone.

• • •

Roya, slumped in the stairwell, had not moved throughout.

She cried quietly for Sanusi, and then in flooding succession for all the misfortunes that had befallen them. She wept for her home, the courtyard with its worn stones and its flowers in pots, the smell of her father and the sound of his weary wisdom, the cries of the food vendors on the street and the children of the neighbourhood running in the dry air, the teasing and the gossip that mattered so much between them and so little now. She wept for her brother, wherever it was they'd taken him. And for her mother on the other side of the door, carrying her sister to who knew where.

Canberra

Cassius walked the streets of Barton under a mist of light rain.

Voicemail: Stella, saying Waldron wanted to know why he had Border Integrity people trying to get through to Cassius's confiscated phone. Stella again: Waldron was hassling her about Cassius's whereabouts. Rory, bored and wanting takeaway for dinner, then holding the phone to the chicken, which appeared to vote for Thai.

He swept the speckles of rain off the screen each time he punched delete. Corners, streetlights, nature strips. Barton's stubborn trapezoid pointed, like everything, at Capital Hill. He walked faster with the phone in his pocket until it rang. The department.

'We have the results. Grid survey, high altitude, two-hundred-kilometre range over Dana—that was right, wasn't it?'

'Yes.' He swept the moisture from his hair with his free hand. Waiting.

'We've found a vessel. Heading north. It's timber, probably another *phinisi*, but if it is, then it's going at top speed.'

'North?' It didn't make sense.

'Yes.' Cassius could hear the small sound of a mouse on a desktop in the background. 'The heading would take them...straight between Sumba and Raijua, into Indonesia.'

'Okay. What else?'

'So this was a Core Resolve job: we asked them, like you said, to run a thermal scan...'

'And?'

'Thirty-eight people. Based on body mass you'd say about four of those are children.'

Something horrible was occurring out there. There was no way of explaining this that didn't add up to horror. His mind wouldn't clear. He stepped onto the road and nearly into the path of a taxi hissing over the wet surface.

'If you draw a line back to the south—you know, if you extend the course backwards, where have they come from on that heading?'

'Stand by.' Insouciant humming on the line, more mouse noise. 'Bullseye. Dana.'

Shit.

His heart was hammering, his hand trembling. He couldn't think what to ask. The boat was going deeper into Indonesian waters, further from his jurisdiction. This was good, this was good...but it also wasn't. All they could do was watch from the sky.

'Oh, sir?'

'Mm.'

'I've been requested to log this call and to report all communications with you to the PMO.'

During the course of the call he'd received a text from the PM—*I'm watching you Cassius*—and an email from his press office, peppered with delirious exclamation points. The major dailies would be syndicating a feature story on Cassius in the morning, alongside an editorial line recommending the government be returned. The headline: *Mr Unshakeable.*

• • •

He climbed the stairs in a daze. His legs were twitching warmly in his rain-soaked pants by the time he opened the door of his apartment. He was briefly shocked to find the hall light on and the heating running.

Rory.

The nanny was asleep in an armchair. She was older, this one, came from an agency that Stella had tracked down. He fumbled and patted his wet pockets, found he had no cash. She reminded him that the agency would send an invoice. Cassius thought he saw her smirk.

When she was gone he headed into the spare room and sat on the edge of Rory's bed. The digital clock said 11:48. He hadn't shopped for days, hadn't arranged the Thai like Rory had asked. What had he eaten? His skull was ringing again and he felt nauseous. He couldn't remember if he'd eaten either.

The light was out but the room was coloured by the sugary glow of the digital displays on the treadmill: Rory must have been playing on it again.

Something wasn't right. It took him a moment to register it: there was a plastic laundry basket wedged up high in the bookshelves beside the bed. He lifted it down and found the chicken stirring irritably on a bed of Rory's clothes. It clucked once or twice and turned its back. There was a note on a piece of printer paper wedged among the clothes. He took it out, recognised Rory's careful hand:

DEAR DAD IN CASE YOU FIND THIS THEY LIKE TO SLEEP UP HIGH

He lifted the chicken out of the basket and placed it on his lap. His hands, he saw, were still shaking. The chicken made a noise that was vaguely like a purr as he ran his palm along its white back, tracing the stiff lines of the quills with his fingertips. He moved his hand up to the bird's neck, closed his thumb and forefinger around it gently, gently. He marvelled at its delicacy, at the bird's tiny fibrillations. Its life, between his fingers in fragile staccato. Dark inchoate thoughts surrounded him, until his tired focus lengthened to the boy in the bed, the covers high under his ears. He was only complex from the outside. From within, Cassius suspected, Rory's adoration of him was as close to uncomplicated love as a human could manage.

He replaced the bird in the basket—it *rrrooked* at him tetchily—and put the basket back where he'd found it. Then he sat himself down on the foot of the bed, below the ridges made by Rory's feet.

And the boy slept so wonderfully, unburdened by anything at all. His mop of hair, rubbed by his movements on the pillow, was spiked into chaotic peaks. His mouth open, top teeth visible below his upturned lip. The deep rhythm of his breathing, his pure, unmarked skin. What had he ever done for his son? Cassius was crying, silently. His love for Rory was a call down lonely wires, over an empty land-scape. Maybe the boy knew he was loved, maybe he desperately wanted it to be so. Probably he idolised his father, but how many years of that could there be left? And then, the torrent of adolescent disdain for the busy narcissist who'd flicked him morsels of his time.

The chance to be a worthy father would only come once in his life, and it was slipping away from him.

Cassius stepped quietly from the room and stood in the kitchen with the door shut, the light hurting his eyes. He had the phone in his hand, weighing an idea briefly as he rolled down the contacts to C.

Carmichael.

The minute he dialled, he would become the traitor that the PM believed him to be. So he savoured the last untainted seconds of his career and poured himself a glass of wine; then dialled anyway.

Savu Sea, West of Pulau Raijua

There was no warning when the *Java Ridge* struck the log.

The cries after Sanusi had gone overboard had gradually subsided and the thick, barometric silence of the tropical night pressed against the racket of the straining engines.

In the bunkroom, Finley had arranged his patients in the bunks nearest to the door. Tim woke infrequently, the change in his consciousness signalled by stifled grunts of pain. Leah had become confused: she gripped the rails of the bunk as though the vessel's motion was now unbearable to her. Shafiqa bore her exhaustion without complaint, only her terror for her daughter etched in her face. Finley had negotiated to have the buckets of human waste removed. Ali Hassan, relenting after Sanusi's death, had brought in new water and rice. The water was offered first to Leah, then both were passed through the bunkroom in small cups and bowls, after which Radja was dumped back through the door to join them. An atmosphere of weary acceptance now prevailed.

It was into this torpor that the giant impact suddenly asserted itself.

The front of the boat slammed into something solid, shuddered massively and lurched, the entire hull riding up high and over the object. There was a loud sawing sound below the bunkroom, the props screaming in the air then gnawing into the thing. Crockery smashed loudly in the galley, and in the bunkroom, everything and everyone tumbled forward, collecting each other and striking random objects as they went, until they were piled in an ungainly heap against the door, Tim screaming with pain underneath them, Shafiqa struggling to breathe. Isi was aware of smaller characteristics within the cacophony: metallic clanks and thumps that indicated secondary damage, damage to machinery. The boat pitched downwards then corked around before it settled. Amid the cries of surprise and pain in the room, Isi listened intently to diagnose what had happened.

'He's either run us aground, or we've hit something,' she said to Leah, who had wound up beside her on the floor.

The engines, the engines. They were still running hard; the vibration through the hull told her that. But some kind of asymmetry had emerged, something rolling or spinning off-centre. The beautiful rhythm of the boat's heart was syncopating; each cycle of the engines marked by a sharp off-note, like a coin in a washing machine. The diesels were breathing harder, working harder, and the isolated clangs were multiplying into a chorus of clatters.

'Turn them off!' she yelled, but she knew it was futile.

She focussed again: a subtle list to port told her they were drifting sideways. So it was either the rudder or one of the props, and they weren't aground. The most likely culprit was a log. Joel had often talked about near misses out here, about his preference for anchoring at night so he wouldn't have to chance it. The illegal loggers who towed barges between the remote islands would lose giant lengths of timber—in storms, out of carelessness or under pursuit—which would drift endlessly just below the surface. A decent-sized container ship might plough through them, but not a *phinisi*.

And Ali Hassan might have lessened the damage if he'd been cruising at a reasonable speed. As far as Isi could tell, he couldn't have hit it harder.

• • •

Roya was back in the wheelhouse with Ali Hassan when the crash happened. She was watching him rubbing his arms to remove the drying blood on them. The flakes were falling as a dark dust on the damaged counter in front of him.

One second it was the two of them: him standing, watching out the window, and her seated behind him on the chair, the dim lighting making her eyelids heavy. The next instant they were on the ground, crumpled together. Her ears were ringing, and for a moment she thought he'd attacked her.

But he picked her up and looked her over to ensure she was all right. Then he took her firmly by the arm, the knife in his other hand as always, and led her once again to the bunkroom steps.

He didn't bother with translation this time: he yelled to Isi to come out. Carl tried to follow her and Ali Hassan angrily waved him back.

'No you,' he said. He pointed at Luke Finley, who stood silently in the shadows: 'Him.'

There were gasps among the people in the room as Isi and Luke moved forward; a collective fear that they were about to meet the same fate as Sanusi. But Luke showed no emotion as he closed and latched the door behind himself, and he and Isi followed Ali Hassan and Roya to the engine-room hatch.

Isi didn't often come down here. It had been Sanusi's domain almost exclusively. On rare occasions he would show Joel something that needed replacing, or the two of them would hammer and swear at a seized mechanism. She loved the sense that it was a world within the world of the *Java Ridge*, a greasy tabernacle that was not the business of strangers. Everything was crowded together, everything was steel. Illuminated by bare bulbs caged in wire grilles, it was a space without any kind of human adornment: fuel filters, gauges and hoses, exposed hull timbers, the din like the life force of the *Java Ridge*.

The noise was deafening as they entered, and even to an untrained ear the discordant clamour indicated something amiss.

A steel mesh gangway led between the two great engines. Under their bare feet, flowing beneath the grille, a slick of diesel-stained water sloshed in the bilge. Isi and Luke began to look over all the obvious inspection points on the engines: it was a surprise to Isi that Luke knew where to turn his attention. He was combing along the port side while Isi searched on the starboard.

It took Isi only moments to see the problem: the rev counter was pushing deep into the red, and she could see the exposed head of the driveshaft where it exited the gearbox and passed through the stern— it was spinning without resistance, far too fast. She looked across at Luke: the engine in front of him was vibrating madly on its base. Most of the metallic battering sounds were coming from the port engine. She knew what had happened.

'IT'S STUFFED—' she yelled over the noise, cupping her hand around her mouth. Ali Hassan looked at her without comprehension, looked at Luke, who shrugged.

'The starboard side'—Isi pointed, because the term would mean nothing to Roya—'has lost its propeller. Lost it completely,' she said slowly, then waited patiently while Roya figured out how to translate. 'The other side has a bend in the driveshaft.' Ali Hassan's face was skewed with suspicion. 'But there's no extra water in the bilge: we haven't put a hole in her.'

Again, the wait while this sank in for Ali Hassan.

'You can't push it any further. It's over,' she said firmly. She locked her eyes on Ali Hassan's while Roya translated. His eyes widened as the words crossed the barrier between them.

'No!' he shouted. 'You trick, fucking *pelacur*!' He rattled off a barrage of high-speed Bahasa and Arabic in Isi's face while Roya tried to keep up.

'He saying you fix or he kill me.' Roya's voice was calm and steady. Ali Hassan brought the blade high under her ear.

'He *knows* it's fucked,' Isi groaned. 'What are we supposed to do with a driveshaft out here?' Sensing it was rhetorical, Roya didn't translate.

'I know,' said Luke. 'But he expects us to do something, right?'

'Okay. Turn the motors off and we can take the shafts out and look at them. Yes?'

This was enough to satisfy Ali Hassan. He spoke in Roya's ear and she translated: 'We go cabin.' Then he took her again, up and out the hatch, which he locked behind himself.

When the racket of the engines stopped, Isi muttered to Luke: 'I can't do anything with this. I don't even know why we're doing it.'

His face indicated he'd resolved something, found a strength Isi wouldn't have guessed was there. 'We give him what he wants for now, and when we get an opportunity, we take it. Agreed?'

She nodded; went to work unbolting the covers that protected the two driveshafts. As she'd suspected, the starboard side was slack and loose in her hand. She could do nothing with it, nothing but hope that the whole shaft didn't drop out of its mounts and allow the inrushing water to flood the engine bay. The port side was intact, she thought, but the bend in the shaft was severe.

The wall of the stern was cracked where the shaft passed through the timber and fibreglass. Isi knew it was unlikely that the port-side prop had escaped undamaged. Even if she could straighten the shaft, they would be limping from now on. *Great time to call in a tow*, she thought. *If only we had some fucking comms.*

She searched among Sanusi's carefully ordered tools and found a long wrench. She jammed its head against the driveshaft, picking the spot where she might lever the bend out of it.

As soon as she applied pressure she could tell it was useless. She'd seen the logs they towed around out here, the damage they caused when they broke loose. The mass involved was enormous—she wasn't going to undo its work with her own arms.

Ali Hassan and Roya returned, and the cramped space became even harder to work in. Ali Hassan had given up using Roya as his interpreter, and was now haranguing them directly, his agitation building again.

'No try!' he shouted at Isi. He pointed the knife at Luke. 'He do.'

Ali Hassan watched intently as Luke took the handle of the wrench and heaved down, leaning back to sling the weight of his whole body from it. He clenched his teeth and sweat ran along his jaw, but the shaft gave no greater indication it would bend than the wrench did.

Isi could see that Roya was now accustomed to the presence of the knife. Ali Hassan pointed it at her from down low with his outstretched left hand. He was concentrating on Luke's effort; barking instructions, wanting him to change angles, to pull harder. Isi watched Roya. Roya's dark eyes were downcast, focussed on that left hand…

Jesus, Isi, what are you thinking? They were already expecting too much of the girl. The more they all burdened her, it seemed, the more capable she became, but this was a *child* for God's sake.

Ali Hassan was shouting at Luke now, pointing and shaking his hands in the air between them. Finally the frustration boiled over and he pushed Luke violently off the wrench. He took the handle in both his hands and funnelled all his rage into it. His left hand still held the knife—the blade pressed hard against the wrench as the muscles of his arms coiled and gleamed and he crushed his eyes shut with the effort.

For Isi, the seconds opened into orbiting worlds—the struggling man, the wrench and the knife. Luke stood close by him in the small space by the engine block, his back against the shelving that was built into the hull. Ali Hassan drove his face against the top of the wrench handle as he poured the will of his entire body into it and when he shifted his grip, Isi could see the sweat from his forehead glistening on the steel.

He made two more great heaves at the wrench. The second one ended abruptly: his top hand slipped and flew from the handle and his body swung off balance.

In the instant it took for Ali Hassan's body to tip sideways, Luke drew his right hand out from behind himself, whipping it in an arc across his body. There was something in his hand and it connected with the side of Ali Hassan's face. At first it seemed the blow had done him no damage, but his left hand sprang open and the knife fell. It landed near Roya's feet with a small metallic clang that was almost lost in the racket of the labouring engine.

A trickle of blood appeared and started to run from above Ali Hassan's eye. He swayed, senseless. Isi stared in disbelief at the object in Luke's hand: she saw it was the winding rod from the vice on Sanusi's workbench.

Ali Hassan's hands began to respond, swirling around in front of him like a man who has disturbed a swarm of bees. He tilted towards Luke, but he was stunned, off-balance—already falling into the space between Luke and Roya.

Isi saw the child shift, her movements tiny and soft as a cat. She wanted to grab her, hold her, somehow stop the relentless pull of events. *Oh Christ, not the kid.*

Luke had raised the steel rod. He seemed to be considering whether to hit the man again. But the girl had quietly picked up the knife from where it fell—she used both hands because the knife was large and heavy in her grip—and she leaned over Ali Hassan and pushed it into his throat, just under and forward of his ear.

It entered the flesh softly, without resistance. Roya immediately recoiled. She let the knife go and raised her hands to her mouth as Luke dropped the winder and stepped in and down. He pressed the heels of his hands on the knife handle so that it sliced outward, opening the front of Ali Hassan's throat cleanly.

The knife fell away. The coils of his windpipe showed white in the red shock of the wound. A gurgle, a retch, a jet of blood gushing forward. His fingers groped for his opened throat. Pulled feebly at the lip of the wound as the last of his breath bubbled the blood. His eyes moved left and right, unseeing: the eyes of a frightened animal, uncomprehending, already given to death. Then he fell face first onto the grille.

Roya edged herself back behind the engine block as if conceal-ment would undo what had happened. Isi and Luke stood mute over the dead man's slumped back, shocked motionless. So much had passed in that instant that it seemed nobody could move until time caught up.

Then, after a long moment, Luke leaned down and heaved the body forward so that Ali Hassan's face hung in a gap between the plates of the grille and was submerged in the bilge water. A frighten-ing quantity of his blood swirled thick and precious in the oily water around the drifting strands of his black hair.

Something came over Luke then, a breaking wave of suppressed fury. He swung a kick at Ali Hassan's ribs that lifted the inert body as it sank home. He kicked out again then shifted sideways and aimed his foot at the bloodied head. Isi grabbed at him, shouting over the noise of the engines, but his eyes were blank and he shoved back at her. He stood over the corpse once more, heaving great breaths, then turned and ran from the room.

Isi found Roya peering out from behind the engine block with her hands clenched in front of her heaving chest and tears running down her cheeks. Released, finally, to be the terrified child she was.

Canberra

His checking of messages had become frenetic, like a lab rat working the pedal for more amphetamine. Email, SMS, the frog-like hop across four social media accounts, then back to email.

Still nothing from Monica. Ringing her was a breach of the consent orders, Cassius knew, but he'd breached them anyway by keeping Rory overnight and he needed an answer. So he dialled her number: at the third ring it switched to voicemail and he hung up angrily. Why was she doing this? Did everything have to be a game?

Stella put through a call from the PM. He could hear him speaking in the background, shuffling sounds of a hand over the receiver, then the voice directed his way.

'Right: these are the rules, Cassius. They're not for negotiation, and I'm not going to write them down so some fucktard can FOI them. One: you are not to publicise the fact that there's a boat out there. If you are asked directly, you can cite operational security, on-water matters, any shit you like, but you are not to reveal the presence of a boat under any circumstances. Are you listening to me?'

'Yes.' Cassius could feel his chest tightening. The breaths were coming to him in short jabs. He'd needed a break between the Monica call and this.

'You're a deceitful prick Cassius and I'll get to you in good time, but right now I'm ensuring you don't distract the electors from the real issues. Are you still listening?'

'Yes. Real issues.' No air. He clutched at the receiver and one knee. No air.

'Right. Mortgages. Fucking...I dunno, fucking Chinese land investment. Interest rates. Not you, not boats. You can get some junior arseling from your press office to do a media release with nothing but black texta redactions, I don't give a fuck. I can't believe I'm having to hose this shit down with twenty-one hours on the clock, you cunt.'

'I don't care anymore.'

'*What?*'

'You heard me. Do what you want.'

Cassius took the receiver in both hands and stared at it for a moment, heard the miniature static of the cursing PM from the speaker holes. Then the air broke through in a great combustive rush and he brought the receiver down with all his strength on the edge of the desk: two, three and four times. His precisely parted hair broke free and a spike of gelled fringe swung and poked him in the eye and he was still hitting.

Stella looked around the corner, her face full of concern. She took in the shards of broken black plastic, the free-hanging wires.

His mobile rang. He looked at it, looked at Stella and picked it up. The electorate office. Final numbers: a cliff-hanger for the government, safe for him. He listened without comment and stabbed it off.

It rang again.

Departmental liaison. He breathed slowly.

When he'd put the request in, Cassius had been unsure precisely how to frame his question. It was important, since the department followed a strict practice of providing operational information only in direct response to whatever they were asked. For countless reasons, valid and invalid, they would hold back everything about their own activities in the field from their minister until compelled to answer. The question in this case had come from Carmichael.

Ask your people about the program of sabotaging boats.

It was as though Carmichael wanted to compromise Cassius before he'd agree to sit down with him.

The answer was that for some years Indonesian intelligence officials had been engaged in a program of sabotaging boats in port. With the active assistance and training of Core Resolve, they'd punctured fuel tanks, drained lubricants and filed off engine mounts. So boats could get out of the embarkation ports—revealing the trafficking operator and the client list to Australian authorities—but never get far enough for the passengers to claim asylum. Cassius knew enough of the murky scene to be sure the police chiefs would be taking a cut of the profit from each boat that sailed. They would also be on the payroll of Core Resolve, nominating which of the hundreds of *phinisis* lining the wharf were legitimate fishing vessels and which were the caskets of the damned.

The Indonesians would have a fit if this got out, the staffer told him. *And Core Resolve will claim commercial-in-confidence. You cannot use this for anything public.*

Cassius had no idea how he felt about this. Elected by the people to speak for the people and to serve them in executive government, he spent most of his time concealing the septic realities from them. It was no real surprise that such a program could exist: the calculated willingness to risk—even sacrifice—lives to make a point with the electorate. If anything, his surprise was reserved for the surge of disgust he felt.

Twenty hours till they opened the booths. Nothing he could find out now would make the least difference.

...

He grabbed lunch with Rory in the Kings Terrace café among the pensioners in their bus groups. He was watching Rory pull slices of tomato out of his roll, slipping them under the table and through the grille of the pet carrier at his feet, when the phone rang. Stella.

'You all right?'

'Yeah.'

'You sure?'

'What do you want, Stella?'

'Your ex-wife emailed me just now.'

Cassius groaned. 'What'd she say?'

'Ah, lemme see. Right. *Please indicate to Cassius that I am not happy with this arrangement about the football. I have had to think about it very carefully, and I am not satisfied that he will keep him clear of the media. Rory is a sensitive boy and I WON'T HAVE HIM USED AS A PROP FOR THOSE PEOPLE.*

'That bit was in caps-lock. And there's a bit more—

'It troubles me that you have put me in the position to have to say no. Please do not blame me when you discuss this with Rory.

'That's all.'

'Fuck!' His eyes darted to Rory. 'Kick-off's in five hours! She's deliberately waited!'

Stella's tone softened. 'You never know. Could've been she was, you know, struggling with it. Wanted to do the right thing. It's hard to tell with emails.'

Cassius lowered his voice to a furious hiss. 'That's why she shouldn't fucking use them when she's talking about our son.'

'Hey! Don't shoot the messenger boss.'

'Sorry. And sorry about before with the…with the phone.'

Once he'd returned the mobile to his pocket he studied Rory carefully. The boy had his eyes lowered, was picking at some other ingredient in his food.

'Mate, the footy's off,' he said. Rory continued to pick at the roll. 'I'm sorry.'

• • •

Cassius dropped Rory at the apartment for the afternoon. He wondered what the boy would do, but he couldn't think of an alternative. He took himself back to his office and tried to sandbag the tide of paper that was flooding his desk. It felt good, or it felt less bad, to be preoccupied. The boy, the boy.

At five, Stella sent a car to take Rory to the airport, and Cassius booked himself a Comcar to meet him there. He found his son in departures, chaperoned as requested by a woman from the airline. Her jewelled wrist reached into the pet carrier to stroke the bird's feathers. She vanished discreetly when she saw Cassius.

'Mate. You got all your gear?'

'Yeah.' There was no disguising the hurt.

'I can't...look, shi—shivers I'm sorry about this.'

'That's okay. I should get home in time to see it on telly. You gonna watch?'

'Yeah. Give you a ring at half time, eh?'

'Okay.' The boy fell silent, looked away.

'Hey, hug?'

They embraced clumsily, Cassius stooping down from his great height, his son stretching upwards and succeeding only in grabbing Cassius's shirt near his ribs.

I'm not the light, Rory. Don't grow towards me.

Tears warmed his eyes and he resisted them. This wouldn't do. Not in public.

Rory regarded him gravely when they separated. 'Dad, are you all right?'

'What do you mean? Of course I'm all right.'

'It's just you look…you look kinda messy.'

'Messy?'

'Like, your hair's all over the place.' Rory screwed up his face. 'It's always so neat, like a Lego man. And today it's like—' he made thrashing motions around his head with his small hands. 'Your eyes are red. And you cut yourself shaving.' He pointed at Cassius's throat, where a small dot of blood stood out on his collar.

Cassius unconsciously smoothed the hair with his hands. 'Long day, that's all.'

Rory's eyes made clear he wouldn't press any further.

'Handshake, Rorkers?' Cassius proffered his own hand. 'You know, for a bloke your age you're bloody good at all this.'

Rory shook the hand, an enactment and no more. 'What, catching planes?'

And then he was gone and Cassius stood in the middle of the terminal, alone among the milling, distracted mass. He wanted to sob; hoped he could make it back to the car first. Against a wall he could see the woman who had been minding Rory, the airline uniform stretching at the curves of her hips. She was huddled with another woman in the same uniform, talking to her behind a hand and both of them eyeing Cassius sidelong. He was accustomed to being stared at, but under the pinned hair and makeup, their faces were openly concerned.

• • •

By the time the car dropped him back at the apartment the headache had returned. There were bright spots of light, dying fireworks, drifting across his vision and a ringing in his head like a power tool working on plate steel.

He fumbled with the key, passed into the air that normally smelled of home. Now he could detect the differences: the boy, his belongings, the bird.

Somewhere, boats were heading out to sea with their engines hobbled. Somewhere else, people punted on those boats carking it near a safe shore. Somewhere there was a place even lonelier than he was, where a boat-load of bodies rotted on a beach.

Rory had picked up the towel that he'd left on the hallway floor. *Good boy.* Cassius turned left into the spare room, wanting to mourn his absence. It was neat and the bed was made. But his eyes were drawn to the maroon square on the armchair beside the bed. The jersey, folded carefully with the beanie and the scarf placed on top.

Rory was not a kid who folded his clothes. Cassius ran the fabric through his fingers, unwilling to understand. He hadn't forgotten to pack them. It wasn't that.

The folding was an apology. Or maybe a rebuke.

Barton, Australian Capital Territory

The manager at the Menzies gave him a booth up the back. Not entirely private, but at least they hadn't propped him in the window. He worked through missed calls while he waited. The drugs had taken the edge off the pain for now.

People were looking at him. And not in admiration. He touched his hair, drank some water.

Carmichael swung through the door in a vintage tweed car coat, glasses on his nose, looking for all the world like a precocious Oxford don. Late twenties but already running a salary north of four hundred grand, funded entirely by benefactors from the Worried Left. When his eyes found Cassius his smile was as much about being seen smiling at a Cabinet minister as about greeting. He lowered himself into the booth and placed a satchel and scarf on the seat beside him.

'Cassius! Lovely to see you. We haven't done this in *ages*.'

'That's because you keep burning me on Twitter. Do you want a drink?'

'No, thank you.'

'Well I'm getting a beer.'

'Good for you. Can I say'—he frowned—'you don't look good. Are you sleeping?'

Again Cassius unconsciously smoothed his hair. 'I'm fine.'

Carmichael shrugged off his overcoat. 'Ugh. Winter in Canberra. I don't know how you put up with it. It's like Boston or something—all those deciduous trees doing colours.' He'd taken his glasses off and was twirling them. 'But there's this feeling the whole thing's landed in the middle of somebody's farm.'

Cassius didn't respond, but began rolling his shirt sleeves. Carmichael smiled. 'So are we playing secret squirrel, Minister?'

'Don't fuck with me. If you fuck with me, this meeting's over. What do you know about boats?'

Carmichael focussed instantly. 'You're talking about the one off Ashmore, up at Dana Island?'

'Keep going.'

'I know a bit. What do you know?'

'I know I'm getting squeezed.'

'What on earth could you mean?'

'I'm not being told everything. PM's giving me no room to move, the department will only answer the specific questions I put to them, and I don't know what to ask. If you know something about that boat I want to hear it.'

'It's Friday night, Minister, what's done is done. The numbers are good—wouldn't matter if you dropped your pants now.'

'It's not about tomorrow.'

Carmichael's eyes lit up. 'Ooh. Don't tell me this is about conscience.'

'It's...' Cassius screwed his face up. Maybe it was about being comprehensively beaten for the first time in his life, but he couldn't say that. 'It's about doing it properly.'

'Of course. You asked them about sabotage, like I suggested?'

'Yeah. But where's that take me?'

'Well, it's partially pragmatic: the boat doesn't make it to Australia, and you spin it for electoral consumption. *What sort of people would put their children on a boat this dangerous?'*

'Bullshit. Who thinks like that?'

'Running quite a risk talking to me aren't you?'

'I haven't given you anything.'

'We both know it's about perceptions, *Minister.'* He cast a look around himself. 'Busy room, known haunt.'

'Ordinarily I wouldn't give a flying fuck what you think about perceptions or anything else, Warren. But right now I'm offering you the ear of the minister, so how about we drop the posturing?'

Carmichael shrugged and smiled. 'I've arranged for someone to meet us here in...' he looked at his watch. 'Five minutes.'

'Who?'

That unctuous smile again. 'A friend.'

Fucking stagecraft. Cassius wanted to solve this problem, and the world wanted to get in the way. 'So what's wrong with what we're doing?'

'On asylum seekers? Where do you want me to start? Trusting the Indonesians to watch the open seas, or outsourcing our human rights obligations?'

'Border protection isn't a human rights issue, it's a national security issue.'

'Of course it is.' His tone was pitying. 'Very *dangerous*, these people. But the two issues bleed into each other anyway, don't they? Immigration control's supposed to be a sovereign function of the state. It's not something you can sell like a fleet of trains.'

'We had to create a harsh regime so that criminal gangs would stop sending people out to die at sea.'

'So the sabotage fits in...where?'

Cassius ignored him. 'The laws are meant to be disincentives. I'm locking you up so that someone else doesn't send another boat. The actual use of the law is secondary. It's about achieving another purpose.'

'Will I find that in the Constitution? *The Commonwealth may enact laws punishing one person for another person's possible future misdeed?*'

'Don't be stupid. Deterrence has been at the heart of our policies since Keating—detention centres are about deterrence. So are turn-backs, TPVs. And so's this policy.'

Carmichael shrugged. 'That's nice. But let's not pretend it's not also about profit. What transparency do you have from these Resolve people?'

'They're subject to KPIs, they report to us monthly. They have to tick off against the various UNHCR stuff.'

'So you know what they tell you. What do you know about what they *don't* tell you?'

'Spicer Ridgway audit them annually.'

'The management consultants?' Carmichael laughed. 'You seriously think they'd risk their fees to tell you some bad news? But let's go back to Core Resolve for a second. They're built from the ground up to resist disclosure. They hire *kids*, Minister. A year or two out of uni—they're given an operations manual and off they go. I'm sorry to get all bleedy on you, but you're reducing human lives to semi-skilled button-pushing.'

'You're assuming that the people pushing the buttons have some kind of animus against asylum seekers.'

'No, no. They're not partisans like you and me. But here's what you're missing: in these situations indifference is more dangerous than malice. It's the same sort of dead-eyed arrogance you get in the finance game; the kid in the suit with the hair who says, "I *am* the fucking High Court."'

'Bah. There's people like that in government. There's another whole limb to this argument anyway, and that's resources. The reason we have a navy is to protect us from sovereign risk. We can't have them endlessly tied up deflecting boat people.'

'Well, in saying that, you're basically admitting these people pose no risk. Which makes me wonder why we're so interested in repelling them in the first place.'

'One of them stabbed one of ours. Speaks for itself, doesn't it?'

'That's a basis for action against that person. It's not a basis for a policy on national borders.'

'To take your line, we're repelling them because they didn't come here through the normal channels and the electorate quite reasonably resents that.'

'So there it is—that's the bottom line isn't it? It's electoral in the end. You're pandering to a fear that you're also stoking. Kero in one hand, extinguisher in the other. But see, the other thing, the *other* thing is…you lot think it's about making sure the public can't peer in. But we're getting to the point where you'll find you can't peer in either. What will you do then, Cassius? How much do you actually know about these people anyway?'

'Core Resolve? They won the competitive tender and it was assessed by…'

'Spicer Ridgway. *Duh.*'

'Yeah. They're a multinational, listed here and in New York, market cap around four hundred million, employ something like seven hundred thousand people. Signatory to the UN Global Compact on Social Responsibility. I know that one because I insisted on it. So I'd say I know them pretty well.'

'If you read that inquiry report I sent you, you'll also know they had those people in the van in restraint positions. They died of asphyxiation. Slowly.'

'That was in another jurisdiction. Completely separate management.'

'It's what they're capable of. Same culture, Minister. They're happy to see a couple of thugs go down for heavy-handed restraint if it means no one looks any further up the chain. Those bodies in the van, that's where your department's heading.'

'Don't be so melodramatic...'

'Melodramatic? Can you look me in the eye and tell me you know how Core Resolve's going to handle the next boatload that wanders into our waters? Of course you can't, and you're not supposed to. And now you've got yourself in a situation where the flow of donations from these cretins to your party would dry up overnight if you tried to get rid of 'em.'

'You're overreaching...'

'Look out wider, Minister. Forget about the boat people for a moment. This dependence on the private sector, it's creating cracks for things to fall into. The mark of a totalitarian state isn't all the picaresque violence and the rallies: it's the fact that things start to *vanish*.'

'That's all undergraduate posturing.'

'Is it?' His eyes climbed all over Cassius's face. 'You've got a problem out there at sea.' He looked up from slightly below Cassius's nose and locked onto his pupils. 'You're hours out from a federal election. Core Resolve's going to fix it, but the idea kind of *disconcerts* you, doesn't it, Minister? You've called in the cleaners, like Winston Wolf in a tux. Problem goes away, but in the process you've lost control.'

Cassius was silent, watching. Carmichael toyed with a fork, tapping its tines so they rang.

'Once you know this, you can't un-know it, you understand? Okay. First up: the photo you've got, the land shot?'

Cassius nodded minutely.

'There's two boats. I don't know why you can't see the other one in that pic, but there's two. There's Australian surfers out there at that island and they've blundered into these asylum seekers somehow. The photographer, they call him Fraggle, he posted a message with it explaining where they were and what the situation was. The caption got separated from the image, I don't know how. Don't know if it was malicious or what it was.'

Cassius desperately didn't want to betray any reaction but his head was spinning, the pain lasering in over his brow.

'Now there's something else. We think we know that boat. It's called the *Takalar*, and it came from Sulawesi. You know that sabotage program? Well this is one of them. They did the engine, or the steering or something. Sabotage might be cheaper than interdiction, but it depends on the damage taking effect early in the voyage. If the boat gets to open sea and it hasn't fallen apart yet, then it's a serious fuck-up.'

Cassius realised that much of this was merely Carmichael admiring the sound of his own bullshit. He needed to press him harder. 'Do you have proof of any of this?'

'The rumour's been around for years. I don't need proof. You do.'

'Even if you're right, what's the relevance of the photo?'

'Well, I agree, I'm joining dots. But let's stand back and admire the worst-case scenario. The boat's been tinkered with. It falls apart mid-ocean under a bit of pressure, gets to the island, then sinks. There's casualties: men, women and children. These Australians have found them, and for whatever reason they haven't been able to communicate that to anybody. Now is that because they can't, or because it's been suppressed at this end?'

'That's fanciful. That's...that's a conspiracy theory.'

Carmichael pushed his mouth upwards in an exaggerated arc of ambivalence. 'It might be unlikely. But the steps are all perfectly plausible, you know it yourself.' His eyes darted left as the restaurant door swung open.

Cassius looked the same way. A young man walked in, searching the room for a familiar face. When he saw Carmichael, he nodded and began to head for their table. Carmichael leaned in and whispered.

'Just quickly Cassius, this chap doesn't know any of the stuff we've been discussing. Best keep it that way.' He winked.

•••

Joel Hughes took the seat next to Carmichael: opposite Cassius. He was young but weathered, stubbled and long haired. Pale eyes, green against the brown of his cheekbones. Big hands, chipped like a tradesman. His face appeared naturally inclined to friendliness, but he was clearly stressed. He muttered his greetings nervously as Cassius, normally so good with names, struggled with a maddening sense that he'd seen this particular name somewhere.

'Have we met?' he asked helplessly.

'No.' Cynicism in the younger man's eyes. 'I think I'd remember.'

Carmichael intervened. 'Joel runs a business in Indonesia, Minister. A boat charter business for Australian surfers. And he uses a particular kind of boat, a timber fishing boat called a *phinisi*.'

'Why don't you let him speak?'

'Oh, I can speak, mate, don't worry about that.' Joel's voice was bitter and forceful. 'My boat was headed to Pulau Raijua, between Sumba and Rote. Know where that is?'

Panic suddenly gripped Cassius. He was starting to understand. 'Yes. Yes of course I do. Look if this conversation is going to relate to my portfolio, then I think...'

Carmichael cut him off. 'Zip it, Minister. You need to hear this.'

'My girlfriend Isi Natoli took a group out eight days ago from Benoa Harbour on Bali. I haven't heard from her since.' His eyes, which had roved over the surface of the table as he spoke, settled now on Cassius. 'The photo, the aerial shot the prime minister had. That's my boat.'

'How can you tell? There must be thousands of timber boats out there.'

'Three reasons. Don't suppose you noticed the red Zodiac on the beach? That's mine.'

He held up his phone, the screen facing Cassius. It showed a Zodiac on a crane at the back of a timber deck.

'I'm sorry, that doesn't prove anything.'

Joel bristled. 'What, you fucking *doubting* me?'

Carmichael laid a hand over one of Joel's clenched fists on the table. 'Easy mate.' Joel pressed on. 'Second reason: four tents. Square ones with beach pegs. I shipped them from a guy who makes them custom in Marrickville. You want his number?'

Cassius didn't reply. His mind was racing for an exit but he couldn't concentrate.

'Third.' He retracted the phone, swiped across a few photos and held it up again. 'There's the shot the prime minister had. I took a screen grab off the net. See the green on the boat? You don't know what that is, do you.'

'Paint?' Cassius snorted. 'I assume it's painted green.'

'No, it's not painted green. Isi planted herbs and salad greens in big pots all over the cabin walls. That's what you're seeing. I'm telling you, it's my boat.'

Carmichael ran a finger around the rim of his glass. 'Take one of those things, Minister, even two—coincidence. But all three?'

Joel Hughes. Joel Hughes. Where had he seen that name? 'Let's say you're right: which way would the boat ordinarily be going?'

Joel started drawing a map on the table, his fingertip dragging a streak of condensation from one of the glasses. 'They would've gone over from Bali, east to Raijua, then depending on the weather, around to Timor, maybe back west to Sumba on the way home. Here's a copy of the passenger manifest: six Australian guests, Isi and two Indo crew. If you check the passports you'll find the Australians are all listed as being in Indo right now.'

Joel pushed a piece of paper across the table to Cassius. He looked at the home-made letterhead—*East Indo Surf Charters: Perfection Starts Here*—and below it the list of names. Cassius had no doubt this was all genuine: there were Australians on board this boat. But now he understood Carmichael's warning: this bloke had no idea there were two boats.

'You know where Dana is?' he asked.

'Better than you do. And I can tell you for certain that's Dana in both photographs.'

'Would they be going north of there for any reason?'

'Into the Savu Sea? No. There's nothing of interest up there for surfers.'

Cassius formed, but chose not to deliver, the obvious next question: *And what about going north at high speed?* Instead he took a safer path.

'So what do you want me to do?'

'I want them rescued.'

'Whoa. *Whoa.* How do you know they're in trouble? How do you expect the government to do anything when they're in Indonesian waters? Why are we even…Warren, why are we having this conversation?'

Carmichael lifted a placating hand.

'Joel's been to the federal police. He's been to Coastwatch: he's even tried ringing Basarnas, the Indonesian search and rescue people. No one's touching it. It's as though they're all in lockstep.' He smiled mischievously. 'You might have some idea why.'

Cassius poked a dismissive finger in Joel's direction. 'He hasn't turned up in the media.'

Another derisive laugh from Joel, and Carmichael put a hand on his shoulder, silencing him. 'He tried, Minister. You put a gag order on him.'

Joel Hughes. That list. 'Get him out of here.'

'What?'

'I can't talk to someone I've taken an order against. It's a clear contravention of the Act. Get him out.'

Christ, the pain. The stress or something had brought it on. Carmichael started laughing. 'Oh Cassius, what were you saying about melodrama?' He tossed a napkin across the table. 'Your nose.'

Cassius stood up, held the white linen to his nose and saw a bright flower of blood.

'He goes or I do.' People were lowering their cutlery. Someone held up a phone. This meeting was being broadcast to the world. Joel stood, leaned forward with a sneer on his face. Now Carmichael was on his feet, a hand on each of their chests.

'You know where that boat is, don't you?' Joel's voice was loud enough to be overheard, tense with hate. He shot out a fist and grabbed the front of Cassius's shirt, bunching it up under his chin. Cassius was paralysed with horror. The whole room was transfixed. He took hold of Joel's T-shirt, twisted it into a ball and shook him hard. The table rocked. A glass fell to the floor and smashed.

'You do. You fucking know it!' Joel was almost shouting. He pointed a finger of his free hand at Cassius as he shrugged himself loose and edged away from the table. 'Fuck your gag order. I'll go to jail if I have to.' He swept his chair away with enough force that it rocked on its legs and toppled. Before the chair had settled, Joel was across the room, diners rearing back out of his path. He slammed the door so hard the windows rattled.

Cassius frantically assessed his position: he couldn't follow Joel out into the street, there'd be paps racing in already. As long as he stayed in here the management would protect him. He sat down, slumped with his head in his hands. His arms were shaking uncontrollably.

Carmichael watched him as he dabbed again at his nose. The blood was slowing.

'What?'

'Does it feel a little sharper now you know it's Australian lives you're fucking with?'

Greasy sweat on his back, sticking to the shirt. 'This is all just speculation.'

Carmichael's voice fell soft and intimate, insinuating itself like a virus in his gut. 'It's fact. You, my friend, could well be leaving seven Australians to die at sea so you can win an election. Is there any other way to look at this?'

Cassius thought about drinking the water in front of him. It slopped all over the place as he raised the glass.

'You'll slink away, take your re-election and get over it. A few dead brown people, that's just the price of doing business. It's the Bangladeshi ferry principle. But *Australians*, Cassius! Young, happy ones...if they're in danger—oh my.'

There was a metallic taste in Cassius's mouth; and nausea, the ringing sound. Carmichael wasn't done with him.

'One day there'll be a Royal Commission and they'll haul you and your PM in, old pissbags in wheelchairs. *I don't recall, I don't recall*...No accountability, is there?' He pantomimed dismay. 'But on the other hand, no solace.'

Cassius finally felt a glimmer of defiance. 'If you actually cared about the brown people you'd be screaming this stuff in the streets.'

'You're right. Yes you are. Fact is, I need to drip-feed it into the media so the rage boils at the right level. Too much and it spills over and then it's done and people move on. Also,' he smirked, 'what would our institute do all day if we lifted all the lids at once?'

What stayed with Cassius, what haunted him through the long night that followed, was the sound of Carmichael's easy laughter, fading and rebuilding. Endlessly entertained by the absurdity of it all.

North of Pulau Dana

Isi opened the bunkroom and released everyone, then went straight to the wheelhouse to assess the damage.

At first she couldn't believe the violence of Ali Hassan's assault on the bridge: cracked panels and shattered screens, curls of electrical loom and sharp fragments from other breakages littered around her bare feet. She tried to concentrate on what she did have: he'd left the GPS, the sounder and the auto-pilot, presumably hoping they'd guide him to somewhere quiet. She lit up the screens and tried to think.

He still had them bearing north, and from what she could work out they were roughly level with the eastern tip of Sumba. There was no help of the kind they needed anywhere in the great basin of the Savu Sea. So she started the port engine again and gingerly brought the *Java Ridge* around to face south, then set the revs at walking pace and left the auto-pilot to guide them. Radja sat in the captain's chair beside her, watching the sea. She had no way of knowing how the loss of Sanusi affected him. Had they been life-long friends? Were they nothing more than a couple of strangers hired by the same employer? Joel had never said. Radja smiled each time she looked at him: deflection, she thought. She left him to his vigil.

Roya and her mother, reunited, were holding each other on a day-bed in the lounge. The girl was curled into her usual protective pose, hand on Shafiqa's belly, but the balance of their embrace expressed reciprocal comfort. The mother's consoling touch as her long fingers drew locks of hair behind the child's ear.

Isi glanced at them as she passed. She felt no sorrow at all for Ali Hassan, only a fervent wish that Roya could have been spared those minutes. What kind of ten-year-old could she become after this experience? What kind of twenty-year-old? She thought about the child's singularity, and her ubiquity. A million Royas in transit over the stateless planet, damaged and seeking a way to heal.

Carl and Fraggle were clearing the mess out of the bunkroom, glad to be occupied after the hours of their captivity. The *Takalar* survivors had resumed their places on the deck, on board bags and mats, bewildered but uncomplaining. Word had spread among them that the boat was again headed for Australia, and their demeanour indicated that this suited them. They had to know about the detention regime. Their ongoing preference for it said plenty to Isi about the alternatives.

A group of men had formed a circle on the floor of the lounge. One of them, sufficiently ancient-looking that Isi wondered how he'd survived the traumas of the wreck, was reading from the Qur'an. The others listened in patient silence, occasionally raising a deferential hand to interrupt. A discussion would ensue, then the old man would resume his reading. His voice, she thought, was meant to mesmerise them; barely more than a whisper but propelled by rhythm. He was taking them back to the comfort of the familiar, as much as he was praying with them.

Near them Isi could see Hamid, huddled with another boy about his own age. They had taken a surfing magazine from the lounge upstairs. The open spread before them featured a wetsuit ad on the left, and on the other side a girl in a bikini laughing at the sun. They'd positioned themselves, she now realised, with their backs to the praying men and out of sight of the women. It was extraordinary to her that

Hamid was now up and walking about. The only sign of his ordeal that remained was the bandaging around his head. Never before had she seen a human being in such desperate danger, and so quickly made safe from it. But the sight of him made her shudder, as the sight of her, and especially of Finley, must do the same to him.

There was enough water and fuel. There was enough food. The boat was wounded but not mortally so. If they were careful, she told herself, they could limp south and help would come to them. She knew Tim and Leah were in trouble but she couldn't gauge how much. As for Shafiqa, she showed no sign of distress now. The impending birth might cause the authorities to evacuate her and Roya to the mainland rather than leave them to stew in the offshore camps.

The body. She hadn't dealt with Ali Hassan. They'd left him there on the floor of the engine room while they attended to everything else. She wondered momentarily if she should throw him overboard, or even stuff him in the chest freezer in the galley, but she decided he wasn't a priority. As long as the hatch remained locked, no one would have to deal with the corpse. Maybe it was a crime scene—she wasn't sure. Some part of her worried that this was disrespectful, but so were the alternatives. The Muslims among their passengers had not asked to give him funerary rites, and she was no longer confident in her own assumption that he'd even been a Muslim.

Luke had been running to and from the galley with a fixed grimace on his face, boiling water and carrying tea towels down to the bunkroom. When his father called imperiously for some minor assistance Luke had reacted sharply. *No. I'm busy.* There had been no open discussion about what had happened to Ali Hassan, although word of the killing had no doubt passed through the boat. How it affected the balance of power between Neil Finley and his son she could only guess.

A group of women among the survivors were in the galley too, cooking rice and onions. They hassled each other loudly in one of the languages they shared, and Isi stopped a moment to puzzle over why they looked so familiar to her. Then she realised: they'd cut and tied the bedclothes from the bunkroom to make headscarves for themselves. Like the men, solace in routine.

Isi prowled the upper decks and the lounge, avoiding the bunkroom. She knew that she had to see Finley, had to see what was being done for Tim. But she struggled to face it. The scale of the practical problems was enough on its own, but Tim's plight was even more daunting. She locked the engine room, and went forward to check the damage to the bow. Although the plating was stove in, the *Java Ridge* was still watertight. She ran diagnostics on the pumps, checked that the fuel storage hadn't been compromised by the impact.

Then she took herself upstairs and opened the door behind the wheelhouse, the one that she never used. Radja and Sanusi's room. She wasn't sure what she expected to find there—or whether it was her business to be there at all. The gloomy bunkroom was the same size as hers and Joel's, but was set up with two single bunks instead of their double bed. The beds had only plain sheets on them, and Radja's was easily identified by the wall above it: his Man United flag and a poster from some victory. He was besotted with the club: on shore he would never be seen without the red jersey.

She turned her attention to Sanusi's bed, quieter and plainer without the football regalia. She understood by the difference that he was much older than Radja, something she'd never considered before. Just as Isi herself had done, Sanusi had pinned a handful of photos to the wall near where his head had lain. Some were commercial prints of flowers on cards: orchids, lotuses. There was a shopping mall booth series of Sanusi with a woman: Isi presumed she'd be his wife. But the largest image, the one that drew a sob from her chest, was of him and two boys. They were maybe ten and twelve, in neat school uniforms. He squatted on his haunches between them, beaming, with an arm draped over each. Their hair was plastered onto their foreheads, carefully combed for the photograph. Isi realised the particular context—the surfing, the wealthy tourists—was not important once you came down to this lonely intimacy. Sanusi may as well have been on a container ship: he was a seafarer, and his family were waiting for him.

She wept for a short while, alone. Then she knew she had to keep moving. She'd done everything she could think of to avoid it, but in the end she forced herself downstairs to the bunkroom.

The Finleys had taken ice cubes from the galley and made cold compresses with them, one on Tim's forehead and one on his bare chest. He was shaking violently now, shivering and convulsing. Leah had been removed from his bed; she lay on the bunk above. Now it was Luke Finley's task to hold Tim down, freeing a hand now and then to sweep back his drenched hair. A thick lather of saliva had formed at the corner of his mouth, and as Isi looked on, Luke wiped it away with a tissue. Tim ground his teeth. The saliva pooled again in seconds. The bandages were gone from the stump of his leg and it had turned a livid purple colour. She could see where Finley had lanced it, and where he'd dumped the bloodied towels in a pile on the floor.

'Can I do anything?' Isi asked.

It was Luke who answered. 'Not anymore.' His words came from faraway, the voice thin. 'Does anybody know...about us? Where we are?'

'We don't have any comms at all,' Isi responded. 'Far as I know, we're on our own until we get to Australian waters.'

'And we can't go any faster?'

'No. We're on one prop, and the engines are on the verge of packing up completely.'

'So,' Luke persisted. 'How long?

'Thirteen hours or so.'

'Okay Isi.' Neil Finley's pink, scrubbed hand lay on Tim's wrist. Following his pulse, or maybe communicating a tenderness he hadn't revealed until now. 'You'd better go.' He looked up at his son.

Isi felt guilty at her own relief. She quietly closed the door behind herself.

• • •

She took a brush and swept the fragments of glass and plastic off the floor of the wheelhouse, then dragged her bedding out and tried to catch some sleep. Joel had done that the first night they spent at sea on the *Java Ridge*, after they'd collected her from Sulawesi. They'd hit a storm out in the middle of the Java Sea and bloody Joel thought the whole ordeal was a great adventure. He'd rolled joints and yelled at the lightning as they pitched and rolled all over the place. Eventually he collapsed in a happy, stoned slumber, and she'd spent the night stepping over his roost to get to the doorway so she could throw up in the thrashing darkness.

They were buccaneers back then, living on borrowings in a foreign currency, lashed to the mast in an unknown sea while their friends applied for home loans and bitched about traffic. If they were in accord about their manic lives at that point, it was her who'd pulled away since, her who'd veered back towards responsibility. It was her who'd scoured the bank statements, who'd read the insurance policies, paid the workers. It was her who'd grown up, while Joel remained stuck in a *Morning of the Earth* idyll that bore no resemblance to reality. Even now, he could have no idea what had gone on out here. Friday night. Friday night at—she looked at her watch—at ten. He'd be six stubbies and three joints into a bear-hugging frenzy of exaggerations and outright lies, blithely certain that no one wanted the dull truth anyway.

But she missed him. She missed his warmth, the way the sun radiated from him, as much as onto him. His indomitable capacity to laugh it off, whatever it was—to enjoy the idea that no one knows what's going to happen next. There are so few people, she reflected, who revel in uncertainty.

Radja didn't. Radja sat beside Isi watching the fading sky and the great unanswering convex sea. Separated by a gulf of language, they saw the same emptiness and took from it different truths: his she would never know. He shuffled slightly, shook out a cigarette and padded silently outside on his bare feet to smoke.

Roya slipped into the wheelhouse. She touched the captain's chair. 'I sit here?'

'Yes, mate. Where's Shafiqa?' Isi asked her. Roya shuffled herself up onto the chair and swayed her hips to make it swivel.

'She praying.' Someone, maybe her mother, had tied Roya's hair back neatly from her forehead. She was wearing a large clean T-shirt as a dress—Isi remembered Leah wearing it the first night of the voyage— and Roya's open face seemed untroubled. Or at least accepting.

'Are you all right, Roya?' Isi asked. But the girl didn't answer, at least not directly.

'Do you want to see my things?' she asked in return. She had slung a plastic bag by its handles over her shoulder as though it was a handbag. She delicately placed it on the floor, sat cross-legged next to it and picked her way through its contents. Isi switched on the light above their heads.

'I have four, hmm. Shells. From the island,' Roya said, placing them in a neat row for Isi to inspect. They were whelks and a cowrie. 'I keep them to remember.'

Her face brightened then as though she'd been struck by an idea, and she reached a hand into the bag. Her dark irises rolled upwards as her hand searched and then came forward, palm flat. A ring. A heavy signet ring made from some dark metal—brass maybe—inset with a stone. The shoulders beneath the stone were scrolled heavily, the patterns marked out in grime. 'And this,' she said, extending her hand, 'this ring my father.'

Isi looked at the ring for a long moment. Unpicking the strange grammar the child had used: *this ring my father.* She took the heavy thing from Roya's outstretched hand and examined it, the scrolled curves and the red stone. She held it up to the light once, turning it over slowly, then handed it back.

'Where is your father, Roya?'

The girl looked down at her crossed feet.

'He is go away. Taliban come, take him. So maybe alive, maybe... not.' She sighed in a way that sounded older. Then her face brightened. 'I show you.'

She reached again into the plastic bag and this time she brought out the small traveller's dictionary.

'Is this how you learned English?' asked Isi.

'Yes,' she said proudly. 'Look...' she thumbed through the thick little book until it fell open about halfway through, revealing a small colour print, washed out and creased. The edges were burred by hand-ling: Roya's searching fingers. The picture showed two people, a man and a woman staring fixedly ahead, their shadows stark behind them on a brightly lit wall. It reminded Isi of historical shots she'd seen; serious-faced portraits from before self-adoration became the default. Why smile, after all? The portrait is about life and this is what life looks like.

Isi immediately recognised Shafiqa, slightly younger; tall and calm and gazing proudly into the lens.

'Your mother is so beautiful, Roya.'

'Yes. This is wedding day for them.' Roya smiled at the recollec-tion of something she'd been told so often, and with such love, that she'd built it into her own experience. 'Dancers, very feast. All of the family and the mullah. So much food.' She patted her own belly as though she was still digesting it. Isi was struck by how young Roya's parents were—how swiftly life had ushered them through descriptors of joy and then loss. Husband and wife, parents; widow and refugee.

'I have brother too,' she continued. 'But he is gone. Maybe Talibs take him to fight.'

Her lip quivered. Presenting the ring had been the wrong decision. Isi took both her hands in her own. They were soft and warm, still clutched around the ring at the centre of their four hands. The girl's eyes filled with tears and her shoulders shook once. She withdrew her hands and shoved the ring back into the bag. She looked at her feet and would not look up. Isi's mind worked its way from the photograph to the ring and she felt she understood: enough of it, anyway.

In all the lonely passages of her long journey, Roya must have pondered the possibilities for her father. That he'd been taken and tortured. Shot and pushed into a ditch. Or that her brother had been forced into military service and had simply never come home. And the unspeakable burden she'd had to assume in the engine room. Why, Isi asked herself, fucking *why* did this lovely child have to carry it all?

Isi withdrew to the private cabin and peeled a photo from the wall, brought it to Roya.

'My grandparents,' she said, as Roya took the picture in her fingers and studied it. They stood close together in the picture, the man and the woman; her with hands at her sides, his left arm obscured by her clothing so that he might have had an affectionate arm around her waist. Him wearing a formal white shirt with the sleeves stiffly rolled up to his biceps, his trousers hitched high and baggy on his small belly. His exposed forearms thick from a life of labour. The woman stood slightly taller than him, thin and square-shouldered in a dress patterned with spiking ferns or flowers. She wore a cardigan, and her short, dark hair tumbled forward over her forehead. She grinned broadly: he looked less confident.

'They're from Italy,' said Isi. 'Do you know where that is?' Roya shook her head, but then, with a sharp intake of air, began to peel through the dictionary. She stopped at a page and opened it for Isi— the flags of the world. She pointed a finger at the Italian flag. 'This one?'

Isi smiled. 'They are both very, very old now. Lovely people. But you know, I think your English is better than theirs.'

Roya's mouth made a perfect O shape as she thought this through. 'Do they speak Dari?'

'No. They speak Italian. I think it's because they still miss their home.'

'I will speak English in Australia,' said Roya. 'But I think of my home.' As she formed the word *home*, Isi saw the light catch on her lower lip. 'My mother maybe speak Dari.'

Isi wanted to keep listening to Roya. But the weariness was more than she could bear. The *Java Ridge* was staggering onwards, 192 degrees south-southwest. Straight off the bow and fifteen hundred miles away across all that darkness she imagined Joel, laughing with beer on his shoes.

Canberra

Cassius remained at the table for another hour and a half after Carmichael sardonically bade him good luck and left. He knew there'd be crews on the footpath awaiting his exit, and he wanted them to freeze for the pleasure of nailing him. He called the waiter over to settle the bill and discovered that Carmichael had picked it up. Cassius asked to have a look at the account: the receipt stapled to it was made out to a credit card in the name of the Institute of Social Justice Advocacy.

'Is this account still open?' he asked. The waiter confirmed that as Mr Calvert was the guest of Mr Carmichael, the tab could certainly be reopened. So he ordered a Japanese whisky—not his normal habit— then shortly afterwards, another. The hot alcoholic trickle muted the headache. At first he was conscious that the diners around him were still looking, were still discussing the scene from earlier on. So he thumbed through his phone, pretending to be occupied and making tired attempts at replying to its various demands. The demands were coalescing around the Joel Hughes incident already. *Draft Minister's Statement Regarding Restaurant Incident.* He gave up and stared into the middle distance.

After a while he rang Stella. He knew it was late but he also knew she'd pick up. He told her he needed printouts of the Australians' passports. He read her the list and their dates of birth. She hesitated only for an instant—*I'll have to get Waldron's permission*—before she assured him she could make it happen. But then her tone changed.

'Do you want to tell me what's going on?'

'I want to see their social media too.' He was looking around the restaurant, assessing the eyes assessing him. The room was nearly empty.

'What, like their Facebook?'

'I want to see them. I want to see *them*, do you understand? Not just the official shit.'

'Why are you doing this?' She was almost pleading with him, but he ignored her.

'Cassius, what's wrong?'

His mind was whirling. He wanted her there beside him, wanted to collapse sobbing in her arms.

'You're supposed to refer to me as *Minister* at all times, you understand? Get me the printouts.'

There was silence on the other end of the line: a chance to retract. He didn't take it.

'All right,' she said simply, and hung up.

A couple nearby got their coats and walked out. Now he was the only patron left in the place, the staff working discreetly around him, clearing tables and restocking the bar. The waiter approached again to relay a reminder from the Comcar driver that he was still out there. Looking across the restaurant, Cassius could see the car outside the front door, where it had been moved in an attempt to draw his attention, or maybe to ward off the press. Steam curled from the exhaust—the driver had the engine running to stay warm.

Cassius mumbled his thanks and a half-hearted apology—they'd seen such things before—and crashed out through the door to the waiting car.

...

His restlessness stirred in the silent car: the story woven by Carmichael, the raw fury of Joel Hughes, who knew nothing of how grave—for how many people—the situation actually was. The circles of insiderness, his corresponding outsiderness, keeping him from working out what was going on. And the day that tomorrow would be; the shrugging acquiescence of the electorate—because what fool would call it a mandate?

He was tired, drunk and dizzy with pain, but his head was alive with feral creatures that barked and gouged. There was no refuge to be had in sleep. Nobody was waiting for him anywhere else: the whole universe echoed with apathy. He directed the car to the office.

It took him forever to get through security. He staggered into the reception area and peered along the corridor to ensure no one else was around. It wasn't that he had anything nefarious in mind, but he knew how he looked. He touched a finger to his nostrils. No blood. Past Stella's cubicle he could see that the overhead lights in his office were all out, though someone had left the table lamp burning.

Probably Stella, he thought. *So considerate.* He stopped at her desk and realised he had no idea how to turn the overhead lights on. He wanted painkillers. He couldn't think straight. He rubbed the palm of one hand up and down the door jamb, hoping to hit a switch. But there was none. *Everything's fucking aut-o-mated.* Every single bastard trying to make his life harder.

He stooped over her desk, ran a clumsy hand around the framed pictures of her and her family, past the pets and the pop stars, the jar of biros and the nail polish remover, the hard drives and seashells and notepaper. His eyes caught the sticky note on the wall, her loud handwriting. It reminded him of something. Then his hand came upon a remote control, and again, a connection clicked somewhere in his mind. He pressed the power button in the top corner and a green LED lit up. Then he squinted some more and found a button that said 'activate'. And the lights came on. He grunted. *Why the fuck*, he muttered to no one, *am I using a remote control to turn the fucking lights on?*

He replaced the remote and walked through into his brightly lit office.

There, perched on the couch with his legs folded one over the other, sat the Prime Minister of Australia. He was in rolled-up shirt-sleeves, tie askew and suit jacket slung over a chair. Despite the overhead lighting, the table lamp made a halo of his thinning silver hair.

The PM watched Cassius with amusement. 'Big night, mate?'

'What are you doing here?'

'The working week's done, Cass.' He stretched extravagantly, prised himself to his feet with a hand on the arm of the couch. 'Let's see: you've got'—he bent over the bar fridge under the television—'Crownies, sav blanc, red...how about a G&T?'

'I don't want a drink.'

'Had enough? Sit down then, mate.' He gestured towards the pale leather couches. Cassius looked at them scornfully. He knew the PM was trying to engage him on his own terms. He headed purposefully for the bar and poured himself a whisky, then took a seat at the conference table. The PM rolled his eyes.

'They're talking no swing against us tomorrow, mate. Maybe even a per cent or two our way. That's enough of a mandate to do some actual governing if we can swing a deal or two. Tax, health, defence...'

Cassius glared at him. 'Stop calling me mate.'

'So I'm going to re-do the Cabinet, *mate*. Starting Sunday, top to bottom. You'll be pleased to hear, no more Border Integrity for you, champ.'

'Why is there no one here taking minutes?'

'Minutes? We're having a chat. We're not launching a military strike.' He pointed at the neck of the beer he'd opened. 'See? No minutes when you've got a beer in your hand. Common sense.'

Cassius took out a pile of printer paper from his desk. He clicked a pen and started writing. The PM chortled. 'This your version of minutes? You with your fucked up—what about these headaches, eh?'

Cassius stopped writing.

'Ah, you didn't expect *that* to get out, did you. Tut tut. How was the Menzies? Did you have the duck, you treacherous cunt?'

'I get approached by a lot of activists in my portfolio.'

'My understanding is that you approached Carmichael, not the other way round.'

Through the fog in his head, Cassius tried to see the PM for who he truly was. He was beginning to understand this method of his: the lumbering joker, a farm lad who'd brought his earthy common sense to Canberra. The bush-battler mythmaking that hid the heart of a volcanic bully, right up to the moment he erupted.

He was waiting now, building, with the beer clutched in his meaty fist like a club.

Cassius tried to light the fuse. 'There were more overhead photos, weren't there.'

The PM sighed. 'You really want to go through this? Yep, every ninety minutes, throughout the whole show. But no one's going to see 'em.'

Cassius had two fingers pinned to the inner corners of his eyes, squeezing like it might somehow hold back the onrush of agony. 'Someone separated that land shot from its caption. There's a caption, isn't there.'

'Mmhm. "We're on an island, reffo boat wrecked...dead and injured, send help." You know, it wasn't like, *explicit*. What else do you think you know Cassius?'

'There's an Australian boat out there.'

'Ah, now I don't want to descend into hair-splitting, but there's no Australian boat out there. There might be Aussies *on* a boat, but that doesn't make it an Australian boat, see?'

'The refugee boat was sabotaged. People acting in our name fucked with the engine...'

'Nah nah nah. NO.' Finally he was raising his voice. 'I've got very little time for this conspiracy crap. Sabotage? It's your department Cassius. If there's some mysterious program, shouldn't you be on top of it? Make yourself a little fuckin tinfoil hat. Simple fact is, there's been a cock-up out there and some people have died.'

'You've deliberately buried all this for the sake of tomorrow.'

The PM laughed. 'Leaving aside the truth or otherwise of that proposition, the public are going to believe *you* did. I'll say it again— it's your department.'

He laughed his mirthless laugh a little more, the laugh that swept aside the fools and believers he'd had to deal with to reach high office. Then he joined his hands behind his head to display sweat-stained armpits and stretched out on the couch. His legs were apart, his balls bulging against his suit pants.

'Let's take it at its most compelling, shall we? You think that a boatload of illegals have sailed south from, where? Sulawesi? Heading for Ashmore Reef, right? A route no one's used for years. But no worries, okay, they're sailing along and they hit a reef, sink the boat and wind up on someone else's boat—someone you and your sources can't identify. Do you know how many people there are on these boats Cass? Do you? On average, about two hundred. So someone out there on the high seas—Australians you say—and what the fuck would Australians be doing up there? This mystery boat, this fucking magical Ark, picks up two hundred crazy fucking stranded reffoes and manages to accommodate them all, and guess what? It's conveniently heading for Ashmore too, and somehow looks identical! And where's the evidence for the existence of this second boat? Hey? Do you somehow deduce it from the two photos you've seen?'

'Someone took that photo of the bodies.'

'Are they bodies? Is it even fucking Indonesia? Don't go leaping to conclusions.'

'Where is it?'

'Where's what?'

'The boat. The Australian boat—the...' he cursed as he tried to correct himself. 'The boat with the Australians on it.'

'Who says any such boat exists?' He stared for a long time into Cassius's eyes. *'If it doesn't exist, I haven't done anything with it. See?'*

'Who's Alan Veal?'

The PM frowned slightly, then recovered. 'Who've you been speaking to? Is this coming from Carmichael?'

'None of your fucking business. Who is he?'

'Veal's an Australian tourist. Photographer, goes by the name Fraggle. He's a nobody. His mother's reported him missing in Indonesia. You think you're onto something there? Do you know how many Australian tourists are missing, hospitalised, locked up or chilling in morgues at any given time in Indofuckingnesia, Cass? I'm beginning to wonder if you might be even more naive than I thought, tiger.'

'How'd you know all that about him if he's a nobody?'

The PM sighed elaborately. 'It's my job to know lots of things.'

'I thought it was your job to remain ignorant.' The pain was back, a knife lodged in the crevasses of his skull. He grimaced as it sparked across his forehead, a current between poles. 'Someday,' he squeezed out, 'when you're old and senile you're gonna realise you're rotting from the inside.'

The PM shrugged. Then he reached over his shoulder to Cassius's side table, the one where he stacked his memos and briefing notes, and picked up an A4-sized envelope. 'You must be wondering why I'm here.' He tossed the package casually at Cassius. 'Got another envelope for you.'

There was no address on it, no identifying features at all. He tore the end off it and slid the papers out. Typed paragraphs, legal letterhead, court registry stamps. It took him a moment to understand what he was looking at. And then his eye caught a series of sentences that couldn't have come from anywhere else:

> 46. *The Husband was always opposed to the idea of us having children. He took an active and intrusive interest in my use of birth control, and when I did fall pregnant he was aghast. He demanded, standing over me and shouting, that I obtain a termination. At that time I was in fear of him.*

Cassius leafed frantically through the pages, knowing all the while that each of the affidavits would be there: Monica, all of her friends, the family doctor, Rory's school teacher. *Domineering. Intimidating. Cold. Insanely ambitious.* But there was more: the report from the child psychologist who described Rory as *emotionally withdrawn in response to disappointment.* And in the grip of a large document clip, the panel recommendation that gave Monica custody, condemning Cassius as *overbearing and incapable of practical compromise.*

Cassius tried to control his face and knew he couldn't.

'You're doing *blackmail* now?'

'Not really.' The PM smiled, enjoying the moment. 'There's nothing to threaten you over. You have no leverage. No, this is personal. From me to you. These have already gone out—to selected journos and trolls who are drooling over their keyboards as we speak. Embargoed to Monday, of course. You're finished, Cassius. You're a washed-up athlete who had a brief career in politics. Remembered only for leaving some Australians to die on the high seas.'

He dug around in his nose with the end of one thumb, grimacing, then regarded Cassius with contempt.

'You know, your pathetic wobbling between pragmatism and principle—you're exactly the reason we privatised this border bullshit. Same with the camps. We can honestly say to the punters'—he raised his open palms with the neck of the beer hooked between thumb and forefinger—'"Sorry guys, private company, blah blah...commercial privilege, fuck off."

'I can look the Australian people in the eye—I'll do it tomorrow for fuck's sake—and say to them I do not know what went on out there and it is not my concern. Now isn't that the best possible position to be in? Do you really think the voting populace gives two shits about whether I'm wilfully blind? Get off your pulpit Cassius, course they don't. They're as fucking stupid as you are. This is Joe Loungeroom, right? "Do I have to worry about brown people invading us from the north today? No I do not. The PM put it in the hands of a corporation and they fixed it."'

He drained the beer and pushed the bottle away from himself, over the glass surface of the coffee table; studying the slumped form of Cassius Calvert, a man who thought he was bigger than politics.

'Goodonya mate. Thanks for the beer.' He belched. 'Gonna grab some shuteye. Big day tomorrow.'

· · ·

After he'd gone, Cassius picked up the bundle of passport printouts that Stella had somehow obtained. She'd moved fast, carried out his instructions to the letter, then presumably gone home.

The faces told him little. Carl Simic, a man with the soft mouth of a boy. Alan Veal, who did not look remotely like an Alan. Isabella Natoli, Leah Hogan, Luke and Neil Finley, Timothy Wills. From the copies he could glean dates of birth and therefore ages. The two Finleys must be father and son, not brothers as he'd originally thought.

Another page appended after these told him that criminal history searches had been conducted and all were cleanskins. A small detail, but it fuelled his rage: why the fuck were they checking for criminal priors? These people were maddeningly obscure to him.

He picked up the second bundle of papers, the social media.

And there they were: the seven of them. Luke Finley playing football, mugging with mates who looked similar to him in striped shirts, beers raised. Leah Hogan on her graduation day at the academy, already the image of a junior cop who'd been the victim of something. Carl Simic on a dirt bike, trying to convey a peak moment with too many exclamation points. Timothy Wills, laying down a lecture about ethical poultry farming. Christ, more chickens.

Veal, who styled himself as Fraggle—he didn't consider himself an Alan either—trying to build a career as a photographer. Never shirtless like the others. He'd met some famous surfers, had covered some stadium rock from side-stage for the music press. Obituaries for a family member of his. Isi Natoli, showing off the dream they were selling: holding a huge fish aloft, surfing a blue wave, lying in a white bikini on the deck of a boat. He studied the planking around her, veined by the seawater that had run off her legs. The shot was probably taken on the same bloody boat.

They were Australians, whatever that meant. They were also young people: self-absorbed, inexhaustible, ephemeral in everything they did. Happy, though they probably didn't realise it. Not broken or cynical. All of them would be the subject, somewhere, of someone else's concern. There would be parents in the dormitory suburbs making food or sorting through something they'd meant to attend to in a quiet moment, the quiet moment that had now arrived. Glancing at a clock at the times of day when these kids would fill the room, the parents had no cause for concern yet. They couldn't know.

It was his burden to know, even if others had conspired to ensure he didn't. It was his place to be the one who held these documents in his hands, somewhere remote from society. At first he'd seen that responsibility as a mere incident of the job: he was first and foremost a political showpiece for the party, a 'leader' in the public's uncritical eye.

Now he understood the gravity. Now he could trace the river backwards to him at its source: the upstream accretion of blame like toxic sediment, carried from the electorate through all those minor officials to the department, the chief of staff and on to him. Him on the bed of that fucking river among the stones with a boulder on his chest.

The pile of bodies on the island, that didn't even enter the political calculus. No, that was his personal horror: the parents, the children who didn't know their warm and breathing loved ones were corpses on a beach. That time would come to them—like a dark angel in their sleep—soon enough. Until then, the arms of the dead would reach to him, fail and reach again. Their voices would plead with him to speak their names to the world. And he wouldn't. Because they'd died as they lived: on the wrong side of an invisible line.

Southeast of Pulau Dana

Tim Wills died at 3:16 a.m.

While Leah sobbed and tried to get up, they closed his eyes, gently removed his watch and the ring from his finger. They wrapped him in bedsheets and took his body upstairs to the chest freezer.

Carl took upon himself the role of pall-bearer, heaving his cousin's swathed body up the steps from the bunkroom and through to the galley. Isi and Fraggle emptied everything but the essentials out of the freezer: fish fillets, fruit and steaks, and piled them on the counters. When there was enough room they lowered the body in, knees tucked against chest, and shuffled some of the loose ice over it.

The *Java Ridge* was grinding slowly south; ever more slowly. Seawater had been leaking into the engine bay for many hours, running through the broken seals around the bent prop shaft. The boat was listing more dramatically to port. Isi adjusted the steering to compensate for the bias.

All the while, the noises from the engine room became more pronounced and more pathological, even to those who knew nothing of machinery.

• • •

As the light broke, a tower of dark cloud loomed over the water. It swelled at its centre through lilac and mauve, shades that hinted at great power but held it close, concealed. Isi moved about the deck, placing buckets of seawater around the signal fire. The angle of the water in the buckets betrayed the steepening list of the boat.

She'd recruited Carl to help her stack all the board bags on the steel deck at the bow. All the luggage they could spare; clothes, towels, anything that would burn slow and smoky. They built a pyre from these items, sloshed some diesel on it and lit the whole thing up. The buckets right there in case the flames ran away from them. It was a terminal strategy, she knew. The choice you made when there was no going back. There was every chance the timber hull would catch anyway and burn them to the waterline, but she needed attention from the outside world and she needed it now.

She added to the fire anything she could find that might burn a vivid black. Wetsuits, a plastic tarp; the curtains from the lounge. All of them she threw on the pile and watched as they melted and bubbled and stank. Eventually she started to add surfboards, and even Carl no longer objected as the colourful logos blackened. He'd spent hours repairing them, but it didn't matter now. People moving around the deck coughed as the fumes wandered over them. In the dead air the sooty column rose almost vertically to a great height, then began to spill sideways.

The men in their tattered *perahan tunban* were slumped by the rail, smoking the cigarettes Radja had given them from Sanusi's stash. They no longer talked in groups, but watched the fire in the casual way you would if it was the burning aftermath of anything—a rubbish pile or a mortar round.

Isi went below and worked her way forward through the following eyes of the old men and the women and children to check the underside of the steel plate that the fire was burning on. It was hot to touch but there was nothing flammable in contact with it: the fire could burn for a few hours more before it presented any danger to the *Java Ridge*. Which only meant the sea was likely to take them before the flames did.

As she passed back through the passageway her eye caught a movement at the corner that led to the engine-room access. Isi stopped and turned, found the huddled form of Roya, sitting with her back to the bulkhead and one hand on the door of the engine room. Isi could see the dimples in her knuckles.

She looked up at Isi's approach but said nothing as she slowly withdrew the hand.

'What are you doing, mate?'

There was a tear forming in one eye. Still Roya wouldn't speak. Isi took her other hand and gently lifted her to her feet, walked her back towards the ambivalent light of the new day.

Back on deck, the atomic burst of the thunderhead had grown taller. Eruptions of brilliant pink cloud lined its edges, clean in contrast against the perfect blue heavens behind. Some other kind of cloud lay in streaks across the base of the storm, parallel to the horizon. But what struck Isi more than the beauty of the building thunderstorm was the effect it had on the sea. The chromed water beneath the cloud was turning an impossible green.

Darkness gathered under the cloud as it reared into the sky, and the green was intensifying. She took the first object that came to hand—a screwdriver she'd left lying on a sill, because it didn't matter anymore—and she threw it as far as she could in the direction of the thunderstorm. It tumbled through the air and splashed briefly through the surface and the white was as she'd known it would be. Not silvery or transparent like ordinary water disturbed, but dazzling—so bright that it seemed to emit light rather than reflect it.

This was what a thunderstorm did to the sea, its most exquisite turning of moods. And she'd become blind to it until now, preoccupied by the everyday and fearful of the future. Beneath the cataclysm in the sky, something perfect inhered.

She'd made choices that went with the shifting atmospheres: between immersion beneath the ocean, or skimming and cutting through its surface, or just looking at it. Usually only one thing or the other would truly feel like being in the ocean. Some days nothing but the pressure of the whole sea in the coil of her inner ear could calm her. Other days it was enough to be slapped by spray and wet to the waist, and that would be an answer to the call.

With the boards consumed by flame, the comms gear gone from the roof, Isi realised that everything identifying them as westerners was eradicated. It hadn't taken much. They were a timber boat on the endless sea, no different from any other seafarers. She looked at Roya, who sat on the deck watching the same cloud. The storm that had consumed her boat had arrived under darkness. She might never have seen the ocean like this. The little girl was at peace as she watched. How separately that moment stood in her precarious life.

Her thoughts shifted restlessly back to the present. Had Ali Hassan been right?

Australia not helping boats anymore.

• • •

Isi was thinking about Joel as she rounded the front of the cabin and saw Carl sitting on the windlass, beyond the oily flames of the signal fire. The vision of him wobbled in the heat—he was alone, lost in thought. She sat beside him on the deck, facing the warmth of the flames.

'Tim was your cousin on your mum's side?'

'Stepmum's, yeah.'

'You were close, huh.'

He laughed a little. 'Close but miles apart. I mean, you saw us—he could be so fucking pompous about all that lefty shit. I'm not political: I'm not, like, the opposite of him or anything. I just get the shits when people start preaching at me.'

'Who were—'

'But I loved him, okay? I did.'

'Who were your parents, Carl?'

He uncrossed his legs and rearranged them, looked out at the faraway storm.

'Dusan, my dad, he landed at Tulla in 1990. I was nine and the twins were, I dunno, still in nappies. He didn't have a wife or a speck of English. He fed and clothed the three of us, educated us, till Margaret came along, that's my stepmum. Never sentimental about the old country, you know? He'd only started talking about it in the last few years once the age mellowed him off a bit. And when he did talk, it was all tangled up in this kinda Euro-Coburg English. Turned out he hated the place, lived in terror of Milosevic, would've gone sooner if he could've.

'And he lobbed up in the new country with nothing, had nothing but his brains and his hands. He was bloody good at making furniture, but. Started at a factory in Campbellfield, then there was a shed he put up in the backyard at home, and then one day—Christ, I remember this so clearly—we were all in the stationwagon and he pulled to a stop outside this industrial shed in Deer Park—you know Deer Park? And there was his name, ten feet high across the front of the building. And suddenly he had people workin' for him. Slavs, Indians, Iraqis, Sudanese. He didn't care. I think he thought that people who were down to the bones of their arse were less likely to sit on it...'

'He still around?'

'Nah. Asbestosis.'

'Oh. Sorry. You remember your mum?'

'Just, just photos.'

'What was your stepmum like?'

'Ordinary Aussie I guess. I knew almost nothing about her before she started arriving on Saturday afternoons for beers with Dusan. She started to be a bit of a fixture, but it always felt like she had no interest in herself, you know? Like she found herself boring to talk about. If she was sick, or once or twice she lost a friend along the way, she'd almost apologise for interrupting normal programming. Dad was—umm—gruff with her. Gruff but affectionate, yeah. She was like a frightened bird around him...What?'

Carl was looking at Isi like she'd made a comment.

'Sorry. I haven't heard you talk this way. About your family.'

'You've never asked me about my family.'

His face changed somehow, turned darker. 'You know we're people smugglers now.'

'What do you mean?'

'We're taking these people across the border. Federal offence, isn't it?'

'But we're not sneaking them in. They're not in shipping containers. We're looking for help.'

'That's what they always say, isn't it?'

'Carl, I don't have the energy for that whole disc—'

'That's okay, neither do I.' He laughed a little, and the sound cracked at the end. 'But Tim would've fucken loved it.'

He turned away from her, eyes downward to study the water under the bow. A big long tom appeared there, in the shadow of the painted timbers. The fish sliced along and across the boat's direction of travel, then jumped out of the water and flew through the air, kinked and whipping. The eerie light flashed on its chrome flank before it splashed in again and disappeared.

SATURDAY MORNING

On the Java Ridge

Thirty thousand feet above the chrome plate of the sea, a solitary object sliced across the sky. The new sun glowed on its sleek white curves like a benediction, like this machine was the bright zenith of human achievement.

It might have been an aeroplane but the wings were slender, the tail fins inverted to spike downwards. Its passengers, its cargo, were circuit boards and fibre optics. The bulbous dome that might have been the cockpit was blind, windowless, occupied by neither human nor conscience. Given to data alone.

Miniature eyes and instruments, absorbing the information. On the belly of the machine a rotating optic: laser-milled glass; aperture and focal length. Tiny papillae measuring velocity and temperature, distance and altitude. Moving over the water and sifting number strings in search of anomaly. Reporting back.

The machine knew what belonged here and what was foreign. It knew the surface of the ocean. It laid a grid over it to measure what was otherwise featureless. The islands, the reefs it knew. The giant seamounts beneath the surface, invisible to all but an observer at this height: it knew these too.

The sensors bristled. There was something on the ocean that did not accord with the known.

...

There was no boat there to greet them.

Isi checked the GPS again. During the slow-motion nightmare of the morning they'd limped nearer the two-hundred-mile line and were now hanging in space over the Timor Trough. Though the ocean was physically unchanged, this was Australia's ocean and she was convinced they'd be watched. Somehow, remotely, someone would have eyes on them.

The gamble of going south into Australian waters for Tim's sake had ended in futility, but Isi still believed it had been the better option. Leah, unconscious now and starved of food for two days, could still be saved. The last time Isi had looked in on her an hour ago, her face had expressed something more frightening than pain—a kind of glazed resignation—but Finley maintained that she had time yet.

As much as Isi would normally have disliked the idea of a warship, some presence out here that indicated authority and homeland would be welcome.

Yet there was nothing in sight but the water's surface and the coronal haze of the sky. Water and air. The *Java Ridge* was the only solid object in the universe.

She knocked the throttles back to idle so the engines stopped their labouring. No hurry anymore, no hurry. She took off her shirt and headed outside.

The guests were slumped in various corners. The wreck survivors had mostly retreated downstairs. The separation of the two groups probably reflected nothing more than their differing ways of coping with the early morning heat. Fraggle had gone inside with them— she'd noticed he was still taking portraits of those who would allow him. Once again he was alone among others.

On the deck next to a hammock he'd left the paperback he'd

been reading—a new edition of the Indonesian surf guide they all read. She picked it up and thumbed out of habit to the index to see if the *Java Ridge* got a mention. But the book fell open halfway through, at a bookmark. She lifted it out: a square leaflet printed on heavy card. A black and white photograph in its centre, of a fair-skinned boy in a suit and tie. And under the image: *Marlon Veal, 13/5/94—28/12/16.*

Travelling's a way of making sure you're not at home, he'd said. She hurriedly replaced the book where she'd found it.

All of them were waiting here, suspended.

From a tub near the stairs she took a facemask and stepped lightly over the gunwale into the sea. It was the temperature of her blood: she felt no change other than the thicker physics when she slipped from air into water. Her feet stabbed downwards, feeling noth- ingness even as they stretched. She took her hands from the mask and watched her silver bubbles slow then climb for the surface. She lay face down, waiting for the aeration to clear.

Then she could see; she could see the great spears of light that angled down into the blue, headed for a vanishing point beyond the sight of the world. She turned her mind to her own buoyancy, spread her arms and legs so she cast a starfish shadow into the great sapphire emptiness below. Her breathing slowed, her heart slowed. She held her body perfectly still on the surface by nothing more than the gentle pressure of her fingertips.

And ever so slowly, she allowed the air to escape her mouth so that her chest contracted and she began to sink. And Joel and the money and Ali Hassan and the asylum seekers and the carnage she'd witnessed and the destruction around her and the uncertain future that lay ahead: in this perfect moment she had sloughed it off and left it to float away.

She descended till her lungs hurt, and then obeyed the instinct to kick for the surface.

When she broke through she saw Roya's face peering down in concern from the port side rail, her mother beside her. Isi took off her mask, smiled away the darkness.

'Hello Roya. Would it be all right with your mother if I took you for a swim?'

The little girl looked apprehensively at the mask, and Isi realised she would be thinking back to her time under the upturned hull of the *Takalar*. She placed a hand over her heart and smiled again. Roya looked at her mother, exchanged a few quiet words with her. Shafiqa nodded and kissed her gravely on the forehead.

Roya disappeared for a moment and returned with a lifejacket and another mask from the tub.

'Leave the lifejacket.' Isi smiled as Roya sat on the gunwale, still in the oversized T-shirt. 'I'll hold you.'

Looking up at Roya as she arranged herself on the edge, Isi felt a fresh wave of admiration. Whether it was nature or experience, Roya had no time for fear. She let herself tumble off the deck and into the water.

Isi swam to her and looped an arm across her chest. She adjusted the strap of the mask over her head, as she had done four days ago.

'Are you ready?' she asked.

Roya nodded.

'Do you know how far a metre is?'

She nodded again, and spread her hands to indicate.

'Well this water is three *thousand* metres deep. Can you imagine that?'

Then she let go of Roya's chest, keeping hold of her hand as Roya laid her body on the surface in the same way she had seen Isi doing.

Isi replaced the mask on her own face and floated beside her. They hung there motionless, two specks on the surface. There were tiny crabs, the size of a little fingernail or less, hitching rides on a broken-off sponge that floated beside them. She poked them with a finger and they scuttled to defend their holey empire. Roya's eyes smiled behind her mask. Isi looked down and out wide, into the abyss, and then turned her head to see the little girl suspended on the surface beside her, her hair and the billowing T-shirt drifting, her eyes alight with joy and wonder.

•••

The operator swivelled side to side in the chair, tapping his foot on the leg of the desk at the end of each sweep. The device he was piloting was a Predator, three or four years old now and no longer the duck's nuts for military use. At his end it was serviceable enough: he had more trouble from the desk interface than he did from the device itself. He'd never actually laid eyes on it. He only ever looked out through its eyes.

This shift he'd taken it out before dawn, from Darwin out over Fannie Bay and over the mangroves and mudflats of the Cox Peninsula; across the Timor Sea, heading absolutely dead straight west. Hours of monotony in his darkened booth.

The length of his attention span wasn't the issue on a shift like this: it was the singularity of the task. He wanted to interact, wanted to run multiple devices and switch between fields. Flick and tap and scan. To sit and stare—at one thing only—required him to suppress every instinct.

The device had reached Ashmore after three hours.

Not his business to know why. Why would you want to tell the guy operating the device what the hell you're doing with it? He could work at 7-Eleven and have more autonomy and as for human interaction…Well, there was the girl on the desk out front—nice eyes but as bored as he was—and a slack-arse manager who was never there.

So there he was, a speck in the sky, looping over Ashmore for twenty minutes when Kieran knocked on the door and brought breakfast in. With one hand he opened the lid of the burger and stuffed the fries in, gluing them firmly to the cheese. With the other hand he flew a circuit of the reef, thirteen nautical miles from end to end, admiring its roseate sunrise colours. There were waves breaking on the southern side, a few tiny islands stranded on the coral like rafts of scum in a sink. He bit into the soft mass of the burger. The ribs of a wrecked trawler lay in the shallows of the atoll like the remains of an eaten fish. A larger island, a kilometre long. He tagged it for future reference: West Ashmore Island.

The orders came through eventually: hello faceless overlords, how's your dark tower?

Bearing 310 degrees. 108 nautical miles at 30,000 feet. Search all anomalies/ grid 80 nautical miles square at that location. DO NOT EXCEED 108NM.

What looked like secretive hocus pocus to them was obvious to him: 108 nautical miles was 200 kilometres—he was being sent to the territorial limit. Three-ten he had to cross-check: it was a straight line to a small island. He zoomed in. *Dana*. Someone's mid-voyage between Dana, whatever that is, and Ashmore. Probably the boat he'd seen the other day.

So the operator scratched his balls and yawned and listened to his own breath under the headphones while he waited for the device to make its way to the search area, occasionally toggling to the video stream to watch the air rushing past its belly.

He flipped rapidly through the images as they came in. Blank sea. Blank sea. Blank sea. He pulled hard at the straw in his shake and tried to keep the slurping sound in the bottom of the cup going until he ran out of suction.

Blank sea.

A boat.

Lying stricken and askew—side on to the course he'd been given—on the great reflective lens of the blank sea. He looked at it a moment, zoomed in and panned round. The phone lit up.

hey n00b wassup

His left hand stayed on the joystick. His right darted from the mouse onto the phone.

yo

quik round of F7?

He dropped the cup in the wastepaper basket. Probably not the time for this.

nuh

hey

nuh

He pulled down a request form from the toolbar at the top of the screen, typed in some details and sent it.

wot thn

He was so bored with Fallout. And besides, he might have to do some work here for a change.

fallouts so 2015. Halo?

ok hey you still at Rslv?

Yes, I'm still at Resolve. That's why you haven't seen me in eight months. That's why the phone's encrypted. That's why I never see the sun, why I'm sitting in a bus driver's chair in a soundproof booth deep in a secure floor in the ugliest building in Pyrmont. Yes I'm at fucking Resolve.

yeah

on console?

Hah. You could say that. A joystick and about three trillion square miles of ocean. Slower than the Xbox on your livingroom floor and you never got to waste the bad guys.

yeah

whatyu do like blow shit up

fk yr imature

?

Cant talk about it

??

They watch me. Srsly

He looked up at the bank of three cameras high on the wall behind him. They were trained on the screens, on him. Reminders, along with the physical searches on the way in and out, that his work was never to be anyone's business.

And he couldn't honestly say he blew shit up. It was mostly a process of image matching—what he got on screen to instructions from above. Mouse clicks and typing. *Finer resolution please. Apply coordinates. Run video.* No different to what the stoner on the end of the phone was up to all night, only the money was fucking royal.

kay login then lez do it

He wouldn't mind an hour on Halo. But this business would have to be dealt with first.

hang on sthingz cumup

An icon flashed on the screen. An answer coming back in response to his request form.

Slow pass at 500 please and boost res on video.

Oh the sheer joy of having something to do. He issued instructions to the device and watched it stripping altitude. There was a protocol for slow passes, and it took some skill. At five hundred feet he drew it around the boat in a wide circle, zooming in on the humans standing on the deck, the plume of dirty black smoke issuing from the bow. His body intuited the G-force and tilted itself unconsciously in the chair.

At first he thought they were on fire. Then he could see the smoke was coming from a stack they'd made: a pile of burning luggage or timbers or something. He pulled in the optical res until it reached its limit and waited for the focus to adjust.

He could look right into their eyes.

• • •

Isi could hear something.

Something other than the slapping of tired water against the hull of the *Java Ridge*, other than the muffled voices from below decks. A faint whining sound, coming from the direction of the thunderhead. Coming from the southeast, and from above.

Roya had emerged from below, drinking in the fresh air. She was dry now, had brushed her hair. The plain fabric of the T-shirt was nearly dry too, patches of salt forming on it. She went first to Shafiqa, who was slumped in the shade, heavy and exhausted. They spoke briefly and Roya went to get her a cup of water. *She must be so close now,* thought Isi.

Roya bent close to her mother and watched her drink. Once she was satisfied, she looked up and saw Isi. She sidled up to her and sat on the narrow ledge that ran around the cabin so that her eyes were at the same height as Isi's.

'What is that sound?'

'I don't know,' said Isi. 'It sounds like a plane, but maybe a small one.' She listened again. 'A jet. You know?'

Roya nodded. Oh yes, she knew about jets.

The noise grew louder now. They both stared into the haze that was its source. The sun was still low but already ferocious in its intensity. A couple of the others came up from the bunkroom, blinking in the sunlight.

The air was nearly still but now and then it would swirl as some pocket of heat stirred restlessly, and the smoke from the pyre on the bow wafted past them. Roya coughed.

'Can you see anything?' Isi asked her.

'No.'

Isi climbed into the wheelhouse and found a pair of polarising sunglasses. She returned to her spot next to Roya.

'Here, try these.'

Roya put the glasses on, admired her reflection in the cabin window. 'I am like a movie star,' she laughed. Hamid was lying on the bow, beyond the signal fire, just as he had done on the *Takalar*. She waved to him through the smoke, imagined herself on a red carpet with cameras flashing.

Isi squeezed her shoulders as Roya squinted again at the distant southeastern sky.

'I see it!' she cried. Seconds later they could all see it: the strange aircraft that didn't quite look like a jet. It was streaking towards them at an alarming speed, but then it banked hard and slowed, large ailerons flaring on its wingtips. It was loud, too, so loud that it was impossible for any of them to hear each other. Now they could see its whole fuselage side-on, could see that there weren't any windows. But it wasn't this that struck Isi as sinister. It was the lack of any kind of livery—not a badge, not a flag or a logo. Plain, clinical white.

'What the hell *is* that?' she muttered. But no one could hear her.

...

The operator had sent the video back, along with another request form. His controller wanted to know if there were any westerners on board. The operator thought hard about that, scrolled through a few frame grabs: the bearded men in their torn robes were without doubt OMEA: *Of Middle Eastern Appearance.*

The pregnant woman and the small girl with her? The mother had her head covered. Dark skin, both of them. A short man wandering around deck barefoot, brown skin, no beard but working on the boat. Likely to be part of the smuggling op. But then there was the younger woman. Short hair, uncovered. Bikini top and shorts. Most definitely not a Muzzie outfit, but he didn't know about the Sri Lankans, they might rock togs. Olive skin but not as dark as the others. Brown eyes. She was borderline: borderline enough that the operator felt entitled to zoom even further and allow the camera to wander a little over her body. A fit, healthy girl. Very healthy.

And indeterminate. But given the context most likely also to be part of the smuggling op. He dwelt a moment on that, but without real concern. On the lanyard around his neck hung an ID card which didn't mention his name: only an alpha-numeric code—N2HD4435. *So.* He sighed deeply. *I am N2HD4435 and you are a timber boat on a faraway ocean.* His fingers raked the keyboard once more. *No westerners on board.*

He tapped the phone to reply about that game of Halo, but the icon flashed on the big screen before he could type. The orders appeared in plain letters but for a moment he thought he'd read them wrong.

He brought up the inquiry field again and this time didn't bother with the formalities. He typed the first word that came into his head.
Really?
The orders appeared again, followed by a curt postscript.
Confirmed.

• • •

The device had completed a slow lap around them, its shadow crossing the deck as it passed before the sun.

Some of the passengers were wild with delight, elated that their ordeal was nearly over. They cheered and embraced, waving their shirts and towels at the craft and offering prayers to the heavens. Others seemed uncertain, watchful.

'What will it do?' asked Roya.

'I don't know,' Isi replied. 'Maybe it can send for help.'

The aircraft widened its circle once the lap was completed and now it headed directly away from them, down low over the surface of the sea, perpendicular to the beam of the *Java Ridge*. They watched the thin stream of exhaust issuing from its tail as it rapidly disappeared.

The noise from its engine faded as it went. They looked at each other blankly. The men who had been waving shirts and towels stopped now: the coloured fabrics hung limp at their sides. No one spoke for a long time as the thick tropical air closed around them and fed upon their collective will. The men who had come up went back below, and others wandered up to take their place. Isi could hear someone urinating over the other side of the boat. There were banging sounds in the galley where someone was making food.

Isi was about to go back to the wheelhouse when she glanced at Roya, sitting with her hands tucked under her thighs as children do. Her head was down. She was looking at her legs, at the paler brown skin of her knees, and she did not look up at anyone as she spoke.

'It is coming back.'

Isi listened hard. Roya was right; the whine of the jet engines was growing louder. Maybe it didn't have the information it needed. It might have to do a dozen of these passes before anyone in Australia would be alerted to their plight.

Shafiqa had lumbered herself along the deck with one hand on the rail until she reached her daughter. She was smiling and squinting at the bright sun, her long hair free of the scarf now and floating lightly when the air moved it. Isi could see clearly for the first time how beautiful she was, how much like her daughter. Shafiqa looped her arms around Roya's neck and nuzzled into her hair, speaking softly in Persian.

'Mother want to know what are we looking at,' said Roya.

She clutched her mother's forearms with her small hands and answered her, her face upturned and her dark eyes trained on Shafiqa's.

The drone had reappeared and was travelling fast, ahead of its sound. It was low and precisely front-on, its wings lowered and spread like the fins of an advancing shark. Although it was only a piece of machinery, a blind canister, it chilled the air with its menace.

In the last moments Isi failed to understand the yellow-white lights that sparked under its wings as it knifed close enough for them to make out the play of light and shadow over its contours, as the surface of the sea began to explode in front of it, as the great towers of water erupted and fell, trained in two straight parallel lines, unerringly seeking the exposed beam of the *Java Ridge*. The percussion of the cannons and the smacking of the rounds on the sea's flat surface; these were only sounds, comparatively slow-moving. The destruction slipped lethally faster.

When the first round ripped through the hull it splintered the rainforest timbers and tore open an old Tajik man and his grandson in the bunkroom. Milliseconds behind it, further rounds punched through two women on beds and dismembered their children, seated on the floor. Ricochets made crazed detours, whirring like saws. The air filled with flying metal.

• • •

The operator was slumped in his seat. He had lifted his hands from the joystick and keyboard when the firing sequence took over, the breath dying in his lungs. He could feel nothing, see nothing but the screens.

Had he closed his eyes he would still have seen them: the brown girl thrown and slammed against the timber, bursting into lurid red against the greenery. The pregnant woman and her little girl, hand in hand as the scything shards tore them to pieces.

· · ·

The rounds cut their tracks through the centre of the boat, smashing their way in: shattering into fragments that sliced through water bottles, scattered books and shoes and ruptured human flesh until one punched through the steel shell of a gas bottle and a bright fierce ball of flame consumed the air inside the hull with an inrushing *whoomp* that catapulted everything and everyone aboard into the hot, still air lying so tired upon the sea.

The fragments spun and drifted and fell, one by one, back to the surface of the sea. And it was only after the last of them had fallen that silence returned to the place. A place beyond sight and hearing, unmarked by anything but the distant presence of a coral reef.

Parliament House, Canberra

The Honourable Member for Walyer, Cassius Calvert, hadn't moved from his seat at the desk through the dying hours of the night. Every two hours, on the hour, the security guard would appear in the doorway to check on him. 'I'm fine, Priya,' he'd mumble. 'How are your kids?' Priya looked more worried each time.

He couldn't feel his feet.

The phone on Stella's desk was ringing. He listened to it through two rings, three, four. He let it ring again, like answering it was optional. Finally he dashed across the office and reached around the doorway to pick it up. As he did so, he saw the sticky note. He loved the girl and her ridiculous ways. Loved her impossibly.

'Mikey and Mel make my morning.'

The voice on the other end of the line was calm, male, quiet.

'Minister?'

He sat down in Stella's chair. 'Yes. Sorry...sorry. I thought you were someone else. I...who are you?'

The man was from Core Resolve. Telling him an unauthorised incursion over the territorial line had been neutralised.

Cassius tried unravelling the jargon but the caller declined to lapse into ordinary human language. The incursion had been confirmed by correlated geo-digital data. The location had been optically surveilled. The incursion was now neutralised.

Cassius put the phone down and didn't move for a long time. When at last he stood, he had to hold the edge of the desk for a moment to regain his balance. Had he slept? He couldn't tell. Daylight streamed down through the light wells in the open meeting area, though he had no memory of the dawn. He looked at his watch: 9:48.

He needed to piss, stood there in the ensuite draining a horsey stream of dark urine that smelled like stale coffee. Ran a hand over his prickly jowls while he waited for it to finish. His face in the mirror as he washed his hands should have horrified him but he barely saw it. It was just someone. Someone who lived in this office.

He tumbled his hands over and over in the warm water, watching the fingers pass over the knuckles, the greenish veins on the backs, the bumps and ridges of scars that proved he'd been a child once. The four lumps at the bases of his fingers where the oar had over so many years worked his skin into calluses. The spill of clear water over his skin.

It took some time for him to knock the lever of the tap to off.

Exhaustion giving way to rage now. The rage threatening to boil over in some unspecified way. The mechanisms of his body were crowding in and mocking him: his eyelids itchy and coarse, flaring each time he blinked. His breath came and went in shudders and a deep, unpleasant chill afflicted his feet while his chest and arms felt prickly and hot. The weight of his hands was wrong. And behind and above and inside and around it, the ringing and screeching in his head. There was no space left for thought anymore. The sound, or the pain or whatever it was, had installed itself and eliminated all else. Escape was the only rational response. He walked away from the holy relics he usually kept close: the phone, his wallet and glasses. He left them all behind, passed ghostlike through the door and down the corridor.

The place was abandoned like there'd been a bomb threat— the campaign staff were all at their electorates, hugging idiots with balloons in their clammy hands, wearing message T-shirts that bulged in awful ways. The ministerial staff would be home among friends waiting for the result: the believers hollering and seeking to draw unsubtle credit to themselves. The agnostics simply enjoying the day off.

But for the candidates—he should have been among them— this was a working day, another round in the ceaseless carnival of falsehood. Wolfing gladwrapped passionfruit sponges in town halls, smiling at people for whom they felt little but contempt. Patting dogs and carefully shaking the hands of wheelchair-bound kids, hand sanitiser at the ready.

He should have been strolling into the grounds of a scout hall this morning wearing a sports jacket over an open-necked shirt. Gorgeous wife on his arm, advertisement-grade children, empty gratitude for the volunteers. But instead, his morning was unspooling like the lost reel of a dark film, and he was powerless to stop it.

Into the lift. Mercifully empty, smelling of cleaning spray. He was hungry. The foyer, with its grand marble and lofty ceilings and cluster of streaky columns. Out through the revolving doors and into Australia.

Australia was sharply cold, the sky clear and still. The sun hung over the airport, trying to hoist itself aloft. He paused on the forecourt, an impossible choice of left or right around the pond. Straight down the barrel he saw the sharp light of the new day on the Old House, and above it the War Memorial. On the induction tour they'd told him there was a straight line of sight from the PM's desk; clean through the viscera of the new building, framing the memorial so it would stare back, a prick to the prime ministerial conscience. He'd never believed it. There was so much you couldn't see from that desk.

A cloud of breath issued from his mouth as he started down the slope towards Federation Mall. The ground soggy and thick: a waterline of mud around the sides of his shoes forcing him to veer left onto the footpath. His thoughts were scattered and slow moving. The PM's face, his voice. The boat, the damn Zodiac. Carmichael, the chicken, Joel Hughes. His child, the trust in his eyes.

Birds clattered and rawked overhead as the soles of his shoes clacked precisely against the concrete path. He looked up to see a currawong watching him, the cruel beak under the poisonous seed of its eye. For some reason it made him think of the chicken; that beak stabbing lethally into its soft body, laying beads of bright blood on the white plumage as the evil bird gorged.

He walked on.

The overpass vaulted the traffic on State Circle, the heavy façade of the Old House growing larger as he approached. The ghosts of Gough and Malcolm frowning on him from the parapets, mocking him in baritone: both of them as huge and permanent as moai. The gravity. He was just a balloon in their company.

He found a new path intersecting his. Leading left, under the trees and through a patch of eucalypts, out onto the long, straight run of Commonwealth Avenue. Across the road he could see the walls of the embassies, flanked by European trees: heavy and dark in the cold light. The Hyatt Hotel, set back from the street, the spectre of Scullin peering out through the heavy drapes, and the Albert Hall passing slowly by and the buildings conceding to open space; Australia revealing itself to him as cut grass and highway.

He felt confused now, lost in time.

A head in a suit, neat hair and white teeth, grinning at him from a corflute. Cassius didn't recognise the candidate. Looked again—it was a real estate ad. The wide concrete footpath lifted gently over Lake Burley Griffin, the waters calm and still. Ducks and swans moved through the haze that lay on its surface.

Halfway across the bridge and surrounded by water, his headache was so severe that for a moment he had to clench his fists around the handrail. Joggers swerved to avoid him, paying little attention. He waited for the bright points of light behind his eyes to fade before he continued.

Captain Cook's fountain, lit by the soft sunshine: so optimistic, so pointless. He leaned his forearms on the balustrade of the bridge and watched it for a moment. The cold air on his cheeks told him he was crying, but it didn't matter; he was pretty sure it didn't matter. He needed to be somewhere but he couldn't remember where it was.

He took his tie off and stuffed it in his pocket. A truck roared past and the driver made eye contact, swivelled his head a little to follow Cassius as they crossed paths.

After the bridge returned to shore on the north side of the lake it passed over a roadway. He stopped to look down at the patterns of shade on the asphalt. Nausea swam with the tilt of his head but he had seen a flight of concrete stairs nearby, passing through the branches of a tall willow. He took these down to the level of the road, where cars were swinging through a bend on the lake's edge at a speed he thought unwise. He skipped across nervously, casting a glance up at the elevated path where he had been a moment before.

Now he was on the shore of the lake, the geyser of the fountain spearing into the sky, high above him. The sky. *Oh no oh no oh no.* He stepped around some footpath blocks that were roped off for repair; the grass slipped under his feet, and he looked behind to see that he was leaving dark prints in the remnant frost. A woman hurried past in jogging gear, pushing a pram. Her ponytail bounced through the back of a baseball cap as she ran. She flashed him a nervous smile and was gone.

Guess what I just did in your name.

He was walking east now, a park on his left and the lake on his right. His feet were beginning to hurt: the shoes were good for a press conference but not much chop over distance. The leather was covered in blades of grass and his feet were wet and cold in their thin socks. He sat down on the concrete lip at the edge of the water and the cold now began to seep in through his trousers and spread over his arse. He untied each shoe carefully and laid them one beside the other. Then he unpeeled his wet socks and stuffed each in a shoe, debating momentarily which one had come from which foot. His toes were pale and soggy. He wasn't entirely happy with the placement of the shoes. He shuffled the right one a little so they were paired neatly on the concrete, the toes pointing at the fountain.

Once he had his belt off he pondered what to do with it. He liked to coil a belt and place it inside a shoe, but the socks were in there. In the end he wound it up carefully and wedged it between the two shoes so that it couldn't unroll.

A cluster of cyclists came past, the expensive bikes hissing faintly through the air rather than whirring and clanging like bikes used to do. Each of the riders wore a helmet and wraparound sunglasses. A couple of them looked at him as they passed, riding with two fingers poised pistol-style over the brake levers, but none of them slowed.

He was shivering now, although the crying had slowed to an occasional sob.

He stood so he could remove his trousers. They came from a good suit: finely made, recently drycleaned. He folded them pleats-inward so the pockets aligned, then folded down the legs until they were pressed into a neat square. This he overlaid on the shoes. The hairs on his legs quivered in the brittle air.

Six buttons down the front of the shirt and then two cufflinks made eight tasks for his cold fingers to fumble and resist. He slipped the cufflinks, St Augustine's—Provehito in Altum, into a trouser pocket. Folding the shirt was more complex but it was a skill practised over many a long trip: rowing regattas with formal commitments, trade delegations. Coathangers. The world's most ubiquitous implement; always elusive exactly when you need one. He succeeded in approximating the way the shirt might have arrived in its packaging. Difficult without pins, but close enough. He placed it on top of the trousers.

His head throbbed as he stood upright again, but he felt now that the worst of it was behind him. He was in good shape, yes, good shape.

The boxer shorts were cotton. Pale blue and pinstriped, as he liked them. He wasn't so concerned about them, so he tossed them loosely on the top of the pile.

Cassius stood to his full height on the footpath and drew in a deep breath of the clean, cold air. He let it out slowly, allowing his fingers to curl and uncurl. Across the water he could still see Parliament House, the hopeful sweep of its flagpole and the bright façade in the hillside. He didn't envy the people who had to work in there.

There were noises behind him. He looked around to see a small crowd had gathered nearby. Keeping themselves at a safe distance, although from what particular danger he couldn't imagine. A teenage boy was holding up a phone. Filming him, he guessed—people filmed him sometimes. He found himself talking to the boy, though he was having trouble following the conversation. The boy's expression was changing from amusement to discomfort; he was backing away. The other faces in the crowd didn't betray any real concern; only a dumb, bovine curiosity.

He looked up to where the land met the sky. Out there, the tortured eucalypts kept vigil beyond the oaks and elms of the pasted-on empire. They watched from the ridges, out wide in the plains. In a thousand years they'd be down here again, erupting through the concrete after all this had passed into memory.

The first step, down off the concrete and into the water, was so cold that it felt hot. Both feet suffered this shock before they surrendered to numbness, making it hard for him to feel the stones on the bottom among the velvety silt. As he shuffled forward a few steps he could see his feet were making muddy swirls in the clear water. The ducks came towards him, and he smiled because they thought he was a benefactor of some kind. He was nothing of the sort, of course, and he shushed them away with his hands.

He felt awkward about the water reaching his balls—that moment when he'd squealed and retreated as a kid at the beach. He gritted his teeth and strode forward. It was as bracing as he'd thought it would be, and he let out a gasp. There was some muffled laughter from behind him. Never mind them.

As his chest submerged the muscles around his ribcage contracted forcefully. His hands finned to keep him balanced. The cold took his breath away, but there was a strange relationship between the temperatures of air and water, and the parts of him that were underwater felt more comfortable than those exposed to the air.

He never dived under, never heaved a giant breath to prepare for immersion. He walked steadily onwards through the lake as the ground fell away beneath his feet. He looked around briefly as the surface tension made bubble noises in his ears, saw the trees and the park, the traffic above on the bridge, the fountain and the House on the hill. He turned a little and he could see the onlookers, a larger crowd now, people slowing their walk and stopping to join them, people on phones. A child wheeling a tricycle in a precarious beeline.

A long, slow exhalation to ensure he didn't float. The water had frozen his eyeballs but he made sure not to blink.

It was Saturday morning in Australia.

His head wasn't hurting at all now.

Parliament House, Canberra

When she walked into the office at ten-fifteen on election day, Stella Mullins was surprised to find the lights on. She'd expected everyone would be out voting, checking polling stations or getting ready for the night to come. Maybe the minister had been in last night; she hoped not, because he hadn't been looking well lately. The pressure must be awful, she thought. No wonder he smashed the phone.

Stella was wearing jeans and boots, a Parramatta Eels top under a puffer: the clothes she liked to wear and couldn't between Monday and Friday. She was heading out to Goulburn after lunch to stay with the cousins and she wanted to make sure the minister had his briefing notes and his timetable sorted for Monday. Tasks she could clear by email, of course. But she knew he liked a handwritten list sometimes. A joke and a smiley face.

She sat herself at her desk, turned the radio up loud and logged on. The screensaver was a shot of her nephew Charlie waterskiing at Tumut. In the arc of the spray from his ski the icons lined themselves up as the system booted.

One of them was flashing.

She squinted at it: it was an icon she hadn't used before and it took her a moment to recognise it. The video conferencing. When she clicked on it the screen filled with a coloured panel: tools and options along the top, and a large empty box in the centre containing a one-line entry. The system had made a recording. She recognised today's date, but it started at 1:06 a.m. and ran until it timed out automatically at the three-hour mark. Even measured by the minister's odd working habits, it was an unusual time to be fiddling with the conferencing system.

She checked for the remote. It had moved from beside her thesaurus, where she'd put it after last week's installation. It now lay at a haphazard angle by the bright plastic filing tray. She was someone who by habit squared everything on her desk. This was not her.

By now she was curious but still not concerned. Was this her business? Plenty of what went on in that room was not her business, but this, she figured, was another example of the minister's fraught relationship with technology. She'd have to take him through the manual.

She double-clicked the entry and waited. The screen now showed the interior of the minister's office. The couch. A figure on the couch, backlit by the table lamp, who was not the minister. She leaned forward in disbelief, scrolled on the speaker icon until the volume was turned up to full.

The man on the couch was the prime minister.

• • •

In half an hour, Stella Mullins had heard the entire conversation between Cassius Calvert and the prime minister. She'd watched the PM leave the room, tailing his suit coat over one shoulder, had seen Cassius disappear off-screen into the bathroom and return to slump in the chair behind his desk, dazed and broken. She had watched him sit there, running his fingers endlessly through his hair and sobbing. She fast-forwarded through the remainder of the recording and she could see that he never moved. Tears ran down her own cheeks: she would later reflect that she was crying not just for him but for the impossible situation he'd placed her in.

She dialled his number—the mobile she'd given him—and it rang out loud in his office. She stuck her head around the corner and saw the room was vacant. There was an empty beer bottle on the coffee table. Wherever he was, she had no doubt he would be in terrible distress. She tried to calm her racing mind and work out what to do about this recording before she started thinking about finding the minister.

She clicked back to the home screen of the software and looked at the settings. *Lights, Zoom, Volume, Save To, Live Play, Share Level.*

Share Level. She tried to remember what the technician had told her about the system as she clicked on the words: *'Share level' is who gets to see the video.*

A list appeared: *Private, Archive Only, Administrator, Ministerial Staff, Cabinet.* None of these was highlighted.

The last option on the list was highlighted, but the thought of it paralysed her.

Sydney

The rich blue velvet curtain. The flags again, always the flags. Flags that will never feel a breeze, made to be hung indoors and propped with clips and tape.

The prime minister-elect stands behind a lectern badged with the hotel's logo. It has been a long day but, framed between those flags, he is perfectly attired and groomed. He plucks a folded speech from his pocket and sweeps his glasses onto his nose.

The crowd is crammed into the room and it swells and it stirs, individual voices calling above the ambient sound. The PM smiles in recognition of some of them, raising and lowering his palms to indicate he needs silence. But he can't help smiling. The work is done, the faithful seek their reward.

'My friends...'

Hysteria takes over. They *are* his friends, all of them.

'My friends.'

They want to hear it. They want to hear it so much that they contain themselves to create a silence into which he can deliver the words.

'I can confirm that we have been re-elected.'

Uproar. The camera flashes sparkle blue-white over the darkened floor like the night sky is inverted. Balloons and streamers appear from nowhere.

He waits patiently for a full thirty seconds while the release of ecstasy takes its course. They chant his name and he grins in delighted amazement from one side of the room to the other.

'You obviously enjoyed hearing it, so let me say it again: I can confirm that we have been re-elected.'

Another barrage of applause. Someone wolf-whistles with piercing effect.

'The Honourable Leader of the Opposition called me several moments ago to concede the result and to wish me well, and I thank him for his good grace in doing so.'

Polite clapping. This doesn't interest them at all, but it's due recognition of the niceties.

'Ladies and gentlemen, we have been handed a generous mandate. A majority of five seats and another four from which we can anticipate some success in the days to come. The men and women of Australia have given us their approval to continue our reforming work on behalf of this great nation.'

A forest of extended arms holding smartphones, their screens made blue by the curtain backdrop.

'I do not take this result, as one of my predecessors infamously did, as a victory only for the true believers. I take it as a victory for all Australians, and we will strive as hard for the people who voted against us as for the people who voted for us. We are a great nation, a lucky and affluent nation, made greater year after year by our hard work and our fundamental decency. Challenges are thrown at us and we prevail by applying our toil, our common sense and our values.

'Managing a growing economy is one such challenge. Educating the children of tomorrow is another. And so too is protecting ourselves and our borders from those who would do us harm. It has been difficult—difficult and painful—to enact a border integrity regime which is deliberately harsh in its operation, but we have done it for the good of all Australians, and you have willingly joined us in that vital project. I value our conversations around border protection, and I'm committed to better outcomes going forward.'

There's another outburst of cheering, because all of this makes perfect sense on its surface.

'Now—yes, thank you, thank you—now one person in my Cabinet above all others has had to carry the burden of that difficulty and...'

He falters, lowers his eyes and holds a finger against his lips. A hush falls.

'...and you saw the price of that commitment this morning. I speak of course of Cassius Calvert: Olympian, Minister for Border Integrity and a great Australian.'

Thunderous applause. His raised hands call for restraint.

'Who knows, ladies and gentlemen. Who knows what pressures he was under? Maybe some explanation will emerge in the coming days and weeks. We're talking about my good friend here. My mate, and I am hurting right now. And to those commenters online who saw fit to mock his obvious distress, I say to you—politicians are fallible human beings. Underneath the stereotypes that have built up, we are real people with fears and aspirations. We laugh and cry like you do. We worry for our children in the night like you do. We hope for a better future, just like you do. Our collective ranks are not a faceless mass: we are people, real and hurting. Perhaps it would be fitting to think about that before you deride us.'

The silence hangs for just a second as he finishes. Then it's punctured by tentative clapping at the darkened margins of the room. Others join and a tide swells. Before long it is unanimous and deafening. Arms upraised, the crowd pounds out its rapture.

Perhaps in response to the surge of ecstasy, a cannon fires a plume of coloured glitter over their heads. It swirls and settles on their shoulders, in their hair. Some look to the person next to them, a faint crease of confusion in their smiles, answered by a shrug. The PM can indulge himself in a little oratory.

But now something is happening in the room that differentiates the punters from the invited media. While the revellers are looking up at the sparkling fallout, scooping handfuls of it to throw again, the journalists are looking at their phones. One of them taps another on the shoulder and points at the screen. Another runs for the door, phone in an outstretched hand as if it will guide her. Before long there are enough of them with a finger in one ear and their phone pressed to the other that bystanders are beginning to stare.

The entire room has turned its collective back on the prime minister-elect and his speech fumbles its way to a forgettable end. His eyes scan the room nervously. An aide leans in and whispers in his ear before guiding him from the lectern and away to the exit.

• • •

In her cubicle outside the empty office of Cassius Calvert MP, Minister for Border Integrity, Stella Mullins sits at her desk. Her face is in her hands. Tears run between the bases of her fingers and down to her wrists as the sobs roll through her body. She has her earphones on, the cord snaking to her mobile on the desk. The phone is streaming a live feed from the victory party in Sydney.

The only light in the room is the white glow from her terminal, the last screen she opened.

The final option on the distribution list for the video of the previous night. The option that tortured and baffled and terrified her for so many hours. Until she could stand it no more and she laid the cursor over it and pressed the enter key, just as the prime minister-elect was confecting his grief over the loss of his Minister for Border Integrity.

The software has taken over now. Stella's relief that her ordeal is over has been replaced by a mounting realisation that it is expanding infinitely.

The screen is filling and shuffling vertically now, as it adds dozens of names to a list it is building. In parallel planes the names scroll upwards, but the heading at the top of the page never moves.

All of Press Gallery.

ACKNOWLEDGMENTS

After I'd finished a first draft of this story, Text's Michelle Calligaro suggested I read *Between Sky and Sea*, the 1946 debut of Herz Bergner. When I reached the unforgettable end of that novel I wondered how mine could have followed such a similar arc. The answer, I feel, lies in the sad circularity of our political responses to refugees. We may have escalated the stakes over seven decades, but our indifference is nothing new.

There are many people to thank for their valuable contributions to this book. On Indonesia, and the operation of a surf charter boat, I'm indebted to Chris 'Scuzz' Scurrah of Sumatran Surfariis—he was very relaxed about my persistent interest in sabotage. On the medicine, thank you to Jennifer McCarthy and Ian Sutherland, Paul Goggin, Cathreena Jervis and especially Jamie Hurley for his unique insights as a surfing surgeon. Simon Troeth and former senator Judith Troeth AM helped to teach me about Canberra and the inner work-ings of Parliament House. And on Afghan society and culture, my thanks to Heather-Grace Jones. In respect of each of these generous people, the errors that remain are mine and not theirs.

My background reading included (in no particular order) Robin de Crespigny's *The People Smuggler*, Åsne Seierstad's *The Bookseller of Kabul*, David Marr and Marian Wilkinson's *Dark Victory*, the Husain

Haddawy translation of *The Arabian Nights*, the Coleman Barks translation of *The Essential Rumi*, Hemingway's *The Snows of Kilimanjaro and Other Stories* and Najaf Mazari and Robert Hillman's *The Rugmaker of Mazar-e-Sharif.*

I'm grateful to have the support and guidance of the talented team at Text Publishing, and most especially Mandy Brett.

For their careful and constructive readings of the manuscript I wish to thank Robert Gott, Chris McDonald, Dom Serong, Jo Canham and Ed Prendergast. And for their love and endless patience, my wife Lilly and our children Raphaela, Carmelita, Humboldt and Ondine.

Macadamia is a fictionalisation of a real chook called Coconut McCann. We never met, but I'm told she was a good bird.